You Can't Just Leave

John Mulhall

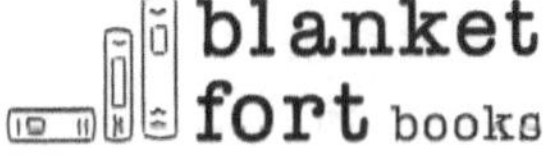

1st Edition. Printed in the United States of America.

Published by Blanket Fort Books

eBook ISBN: 978-1-968340-00-1

Paperback ISBN: 978-1-968340-01-8

Hardcover ISBN: 978-1-968340-02-5

Audiobook ISBN: 978-1-968340-03-2

www.youcantjustleave.com

www.johnmulhall.com

www.facebook.com/authorjohnmulhall

Cover Art by Cherie Fox

Author Photo by Victor Curtis

Editing by Naz Keynejad, Linda Larson, and Dayna Bennett

You Can't Just Leave

John Mulhall

CONTENT WARNINGS

I've never been one to focus on blood and gore in my writing. I tend to find dread, discomfort, and emotional tension far more compelling.

Terror first, horror second.

You Can't Just Leave is my least gory book, but some may find its emotional and psychological weight more disturbing. The themes in this story are challenging. It deals with damaged people whose actions are often cruel, even depraved, and some of the scenes are upsetting.

If you're navigating the aftermath of trauma—especially abuse or childhood harm—this book might not be the right fit. To help you make an informed choice, I have provided a detailed list of potential triggers below. While it's a long list, many of the items appear only in passing or are discussed briefly. Still, I wanted to be fully transparent.

I want to address two entries that might deserve special attention: *Animal Cruelty* and *Animal Death*. These moments are brief, not described in detail, and the animals are not characters the reader knows or connects with. I considered omitting these scenes to make the book more accessible, but ultimately decided it would dim the truth of who these characters are.

Unlike the title suggests, you *can* just leave. There's no shame in that—you know your own limitations. However, if you feel ready to dwell in the darkness for a while, I'll be right there with you. Not to shock or punish, but to guide you through the shadows.

You won't be alone.

<u>Content Warnings:</u>
  - •Ableism
  - •Abuse (physical, mental, emotional, verbal, and sexual)
  - •Addiction
  - •Animal Cruelty
  - •Animal Death
  - •Bullying
  - •Death
  - •Gaslighting

- Homophobia
- Incest
- Mental Illness (including depression, anxiety, schizophrenia)
- Pedophilia
- Rape
- Self-Harm
- Sexism
- Sexual Assault
- Sexual Harassment
- Slurs
- Stalking
- Substance Abuse (drugs, alcohol, smoking)
- Suicide
- Swearing
- Violence
- Weapons

*For Naz Keynejad,
my partner in crime, my friend, my sister.*

(And isn't this better than an inscription anyway?)

The House That Remains

It waits for you.
It watches, unblinking,
keeping vigil,
anticipating your return.

It remembers,
and its old bones
ache from the weight
of all that it's seen.

And though it is silent as stone,
keeping its secrets close,
it still speaks your name,
in whispers only you can hear.

Its door will never shut for you,
and its windows will never truly open.

Its nails are rusted.
Its wood, splintered.

Its air, heavy.
And its corners are thick with dust
and shadows
that bear the familiar shapes
of things left behind.

In every room there are echoes.
In every creaking step
is the ticking of a clock.

It is a witness
to all that's been,
and to all that is,
and to all that will remain
until burdens are laid down
and the foundation itself is split,
and the house,
once necessary, once vital,
can finally fall.

"There is no coming to consciousness without pain. People will do anything, no matter how absurd, in order to avoid facing their own Souls. One does not become enlightened by imagining figures of light, but by making the darkness conscious."

– Carl Jung

Chapter 1

33 Stillwater Lane

Mandy was surprised by how much smaller the house seemed. It had loomed in her memory for so many years, a symbol of everything she'd wanted to leave behind. Now, seeing it again after such a long time, it looked like any other structure, an assortment of wood and brick and plaster. A thing, most unremarkable.

They'd known the house would need repairs, but she hadn't expected it to be quite so run down. Though it had always been taken for granted by those who lived here—neglected and unappreciated, starved of love and attention—the years had been most unkind.

Mandy leaned against her faded blue Corolla, its engine still warm from the drive, and took a breath. The summer breeze was tinged with decay, sweet yet sour, in a way she found unsettling.

She glanced around at her old neighborhood.

The other houses on the street stood in stark contrast, simply by virtue of their upkeep. Some of them had been remodeled and appeared downright cozy, like places where families shared meals and laughed together.

But not *this* house.

Not her house.

Not 33 Stillwater Lane, Rosebury, Tennessee. Home of the

Holloways and the Caulders before them. *This* house stood apart, stagnant, uncared for, touched only by weather and age. As if it had stopped and waited for her to return, biding its time in a state of quiet ruin.

From the car, Ethan asked, "Mom, can we go to the hotel now?" The 14-year-old was sitting alone in the back, his eyes down over his portable video game console.

"We have to get the keys first," Mandy replied, the fatigue evident in her voice.

"I really need to go to the bathroom," Grace said, squirming. The 9-year-old leaned out the front passenger-side window, her long, blonde tresses mussed from a day spent riding in the car. She fiddled with the side mirror.

"You'll have to hold it for a few more minutes, okay?" Mandy said.

Grace sighed. "You know holding it isn't good for you, right?"

Mandy chuckled. "I think you'll be okay."

She glanced down the road, looking for any sign of Chris or the woman. Nothing yet. Sighing, she turned back to study the house again.

It was a single story, ranch-style home, built right after World War II. And, apart from the ravages of time, it appeared just as it had when it was constructed.

On the far-right side of the house was the car port. It was filled with junk: boxes and bags, miscellaneous detritus, and old washing machines and dryers stacked on top of one another. Parked under the carport was her father's 1972 Ford Torino station wagon. The car was once a prized possession for him. It was meant to be his pet project, something he would restore to its former glory. Now it sat weathered and rusted and rotting away. Mandy wondered how long it had been since it had moved.

Large yards were a staple of homes in this area. The front had once been grassy but was now sun-bleached and overtaken by weeds and plants grown wild. The two oak trees were once familiar playthings for Mandy. In the time since she'd been away, they had grown taller, but they too appeared weathered and unfed. Weary.

A solitary car tire, gray and cracked from exposure to the sun, lay in the yard near the black-top driveway. For a moment, she wondered if it was the same one that had been part of the tire swing that had once hung from the oak tree on the left side of the yard.

No, she thought, *surely not.*

In the middle of the house was a set of steps leading to a small porch. The front door was covered in uneven marks, its white paint worn and peeling. Several deep, uneven gouges marred its surface. Seeing them made Mandy wince. Made her stomach ache.

She pushed the thought away.

The frame of the screen door was rusted, the screen torn.

To the right of the front door were two windows of equal size, framed by shutters that were now full of wood rot. One of them drooped on a broken hinge. These were the windows to the living room.

To the left of the front door were three smaller windows that were nearly obscured by the viburnum bushes that were now growing wild. These were the children's bedrooms when she was a girl—hers and her two older brothers. Her focus narrowed on the window on the right, the one nearest the front door. *Her* room.

The memory peeked up again without warning, like an intruder.

The dark of night. Waking with her heart racing. A truck horn blaring outside. An engine revving. Bright headlights aimed right at her bedroom window.

It was a momentary and uninvited reminiscence, and she shuddered.

How had it come to this? How in the world had she ended up back here? In this town. In this yard. Standing in front of this house. After she'd sworn she'd never return.

So much had changed for her in the last few years. And even more so in the last few months, ever since she'd received the call that Monday morning.

———

"Hello. I'm lookin' for Amanda Jean Holloway," the woman said from the other end of the line. She sounded like an older woman. Her voice was coarse, but pleasant, and tinged with a lilting Tennessee accent.

"Who's calling?" Mandy asked.

"My name's Mary Lynn Kreuger. I work at Martin Puckett's office. He was named executor of your folks' estate after they passed."

Mandy experienced a jolt at the mention of their deaths, a surge of confusing and conflicting emotions that tightened her throat and brought tears to her eyes. The intense feelings passed quickly, leaving behind the vague numbness she most often associated with her parents.

"I'm sorry…uh, *this* is Mandy, but are you sure you have the right person?"

"Um…well, let's see…were your folks Earl and Deborah Holloway?"

"Yes," Mandy said. "Yes, they…*were*. I'm sorry—can you give me a moment to process this? It's the first I'm hearing of it."

"Oh, my stars! I should've asked, hon," Mary Lynn said. "I assumed you knew. I'm not used to the children not knowing. I'm sorry—I didn't stop to think about it, and that was… Well, it was thoughtless of me."

Mandy hadn't lived in Tennessee in almost two decades and hadn't seen her parents in almost as long. She hadn't even spoken to them on the phone in years.

Though the news of their deaths had taken her off guard, she wasn't exactly surprised by it. Their routines had always involved fried foods, chain-smoking, heavy drinking, and no exercise. Her father was an alcoholic and had been for as long as she could remember. Her mother was a drug addict—sometimes functional, though often not— who chased her prescription pills with Mountain Dew and bourbon. Mandy would've been more astounded to learn they were healthy and thriving than that they were gone.

"It's okay. It's fine," Mandy said after a moment. "I'm fine."

Mary Lynn Kreuger explained that her parents' estate was in probate, but that it should be resolved soon.

"Do you know…*how* they died?" Mandy asked.

There was a pause on the other end of the line. "Uh, I'm afraid…I can't say for sure. And I wouldn't want to steer you wrong with…*guesswork*."

"I understand. I'm shocked that my folks even had a will, to be honest. It wasn't in their nature to prepare. Or plan for things. Or *do* things, for that matter."

"Well, it's not *much* of a will," Mary Lynn said. "They didn't have much in the way of assets. Or debts—which is good. So, probate oughta be wrapped up soon enough. From what I can see, they were mainly livin' off your daddy's pension. And they wanted to be buried in the family plot on the property. Does that sound right?"

"Probably, yeah." Mandy hadn't thought of the family graves in years.

"Alright then. It looks like they left some money for funeral expenses to your brother Shane. But…everything else they had is supposed to go to you."

Mandy blinked. "That's… No, that can't be right." Her mind raced.

"It is, indeed," Mary Lynn said. "All assets go to their daughter, Amanda Jean Holloway."

"And there's…no explanation at all?"

"No, nothing like that. It only specifies burial on the family property, sets aside some money for burial and headstones, and leaves everything else to you. It's a short, handwritten will, but it was signed and notarized down at the bank, so everything's in order."

Mandy rubbed her face. "And you're sure there's no other mention of my brothers? Or my uncles? *Anyone?*"

Mary Lynn cleared her throat. "*No one else,* Miss Holloway. Like I said, it's real brief. Not much room for misunderstandings."

"I don't…huh. I'm having a hard time understanding this," Mandy said, more to herself than to Mary Lynn. "Please forgive me. This is all very…unexpected."

"Of course, of course," Mary Lynn said, her voice softening. "As I mentioned, there's not much in the way of cash savings. But there is some real property. A few vehicles. Some jewelry. Furniture. And, of course, the house at 33 Stillwater Lane, which has no mortgage."

The mention of her childhood home hit Mandy right in the gut.

Her first, most primal thought was to destroy it—a visceral urge she didn't quite understand. That was followed by a flood of emotions, a confusing concoction of resentment and guilt.

Mandy exhaled, trying to process everything she was learning, everything she was feeling.

Mary Lynn's voice cut through her chaotic thoughts, steady and pleasant. "Any smaller items, like the jewelry, can be shipped to you. And, if y'all need help getting the vehicles or the house ready to sell, I can assist you with that. Judging by your area code, you're not local anymore?"

"No. California," Mandy said.

"Ahhh," Mary Lynn lingered on the word, letting it stretch out.

"I know, it's not really the same…vibe," Mandy said.

Mary Lynn giggled, "No, I s'pose it isn't."

———

After a few minutes, Mandy saw two vehicles approaching. One was Chris's truck, pulling the rented trailer. The other was a red sedan, which Mandy hoped was Mary Lynn Kreuger.

She hoped it wouldn't take long to conclude their business. Chris had to be as tired as she and the kids were. They had been on the road all day and had come a long distance. They were all due some rest.

The truck and trailer pulled up in front of Mandy's car. The other vehicle, an off-red, older Mitsubishi Galant, pulled onto the blacktop driveway.

Chris climbed out of the truck and began stretching his back as he walked toward Mandy and the kids.

A squat woman in her early sixties exited the Galant. She had a head of blonde ringlets and was sporting a bright pink coat. If this was Mary Lynn Kreuger, her appearance was just as Mandy had imagined.

"How are you doing?" Chris asked.

"Same as you, I suppose," Mandy replied. "All gassed up now?"

Chris shook his head in disgust. "I *almost* made it. Figures."

"At least you don't have to do it in the morning."

"Glass half full." He shrugged.

"Hi, hi, hi," the woman in pink said. She extended her hand. "I'm Mary Lynn. Are you Amanda Holloway?"

"I am," Mandy said, returning the handshake. "And this is my partner, Chris Ashford. And that's our brood in the car."

"Oh…Ashford?" Mary Lynn asked, giving Chris and the kids cordial waves. "I need to make sure to update all the paperwork with your married name, so that there are no issues down the line."

"No, you have my name right," Mandy said.

"Oh. Well…okay then," Mary Lynn replied. She tugged at the bottom of the too-tight, Pepto-Bismol colored blazer. Her vivid red lips pulled back in a forced smile, revealing a decent set of cigarette-stained teeth.

While it would have been easy to dismiss the notion of a law degree based on Mary Lynn's appearance—the yellow ringlets dancing around her face; the thick makeup, bright around her eyes and rosying her cheeks; the attempt at professionalism marred by scuffed shoes, ill-fitting clothes, and coffee stains—Mandy could recall a great number of professional people from her childhood who looked an awful lot like Mary Lynn. Her Aunt Lisa came to mind, for one. Lisa had been a Mary Kay saleswoman for a brief time and had driven around in a car very similar in color to Mary Lynn's coat.

"I don't need to tell y'all that you're in the right place, now do I?" Mary Lynn giggled.

"I suppose not." Mandy tried to smile, but she felt far away, disconnected, almost out of body. Did her smile appear false? Did her mouth move right? Had her eyes seemed distant? "The place is the same," she said, after a moment, "and I do *not* mean that as a compliment."

"Yes, well…it's all original. It *will* need a bit of love and some elbow grease, but I think the bones are all still pretty good. Would you like to go inside and take a gander?" Mary Lynn didn't wait for them to answer. She was already extracting a ring of keys from her blazer and moving toward the front door.

Mandy didn't follow. She waited for Chris, who'd stopped at the car to talk to the kids.

"You guys stay here in the car, okay?" he said.

"It's too hot in the car," Ethan protested. "Can't we go inside?"

"Your mom and I are gonna go in and check it out first. If it's too hot, take your sister and go explore the yard."

"It's too hot *outside* too,"

Chris huffed. "Jeez, it's not that bad. Go and stretch your legs. But watch out for rusty metal and snakes."

"Wait—really?" Grace said, concern creeping into her voice. "Like, real ones? *Poisonous* ones?"

Ethan scoffed. "We'll be fine."

"Look out for her, bud," Chris said.

"But…are there *really* snakes?" Grace asked as she climbed out of the car.

Mandy watched the two kids hurry toward the side yard before turning back to the house. She attempted to moisten her lips with her tongue and put a hand to her chest where her heart was pounding.

This place had haunted her.

Not a day had passed that she hadn't thought of it. In fleeting memories. And in nightmares. Now here she was, standing in its shadow, waiting to step inside. Preparing to *live here* once more. The thought was almost unbearable.

"You doin' okay?" Chris asked, placing his hand on the back of Mandy's arm.

She jumped at his touch. "Yeah. But it's kind of…*surreal.* To be back, you know?"

Chris rubbed her arm through her top. "You look a little peaked. You feel alright?"

She took a small breath. "From being cooped up in the car all day." Then she added, "Just…lie to me."

"But we promised we would never." He said it with mock drama, smiling.

"It's okay. I give you permission this once. Lie to me."

Chris squared his body with hers, his hands firm on her shoulders. "I don't have to lie. It's *all* going to be okay."

Her lip twitched. It might not have sounded like a lie, but it felt like one to her. She tried to avoid his eye contact, but when she finally gave in, she saw a familiar earnestness. She wondered why she often avoided his gaze when it was always reassuring. Kind.

"It's *only* temporary," he said. "We fix it up and we sell it, like we planned. A means to an end. We'll be back on our feet in no time."

Mandy nodded, but not because she believed him. It was going to take a *lot* to fix this place…if it *was* fixable.

Some places are built on bad foundations, she thought. *Some places are too far gone.*

"C'mon," Chris said, reaching out for her.

Mandy took his hand. His warm, calloused fingers were familiar and comforting. Together they began to walk toward the house, the white front door looming ahead. With each step, the grass crackled beneath their feet, brittle and lifeless, and the air grew heavier, thick with the scent of damp wood and mildew.

As they approached the uneven steps leading to the front porch, Mandy stopped. How many times had she sat right here, playing alone, either by choice or because no one else cared?

"You go in first," she said, her voice unsteady. "I'll be right behind you."

"You sure?"

She hesitated. "Yeah, go. She's waiting on us. I…need a moment."

Chris nodded and squeezed her hand before walking up the steps where Mary Lynn was waiting by the door.

He exchanged quiet words with the woman, and they entered. Mandy listened, and after a moment of silence, she heard Chris say, "Ohhhh—oh, man."

Mandy clenched her jaw.

They'd been through so much already over the last couple of years. And Chris had been their rock, the steady one, always finding a way to move forward. Now, for the first time, she could hear the weight of defeat in his voice, and that was devastating.

This move was supposed to be a fresh start for them, and this house was meant to be a life raft, something to keep them afloat after years of treading water. But she worried it was only another weight that would drag them down.

From inside, Mary Lynn cleared her throat. "Travis—uh, that's the brother—certainly did his worst on his way out the door."

Mandy waited for Chris to make a joke. Waited for him to start processing out loud.

His silence was so much worse.

Mandy took a deep breath. And as she did, she was surprised by a familiar scent. It was that unique scent that sets upon a place after years of continued habitation, like a stamp of identity, the marriage of a place and the people who dwell within. Mandy hadn't taken in this specific scent in close to two decades, but there it was, vivid and recognizable. It rushed through her, transporting her back in time as random memories flashed through her mind like snapshots.

It was the smell of her childhood.

And she loved it. And she loathed it.

And here she was again, bathed in it.

This was her home. Different, but also the same.

Mandy took a few small steps forward, opened the screen door, and pushed her way past the gouged front door. She stopped at the threshold, taking a moment to compose herself, then stepped inside and looked around.

Oh my god.

CHAPTER 2
GOOD BONES

The house was still.

From her place in the doorway, Mandy could only see the family room to the right and the kitchen dead ahead, but it was clear that the house was a disaster.

Chris was the one who was pale now. It was unusual for him to be speechless. Mandy wondered if he needed her to tell *him* lies . To tell him that it would all be okay and that it was only temporary.

The house had always been a mess. Even when she was a girl. But now...

Jesus, Mandy thought.

The house looked as if it hadn't been cleaned in years, and that very well might have been true. The carpets were stained. The wood was gouged and splintered, weak from rot. The walls were cracked, and the paint—layer upon countless layer—was flaking away, each coat revealing another color underneath. A coating of dirt and dust obscured the true shades of furniture fabric and countertops. Broken glass marred the cabinets in the kitchen.

Most of this was due to neglect.

But there was an extra level of nastiness here.

According to Mary Lynn, Mandy's brother, Travis, had been living in the house when their parents had died. Though he had no legal right to the property, and no means with which to challenge their parents' will in court, he'd stayed until he was evicted. Before he left, he stripped the house of anything of value. Appliances had been sold and wheeled away. Some of the lights and plumbing fixtures had been removed. Even some of the wiring had been pulled from the walls.

A simmering anger took its place among the already chaotic mix of emotions within Mandy—nervousness, resentment, grief, fear.

Travis had always been a disaster, but this was vicious. *Personal.*

"What a complete asshole," Chris whispered.

"Uh…yes, well," Mary Lynn cleared her throat. "He did *not* want to go."

Chris nodded. "Yeah, I can tell."

"I did mention on the phone that the house needed *a bit* of work. I hope y'all didn't plan on stayin' here tonight?" Mary Lynn asked.

"No. Thank God," Chris replied. "We're staying at the Briarwood hotel in town tonight. But we had no idea the extent of things, so we may need to extend that…a couple of nights, I guess? Until I can make sure this place is safe, at least, and that we have electricity and water and…what not."

More money, Mandy thought. *More money we didn't budget. More money we don't have.*

"I reckon that's a good idea." Mary Lynn offered Chris the keyring. "The locks are brand new. Got you three sets of keys. All doors are keyed the same—front, back, work shed, and…uh, what was the other one again? Oh, right, the basement."

The basement.

Mandy's eyes drifted to the basement door, almost reflexively.

As Chris moved to Mary Lynn, the floorboards creaked under his weight.

"Thank you," he said, taking the keyring.

Something about the combination of the creaking floorboards and the jingling of the keys scratched at something deep within Mandy, an unease she recognized but couldn't place.

Every sound, every detail—the pervasive smoky stench, the way the interior of the house carried sound, the uneven fading on the carpeting—triggered new memories, fragments of moments she hadn't thought about in years or reminders of things she'd long forgotten.

Mandy swallowed hard and refocused her attention on Chris, as his gaze darted around the interior of the house. She wondered what was going on in his mind. Chris had always been stubbornly optimistic and earnest, determined never to let life wear him down, greeting every obstacle with a smile. It was this quality that had first drawn Mandy to him. Now, for the first time, she wondered if this house—the mess of it all—would be the thing that broke him.

Instead, he turned to her and asked, "How are *you* doing? Being back in this house?"

She shrugged it off, pursing her lips and nodding.

As if to punctuate his question, a cockroach scurried out from under the living room sofa.

"Oh. Uh, I can get you the name of a good pest control fella, if you need it," Mary Lynn offered. "You know, just in case."

"Uh, yeah." Chris nodded. "Probably gonna need that."

Mandy stepped forward. The floorboards creaked again, the sound reverberating through the still house and piercing through her. Another memory peeked out. Not in full, but enough for Mandy to catch its shadow before it disappeared again.

Being back here made her feel sick inside. She wanted to run. To jump in the car and speed back to California, back to the apartment they'd all once shared. Where they'd laughed and smiled, and where life had been manageable…before it wasn't. It was so hard to accept that doing that wasn't possible. She still felt as if she'd wake up any moment and shake off a bad dream to find herself back in a life she loved and missed.

But that wasn't going to happen.

This was her reality now.

Then—a loud *thunk* came from somewhere down the hall.

Mandy froze.

Something had moved.

Chris spun in the direction of the sound, his eyes turning steely, his usual casual demeanor giving way to something more guarded.

"Is someone else in the house?" he asked.

———

Grace kicked at the dirt as she followed Ethan toward the side yard. There, the weeds and wild grass were interrupted by stretches of gravel and red clay. And it smelled different—like metal, damp wood, and something bitter. She didn't like it.

"Can you believe this?" Ethan asked, glancing back at her over his shoulder.

"Well, it's big," Grace said. She couldn't believe the amount of space between the houses. In California, they'd lived in an apartment and had no yard of their own. And most of the houses she'd visited were sandwiched together, with not a lot of breathing room.

"Yeah…a big pile of crap," Ethan laughed.

The first thing they encountered was an old brown car sitting on bricks where its wheels should be. Its paint was peeling, its edges were rusty, and its hood was propped open like a mouth mid-yawn. As they passed, Grace glanced inside the busted side window. Through cobwebs, she spotted a raggedy blanket stretched across the back seats. The rest of the car was filled with trash, sticks and leaves, and a mess of yellowing newspaper with headlines too faded to read.

Something—*a small animal?*—moved inside, shifting the car. Grace stumbled back, startled, almost stepping in a puddle of water. Its surface was covered in a shiny, rainbow-reflecting sludge, and it had a foul, pungent odor—a sharp contrast to the scent of rusted metal. She wrinkled her nose.

Beyond the brown car was a heap of junk, much of it indistinguishable—a stack of old tires, a pile of cinder blocks covered in moss, an assortment of trash and metal and fabric. Tall weeds wound their way through the mess.

And beyond that was another vehicle: an old, orange pickup truck with white rimmed tires. Its back end was lifted by rusted red jacks and its windows were thick with dirt. Underneath the truck lay various debris and scrap metal. And in its bed was another full truck bed, this one a faded, matte black; it was tied down with fabric straps.

Grace found the image of a truck bed in a truck bed amusing. It reminded her of that kid's book about turtles stacked on turtles.

Ethan knelt near the side of the house and tried to peer through a window near the ground. "What's this room, I wonder. You think this house has a basement?"

Grace shrugged, uncertain and, for the moment, uninterested. She pointed to a rusted refrigerator lying on its side. "What do you think's in *there*?"

Ethan laughed. "Nothin' good, I bet." Nevertheless, he went to it, grabbed the handle, and lifted it open. The door creaked as he pulled —a harsh metallic grind—and a swarm of tiny bugs scattered from underneath.

Grace jumped back. "Gross."

Inside was nothing but dark stains and broken shelves, which seemed to disappoint Ethan. He let the door fall shut with a loud thud.

Grace stepped forward. She didn't notice the patch of shiny mud until her foot sank into it. As she pulled back, her shoe popped free with a deep, sucking sound. "Seriously?" she said, noticing the sticky, brown sludge left behind on her sole. She picked up a stick and began to scrape at it. "It's like poop mud."

"Great job," Ethan said. "Now Mom's not gonna let you back in the car."

Grace huffed.

As she continued to scrape away in what felt like a futile effort, she noticed how quiet it was outside. Not like Los Angeles. No sirens. No traffic. Only the faint buzz of flies, the rustle of leaves when the wind picked up, and the steady drone of cicadas in the distance.

"I'm going to check out the tool shed," Ethan said.

Grace dropped the stick and followed close behind him, game for whatever exploration he had in mind.

The small, windowless shed stood on the far side of the yard. Its roof was sagging, and its metal siding was streaked with rust.

The gravel surrounding the shed crunched beneath their feet.

When they reached it, they stopped short. And Grace's eyes widened.

Bones lay scattered across the ground, pale and brittle. The long incisor teeth of a small skull were bared in a permanent snarl. The rest was half-hidden by an old tarp.

"Ethan," Grace whispered.

———

"I don't see how anyone could be in here," Mary Lynn said, her voice tinged with defensiveness. "We had the locks changed yesterday, and I was here when they did it. I promise you the house was empty at that time."

Chris nodded and began to move down the hall in the direction of the noise. He stepped with caution and Mandy followed.

"Christopher, be careful," she said.

"What's this room?" Chris asked in a whisper, pointing to a closed door on the right.

"Bathroom," Mandy replied.

Chris placed his hand against the door and leaned near it, tilting his head to listen. "Hello?"

He glanced back at Mandy and shrugged.

Then he placed his other hand on the knob and gave it a tentative push. The door, warped and swollen with age, resisted. Chris pushed again, putting more weight behind it. And with a sudden crack, the door flew open, slamming against the bathroom wall.

As it did, something shifted behind it and crashed to the floor. Something heavy. Something *alive*. It landed with a thud and erupted in a high-pitched raspy shriek that echoed through the house.

Chris staggered back.

The bathroom door rebounded and swung shut again on its own.

Mandy's breath caught. That scream—it was familiar.

"Shit!" Chris said.

The thing behind the door scuttled, its movements erratic. Frantic. The piercing scream continued. It was almost otherworldly, blood-curdling.

"What the hell is it?" Mandy gasped.

Chris steadied himself and placed his hand on the door, easing it open again. He squinted into the dim bathroom. Shaking his head, he began to chuckle. "It's just a goddamn possum," he said with a relieved sigh, his voice still carrying a hint of anxiousness.

Of course, Mandy thought. A possum. She knew she'd heard that sound before. She'd encountered many possums in Rosebury as a girl.

"He's a big boy too. Good thing their bark is worse than their bite," Chris said, taking a cautious step into the bathroom. He leaned in and looked around, then recoiled. "Oh, Jesus," he gasped, gagging. He put a hand over his mouth as he backed away, letting the door slam shut again.

Mandy took a step toward him. "What is it?"

"No, stay back," Chris warned, raising his hand to stop her. "There's gotta be a sewer leak or something. It stinks."

"There's no sewer," Mary Anne called from the family room. "It's a septic system."

Oh…right, Mandy thought, remembering the times that the septic tank had overflowed. It had happened often, and she'd forgotten all about it. Another thing she'd blocked out.

Chris pulled his t-shirt collar up to cover his nose and mouth and pushed the door open again. The possum, which had gone quiet, resumed its shrill, defensive wail.

"Damn it," Chris muttered.

"What is it?"

"There's a hole in the floor in here—you can see down into the floorboards. Or maybe even the crawlspace. I'm guessing that's how our little friend here got in," Chris said, glancing at Mandy over his shoulder. He took one more look, gagged again behind his makeshift mask, shook his head, and sighed. "You said there was a basement, right?"

Basement.

"Yeah," Mandy replied, her voice unsteady.

"I need to check it out. This might be a septic backup. If it is, it could be bad. We've got to deal with it right away." He let the door shut and the possum once again stopped screaming. "Which way is it?"

Mandy motioned toward the kitchen.

"I'm sorry to abandon y'all, but I have to get back to the office for another appointment," Mary Anne said. "Will you be alright on your own?"

Mandy nodded. "We'll be fine."

"I have a few more papers for you to sign in person, but we can handle it at the office in the next few days, if that works better."

"That would be best," Mandy said. "It's been a long trip, and we're all pretty tired and hungry." She tried to keep her focus on Mary Lynn, but her gaze kept drifting back to Chris as he moved to the basement doorway and opened it.

As he stood at the top of the basement stairs, he said, "Lights aren't working. Can you hold the door open for me?"

"You go," Mary Lynn said, giving Mandy a reassuring pat on the arm. "We'll talk later."

Mandy nodded again.

Once Mary Lynn had gone, Mandy was left with both relief and fear for what was next. They were on their own now.

She moved into the kitchen, and as she did, the wooden floor groaned again. Her pulse quickened and her hands were suddenly clammy. She swallowed against the dryness in her throat.

"Here, hold the door open so I can get some more light," Chris said, switching on the flashlight function on his phone.

Mandy reached out for the edge of the door, and a shiver ran through her as her fingers brushed the old wood.

"I'll only be a minute," he said.

She held the door open and watched as Chris descended into the basement, phone held in front of him, the old wooden stairs complaining with every step. Each creak was like nails on a chalkboard for her, making her stomach twist.

Mandy watched as he reached the landing and turned, disappearing from her view. The residual light from his flashlight was engulfed by an oppressive darkness. She kept her eyes fixed on the landing, on the dark, as if something horrible might emerge if she dared to glance away. Her heart began to beat harder, and an inexplicable sense of dread seized her.

"You doin' okay down there?" she called, her voice wavering. "Chris?"

After a beat of uneasy silence, he responded. His voice was distant and uneasy. "Well…sort of."

A feeling of relief washed over her when she saw him on the landing, climbing back up the stairs toward her, the collar of his t-shirt covering his nose and mouth.

"It's hard to tell how bad it is with just the light from my phone, but there's definitely a septic back up," he said, shaking his head. "Let's hope for the best."

Chris arrived at the top of the stairs and pulled the door shut behind him. Only then was Mandy able to exhale, glad to be done with the basement, at least for now.

"This is too much, isn't it?" she asked, her voice low and soft. "We're in over our heads."

"Well, it's…a lot," he admitted. "More than I expected, that's for sure."

"Right. Too much."

Chris looked at her, his gaze distant for a moment, as if seeing right through her. Then his focus sharpened, and a familiar glint of optimism flickered back into his eyes. "It's an opportunity," he said with quiet conviction. "That's how we have to look at it. Opportunities need to be met with effort. So, that's what we'll do."

"We can all help," Mandy replied, her voice steadier now.

A slight smile returned to Chris's face, forming familiar creases at the corners of his eyes. "I'll call a few local septic services once we're at the hotel. I'll make sure everything is safe for you and the kids before we do anything else. After that, we'll tackle it together. We'll each do our part. It'll be a…*bonding* experience." He nodded. "We can survive this."

"We can," Mandy said.

I have before.

———

As MANDY WALKED toward the side yard to find the kids, she was startled by an unexpected voice.

"Amanda Holloway?"

Mandy spun around.

A woman was standing only a few feet away. She was of average height, but heavy, her white tank top and brown sweatpants clinging to her curves. The skin around her mouth was pocked with acne. Her hair, a dirty brown, was pulled back into an untidy ponytail, with loose strands hanging over her forehead and eyes. She was barefoot. It was hard to guess at the woman's age, but Mandy figured maybe ten years older than she was. Early fifties perhaps? She didn't recognize the woman.

"Amanda?" the woman said again. "It's me. Cheryl."

Mandy blinked, scrambling to place the face.

"Cheryl *Stilton*," the woman continued with a nervous chuckle, fidgeting. "I used to live next door. Still do, actually. We were in the same grade over at Woodson Elementary. We were…friends."

Cheryl Stilton. How was that possible?

Mandy's mind struggled to reconcile this nervous, fidgeting, over-weight woman with the sweet little girl who used to play with her by the creek.

"Oh my gosh, of course," Mandy said. "Forgive me, Cheryl."

"No, it's fine," Cheryl said. Her speech was slurred somewhat. Mandy thought she saw a glint of metal behind her lips—a retainer, perhaps. "It's been…well, Lord, I don't know…a long time."

"Decades, yes. How are you?" Mandy asked.

"I'm okay. Surprised, I s'pose," Cheryl said. "I didn't 'spect to ever see ya back 'round here." She swayed, toying with her hands, her hair, her tank top. "Little Amanda Holloway back in Rosebury, all grown up. Who woulda thunk?"

The two women stood facing each other, the silence stretching on too long. Mandy struggled to think of something else to say. Until Chris appeared beside her, offering her a way out. "Oh…this is my partner, Chris," she said, relieved. "Chris, this is Cheryl. She grew up next door. And still lives there."

"My pleasure," Chris said with a small but friendly wave.

"Hey there." Cheryl smiled at him, her pale cheeks turning pink. "Partner, huh? Like in a business or somethin'?"

Chris chuckled. "No, I'm her boyfriend. And her baby daddy. But she refuses to make an honest man out of me."

Cheryl paused, her brow furrowing. "Oh, I see," she said, half-smiling.

"Life partners," Mandy added, as if to clarify.

"Oh, okay." Cheryl changed the subject. "Y'all stayin' in the house?"

"Well, not tonight," Mandy said. "We're staying at the Briarwood until we can fix the place up a bit."

"Y'all are fixin to…move back?" Cheryl asked.

"Well…it's a long story," Mandy replied, glancing around. "Sorry to cut this short, but we just got in and we're beat. We really need to find the kids and get to the hotel. But maybe we can catch up more later this week?"

"Uh, sure," Cheryl said, her expression a mix of curiosity and confusion. "I would love to hear what you've been up to. It's been a long while."

Before Mandy could respond, the sound of the kids' voices came from the side of the house. They were calling for her. Mandy began to move. "To be continued?" she asked over her shoulder, a forced cheerfulness to her voice.

"Okay…uh, sure," Cheryl muttered. "Pleasure meetin' you, Chris."

As Chris and Mandy hurried toward the kids, Chris asked, "So you…grew up with her?" He seemed almost confused by the idea.

"Yup. Same grade, even."

"Man," Chris said under his breath. "That's rough."

"You be nice," Mandy admonished. And while she kept her tone playful, something about the idea of pitying Cheryl made her uncomfortable. The two of them had been friends once. If Mandy had never fled from this place, the differences between them might not have been so stark.

Mandy called for the kids again.

"Mom! Over here!" Grace called from somewhere amidst the debris.

As they followed the sound of her voice, Chris and Mandy weaved past the clutter, the cars, and the piles of junk. A graveyard of forgotten things.

Just as it always was.

"Mom, c'mere!" Grace was calling.

Mandy increased her pace, jogging ahead of Chris, and found both kids near a work shed on the side yard. Grace was waiting for her. Ethan was kneeling nearby, his chin resting on his knee, his hands wrapped around his shin.

"What is it? Is everything okay?" Mandy asked, rushing to Grace's side, placing a hand on her hair. "What's going on?"

Chris arrived behind her.

Grace pointed to the ground in front of Ethan.

Mandy moved closer to see what the kids were staring at.

She stopped cold.

Bones.

"Ethan says it's a dinosaur," Grace said, shrugging, her eyes uncertain.

Mandy's heart sank. Though the bones were scattered, disturbed by time and scavengers, she knew what they were. She only *wished* it was a dinosaur. But the rusted chain attached to an old leather collar—half-buried in the dirt nearby—made her stomach turn. The chain stretched only about ten feet, its other end attached to a corroded pipe jutting from the side of the work shed.

"Maybe we discovered it," Ethan lied, his voice hushed.

A wave of nausea hit Mandy, but she swallowed it back, forcing it down, hiding it away. She wished that they'd done an inspection of the yard before letting the kids explore on their own. How could she not have foreseen something like this? At some point, she'd gotten used to people behaving in a halfway decent manner and forgotten how cruel this place could be.

Mandy didn't know how long the skeleton had been there, but she knew that in the sweltering heat of a Tennessee sun, it wouldn't have taken long for a chained creature to die.

She didn't want her children to ever have to experience this kind of cruelty.

"Maybe we'll call someone," Mandy said, trying to disguise her disgust with a cheery smile and bright voice. "Maybe they'll want to come take a look." She pulled Grace tight against her and gave her a squeeze. Grace glanced up at her, squinting against the late-day sun. She smiled, but the corner of her mouth twisted.

Ethan remained where he was, kneeling, his arms hugging his leg, his eyes fixed on the bones.

Mandy looked at Chris, an apology in her expression.

Chris shook his head, slowly.

"I told you. You didn't know what you were getting yourself into," Mandy said. "Welcome to Rosebury."

CHAPTER 3
THE BRIARWOOD

MANDY COULDN'T REMEMBER THE LAST TIME HER ENTIRE BODY had been so tense. Already bone-weary from the cross-country drive, she hadn't anticipated how stressful being back here would be. The moment they crossed into Rosebury—the moment she saw the sign marking the city limits—her muscles had tightened, as if trapped in fight-or-flight mode, locked on high alert.

She was relieved to be in the hotel. The old air conditioner rattled, doing its best to cool the humid room. The faint scent of mildew lingered, mixed with the sharp odor of bleached sheets.

Chris and Grace had gone to pick up dinner and a few groceries, and Ethan was absorbed in his video game. Mandy had done the bare minimum unpacking, and now sat on one of the two queen beds, enjoying a moment of stillness as she stared at the television without actually seeing it.

Her skin was grimy. She had to stink. And though she dreaded the effort it would take to shower, the thought of sleeping in her current state was worse.

As she started to rise, Ethan spoke up. "Mom…that dog we saw earlier…"

Sitting on the edge of the bed, Mandy stared straight ahead. "Yeah?"

"Why would someone do something like that?"

"I don't know," she said, her voice flat. It was the best answer she could muster at the moment.

"It makes me angry," he said.

She turned to look at him—his upturned nose, narrow lips, close-set eyes, and the scowl etched on his face. When he was mad, he looked like her mother's side of the family—her brothers when they were young, and her uncles in some of the old photos she'd seen. Sometimes, she had to remind herself that he wasn't them. "Don't be *angry*," she said. "Angry people are the ones who hurt animals. Just be better than they are."

"It must have suffered," he said, his voice small.

Mandy stood and sighed. "I'm sorry. I don't want to talk about the dog anymore, Ethan. It's been a long day and I'm tired. I'm going to take a shower." Before he could respond, she grabbed a t-shirt and shorts from her open suitcase and slipped into the bathroom, shutting the door behind her.

The hotel shower wasn't strong, but it was warm. It felt good to wash the day away, even if only a little.

Mandy closed her eyes under the water's flow and let herself sway, sounds and images looping through her mind—the state of the house, the bones in the yard, the creaking of floorboards, the jingling of keys.

A loud knock on the bathroom door pulled her from her thoughts. She blinked, unsure of how long she'd been daydreaming. She put a hand on the shower wall to steady herself, then turned off the water.

"Yes?"

"Mom, are you almost done? I have to pee so bad!" Grace's small voice called out.

Mandy climbed out of the shower, wrapped herself in a hotel robe, and unlocked the door to let Grace in.

"Finally," Grace said, hurrying past her to the toilet. "I was about to explode."

Mandy frowned at the robe's flimsy material. It clung to her body in a way that was neither comfortable nor family appropriate. She dried off and began changing into her clothes.

Behind her, Grace hummed a tune as she sat on the toilet. Mandy reached for the bathroom door to give her more privacy, then hesitated. From the other room, she could hear Chris talking with Ethan. She waited and listened.

"Some people are just not good people, bud," Chris was saying.

"It makes me mad," Ethan replied.

"Yeah, I understand. But does it make you mad, or does it make you sad?"

Ethan paused. "Both, I guess."

"Me too. But, sometimes, when we're sad, it's much easier to be mad. When we put ourselves in other people's shoes and think about what they're going through, that can hurt. And hurting isn't fun. In this case, if we think about what that dog must've felt, that's sad. It probably only wanted to be loved, and didn't understand why people were mean to it, or why they abandoned it like that to fend for itself. When we feel for others like that, it's called empathy. And even though it may hurt at times, it's a good thing, buddy."

"Yeah, I guess…"

"But I do think it was real nice that you didn't talk about it in front of your sister."

"Do you think Mom is upset at me about it?" Ethan asked.

"Why would she be upset with you?"

"Because we're not supposed to lie."

"Nah. She's not upset about that, I promise. We're not supposed to lie when it's hurtful. But you lied to be kind, and that's different."

"Grace loves animals. I didn't want her to be sad," Ethan said. There was a maturity in his voice that surprised Mandy.

Chris took a deep breath. "I know. And that's why I love you, pal."

Mandy lingered at the door, her hand on the knob, a pang of guilt running through her. She wished she hadn't cut Ethan off earlier.

But she told herself it was better this way. Chris was so much better at talking about feelings, reaching the kids in a way she couldn't. She envied his ability—his patience and capacity for communication. She hated that her instinct was to run from these conversations, fearing she might say the wrong thing. But Chris was there, always. He was never tongue-tied, never struggled to find the right words. She was grateful for that, even if sometimes it made her feel like she was falling short.

———

After they'd eaten and the kids had gone to bed, Mandy went out onto the balcony of their hotel room. She sank into one of the awkward patio chairs, propped her bare feet on the wrought-iron railing, and lit her cigarette. She took a long, satisfying drag, sighing as she stretched the taut muscles in her aching neck. Her long hair was still damp. The shower had been a welcome relief, and her stomach was full, but she still couldn't shake a general apprehension.

She sat alone for a while—the balcony railing cool under her toes—and marveled at how little the town had grown since she left. Despite some new buildings, updated signage, and a fresh coat of paint on old, familiar storefronts, it was still small and quaint. Still Rosebury.

She listened to the steady, ever-present hum of cicadas and crickets, only interrupted on occasion by the sound of a passing car or semi-truck on the street below.

A warm breeze carried a hint of diesel.

In the distance, a train rumbled along the tracks at the far side of town—a sound that would always remind her of her father. She pictured him in her mind's eye: a tall, weathered man with tan skin and a face carved from stone. He always appeared either worn down or simmering, ready to explode at any moment.

When Chris had finished saying goodnight to the kids, he joined Mandy on the balcony, two beer bottles clutched in one hand, his phone and a bottle opener in the other. He sat in the chair beside hers, popped the caps, and handed her one of the bottles.

"Oh, thank god," Mandy said, wasting no time in taking it. "Where the hell did you find beer? Do they sell it in grocery stores now?"

"Nope, still only wine, I guess, and only in certain stores. But there's a liquor store on the main road…a *drive-through*, no less! This place is going to take some getting used to."

"Yeah, well, I hope we won't be here long enough to get used to anything." Mandy took a swig and let out a contented sigh. "Oh man. *This* is why I love you."

"*This* is why?"

"Yes, just this," she said, grinning. "And a…*few* other reasons."

"Are you…smoking?" Chris asked.

Mandy held the cigarette up in front of her, with mock surprise, as if she were seeing it for the first time. "Oh golly! I think I am."

"Jesus, you *must* be stressed."

"Fuck, I really am. I think I'm about to explode," she said, waving the cigarette in his direction. "Just this one, though. I don't want to make it a habit, so keep me honest."

Chris nodded and took a sip of his beer. "You doing okay with all of this? You *can* talk to me, you know."

"I know," Mandy said, shaking her head.

Chris coughed into his hand. "Yeah, well, you say that, but we haven't talked much since we started the trip."

"We've been in different cars."

"You know that's not what I mean."

Mandy's jaw tightened. Her instinct, as always, was to shut down and avoid the entire conversation. After all, what would talking about her feelings accomplish, aside from making them real?

"Let's not do this right now," she said, taking another quick drag from her cigarette and another swig from her bottle.

"Do what? I'm not trying to start a fight. I'm just worried about you. And…about *us* too. It's hard for me to tell what's going on with you these days."

Mandy sighed, the smoke swirling around her head. As much as she wanted to open up, the thought of it made her uneasy. Anxious. "I don't… I'm not like you, okay? You're a pro at *using your words*. And I don't… I'm not…it's not my thing."

"After seventeen years, I know this about you. I do. But ever since you found out about your parents and the house, ever since we decided to do this, it's like I sense you slipping away a little more each day. And I want to understand."

Mandy realized that her body had begun to tense again, and she tried to relax. She glanced over at Chris, then reached out to him. Chris took her hand. "I'm not slipping away," she said. "You don't understand how it was here when I was a kid."

"That's because you won't tell me. But I'm here. I want to be. I want to support you through whatever this is."

"You are," she said. "You're already doing that. I'm sorry. I just don't process things like you do. You're very…"

"External?"

"*Yes!*" Mandy chuckled. "And I'm very…*not*. But I love you anyway."

"I love you too." Chris squeezed her hand, taking another sip of beer. "I'm just doing my best to make sure this whole thing doesn't destroy us. I worry that we did the wrong thing."

"I hope not. But it's not like we had much choice," Mandy said.

Chris raised his eyebrows. "Comforting."

"Yeah, sorry," she muttered.

"Oh, by the way," Chris said, leaning forward in his chair, "I talked to a septic guy. He was familiar with the property already, which is good…I guess? He's gonna meet me early tomorrow morning to take a look."

"Jesus…I'd almost forgotten about the septic mess."

"One day at a time, babe. That's all we can do."

Mandy nodded. He was right, but it did little to ease her mind or loosen the knot that had been tightening in her chest. "Tell me you love me."

"Till the wheels come off."

She smiled despite herself. Then she downed the rest of her beer and dropped her cigarette into the empty bottle. "Do you want me and the kids to come over early with you?"

"Nah, sleep in, have some breakfast. Come over when you're ready."

"Then…can you take care of the bones before we arrive?"

"I already planned on it."

"You're the best."

"I am. It's true."

"We okay?" Mandy asked.

"I don't know. Are we?"

She nodded.

He took her hand again. They sat in silence for a while and listened to the cicadas, as the sun set behind the mountains.

———

AMANDA RAN BAREFOOT through the yard, the sun hot on her bare shoulders, her hair bouncing behind her in a messy ponytail. The grass was soft between her toes, the breeze warm on her face.

It was in these rare moments that she was happiest. She was free. Unburdened. A girl enjoying the world. A child reveling in her summer.

Cheryl, her little friend from next door, was right behind her, hot on her heels. Together, they sped toward the grove of oak trees that lined the back of their yards. It wasn't a race, but it felt like one, and Amanda became determined to reach the trees first. Whenever Cheryl gained ground, Amanda pushed herself faster, a smile plastered to her face. Their laughter filled the air.

As they neared the tree line, Amanda glanced up into the sky. Dark clouds had appeared without warning, creeping in, overtaking the blue, draining it, consuming it, swallowing it whole.

She was so close to the trees now.

The rain came in a downpour, drenching her face and clothes.

But where had Cheryl gone?

Alone now, Amanda came to a halt beneath the massive oak trees, finding shelter from the deluge under their broad, protective canopies. Her feet ached from running. They were sore and covered in mud. She was out of breath and perspiring, and her tank top and jeans were soaked through.

She huddled near the trunk of one of the giant trees as the water poured down around her. When she glanced back toward the house, its outline was blurred, obscured by sheets of rain.

In the distance, a dark figure—a man—was coming her direction. He moved slowly, almost strolling, as if undeterred by the sudden cloudburst, as though the rain wasn't affecting him at all.

His arms hung at his sides and a hat cast dark shadows on his face.

A wave of déjà vu swept over her, as though this had all happened before. As though it were real, somehow. But it wasn't a memory.

She began to panic. She should *flee*. But to where? Where could she go that he wouldn't find her?

Lightning flashed, and in that moment, the man appeared closer, as if he'd jumped in time. The thunder rolled close behind, rattling her ribs and shaking her heart.

You should go. Now.

Without another thought, she bolted through the trees, following the narrow creek bed, mud thick between her toes as she traversed the rocks and brush. The creek water was dark and murky.

Another flash of lightning illuminated the grove. The surface of the water lit up, and the creek became an eerie reflection of the woods. The trees closed in around her, their twisted branches casting skeletal shadows. They appeared alive. The shifting light disoriented her, making it hard to run. As the shadows faded, there was another deep roll of thunder.

Amanda kept moving, skirting the creek. She glanced over her shoulder, her heart pounding, fearing that the man might be right behind her, pursuing her. But she saw no sign of him.

Still, a familiar sense of dread permeated her, thick and unshakeable.

Then—a *third* strike of lightning. This time, the thunder crashed in near-perfect synchronicity, a sudden deafening explosion that shocked Amanda and sent her flailing forward, sprawling into a mess of mud and brush, her forearms taking the force of the fall.

She struggled to rise, slipping in the muck. She had to keep moving.

Through the sporadic flashes of light, she realized she was face to face with the skull of an animal, half buried in the mud. It seemed to be staring deep into her with vacant sockets.

Left behind.

Gasping for breath, she fumbled for a foothold, scrambling.

When she looked up, he was there.

He was standing over her, the dark hat low over his eyes, rain dripping from its brim. From this vantage point, he appeared almost impossibly tall.

He reached down toward her, and as the next lightning strike lit up the darkness of the grove, she glimpsed his face—his jaw long and thin, his teeth protruding, his deep-set eyes gaunt and hollow.

Mandy's eyes flew open, and a scream caught in her throat, escaping her lips as only a faint wheeze. Her pulse was racing, and her t-shirt and shorts were soaked in perspiration.

Her eyes darted around the room, half expecting to see skeletal shadows or the remnants of raindrops on the patio door. But there was nothing.

She was in the hotel. The Briarwood. In Rosebury.

She clutched her chest, blinking against the darkness. Already the images were beginning to fade, the man's gaunt face becoming hazy. But she struggled to shake the lingering dread of her nightmare.

"*Fuck me,*" she whispered to herself, trying to slow her rapid breathing. Was this what a heart attack was like? Should she wake Chris?

She propped herself up, leaning against the headboard.

"Mom?" the small voice said, startling her.

Mandy turned to see her daughter lying next to her, holding a pillow, her eyes open wide.

"Did I wake you?" Mandy asked, her voice deep and hoarse.

Grace shook her head.

Mandy nodded. "I had a bad dream."

"Me too," Grace whispered.

Mandy swallowed hard, her pulse still rapid. "I'm sorry, honey." She opened her arm, and Grace moved closer to her, cuddling in. "Do you want to talk about it?"

Grace shook her head again. "I don't remember. Just that it was scary." She glanced at the patio slider. "Is it raining?"

Mandy shuddered. "No, honey. Why?"

"I dreamed it was raining really hard."

Grace turned back and nuzzled into Mandy's side. Mandy kissed the top of her head, taking in the familiar scent of her hair. Within a few minutes, Grace was asleep again. But Mandy sat in the dark, unsettled. The feeling of the dream clung to her, as heavy and damp as the clothes she'd sweated through. She kept reminding herself it had only been a dream. Reminding herself that the shadowy man wasn't there, lurking in the darkness of the hotel room, waiting for her to sleep.

———

When Mandy finally nodded off again, her sleep had been deep and dreamless. She woke confused about where she was. But the generic artwork and constant noisy hum of the air-conditioner reminded her.

From the light, she realized it was much later than she was used to. She blinked off the sleep and examined the room. Chris had gone. Grace sat on the bed beside her, changing the channels on the hotel television, remote in hand. Ethan was on the opposite bed, scrolling through his phone, still half awake.

Mandy was shocked she'd slept so late. On most days, she woke on her own, long before the kids. Even Chris's alarm hadn't roused her. She must've been more tired than she'd realized.

The blackout curtains on the patio door were closed. Chris must have done it before he left. Though they didn't do an amazing job of keeping the morning light out of the room, they must've done the trick.

What day was it? Friday? The days had started blurring together since they'd started the move.

"Hi," Grace said, her voice chipper.

"Dad told us to let you sleep," Ethan added.

"What time is it?" Mandy asked, reaching for her phone and watch, which were charging on the nightstand.

"9:04," Ethan said without looking up from his phone, adding, "A.M."

Wow.

Though she wasn't looking forward to it, Mandy knew she should get up and get going. There was much to do, and she was wasting valuable time.

She stretched and pulled herself up in her bed. She winced at the persistent stiffness in her neck and shoulders, no doubt in part from the long drive. Even after some much-needed rest, she was still fatigued. Achy.

For a moment, she thought of the dream she'd had. It had been so vivid. So frightening it had woken her up. Now it was fading from her memory, more with each waking moment, leaving behind only a faint unease.

"I can't remember the last time I slept in this late," she said.

"Me either," Grace giggled. "You're a Lazy Bones Jones!"

"Hey, punk!" Mandy chided. "I'm still bigger than you, you know? For now."

Grace laughed again.

"Do you guys want breakfast? McDonald's?"

This got Ethan's attention.

"Oh, yeah…Happy Meal!" Grace said, and began doing a version of her happy dance—the one she did whenever she was excited about food—without ever moving from the bed.

"Too early for that, but you can get pancakes."

"Yes, pancakes!" Grace said, her enthusiasm in no way diminished.

Mandy rolled to the edge of the bed and stretched again. Her back cracked. She thought of Chris, who was already at the house, hard at work, and had a twinge of guilt.

After some prompting, they all got up and began getting ready for the day, though Ethan needed occasional reminders to put his phone aside and finish getting dressed.

"Remember to take your backpacks today," Mandy reminded. "Did you charge all your devices?" she asked Ethan.

"Uh…sort of?"

"I told you guys that there might not be any electricity at the house for a couple of days."

Mandy could tell the prospect of this dismayed him.

"Who cares," she said. "You need to get out of your phone and look around. It's a whole new place. A whole new city. Gotta figure things out. Maybe there'll be other kids in the neighborhood. Gotta seize the day! Or YOLO! Or whatever the current thing is."

"Ugh, Mom. Please don't do that," Ethan said.

They carted their stuff downstairs and loaded it into the car.

"Shotgun," Grace said as she opened the front, passenger door. Ethan didn't protest and climbed in the back seat. They'd been good about taking turns.

The McDonald's wasn't far away—in fact, they could see it from their hotel—and the line for the drive-through wasn't long. After receiving their order, Mandy pulled into a spot in the parking lot and left the car idling as they distributed and prepared their food.

"Where's the syrup?" Grace asked. As Mandy dug through the bag, Grace patted the dash, and began to chant, "Syrup! Syrup! Syrup!"

"You're a nutball," Mandy said. She started to hand Grace the small plastic container, but jerked it back, warning, "No spilling this in the car. It's sticky."

"I know, I know. Jeez," Grace said.

Mandy wrapped the Sausage McMuffin so that she could eat it while driving. And once everyone was set, she pulled out and they were on their way.

Mandy was amazed at how fast everything was coming back to her. Without touching the map, she navigated the route back to the house with an ease and familiarity that surprised her. She hadn't been in Rosebury in almost twenty years, yet she knew the town as if she had never left.

As she turned onto Stillwater Lane, a familiar queasiness returned, a tightening in her stomach. All the memories that were tied to this place gnawed at the edges of her mind. She did her best to push the feelings aside, dismissing them as nervous jitters, but she knew it was more than that. She wondered if she'd ever be able to return to the house without it being this way.

CHAPTER 4
DUST AND CLUTTER

CHRIS'S TRUCK WAS PARKED IN THE DRIVEWAY, THE RENTED trailer still attached. In the bed of his truck was a stack of assorted lumber. A white truck with a cylindrical tank was backed up on the grass. Big, black, blocky letters spelled out SEPTIC on the tank. It was what Mandy's parents had always called a "pumper truck."

Mandy pulled the Corolla in front of the house. She supposed she could park in the driveway, but decided it was better to leave the car on the street, out of the way.

Chris was on the porch. He was talking to a sinewy, bearded man wearing a yellow safety vest over blue overalls, a hard hat, and black work gloves. The man was animated, gesturing back toward the side of the house. Chris was nodding, his arms folded in front of him. Mandy scanned Chris's expressions for any hint of his mental state, but he kept a good poker face.

"Can we go inside now, Mom?" Ethan asked.

"Uh, we need to make sure it's all safe first. Take Grace and explore the back yard."

"We already did that."

Mandy turned and frowned at Ethan in the back seat. "Really? So you've seen everything already, huh? The whole yard? The neighbor-hood? Everything in Rosebury?"

"Kinda."

Mandy sighed and rolled her eyes at him. "Fine, hang out on the back porch and be boring. But watch for spiders."

"Snakes *and* spiders!" Grace said, shaking her head in disgust. "Seriously, what is this place?"

"Yes!" Mandy said. "*And* salamanders *and* frogs *and* crickets *and* bugs *and* crawfish *and…!*"

"Ew. Please. Can you not?" Grace wrinkled up her nose, her upper lip pulling back from her teeth.

Mandy chuckled. "You're a big girl. You'll survive."

They all got out of the car. The kids meandered in the direction of the back yard, while Mandy went to the porch.

As she got close, she heard Chris say, "So, we should stay out of the basement? What about the rest of the house?"

A wave of relief washed over Mandy when she heard they'd need to *stay out of the basement.* Then guilt, as it meant they had more to deal with.

"Well, it *oughta* be all right," the man said in a thick southern accent. He rubbed the back of his neck with his gloved hand. "I'd open all the doors and windows, for a while, though, if y'all are gonna be inside."

"And how long will it be before the basement is accessible?"

"At best a few days, maybe a week. If all goes well, shouldn't be longer'n that. We'll need to get an inspector out."

Chris nodded. "Well…*crud.*"

"Coulda been a lot worse. Be glad y'all caught it early. We'll finish up out here, and I'll let y'all know when we're done."

The man moved off the porch and Chris turned his eyes to Mandy.

"Hey, cutie," he said.

She knew this move—the pivot. He was attempting to soften the blow of the bad news. She attempted a smile but managed only a half-smile at best. "So…it's going to be expensive, huh?"

Chris waved it away. "Yeah, well…like the man said, it could be worse. Could be a family of raccoons living down there, right?"

Ever the optimist.

"So, no raccoons, only possums?" she asked.

"Oh yeah...that." Chris shrugged. "Did you get some sleep, at least?"

"Yeah, I guess I really needed it. I slept okay, except for some bad dreams. Thanks for letting me sleep. That was sweet of you."

"What were the dreams about?"

"I don't really remember now."

———

As soon as the septic truck left, Chris got right to work. He set up a pair of sawhorses in the front yard under one of the oaks, and began pulling the lumber from his truck, making a pile on the remnants of the lawn.

"So, what's first on the list?" Mandy asked. "You need help with the wood?"

"No, I think I'm okay on that. My top priority is getting that floor in the bathroom fixed. I don't want anyone to hurt themselves."

"What should I be doing? I'm a decent cheerleader, but I'd better be more useful than that or this project's gonna take forever."

Chris stopped what he was doing and wiped the sweat from his brow. "Man, it's already hot. This is gonna be fun. Let's see... I was thinking that it would be helpful to do an inspection of the house and make up a list of all the major fixes. No paint or cosmetic stuff, only repairs. It doesn't need to be complete, but it would be great to get a sense of what we're looking at."

"Sounds like something I can do."

"Oh, and can you open all the windows to air it out?" he asked.

"Sure."

"Also," he added, "while you're looking around, maybe do a mental inventory of furniture and what not. See what your asshole brother left behind and what's still usable. After that, we can make a game plan. Sound good?"

"Sure thing, chief," Mandy said, with a wry smile.

"Thanks...uh, sport," Chris replied, chuckling.

Mandy grinned. She loved that they were still playful, after all this time. They had always worked well together.

"When do the movers arrive?" he asked. "Today or tomorrow?"

"Saturday," she said. "That's tomorrow, right? I'm all mixed up."

Chris nodded. "Yeah, tomorrow. We have a helluva lot to do before we move anything inside."

"It doesn't matter. They're only going to drop the storage pod thing. We can get to all that stuff when we're ready." As she reached the front steps, she turned back. "Should I do the list on my phone? Or paper?"

"Whatever's easiest."

"Phone it is," she said.

Mandy walked up the steps and placed her hand on the screen door handle. As she pulled it open, her eyes went to the gouges in the front door. They had faded over time. Others might assume they were from age and nothing more, but to her they were sharp and unmistakable. Somewhere in her memory, she heard the sustained honking of a horn. Her grip tightened, and her heart began to beat faster. She closed her eyes and forced herself to breathe. Only when the heat began to drain from her cheeks, did she go inside.

———

MANDY STOOD STILL, right inside the front door, and took a moment, taking in the musty scent of the house and listening to its echoey stillness. The air was wet, heavy with age.

Are you ready for this? she asked herself, knowing she had no choice.

She scanned the living room. It was the room her mother had always called the parlor, as if that made it any fancier. It was the biggest room in the house.

On the front wall were two large windows, letting in light. Dust floated in the sunbeams. A rusted metal screen and a set of fireplace tools sat in front of the woodburning brick fireplace.

If Mandy's suspicions were right, her brother had only taken what he thought might be valuable, so he'd left behind a great deal of her parents' old furniture and personal items.

Some things about the living room had changed. Once, it'd housed a grandmother clock and her father's La-Z-Boy chair, but both were now gone, leaving the wood floor discolored where they had been. Other things were the same as they had been when she was a girl, like the blue chair by the front window, where she would often sit and read after school. An old credenza covered with framed photos—most of them black and white—still sat against the wall near the kitchen. The collection of pictures was very much as she remembered.

Mandy moved to the credenza. She swallowed hard seeing the faces. Several were posed family photos. Some were her grandmothers and grandfathers. One showed her maternal grandfather in his army dress, newly returned from World War II. She'd never known him. Another was of her mother and father, young together. Even then, there was a coldness to them, a distance in their eyes. She wondered if they'd ever been happy.

One photograph, in particular, drew her attention. It was her mother as a young woman, posing with her two brothers, Harlan and Malcolm. Mandy picked up the picture. The Caulder side of the family all had such similar features. And, while she didn't resemble that side of the family much, she saw them reflected in Ethan. It was a strange thing seeing traces of people you'd prefer to forget every time you looked at your own son.

She set the picture back, turning it face down, then moved toward the kitchen.

The door to the basement was between the kitchen and living room. A plastic seal covered the door jamb near the doorknob, and caution tape stretched across the doorframe in an X shape. Taped to the middle of the door was a pre-printed sign warning about potential contamination: DO NOT ENTER.

Mandy was perfectly fine with that. She didn't even like being near the door, though she genuinely had no idea why.

The floorboards squeaked under her weight. God, she hated that sound. She didn't think she'd ever get past it.

From outside, on the back porch, Grace and Ethan were laughing.

Perhaps she was only putting off an unpleasant task, but Mandy decided to check on them anyway.

As she moved across the kitchen to the back door, another memory leaped out.

Her heartbeat throbbing in her jaw. Her breaths coming in short gasps. Racing against time. Desperate to reach the kitchen door first, to make sure that it was locked before *they* found their way inside. And the sheer terror when she saw the back door ajar.

But it wasn't ajar now. It was sealed. Locked up tight.

How long would the constant stream of unwanted memories last? As long as she was back in this house? She didn't even want to entertain the thought.

As the memory faded, Mandy turned the bolt on the brand-new lock and pulled the back door open. It stuck, so she pulled with more force. The door scraped against the doorframe, stalled a moment, then flew open wide, slamming into the kitchen counter.

Ah, yes. She'd forgotten how stubborn the back door could be.

Grace and Ethan sat on the back porch steps, with Ethan showing Grace something funny on his phone. As the door opened, they both stopped what they were doing and glanced up at Mandy.

"Are you guys…alright?"

They nodded.

"Okaaaay." Mandy nodded back. "Good chat." She turned and went back inside. The laughter immediately resumed behind her.

Her mission of distraction had failed, but Mandy lingered by the back door. The carefree laughter of her children outside only made the stillness of the house seem heavier by contrast.

But she still had a job to do, and a long way to go.

The kitchen was in much worse shape than the living room. The ceiling above the dining table was dark yellow from decades of cigarette smoke. The wood floors were gouged from heavy use and carelessness, stained from beverages and paint.

And blood, yes?

She tightened her grip on the phone and forced herself to focus on the list.

The walls were marred by handprints, and in one place, the

drywall had been broken by something. *A fist?* Much of the cabinetry was dinged and gouged. One upper cabinet door hung loose, drooping on its hinges.

Mandy typed every issue she spotted into a FIXIT list she'd created on her phone.

The stove was as old as she was, most likely. The refrigerator was gone—sold by Travis, she assumed—leaving behind discolored drywall, mildew, and a mess of sticky black grime on the floor where it had stood. She caught a whiff of something foul—perhaps a dead mouse in the wall or ceiling.

Every stain and blemish held a story. Some of them she knew well. Others she'd forgotten. And some had occurred since she'd been gone.

Since you escaped.

———

MANDY LEFT the kitchen and headed down the hallway. The first door on the left was Mandy's childhood bedroom.

But it wasn't your first bedroom, was it?

She paused at the door, gently running her fingers over the familiar metal of the doorknob. It was strange how the past could feel so far away and still be right under your fingertips.

As she pushed her way inside, the door creaked and bumped into the drywall. Mandy noted: *BEDROOM 1, DOORSTOP.* But as she looked closer, she noticed that the drywall was already broken where the doorknob hit. And she suddenly remembered why. It was a day burned into her memory, but one she'd be happy to forget forever.

Holy hell, this is going to be hard.

She put it on the list: *BEDROOM 1, REPAIR DRYWALL.*

Mandy took a moment and scanned the room, taking it in. Though it was cluttered—strewn with stacks of packing boxes and mismatched furniture—so much of her personality remained that it surprised her. It stirred emotions that hadn't surfaced in some time. This had been *her place* for many years, and though it was clear that the room had become nothing more than a storage area—maybe even a guest room—it still felt like her.

On one wall was the painting she'd done as a teen, in a desire to distinguish her room—an attempt at a mural, for which she'd been punished. The bed was the same one she'd once slept in. And the dresser and bookcase were the ones her father had picked up at a local garage sale.

Several familiar books lined the shelves, ones that she remembered reading when she still lived at home: *The House of Spirits*, *Song of Solomon*, *One Hundred Years of Solitude*, and *The Secret Garden*, one of her favorites.

Behind the musty bouquet of old wood, dust, and paper, Mandy caught the faint hint of waxy crayons and markers, a reminder of many a day spent lying on the floor, lost in her own world, drawing away.

A music box sat on the dresser. Mandy went to it and opened it. A tiny, plastic ballet dancer sprung up, and the music began to play: *Music Box Dancer*. However, it played slower than it should, needing to be wound. Mandy's brow furrowed. Something about the familiar melody made her skin crawl, made her queasy. She snapped the lid shut, cutting the eerie melody off.

The packing boxes had been rummaged through and left in disarray. Strewn about were some of her old things: a stuffed bear, a few Polaroid photos, some art supplies, and an old porcelain harlequin doll, half black and half white, with a white cone-shaped hat. Mandy picked up the doll and examined it. The glossy paint on its white face glistened in the light of the room. She'd always hated this doll. Something about it disturbed her—its bright lips and the way the accents on its cheeks and eyelids made its dark eyes pop. Like it was watching her.

Without much care, she tossed it into one of the open boxes, then brushed her hands on her jeans and turned to the window. Again, she was reminded of how the bright headlights had shone through her blinds that night as a girl, illuminating her room, casting strange shadows. The constant sound of a horn outside.

Mandy pushed the memory down.

Shuffling her way past the boxes, Mandy went to the window and cranked it open. There were no screens. Never had been. She'd forgotten about that too. If the windows in the house needed to be open for ventilation, they'd all need to look out for critters.

Mandy hadn't anticipated how strange it would feel being back. A small, optimistic part of her hoped a return to this house would be cleansing, a way to put the past to rest, once and for all. But this didn't feel like closure. It felt more like ripping open old wounds. Each new discovery only reminded her of things she'd been more than happy to forget. And she couldn't help but wonder how much more the house was waiting to unleash upon her.

No sooner had the thought crossed her mind than she noticed the stain on the carpet and shuddered.

Jesus.

Thinking about how it had come to be there still hurt.

The carpet had once been white but was now a dingy yellow at best. The stain had once been bright red, but was now a murky, faded brown. It was a blood stain. She'd never been able to get it out, though she'd scrubbed as hard as she could. As if removing the stain might remove the memory as well. But some stains never come out, no matter how hard you try. Some stains are for good.

She shook her head and typed on her phone: *BEDROOM 1, NEW CARPET.*

Mandy continued to note various fixes around the room. Before leaving, she inspected the closet door. A tall piece of furniture stood nearby, covered by a painter's cloth. Out of curiosity, she pulled the cloth away and let it drop to the floor.

And she gasped.

It was her mother's mirror. Her mother had always insisted it was an antique, and it certainly looked the part. It was heavy and the thick frame was ornate. Intricate hand-carved floral patterns adorned the wood, with weathered silver-leaf inlays. The glass was uneven, and darker spots speckled its surface due to age.

As a little girl, Mandy had been fascinated by the mirror, the way it slightly distorted reflections, making them seem almost otherworldly. But her mother had been protective of it, keeping it in her bedroom, calling it off limits. Mandy had been disciplined more than once for even going near it.

She wondered how much the mirror was worth and whether they should have it appraised. Given the state of the house, they needed every penny. She smirked at the irony that Travis—desperate to strip the house of anything of worth—had likely passed right by it, incapable of recognizing something as lovely as this for its value.

Mandy stepped closer to the mirror and examined her reflection. The uneven glass added an ethereal, almost ghostly distortion. She stared at herself a moment, then shifted her gaze to the patterns on the frame. As she ran her fingers across them, she thought of how her mother would never have approved, and she delighted somewhat in the act of disobedience. The woodwork was so beautiful, so complex, yet it retained the sublime imperfections only a human craftsman could imbue.

Something moved behind her in the reflection. As if someone had passed by the doorway in the hall.

Startled, Mandy turned.

"Chris?" she called, her voice timid, uncertain. "Is that you?"

But no. It wasn't Chris. Through the window, she heard him outside, sawing lumber and humming along to an 80's song on his portable radio.

"Hello?" Mandy said, a bit louder.

Maybe it was another possum, she rationalized. But if she'd seen something, it had been much bigger. More like a person.

"Kids?"

She listened, but all she heard was the sound of Chris working outside.

You're being crazy. You're seeing things. No one's in here.

Mandy sighed, scooped the painter's cloth from the floor, and turned back to cover the mirror. But as she glanced into the glass this time, the reflection had changed. It was still her in the mirror, but she was covered with bruises, on her face and down her arms. Blood was streaming from her nose.

She shrieked and jumped back, stumbling into the packing boxes. Her knees buckled but she caught herself before she fell. When she looked up again, the image of herself had returned to normal.

Mandy wiped at her eyes, her breathing shallow.

I'm tired. I'm still tired and I'm seeing things.

Her watch beeped, alerting her to a spike in heartrate.

"Gee, thanks." She dismissed the alert screen. "Like I didn't know."

Mandy didn't attempt to cover the mirror a second time. She dropped the painter's cloth on the floor and peeked out into the hall to check for any potential intruders.

"Hello?" she said again. But there was nothing.

She took a moment to steady herself before continuing her inspection.

———

THE SECOND ROOM on the left was the one her brother Travis had occupied as a kid. And based on the state of it now—the assorted items left behind and the still lingering stink of drugs—he'd occupied it as an adult as well. Mandy didn't spend much time in this room. She added a few items to her list and moved on.

The third room on the left, the final room along the front of the house, was once her oldest brother Shane's room. Well, it hadn't *always* been his. It had been hers once, when she was small, before—

Mandy cut off the thought before it developed.

She placed her hand on the doorknob but didn't turn it. Her palm was sweaty against the metal, and her mouth had gone dry. *No reason to go in right now*, she told herself. Another time, when she wasn't so jumpy.

On the other side of the hall was the door to her parents' bedroom. However, Mandy found it was locked. It didn't require a key, so it was likely latched from the inside.

She figured Chris would have a tool to get the lock open, so she put it on the list: *PRIMARY BEDROOM, LOCKED*. But if not, there was another entrance to this room from the outside through the attached bathroom.

Okay, two rooms would have to wait. Or...three, counting the base-ment. Well, four, technically, counting the primary bathroom.

Mandy sighed. She wasn't exactly making stellar progress on this list.

Before moving on to the exterior of the house, she decided she'd pop into the hallway bathroom. Though Chris was already planning to work in that room, she figured she would find a lot more to put on the list, aside from the hole in the floor. Plus, the exterior of the house was going to take considerable time to go through, as there was a lot to fix. If she gave it all too much thought, it was overwhelming.

One room at a time.

The hallway bathroom had no exterior walls, which meant no windows. Since there was no electricity yet, Mandy decided to use the flashlight on her phone for her inspection.

But she'd forgotten about the sewer smell, and, as she opened the door, the stench hit her square in the face, making her gag. Tears welled in her eyes. She yanked the front of her shirt up over her nose, as Chris had done.

Deciding to soldier on, she stepped forward. The floor was grimy under her feet. And a damp, cold breeze moved past her. She moved the beam of light around, examining every part of the room.

What a shocking mess.

The floor, alone, was a nightmare. Aside from the hole near the stained toilet, most of the tiles were cracked and some were missing.

The walls were riddled with gouges, and the clawfoot bathtub was covered in corrosion and mildew. The light fixtures were gone, and the wiring was exposed where they had once been mounted. Rust covered the shower head, the towel racks, and lined the edges of the mirror over the sink. Most of the walls had water damage, and what appeared to Mandy to be spreading mold.

The wallpaper—a yellowish background with a repeating blue pattern of bouquets with faint pink flowers—was likely original to the house when it was built in the 1940s. She remembered it from when she was small. Even at that time, her parents had joked that it had seen better days. Now, it was destroyed. It would have to be stripped completely.

And to top it off, both the sink and the shower appeared to be leaking, dripping in an off-putting cadence, echoing in the small space as if the room had its own staccato heartbeat.

Mandy stepped back, starting to despair. They'd barely begun and already the task felt impossible. What was she thinking, agreeing to this? Why had she brought her family to this place? She knew it wasn't productive to think this way, but it was hard not to feel defeated.

After a moment, she steadied herself and repositioned her shirt over her nose. She didn't want to go back inside, but she would in order to finish her notes.

Or I could just write REDO THE ENTIRE GUEST BATHROOM and be done with it! she thought.

She stepped back in, alternating between taking notes and using the phone as a light. She swept the beam around the small room, noting everything as she went. As the light passed over the hole in the floor, she stopped and held the beam on it. She wondered how it had come to be and smiled momentarily at the thought of Travis on the toilet when the floor had given way. The mental picture made her happy.

Wait...what the hell?

She blinked against the darkness, moving closer to the hole, testing each step before committing her full weight.

Had she seen something inside?

Mandy leaned in and squinted. It was hard to tell with the weak camera light, but...was that...? No, it couldn't be.

What the...?

Mandy turned the flashlight off and switched her phone into camera mode. She aimed the phone down into the hole to the best of her ability and pressed the camera button, hoping the picture would turn out in the dim light of the bathroom.

You're being ridiculous.

As the flash went off, she felt the familiar pressure of a hand on her back. It startled her at first. Chris, she thought, worried she might fall through the floor and hurt herself.

"I'm coming out right now," she said, her voice shaky. "I just wanted to see something."

He leaned in closer to her. *Too* close. Confused, Mandy opened her mouth to speak—then caught the faint, stale scent of cigarettes.

It wasn't Chris's voice that spoke to her.

"*You can't just leave,*" it said in a whisper, right next to her ear. There was warm breath against her neck.

For a moment, Mandy froze, muscles locked, gooseflesh rising on her nape, running down her arms. Then she jumped, tripping, falling forward. Her hand scraped against the gritty floor, and her shoulder slammed against the cabinet under the sink. She spun herself around as quickly as possible, her hands rising, ready to defend herself, her heart hammering in her chest.

But there was no one.

She was alone in the bathroom.

From outside, the sound of Chris's humming continued.

Mandy sat on the dirty floor, unnerved and frightened, waiting, trying to comprehend what had happened. Her breaths came in short, ragged gasps.

After a moment, when she was sure she was alone in the house, and her heartrate began to slow, she glanced down at the phone in her lap, still open to the camera, and the photo she had snapped.

Her stomach dropped and a strange disquiet swept over her.

She blinked, staring at the screen, willing the image away, wanting it to make sense somehow. But it didn't.

It was a perfect picture of the uneven hole in the floor. And sitting inside of it was a baby doll's head. Its plastic face was cracked and worn, half-hidden in filth. Its blonde hair was tinged with grime. One eyelid was stuck closed and the other hung open to reveal a bright blue eye that seemed to be staring right back at her.

She remembered the day it had happened.

How old had she been that Easter? Six? Seven?

For years, she'd put the whole thing out of her mind. But here it was, all flooding back again, whether she wanted it to or not.

CHAPTER 5

EASTER, 1988

AMANDA HOLLOWAY WAS SIX YEARS OLD WHEN HER MOTHER announced she was going to host a group for Easter and do the cooking. This was big news for Amanda. Seeing her mother cook or clean was an unusual occurrence in and of itself, so the idea of her hosting a group at their house was entirely new. Though Amanda was confused by the announcement, she was also excited at the prospect of helping.

Amanda's father, Earl, worked as a freight engineer for the railroad, which meant he kept an irregular schedule. Though some of his trips lasted as long as a week, he was typically gone for one or two days at a time, most often making runs to Bristol and back. When he was home, watching television and snoozing in his La-Z-Boy chair, it was only for a few days at a time. Then he would leave again. The family had gotten used to it. He was either not around at all or around too much, and there never seemed to be a happy medium.

This meant the day-to-day rearing of the children had been left to Amanda's mother, Deborah. And, to say she took a hands-off approach would be an understatement. Deborah was self-focused and self-medicated, which made her both undependable and unpredictable. Sometimes, she would wake with boundless energy. She might start a new project, such as painting a random wall in the house with an unusual, clashing color. Or she might disappear with Earl's paycheck to go shopping or gambling—she liked to play Bingo at the hall in Alcoa. Some days, she stayed out all night, only to return the following morning. Other days, she never got out of bed at all.

This way of living wasn't new to Amanda. She'd never known anything else.

Early on, she'd learned she couldn't rely on her parents to be there for her when she needed them. Even at six, she was used to fending for herself. She'd grown accustomed to waking herself up in the morning, getting ready, and getting herself to school. Sometimes, she was proud of her independence. And while it wasn't a happy way to live, or reassuring for a girl her age, it seemed almost normal. It was only when she saw her classmates with their own families that she was reminded how unusual her life actually was. That would make her sad, and jealous, and a bit confused.

Her two older brothers, Shane and Travis, were no help. Shane was always distant, like he was somewhere else, even when he was sitting right next to her. And Travis was always in trouble for something— skipping school, getting in fights, stealing.

What she couldn't comprehend at her age was that they were doing the same thing she was. Trying to cope, parenting themselves, figuring out who they were, and trying to get by, with varying degrees of success.

As Easter neared, Deborah's energy level was high. And when she announced her plan to host an Easter gathering, Earl tried to talk her out of it, reminding her he'd be gone for work until Easter morning and unable to help. He told her she wasn't focused enough for such a thing. She was, as he put it, "too flighty."

But she would not be deterred.

In the days leading up to Easter Sunday, Deborah talked endlessly about her plan for them to attend church services together. Though her mother made every attempt to go to church on a weekly basis, and encouraged her family's participation as well, she usually didn't get this worked up about it.

In addition, Deborah cleaned the house and had gone grocery

shopping, both of which were surprising and unusual. It was the first time Amanda had seen a decent amount of food in their refrigerator.

Her mother had even bought Amanda a brand-new dress.

Ah, that damn dress.

While some of Amanda's clothes came from yard sales or thrift stores, most were hand-me-downs from neighbors or family—her older brothers or her Aunt Lisa. Amanda was used to wearing whatever fit, and whatever she could *make* fit.

A *new* dress…well, that was a luxury.

And this one was lovely. It was bright yellow, with white ruffles and a white sash. She'd also gotten a pair of white ruffled socks and patent-leather Mary Jane shoes.

While Amanda loved her new dress and found it beautiful, it also was strange to have it. She never got new clothes, so wearing it was like wearing something stolen. She felt as if she might get in trouble for having it. She wasn't used to new things, especially not dresses. Most of her wardrobe consisted of boy clothes, and since she liked being outdoors, that suited her fine. She was very comfortable in long pants.

Her brothers had received new clothes for the occasion as well: black dress pants, black lace-up dress shoes, white button-up shirts, and thin, black clip-on ties. It was obvious to Amanda they hated all of it.

What Amanda didn't realize at the time—and what she would only understand much later on—was that her mother was hoping to impress people that day, the people at church and the guests she'd invited for dinner. The Holloways didn't have the best reputation in town, and Deborah had convinced herself this was her chance to prove to everyone how respectable they were.

Amanda found it all out of character and confusing. Her family wasn't often concerned about appearances.

Her father had been gone for work for nearly a week by the time Easter morning arrived, which was a long stretch for him to be away. Amanda's mother paced the living room, wringing her hands. She kept checking the grandmother clock, worried he wouldn't arrive home with enough time to get showered and dressed and accompany them to church. It was important to her they arrived as a *family*. While muttering to herself, she repeated it several times.

When Earl finally arrived home, Deborah immediately began pestering him about the time, which quickly turned into a full-blown argument. Hearing their raised voices that morning from her room—hearing them scream and swear at one another—was how Amanda realized her father was home.

Though she hated the sound of them arguing, it didn't surprise her anymore. It was how they interacted with one another. Her father was not a patient man, and her mother was good at testing people's patience. If her father was home, a constant level of tension between them was normal. It was just how things were.

Once her father had showered, and everyone was dressed to her mother's satisfaction, they climbed into her mother's van and drove to church. As they walked into the morning services, her mother looked proud. Her family was all dressed up in new clothes, looking dapper. She was sporting a new lavender Easter bonnet herself, and a handbag no one would know she had borrowed. Why, they might as well have been upper crust.

Amanda thought the services were long and dull, even more so than normal. *More* hymns. *More* prayers. And a tedious sermon, extolling the glory of the Risen Jesus.

Amanda found it hard to sit still. She realized that morning that fancy dresses, unlike pants, were built to be fashionable, not comfortable. So, she was relieved when the choir began singing *The Old Rugged Cross*, knowing it meant the service was likely nearing the end.

She was pleased with herself for having managed to make it through the entire ordeal without reprimand, pants be damned. The same could not be said for her brothers. Her mother had to hush and scold them several times, which appeared to bother her more than usual. After the fourth incident, she separated them and made Travis —most often the instigator—sit next to their father. Misbehaving in church typically meant a punishment was in store, but after they returned home, her mother began readying dinner and all was forgotten.

Amanda was hoping to stay in the kitchen, to watch and maybe help. She liked the idea of them working together to prepare dinner. But her father wasn't having it, and, though Amanda was frustrated and disappointed, she knew better than to argue.

"Y'all outta the kitchen and let yer mama cook," her father warned, wagging a beer bottle at her and her brothers, "and don't go messin' up them new clothes 'fore supper."

She should have taken the dress off right then.

———

TRAVIS AND SHANE were quick to leave the house together that day.

The boys were close in age—only two years apart—which meant they'd grown up together, both rivals and reluctant allies. Sometimes, they acted like enemies, wrestling in the yard, beating each other up, stealing from each other. Other times, they were more like friends and conspirators, hatching plots and schemes. But even their best moments were fleeting and uneasy.

Though they were brothers, they'd had to fight for everything they had, struggling to find their own voices and identities. Whatever love they shared came tangled in competition, animosity, and distrust.

On rare occasions, their agendas included Amanda. But, most often, they did not. They were both older and not interested in the same things she was, and they made it obvious her presence was inconvenient for them.

So, with Amanda's plans to help in the kitchen derailed, she did what she normally did when left to her own devices on a Sunday. She retreated into her imagination. In many ways, she behaved like she was an only child. Her own best friend.

That was okay with her. It allowed her to avoid the harsh realities of her life whenever possible. The stinging indifference of her mother, the unforgiving glare of her father, the potential torment of older siblings. She kept to herself, learning to find entertainment in her own company.

Around midday, Amanda took one of her favorite stuffed animals and wandered out toward the work shed in the back yard.

Amanda's parents didn't allow her to have pets. Several feral cats came and went, but mostly called their yard home. And Amanda fancied them her adopted pets.

One of her favorites, George, had gotten pregnant. This was when Amanda realized George was a girl. Amanda had created a comfortable bed for her in the work shed, and there, George had given birth to a litter of five kittens. Amanda would go to the work shed daily and check on them. She wanted to make sure everything was going well, so she'd bring scraps of food when she was able and watch George nurse the kittens.

But that day, Amanda arrived to find the work shed door standing open. George was there. But her kittens were gone.

Amanda panicked.

She rushed around the yard, searching for them, calling for them. She checked under the car in the carport. And around the garbage bins. And in the small tool shed on the side yard. Her heart raced. She was so flustered she almost couldn't think straight.

But then she heard the laughter of her brothers.

It was coming from the grove. From down by the creek at the back of their yard.

Amanda ran.

She ran as fast as her new shoes would allow, hoping and praying their laughter had nothing to do with the kittens.

But it did.

She was aghast at what she witnessed. It made her sick.

Shane was on the rickety wooden foot bridge, placing the kittens in the water, one by one, letting the small but steady current whisk them downstream. And as they tumbled down a miniature waterfall, struggling to keep their heads above water, Travis was taking aim with his pellet gun.

Amanda froze, almost unable to comprehend what she was seeing.

And she cried out.

She screamed so loud it hurt her throat.

Tears sprung into her eyes and began streaming down her face, a potent mixture of sadness, abject horror, and white-hot anger.

"NO!" she cried out. "No! How could you?!"

She barreled into the creek without a thought, splashing through the water, racing to rescue the nearest tiny newborn kitten.

Behind her, Travis was laughing.

Maybe Shane too?

Many years from now, she would come to think of Shane as the reasonable brother, the strong one, the kind one. But he'd gone along with enough of Travis's reprehensible plans to be considered, at the very least, complicit. He wasn't kind enough—or strong enough—to say no.

Amanda ran through the creek, sloshing through the cold water, almost falling on slick rocks. She searched for the other tiny cats but was only able to pull two of them out alive. She wrapped them in the white sash of her new dress and carried them out of the water to safety. The remaining kittens had not been so fortunate.

Looking at their tiny faces, wet and smeared with slimy creek mud, gasping for air, Amanda found herself consumed by an anger she'd never experienced before. She cursed at Travis, only for him to laugh at her again. And the laughter stoked her anger more.

"What are ya fussin' 'bout? Ain't nothin' but dumb ol' cats," Travis sneered.

Amanda turned and started to leave, tears streaming down her face. The two surviving kittens were mewing in her hands, wrapped up in her sash. Their hearts were pounding in a tiny, frantic flutter.

Just then, her father called from the house: "Supper's ready! Y'all come get cleaned up!"

But still, her brother's laughter was ringing in her ears.

Once she was a safe distance away, she set the kittens down near the base of a tree.

Then she turned back and, without thinking it through, she ran at Travis. She mustered all her anger and she hurtled toward him as fast as she could, launching herself at him with all her strength and fury.

At first, he looked surprised by her display, but as she reached him, he stepped aside effortlessly. He placed a hand on the top of her head, pushing her down. Amanda landed hard in the mud, her face sliding through the muck. She tasted it, earthy and foul. The slickness of it was on her teeth and tongue.

Travis's laughter continued the entire time. Laughing at her. At her pain.

Amanda lay on the ground, bruised and trembling. Her dress was covered in mud and her face was coated in filthy tears. She stayed in that position as the boys walked away toward the house, the sound of their mockery gradually fading away.

After a few minutes, she pulled herself up and wiped the filth from her face and her mouth. She stood and went to the two surviving kittens. Though she was already late for dinner, she took the time to find them a temporary hiding spot inside a stack of old tires.

As Amanda walked back toward the house, she knew she would be in trouble. She was covered head to toe in bruises and mud. Her hair was a tangled mess. And her new dress was ruined.

Amanda took a moment before she walked through the back kitchen door.

Everyone stopped what they were doing.

Her Aunt Lisa and her cousins had just arrived; Lisa was taking off her Easter bonnet. Her Papaw was sitting at the table, his face tired and stoic. She didn't recognize a few of the faces, people from church no doubt. In the parlor beyond the kitchen were her uncles, Harlan and Malcom; they were sitting with her father, all of them holding bottles of beer.

Every one of them stopped and stared at her.

In the kitchen, her brothers stood by, smirking, as if they hadn't been a part of this. Amanda scowled at Travis but he only grinned.

But worst of all was her mother. She was standing at the dining table, hair up, oven mitts on. She was setting out food when Amanda came in. Her jaw dropped and her eyes went wide. She gasped, and her color went an ashy white.

Anger flashed across her father's face. His eyes darkened. She hoped the fact they had visitors would be her saving grace.

But her father jumped up and charged across the floor into the kitchen. He grabbed Amanda by the arm, snatching her from the doorway. He dragged her out past the company, down the hall, ignoring her quiet pleas that he was hurting her. He opened the door to her bedroom and shoved her inside. Then he began to unbuckle his belt. Amanda was well aware of what that meant. The last time he'd used the belt on her, she hadn't been able to sit for days without her backside aching.

But he stopped.

He glanced back toward the kitchen and grumbled.

"You're gonna keep yer tail right here in this room while the rest of us have supper, and ya can best think long and hard 'bout what ya done." He started to leave but he stopped and turned back to her. "We buy ya somethin' nice, and this is how ya thank us, ya ungrateful little bitch?" he snarled. "Never again."

As he left her room, he slammed the door so hard it knocked a picture from her wall. The glass cracked in the frame as it hit the floor.

Amanda began to sob.

His words—*never again*—repeated in her mind. In some ways, they were worse than any beating.

Her tears came in waves. And when she thought they were done, she'd cry again.

Only once more did the door open that night. This time, it was her mother. Amanda was hoping she would come. She wanted to apologize for what had happened. Maybe her mother would realize how hungry she was and bring her some of the Easter ham and deviled eggs. But her mother had no dinner for her. She stood in Amanda's doorway motionless, silhouetted against the hall light, a bottle of beer in one hand and an Easter basket in the other.

"You done ruined today," she mumbled. "I was hopin' for a nice, normal Easter, but ya went and wrecked it. You wreck everything." She tossed the Easter basket into the room, then turned and closed the door behind her.

Amanda cried again.

Her mother had never gotten her an Easter basket before. And, though Amanda didn't know it, she never would again.

With her eyes still full of tears, Amanda got up from her bed and went to the Easter basket on the floor. She set it upright, gathering up the spilled contents, fixing it, adjusting the faux plastic grass, until it looked just as it should.

Inside was a large chocolate bunny wrapped in foil, two Reese's

Peanut Butter Eggs, two Cadbury Cream Eggs, a few Tootsie Rolls, assorted jellybeans, and the centerpiece—three baby dolls wearing matching dresses. A brunette doll wearing red, a blonde doll wearing blue, and a redhead doll wearing silver.

Amanda put the Easter basket against the wall opposite her bed—under the nightlight, next to the rocking horse—where she could see it.

She got back into her bed and stared at the basket for a while. She wished it *had* been a normal Easter, just as her mother wanted. They'd never had normal before. Perhaps it was silly for any of them to expect it now.

She lay there in the dark, the sound of laughter in the kitchen and the clinking of dishes a reminder she was truly alone. It was only when all the guests left that Amanda was able to fall asleep, despite her tears.

But her sleep didn't last long.

She woke in a panic, covered in sweat. It felt like something was there in the room with her. Something…or *someone* scary.

She held her breath and waited for her eyes to adjust.

The darkness of her room seemed almost alive, as it shifted and pulsed.

And then she heard something. A whispering in the dark.

Tiny voices.

Terrified, Amanda sat straight up in her bed and pushed her body close to the wall, pulling the covers up to her chin, peering through the darkness.

They were hushed whispers. Words she couldn't quite understand.

Then she realized where the voices were coming from. They were coming from the other side of her room. From under her nightlight.

From her Easter basket.

The three dolls were all lined up under the light. Amanda watched in horror as their plastic heads began to swivel from side to side. It was as if they were speaking to one another, whispering in small, low voices.

Then her rocking horse began to rock, all on its own.

It was in that moment that Amanda sensed the presence again. A darkness in the room. Surrounding her. It made her flesh crawl. The air grew cold around her face and neck, until she could see her own rapid breaths.

She sat in bed, her hands trembling, teeth chattering, frozen in fear. And the whispers grew louder—*slowly, steadily*—indistinct murmurs, building into a cacophony of white noise, swelling and swirling together into a singular voice, loud and shrill, like a tea kettle boiling.

A scream.

GET OUT OF MY HOUSE!

The words reverberated through her skull, and made her ears ache. For a moment, she thought she might faint.

Instead, she *ran*.

She flung the covers from her bed and bounded from the room. Slamming against her bedroom door, she darted out into the hall.

And, not knowing what else to do, she ran to Shane's room.

In near hysterics—in a short, hitching, hushed voice—she told him what had happened. Through a stream of seemingly endless tears, she confessed she was terrified.

Though she had expected Shane to mock her again, he didn't. He was kind to her that night. He apologized for making her sad, and for what he'd done with Travis and the kittens. He calmed her down and told her she could stay in his room.

Before they went to sleep, he promised something. He promised that he would swap rooms with her the following day. That she would never have to sleep in her old room again.

And she never did.

Chapter 6

Sweet and Sour

Mandy raced from the house, slamming the door behind her. Chris looked up from measuring a 2x4, startled by the noise.

"What's wrong?" he asked.

"Uh…nothing." Mandy's voice shook as she hurried down the front porch steps and onto the lawn. She didn't want to talk about it. How could she explain it without sounding insane?

"You're as white as a sheet. Are you feeling okay?"

She nodded, blinking against the sunlight. "Yeah. Yeah, I just… The smell of the bathroom got to me, I think."

"Aw, man. I should've told you to wait on that room. I'm gonna set up some work lights in there in a bit. It should be a lot better after I fix the floor."

"I should've waited. It was dumb of me."

Chris studied her face. "Are you sure you're alright?"

"Yeah. I think I'm going to go for a walk and get some fresh air."

"Good idea," he said. "Where are the kids?"

"Back porch. Playing on Ethan's phone."

He shook his head. "Of *course* they are. Take your phone with you, okay?"

"I have it." She held her phone up, gripping it with sweaty hands.

But she began to worry he might see her hands trembling, or the picture of the doll's head, still on the screen. Before he could do either, she rushed from the yard and started to walk down Stillwater Lane.

Mandy was unsure of where she was headed. She needed to clear her head.

Though it was already getting warm outside, a gentle breeze was blowing and the trees along the street provided a great deal of shade. But Mandy was oblivious to the scent of honeysuckle, the sound of the birds in the trees. Her mind was busy, trying to unpack what she'd experienced.

It had been a long time since she'd thought about that Easter Sunday. As with so much of her past, she'd tried not to. She glanced down at the photo again, her fingers tightening around the phone, and a little voice inside of her whispered: *It was a mistake to come back.*

The voice hadn't spoken to her for years, but since they'd arrived in town, it had returned. She tried to make it stop, but it was only growing louder, more frequent.

When Mandy looked up, she was already at the corner.

The house across the way was familiar to her. She couldn't remember who'd lived there, not anymore, only the rusted swing set on the side yard where she'd played with other kids from the neighborhood. This had once been a simple, carefree place for her, full of smiles and laughter. And she was relieved to be thinking of something pleasant for a change.

The house was the same, but different. It had been painted. The walkway and landscaping were all new. And the swing set was gone now, replaced by a neatly tended garden. Just like her memories of it, only the vaguest hint remained of what this place had been.

She wondered why it worked that way—why the pleasant memories blurred and faded, leaving only a faint impression behind, while the awful ones would resurface without warning, sharp and vivid, refusing to die.

The gentle breeze blew across her face and through her hair. She took another look at the house, turned, and started back.

———

WHEN MANDY GOT BACK to the house, Chris was no longer in the front yard. She called his name, but he didn't answer. As she went to the front porch, she began to get nervous again. She didn't want to go back inside alone.

Yeah, you should be worried. But what are you gonna do? Sleep in the yard? You agreed to this.

Don't be silly, she told herself. Moving back to a place that held so many troubling memories was bound to be stressful for anyone. It was normal…right?

She pulled the door open, hesitating as her logic wrestled with the lingering unease. There were voices inside—Chris's baritone and a woman's voice, thick with a Southern drawl. Mandy let out a heavy sigh. She wouldn't be alone, after all. But her relief came tinged with a hint of annoyance. She wasn't in the mood to interact with other people. Not right now, not after the morning she'd had. Putting on a polite face and making small talk was the last thing she wanted.

"Hello?" Mandy called.

Chris leaned back in his chair and poked his head around the corner of the kitchen. "In here. Cheryl came for a visit."

Taken off guard, Mandy entered the kitchen to find Chris and Cheryl sitting together at the dining room table, red plastic party cups in hand, a pitcher in front of them. Cheryl was wearing an oversized, white, graphic t-shirt promoting the 2015 Knox County Fair.

"Hiya," Cheryl said.

"You brought lemonade?" Mandy asked.

Cheryl nodded.

"That was real nice of you," Mandy said.

Cheryl smiled, and Mandy realized that she did indeed have braces. "I don't mind. I saw your husband workin' in the yard and figured some pink lemonade was the least I could do. Southern hospitality and all. You want some, hon?"

Mandy bristled at the mention of her "husband." She realized most people didn't mean anything by it, but it always bothered her. It felt like being forced into something she hadn't chosen for herself. And she didn't like that.

"Uh, sure," Mandy said, taking the seat near the back door. "Are the kids—"

"Still out back," Chris said.

Mandy nodded. "I don't want them in the house."

Chris shot her a questioning glance.

"Uh, I mean…until you fix the bathroom floor."

Cheryl finished pouring some lemonade in another red plastic cup and handed it to Mandy.

"Look at you," Mandy said. "You even thought to bring cups. How thoughtful."

"I figured you might not have much in the house yet. I was tellin' your hus—"

"We're not married," Mandy cut in, but immediately regretted her response. It was too fast, too forceful.

Cheryl's face dropped. "Oh, I'm sorry. Outta touch, I guess. Bad manners."

"Not at all," Chris reassured her. "Happens all the time. We're used to it."

"Yeah, we get it a lot," Mandy echoed, her tone softening. She hadn't wanted to make Cheryl feel bad.

"Well, to be honest, I don't blame y'all," Cheryl said. "After two divorces, I can't imagine gettin' hitched again neither. I suppose y'all might be doin' it the right way."

Chris finished his lemonade and smacked his lips. "Cheryl, thanks again for the lemonade and the chat. But there's a lot to do, so I better get back to it." He got up from the table, then leaned over and kissed Mandy on the forehead. "No rest for the wicked."

Cheryl laughed. "Ya got that right."

"Don't you need my help?" Mandy asked, doing her best to avoid the conversation with Cheryl.

"No, it's fine," Chris said, pulling his work gloves back on. "I'm still working on patching the hole in the bathroom. You two go on and catch up a bit."

"Okay, but…let me know if you *need me*," Mandy said, hoping Chris might pick up on her signals. But either he wasn't catching them, or he was ignoring them.

Before Chris was out the front door, Cheryl had turned her chair toward Mandy and leaned in. "Amanda Holloway. Boy, it's good to see ya again."

"Is it still Cheryl…Stilton?" Mandy asked.

"Taggerty now," Cheryl said. "And before that, it was Foxcomb. Taggerty's better, don't ya think? Foxcomb sounds kinda…off."

Mandy chuckled. "I agree."

"I gotta tell ya, once you got outta here, I didn't think I'd ever see ya again."

"You make it sound like I escaped." Mandy tried to hold a casual smile, hoping Cheryl wouldn't notice the quaver in her voice. An escape is exactly what it had been.

"I knew ya weren't happy," Cheryl said. "I was proud of ya for leavin'."

Mandy winced.

And now you're back.

"Was it so obvious?" Mandy asked.

"Oh yeah," Cheryl laughed. "Least to me, it was. Maybe not to no one else. Your family went through a lot of strange and awful things, but you were always so sweet to me. Always smilin'. That's how I 'member you."

"Strange and awful things." Mandy repeated the phrase, almost to herself. "That's how you remember my family?"

"I mean, like how your brothers were always actin' up and getting' into trouble. And Travis sellin' drugs," Cheryl said. "And how your uncles used to have fights with your daddy. Didn't they hurt him real bad once?"

They did.

"And how your mama would go off on tears. And how she never bought y'all no food," Cheryl went on. "Seemed like you were at our house eatin' dinner whenever ya could sneak away."

Mandy nodded. "Yeah. Mom was somethin', I guess." A bead of sweat trickled down the middle of her back. For years, she'd tried not to think about these things, but now Cheryl was dragging them into the daylight without a second thought, as if they were no more than tiny nuggets of nostalgia for them to share.

"You remember the night she wandered outside in her white night-gown and climbed up in that tree?" Cheryl asked.

"Um…no," Mandy said quietly. "I actually *don't* remember that… Did that really happen?"

"I'm real surprised you don't recall it. Your daddy was outta town workin'. We had to call your uncle over to get her down. She looked like a ghost up in that tree. I was worried she was gonna take a tumble."

Mandy's little voice roared back.

Don't you remember, Amanda Jean? Don't you remember the night your mama climbed up in a tree? Don't you remember the cockroaches on the silverware? Or the headlights shining on the window in the middle of the night? Or your daddy grabbing his bloody stomach? Or the handprints on the wall? Or wearing long sleeves to hide all them bruises? Don't you remember Duck and Donnie? Or the Ouija board? Or the little girl? Don't you—

"Let's talk about you," Mandy said, cutting off her own internal diatribe before it spiraled out of control.

Cheryl laughed. "Not much interestin' to say, I 'spose. Still livin' in the same house with my kiddos. Moved out young when I married my first husband, Troy, and had my two girls. I divorced him and moved in with my second soon-to-be-husband, Roy Dean. He went to high school with us—you might remember him. Roy Dean Taggerty? Big boy? His daddy owned the scrap metal yard?"

"Not ringin' any bells."

"Well, when my daddy passed, Mama went to live with her sister, and Roy Dean and I moved into the house. He's the daddy of my boy, R.J."

"Roy Junior?"

"You got it."

Mandy smiled. Some things truly did stay the same. "So, Roy Dean isn't around?"

"Oh, he's around, alright. Makin' my life miserable whenever he's able." Cheryl chuckled. "Luckily, there ain't many expenses on the house, so I manage without his help. I still do hair—did I do hair when you were around here?"

"I don't think so. You might have been going to school for it. I don't recall."

Cheryl nodded. "Well, I do hair now. And other glamour-type things, on occasion."

If she was being honest, *glamour* wasn't the first word Mandy would've associated with Cheryl.

"If it's not too nosy, why'd ya come back here?" Cheryl asked.

Mandy took a moment, debating how much to say. Whether she went with the long version or kept it short, it was still daunting.

"Well, jeez, let's see," she said, hesitating. Where should she begin? "When the pandemic hit last year, Chris and I both lost our jobs."

"Oh, man…don't get me started on that whole thing." Cheryl huffed, shaking her head.

Mandy chose to ignore the comment and went on with her story.

"We had some savings," she said, "but it's rough watching money you worked hard for—money you hoped to invest—just disappear. It's like seeing your whole life unravel strand by strand. We moved into a smaller apartment, cut unnecessary expenses, and tried to find work, but…it was hard.

"Chris was in 'the industry'—that's what they call the movie business in L.A. He worked in the scenic department, building props and sets. But, after COVID hit, it seemed like Hollywood wasn't the same. He tried to find other work, but construction took a hit too. He did a few handyman jobs, but we couldn't afford all the proper insurances, so it was always risky.

"I'd been working in events, which was another industry that took a major hit. I mean, *everything* shut down for a while. Right before 2020, I took a job at a hotel not far from us, booking parties and weddings and business meetings. I figured…less travel, closer to home, more time with the kids and Chris. But I got laid off within the first few months of the pandemic."

"Bastards."

Mandy paused, recalling the panic of those early months.

"No one was hiring after that. Not for what I did. I had a couple of contract jobs—short term, but nothing real. Nothing close to it.

There were only a few jobs and a whole lot of people fightin' over them."

"Then ya heard 'bout your folks?"

"I got the call a couple of months ago. Given our situation at the time, Chris and I talked about it and realized…well, we didn't have a lot of choices. So, here we are."

Cheryl took a sip of her lemonade and smacked her lips. "Are y'all plannin' on stayin' for a while?"

"The plan is to fix up the house, live in it while we look for work, probably back in California. Then sell it and move back."

Cheryl frowned. "I figured it was temporary."

"Well, that's the plan," Mandy said. She crossed her fingers. They'd made many other plans in recent years, and none of them had gone well. "Nothing against Tennessee. It's just not my home. Too many bad memories. My life…it started when I *left* this place."

"I getcha," Cheryl said. "Sad about your folks."

"Well, they *were* both in their seventies, and neither of them lived very healthy lives."

"Sure, but it ain't like age had much to do with their dyin'," Cheryl said.

Mandy's eyes narrowed. "What do you mean?"

Cheryl's expression changed, suddenly apprehensive. "You don't know?"

"I heard it was natural causes."

"No one mentioned nothin' else?"

"Cheryl, what aren't you telling me?"

Cheryl jumped up, her chair squeaking against the wood floor as it slid back. Her eyes darted to the front door and she began moving around the table in that direction. "You never mind me. It ain't my business. You go on and keep the lemonade and the cups. I'll get the pitcher from ya tomorrow."

Rattled, Mandy rose too. She couldn't let Cheryl run off, not if she knew something. Mandy circled the table in the other direction, blocking Cheryl's path. "Please, don't go. If something else happened, I need to know!"

"Probably better if you talk to Shane or Travis or—"

"I *have* talked to Shane. He told me it was natural causes."

Cheryl looked around, fidgeting. "It ain't my place, Amanda."

"Please," Mandy pleaded.

Cheryl hesitated, then nodded. "Alright. Well, I only know what I heard. Roy Dean and Travis both hang out at the same bar. One night, after a few drinks, Travis tells him…that your mama didn't give your daddy his heart medicine, so he had a heart attack and died. Then she took a bunch of her own meds…and went to sleep."

Mandy's face was numb. Her thoughts were fragmented, her mind struggling to process it. None of the words were making any sense to her.

"What is the…? *What?*"

"I'm sorry, hon. I hope it ain't true."

"But, why would she… Why wouldn't anyone *tell me this?*"

Cheryl shook her head, her expression sympathetic. "I don't reckon I know."

———

Chris leaned against the balcony railing of the Briarwood hotel, cold beer in hand, listening to her.

"Maybe Travis was lyin'," Mandy said. "He's obviously bitter about gettin' kicked out. About our folks leavin' me the house. Maybe he was talkin' shit." She put the cigarette to her lips and pushed back in her patio chair.

"I'm assuming you do *not* want me keeping you honest about the cigarettes right now?"

"Astute."

He nodded. "Yeah, I'm smart like that. Listen, this might be nothing, but why don't you request their death certificates? Ask for the police or toxicology reports? And…I mean, can't you just talk to Travis?"

She huffed. "I don't wanna talk to him." She took another drag and reconsidered the suggestion. "No, I don't wanna open that door right now. When I talked to Shane, he told me what I told you—that it was a heart attack for dad, and multiple organ failure for Mom—

but nothing about a… *Jesus*, would it be considered a murder-suicide?"

"Let's not go to dark places."

"It might be too late for that," she said. "My brain tends to go dark pretty quick."

"Oh, I know." Chris chuckled. "But we don't know that this is nefarious. Or that people are keeping things from you. Maybe it's only miscommunication. Or speculation. If it was an overdose—even accidental—I'm sure multiple organ failure could've been listed as a cause a death."

"I already called the sheriff's office," Mandy said.

"Proactive. That's good. What did they say?"

Mandy shook her head. "Nothin'. The woman took my info and said someone would contact me. Told me I should call the county office if I wanted a death certificate."

"That's great. See, you're already on your way to answers."

"I guess," Mandy said. She took another long, slow pull from the cigarette and leaned her head back in the chair, blowing the smoke out through her nostrils.

"I've never seen this much of 'Smokin' Mandy.' It's like a whole other side of you. Like a…mirror universe version, where you hang out in dive bars."

Mandy didn't laugh. She just looked at Chris. "I'm…sorry. We've been back less than two days and I feel like I'm already dragging us into another mess. I didn't want it to be like this."

"Don't do that. This is a lot for you to process. Losing your folks. Coming back here. And now this…*twist*. I appreciate you talking to me about it. Let me know what else I can do to help."

For a moment, Mandy considered telling Chris about her experience in the bathroom—hearing the whispers, seeing the baby doll head, the memories of her childhood flooding in. She wanted to tell him. He wouldn't judge her. He never had. So, why was it so damn hard to let him in?

"I'm fine," she said. "I'm a big girl. You've got enough on your plate."

Chris finished his beer. "True. Speaking of my plate, I'm going to start early again tomorrow. Can you help me get the trailer unhitched before the movers arrive?"

"Sure."

"I'm going to go lie down and scroll through my phone for a while before I crash."

"I'll be in in a bit," Mandy said.

Chris stopped at the patio slider and turned back to her. "You don't always *have* to be so strong, you know. I realize you're used to dealing with these things on your own. But you don't have to. It's okay to lean on me. On all of us."

Mandy closed her eyes.

She heard his words, she understood him, but it was hard for her to let the message in, so she nodded.

When the patio door clicked shut, she opened her eyes again and exhaled.

Smoking usually helped calm her, but her thoughts were still scattered, her anxiety still high, and the damn cigarette was almost gone. But she wouldn't have any more today, she promised herself, no matter how stressed she was.

In addition to the lingering smoke, there was something else familiar in the air. The scent of impending rain.

There was a rumble of thunder in the distance. Mandy stood and moved to the railing for a better view of the horizon. Faint, dark clouds were forming. She'd almost forgotten how common summer storms were here, rolling in late in the day without much warning.

Living in Los Angeles, she'd grown unaccustomed to rapid changes in the weather. Storms were rare as it was. Summer storms were almost unheard of. But standing here on the balcony—the dark clouds gathering over the hills, the first patter of raindrops landing on the concrete, the dampness on her skin—it all felt so normal.

Though the raindrops were light so far, she knew from experience that it wasn't good to be complacent. Thunderstorms could come out of nowhere and turn your world upside down.

Mandy shook her head. As if she could feel any *more* upside down right now.

She didn't know what to believe, but the idea continued to gnaw at her.

No one would argue that her father was an easy man to live with. Could she put it past her mother to reach her limit after so many years together? To withhold his medicine and then cash in her own chips? Yes, her mother had always been unpredictable, unreliable, and hard to understand, but was she capable of what amounted to *murder?*

Perhaps there was more to her than Mandy understood.

But she didn't want to think about it anymore today. She dropped the cigarette onto the damp balcony floor and crushed it under the toe of her shoe, then turned back to the patio slider, ready to go inside.

That's when she saw it.

Reflected in the glass was a little girl with long blonde hair. She was small and pale. And she was standing right beside her.

Mandy gasped and spun around, pulse quickening.

But the balcony next to her was empty.

She turned back to the patio door, but now the glass showed only her own reflection.

She'd seen her, though, hadn't she? The little girl? Glimpsed her, if only for a moment?

Mandy pressed a hand to her chest, willing her racing heart to slow. She slid the patio door open and stepped inside. After shutting it, she locked it for good measure. Leaning in, she took one last look outside, the cool glass pressing against her forehead.

She hadn't seen the little girl in decades—hadn't even thought of her in years—but as a child, she'd seen her often, in and around the house on Stillwater Lane. A ghost. Or a vision. Or perhaps merely a figment of her imagination.

But whether real or not, seeing her now made Mandy feel like she was nine years old again, and seeing her for the first time. She could almost hear the lightning storm raging outside, almost feel its cold seeping through the house's thin walls.

Chapter 7

The Night of the Storm, 1990

Raindrops thudded against the roof, and the runoff rushed through the gutters like a river. The house creaked and the wind whistled, rattling the windows, shaking the doors in their frames. The shutters banged against the side of the house, with no discernible rhythm.

This storm was one of the worst they'd had in some time, and by far the worst Amanda had experienced in her nine years of life.

As she left the bathroom, she was careful to avoid the bucket in the hall collecting water from a leak in the roof.

Plink, plink, plink.

A cockroach scurried across the floor in front of her and she stomped on it. Amanda sighed, shaking her head, annoyed. Cockroaches had always been a nuisance. Most of the time, she ignored them or carried them outside, but the storm had brought a veritable army out of hiding, making it hard to live and let live.

As she neared the kitchen, lightning flashed. For a moment, the living room windows glowed bright white. Lit from behind were dark speckles of rain, and, beyond that, the silhouettes of trees, branches waving like spindly arms.

The thunder rolled soon after, a deep rumble that seemed like it might shake the house from its foundation. The lights flickered, threatening to go dark.

Amanda held her breath, hoping they wouldn't lose power. She'd lit a candle in her room, just in case. She didn't like being in the dark. Her imagination was too vivid, always ready to conjure monsters in the shadows.

From somewhere in the distance, she heard sirens wailing. She always hated hearing that sound but hearing it during a bad storm was worse. It meant that someone, somewhere was in trouble.

She shivered.

The house was always damp and chilly in the winter, but along with the storm came a persistent wind sneaking through the gaps and cracks, clawing its way inside with icy fingers, making the rooms that much colder.

"Y'all dish up 'fore it's cold," her father called out to no one in particular.

"What is it?" Travis asked, glancing at the pan on the stove.

"Chickenshit," her mother said. She was already sitting at the table with a plate and a can of Mountain Dew. "And rice."

Amanda was surprised Travis had to ask.

Most nights, when her father wasn't at work, he was in his chair watching TV, oblivious to anything or anyone else. This wasn't a bad thing in Amanda's opinion—when he paid attention, it often meant trouble. On the rare occasions he decided to cook, it was almost always one of three things: scrambled eggs, chickenshit, or creamed chipped beef on toast—also known as S.O.S., or shit on a shingle.

Chickenshit—a casserole featuring canned chicken and cream of mushroom soup—was not only one of the few things their father cooked, but it also had a distinctive, often lingering aroma. Amanda didn't know if he'd made up the name or if it was a real thing. Either way, it wasn't her favorite.

Still, it was always good to be fed.

Her mother was capable of whipping up a larger menu when she put her mind to it, but most of the time, she made nothing for dinner, leaving the others to fend for themselves.

Sometimes, when Amanda was hungry, she'd sneak into the pantry and throw together whatever she could find. That meant dinner often consisted of something like stale white bread smeared with mayonnaise and a can of pork and beans.

That was *if* her mother remembered to buy food.

Amanda would grow up thinking that her family was poor. Hand-me-down clothes and an empty pantry. It would be many years before she realized that it wasn't poverty. Only laziness. And neglect.

If dinners were rare, shared dinners were even more uncommon. Most of the time, someone was missing—away at work, off with friends, or simply *uninterested* in being around.

"Where's Shane tonight?" Amanda asked.

"Over at Luke's," her mother replied.

As Amanda opened the kitchen cabinet to retrieve a plate, another cockroach fell on the countertop, tumbling to the floor. Their constant presence was aggravating. She crushed it under foot, then got a paper towel and cleaned it up, tossing it in the garbage.

The trick with killing cockroaches was to stomp down fast with the heel of your shoe, before twisting and dragging a little. Otherwise, the suckers would lay out flat and fool you, only to pop up and wander away when you weren't looking. It was also important to have a hard surface, and to aim right at the center of their body.

Amanda didn't wear shoes very often, nor did she often kill cockroaches. But tonight it was cold, and they were everywhere, so she'd put some on.

She went to the stove and used the spoon in the pan to stir the sauce, which was developing a thick skin. She scooped some up, letting it slide off the spoon and plop onto her plate.

Yummy.

She added a scoop of rice and moved to the table.

Before Amanda was able to sit, her mother looked up at her and said, "Oh, honey, don't forget to take some to Papaw." Amanda glanced at Travis, who was already eating. *He* was never asked to take care of Papaw. Papaw wasn't staying in *his* room.

Papaw had come to stay a few months prior when his health had begun to fail. They'd put him up in her bedroom and given him her bed. And Amanda had been relegated to sleeping on blankets on the floor.

Every night for the last few months, she'd listened to her grandfather coughing and wheezing—his breathing thick with mucus—his oxygen tank rumbling on occasion. She'd listened to him moan. And gasp. And snore. And fart.

She loved her Papaw. But she didn't want him in her room. And she didn't understand why everyone expected her to wait on him. To be *in charge of him!* She was only nine! She couldn't even keep her room clean, so why was she supposed to be in charge of a full-grown man? The fact that it was expected of her, while everyone else ignored him, was frustrating.

Amanda dropped her plate on the table and went to the cupboard to fetch another.

"So, Papaw…he's *your* daddy right?" Travis asked their father.

"Yup," their father said, focused on his chickenshit, making wet, smacking noises as he shoveled the food into his mouth.

"But Uncle Malcolm and Uncle Harlan are *your* brothers?" Travis asked, turning to their mother.

"Uh huh," she replied.

"And your daddy…he died?" Travis asked their mother.

Their mother stopped eating and stared at him, as if he was being a nuisance. "Why're ya askin' so many questions, all a'sudden?"

Travis shrugged. "Just curious."

"Well…we reckon my daddy passed on. But we don't know for sure. He went missin' back when I was a girl, not much older than you are now."

"Went missin'?" Travis asked.

"Your grandaddy, he had a mind of his own," her mother said. "We reckon he went out huntin' or fishin', like he always did, and…somethin' must've happened to him."

"Or maybe he got fed up with you and your brothers makin' trouble, and up and left," Amanda's father said, licking his teeth clean. He scraped up the remaining bits of food. The sound of his fork scraping along the ceramic dish made Amanda wince. "Couldn't blame him."

"That ain't nice, Earl," her mother said, frowning.

"But ain't he buried out in the yard next to Mamaw?" Travis asked, confused. "Ain't he got a headstone?"

Their mother sighed. "Yeah, there's a headstone alright, but no body. We done it to remember him and keep him close to my mama," she said. She didn't have much emotion about it anymore.

But, you never could tell what mama would get emotional about, Amanda thought. Sometimes it was nothing. Sometimes it was everything.

Amanda didn't really care who was related to whom. Or who went missing when. Or who was buried where. She wanted to sit down and eat.

She finished preparing Papaw's plate, scooping up all the chickenshit left in the pan—a healthy portion—before shoving the spoon back into the pan a little harder than she intended. She added some rice too, what little of it remained.

"I'll be right back," she said, though she was certain no one was listening.

She carried the plate into the hall, stepping around the bucket. As she got to the entrance of her room, the lightning flashed again, lighting up the window by her bed.

Amanda blinked against the sudden brightness, her vision blurred and haloed. Through the haze, it almost appeared that there was a little girl sitting on the edge of her bed—next to where Papaw was lying—facing the window.

She blinked again, trying to clear her vision. But the little girl was still on the bed, clearer than before.

She was wearing a long, white nightgown, and holding a stuffed bear.

A surge of panic rushed through Amanda. The air was thick around her, and she found herself short of breath.

A clap of thunder rumbled the house.

The little girl turned slowly and stared at her. Stared *through* her.

Amanda screamed and jumped back.

The plate slipped from her fingers and crashed to the floor, breaking into several pieces. The chickenshit and rice splattered across her carpet.

When she looked up again, the little girl was gone.

It was only her room, with Papaw taking up her bed, his eyes closed, his mouth agape, his skin pale and loose, almost paper-thin.

Her father appeared behind her in the doorway.

"What the goddamn hell is goin' on?" he shouted. He was so close to her she caught a whiff of his aftershave, and the alcohol on his breath.

Amanda flinched, her heart racing.

"Uh, I…uh…" She gestured back to the bed, struggling to find the right words. Her father was already angry. What words would make him understand?

"Clean it up, goddammit!" He shook his head in disgust. "So goddamn careless. You're gonna replace that plate, or so help me!" He turned to head back down the hall toward the kitchen, but stopped and added, "And dish my daddy up some more food."

"Uh, we're…outta chickenshit," Amanda muttered.

"Then give him yours," her father growled. "Ya still got a plate, don't ya?"

Tears welled in Amanda's eyes. Her lip began to tremble. "Yes, sir."

"Well, give it to him. You'll have to make do."

Amanda didn't let herself cry. What was the point? It wouldn't change anything.

Instead, she did as she was told. She went to the kitchen, retrieved her plate from the dining room table, and brought it back to her room, careful to step over the mess of food on her carpet.

Papaw hadn't been awake through any of it, and she had no idea when he *would* wake or if he'd even be hungry, but she left the plate on the side table, nevertheless.

She looked around the room, at all of her things pushed aside to make room for Papaw and his belongings—his suitcases, his oxygen tank, his walker. It didn't feel like her room now, except for the pile of blankets on the floor. Her makeshift mattress. Her temporary bed.

Her gaze lingered on the edge of the mattress, where the little girl had been sitting. There was something about her. About her face. Her eyes. Her gaze had been comforting, at first. Then sad. And terrifying.

By the time Amanda was done cleaning the mess from the carpet, the family had dispersed from the kitchen. Her folks were in the front room, her father sitting in his La-Z-Boy watching television, and her mother asleep on the couch. Travis was in his bedroom listening to music.

So, Amanda went to the kitchen by herself. In the pantry, she found a can of pork and beans and a loaf of stale bread.

———

When it came time for Amanda to sleep that night, she pushed her bed—or what passed as her bed, these days—as close to the dresser as possible. And when she lay down, she pushed her back against the dresser too.

Though she used to have a nightlight in her room, Papaw had complained that it kept him awake. Now, without it, her room was quite dark.

Amanda peered over the top of the raggedy blanket and scanned the room through the dim light. All she could think about was the little girl's face in the darkness—her eyes, her faraway stare. The image wouldn't leave her mind.

An occasional flash of lightning would light up her window, and the room would illuminate, but only for a moment. When the bright light faded, she'd have to wait for her eyes to adjust to the dark all over again.

She knew she needed to sleep, but every time her eyelids started to close, she'd picture the little girl's face again, and jerk back awake.

She listened. To the steady rain and howling wind outside. The scraping of tree limbs and other bushes against the house. The hum and hiss of her Papaw's oxygen tank, his heavy breaths. The slow trickle of the water as it leaked into the bucket out in the hallway.

Plink, plink, plink.

It was only when the storm began to weaken that she finally allowed herself to drift off. She had maybe been asleep for an hour or two when she woke suddenly to a new sound.

It was Snickerdoodle—one of the two cats she'd rescued from the water that Easter. Now, he was in Amanda's room, and he was hissing.

In the darkness, his white splotches were visible first, then the outline of his orange body came into focus. He was standing near the bed where Papaw was asleep, staring at the bedroom door.

"What's wrong, Snick?" Amanda whispered.

The cat spat, the hair on his back standing up straight. He hissed again, crab-walked to the side, and began to emit a deep, guttural growl—like a siren winding up.

Amanda fought to see what the cat was reacting to in the dark of the room. But she couldn't see anything at all.

Except the bedroom door. It began to open.

Amidst the other noises—the wind and rain, the oxygen tank, and the low growl of her cat—was the slow creaking of its hinges.

Amanda pulled the blanket up over her mouth and made herself as small as possible. Her whole body was shivering. She was terrified at the thought of someone coming into her room in the middle of the night. But not as terrified as she was by the idea that no one was there at all.

Snickerdoodle hissed and spat again, puffing up. He began to bat at the air in front of him, as if defending himself against something. Something that Amanda couldn't see.

The cat reared back.

With a shriek, he ran from the room through the widening doorway.

With Snickerdoodle gone, Amanda was left on her own, lying on the floor next to the bed where her Papaw was in a deep sleep. She realized that *her* breathing was loud too. She did her best to calm herself, to quiet her noisy breaths, but it was little use. She was too scared.

Inch by inch, the door continued to creak open.

Amanda was trapped. For a moment, she thought about running from the room, following Snickerdoodle, but the idea horrified her. She knew she wasn't brave enough to do it.

Then she had an idea.

She didn't know if it would keep her safe, but it was all she could think of.

Keeping herself close to the ground, Amanda inched her way over to the bookcase. She sat up, taking her time, careful not to make any noise, still hidden behind the blanket. With her back against the bookcase and her eyes on the bedroom door, she reached up and began to explore the shelf with her fingers. She was certain she would be able to identify the book by feel alone. It had a firm, textured, faux-leather cover.

It took her a few tense moments of cautious exploration—taking care not to make any sound—before her fingers brushed over it. Gripping it between her fingers, she lowered the book into her lap. She held it tight. There were papers and a bookmark inside, and she didn't want them to fall out.

The bedroom door was open now. The room was still.

Little by little, staying as quiet as possible, Amanda inched her way back to her "bed," and made herself small again, gripping the book to her chest.

She kept thinking of one line from it that gave her comfort.

Get thee behind me, Satan.

She watched the door for at least another hour before she was able to relax enough to go back to sleep. But she never let go of the Bible, not once the entire night. She held it in her arms across her chest, like a shield against the darkness.

CHAPTER 8
THE OFFER

Before she went to sleep, Mandy made sure the blackout curtains on the patio slider weren't shut. She didn't want to sleep late again, not with the movers coming.

What she hadn't anticipated was not being able to sleep much at all. Every time she began to drift off, she'd wake in a start, arms crossed over her chest as if holding something.

Holding a Bible, like it ever did you any good.

Each time she woke, she lay in bed while the others snoozed, watching the numbers change on the hotel's digital alarm clock.

When the clock turned 6:00, Chris's alarm went off and he began to stir.

Mandy decided to get up as well. Soon after, she woke the kids. Though they protested, they rolled out of bed and began to ready themselves for the day. Soon, they were all back at the house on Stillwater Lane.

Before doing anything else, Mandy helped Chris back the rented trailer onto the left side yard, unhook it, and level it. After unlocking the back, Chris pulled out a folding table and some folding chairs, and Mandy helped him set them up in the carport next to the Ford Torino.

He pulled the ice chest out of the back of his truck's extended cab and added it to the scene.

"Since you don't want the kids in the house yet, I figured this would be a decent place for us to gather," he said. "I should be done with the bathroom today though, if all goes well."

He meant it to be reassuring, but a pit returned to Mandy's stomach.

Chris returned to measuring and cutting wood, moving pieces in and out of the bathroom, where he'd set up battery-powered work lights and hung plastic tarping over the door.

Mandy offered to help again, but he declined. Instead, she decided to resume her inspection, this time looking at the house's exterior. She grabbed a baseball cap and her sunglasses from the car and pulled up the list on her phone.

She took a moment to stand outside and loathe the house in silence. Once she was satisfied, she got to work, starting with the carport, taking note of all the copious repairs.

After an hour or so, Chris found Mandy. "I need to go pick up some supplies. I'm gonna try the local hardware shop first. If they don't have what I need, I'll drive out to Home Depot again, but it's a bit of a trip."

"Is the hardware shop still called Rutherford's?" Mandy asked. She recalled a classmate working there in high school.

"No, it's uh," he opened his phone, "Rosebud Building Supply."

"I bet it's in the same place," she said, more to herself.

"I thought I'd take the kids. We can grab some food on the way back. You wanna go?"

"Shouldn't someone stay here in case the movers show up?"

Chris grimaced. "Right! I almost forgot. I'm sorry."

Mandy laughed it off. "It's fine. Where are you going for food?"

"There's a Hardee's near the hardware store. Isn't that the same as Carl's Jr.?"

"Eh. More or less, yeah. Get me whatever breakfast sandwich they have. I'm easy. And hash browns."

Mandy noticed that Ethan and Grace were eager to go. Must be itching for a change of scenery, she thought. They loaded into Chris's truck, and Grace waved at Mandy through the back passenger window as they drove away.

She watched them go. And as the truck turned from Stillwater Lane, Mandy suddenly felt very alone. Almost exposed, standing in the yard. And a bit cold, despite the heat from the morning sun.

Mandy shook it off and refocused on her task, moving around to the back of the house, her phone in hand.

She added to the list: *REAR EXTERIOR—BROKEN AND MISSING SHINGLES, LOOSE AND RUSTED GUTTERS, CRACKS IN PLASTER, ROT IN WOOD SIDING, BROKEN WINDOW FRAMES, BROKEN WINDOWPANES*, and of course *PEELING PAINT*.

So much peeling paint.

As she climbed the steps of the back porch, she noted: *BACK PORCH—LOOSE RAILINGS, ROTTING WOOD*. And was it her imagination or…was the porch itself slanted? She'd need to ask Chris to check it with a level. She added it to the list.

Then she heard a small voice. A girl. A child.

Mandy wondered if Grace was back already, for some reason.

She strained to listen.

No other voices. No Chris. No Ethan.

Maybe it was one of their neighbors, she thought.

There it was again. A little girl playing, giggling. From the direction of the left side yard, where they'd parked the trailer.

Mandy walked down the back porch steps and stopped to listen. But she couldn't hear the voice anymore. She walked across the yard, pausing at the door to the primary bathroom. When she got to the corner of the house, she peeked around, but no one was there. Only the rented trailer.

She listened again for the child's voice, but—nothing.

"Hm," Mandy said, pushing her apprehension to the side.

She went to the primary bathroom entrance and pulled her copy of the house key from her jeans pocket. She'd been meaning to try this but had kept forgetting. She slipped the key into the lock and turned it.

Click.

There was a little rush within her—excitement, but also uncertainty.

Was she ready to go into her parents' private space?

Before she was able to decide, she heard the voice again. It was unmistakable this time. A young girl. She thought of the image she'd seen reflected in the patio slider at the hotel and shuddered.

A breeze blew across the yard, kicking up dead leaves.

Mandy left the key in the lock and went back to the corner of the house, peeking around again.

This time, she saw her. The little girl.

It was only for a moment.

She was standing by the front of the house before she slipped around the corner into the front yard, disappearing from view.

It was crazy to think it was her. The same phantom she'd been chasing since she was a child herself. But damn, if it didn't look like her. Long blonde hair. White nightgown.

I think somethin' about this place makes you a touch crazy. You can turn around and walk the other way, but I bet you're goin' after her, ain't you?

Mandy shook her head.

She hesitated a moment, then followed, moving quickly down the side yard. As she reached the corner and looked down the length of the front of the house, the front screen door slammed shut.

The hair stood up on her arms and scalp.

What the fuck?

She didn't know if she should—if she was more frightened to go inside or to be stuck in the yard, alone with her dread—but she went towards the front door anyway. By the time she reached the front porch, her walk had become a run.

Though her mind was racing, uncertain, she jerked the screen door open and barreled inside.

"I saw you come in!" Mandy called, the anger in her voice barely masking the fear. There was no one in the living room or kitchen. "I know you're here!"

She took a few tentative steps forward. As she glanced down the hallway, she saw her again. For a moment. The briefest glimpse. A hint of blonde hair and a flowing nightgown. Then the little girl disappeared into the last room on the left, Shane's room.

Your room…until that Easter.

The door slammed.

Mandy's heart was pounding now. She experienced a rush of conflicting emotions. Panic and fear, yes. But vulnerability as well. She glanced back at the open front door and considered leaving. Waiting in front of the house for Chris. Waiting for him to help her.

And that made her angry.

She'd worked so hard not to be that person. And yet here she was, after only two days back in Rosebury, feeling like a helpless child again.

Before you stepped up. Before you learned to help yourself.

Mandy forced herself to stop thinking. She moved down the hall toward Shane's room, ignoring the creaking floorboards, her eyes locked on the door. It was almost as if she were pulled—closer and closer—until she was standing right in front of it.

She reached out and placed her hand on the doorknob.

If she went in this room now, it would be the first time since she was a child. Since the day she'd stepped in against her better judgment, bringing food to her recuperating father.

But she was still young then. She was different now. Stronger.

Can't change who ya are. Not really.

Mandy gritted her teeth, held her breath, and turned the knob.

She pushed the door open and stepped inside.

There was no girl in here. It was empty.

The room was just as she remembered it. It was sparsely furnished, old furniture covered in boxes and crates and clutter. Shane's bunk bed was in the same place. His dresser as well. His personality had been stripped away—peeled from the walls, dumped into boxes—but beneath the mildew, it still smelled like his cheap cologne.

Mandy steadied herself. She moved to the closet and opened it. It was empty.

She turned back to the window. In one corner of the room sat her old rocking horse, filthy and worn. She stared at it, surprised it was still here. That it had survived after so many years. It made her uncomfortable.

She half expected to see it start rocking by itself. To hear the whispers she'd heard as a girl.

Instead, there was a voice behind her, deep and weathered, roughened by cigarettes and time. "Amanda Jean."

She jumped and spun around.

A man stood in the doorway of the room.

She knew this man, but she never expected to see him again.

He was in his late sixties. Thin. Bony. His skin was ashen, and his hair was thin and gray, messy around the ears, and longish in the back. He was unshaven, and his facial hair was rough and patchy. His face was thin, his cheekbones severe, and his eyes were dark, set back in his skull under a furrowed brow.

The flannel shirt he was wearing was a mix of grays and whites. It was tucked into his high-waisted jeans, which gathered at the top of his black work boots. Around his neck collar was a bolo tie with a red stone inset. In his hands, he held a crumpled gray baseball cap.

"Uncle Harlan," Mandy said, her mouth dry. "What are you doing here?"

"It's good to see you, Amanda Jean."

"It's Mandy now," she said, straightening her posture.

He cleared his throat. "You grew up right pretty. You look like your mama when she was a girl. Like a—"

"Why are you here, Harlan?"

His eyes narrowed, and he grinned. "Not exactly a hospitable welcome for...*kin.*"

Mandy said nothing but stared at him. She found that she was overly conscious of her body. She reminded herself not to fidget.

The stink of cigarettes and sweat mingled with the mustiness of the room.

"I heard you were back in town," Harlan said. "I'm on the city council now, see. Got friends at the sheriff's office. They told me you called, askin' about your folks. So... I figured I'd pay a visit, say hello, and tell ya what I know."

Mandy waited for him to continue.

"Amanda Jean…all grown up," he pondered, shaking his head. "Say, ya remember how you and your brothers used to help me over at the church?"

"I haven't been a religious person in quite a while, Harlan."

He clicked his tongue. "Well, that disappoints me, Amanda Jean. The Lord's work is never done. 'Behold, he that keepeth Israel shall not slumber or sleep.' Your mama, she never missed a service right up until—"

"Until she killed herself?"

Harlan winced. "Oh, come on. We don't know that," he said.

"But we do *suspect* it, right?"

Harlan shrugged and shook his head, pursing his thin lips. His upper body and head were animated, as if exorcising the answer from within, but his feet remained planted. "Well…no one left a note."

"But she died from pills, right?"

She took Harlan's silence as confirmation.

"And Daddy?" she asked.

He shook his head. "I reckon they don't know *what* happened. They say his heart medicine was here, but it was hidden. He hadn't used it."

"So…the crazy bitch really did it?" Mandy said. "I guess we shouldn't be surprised."

"Don't talk ill, now. Your mama—"

"My mama ain't here no more, Harlan. And this is *my* house now. So, while I appreciate you stopping by to provide this *enlightening* information in person, thanks for nothing."

Harlan huffed—a sharp, bitter little breath of contempt. He didn't move from the door. "Yes," he said, after a long moment, "*your* house. But *I* was born here. In this house. In this exact *room*, in fact. My daddy bought this place when he come back from the Great War. My mama and my brother are buried on this land. This here's been our family's home for near a century. A *Caulder* home."

Mandy's hands began to shake. She didn't know where to put them, so she folded them in front of her to better hide her nerves.

Caulder home, she thought. That was about right. She'd never felt like she belonged in this house. Even owning it didn't change that.

Mandy set her jaw and held Harlan's gaze, refusing to give him the pleasure of a reaction.

But Harlan *did* look away. He scanned the room as if seeing it for the first time, appraising it, taking in every detail, from floor to ceiling. As he glanced up, his mouth drooped open, his upper lip curled into a sneer. His teeth and gums were tinged with gray. He took his time, and when he finished his perusal, he looked back to her.

"Not that you asked, but I'm doin' just fine, thank you kindly. If you *had* asked, I would've told you that Caulder Brothers Construction is the biggest builder in the County now. Makes for a real comfortable livin'. And that brings me to the other reason I came here today."

Harlan shifted his baseball cap into his left hand. He reached into his shirt pocket and retrieved a folded piece of paper. He held it out, offering it to Mandy.

She stayed in place, arms folded, her pulse racing, and asked, "What is it, Harlan?"

He shook the paper, like a treat before a pet, as if that would entice her to take it. When she didn't move, he said, "It's a check. An offer. To buy this property. I want it back."

Mandy did her best not to gasp out loud.

Of all the things he could have said, that was the last one she expected.

"Why?" she asked.

"I told ya, already. It's my home. It's my birthright."

Mandy scoffed. "I bet it killed you to learn they gave it to me, didn't it?"

He ignored her question. "You'll find my offer real generous. More than you'd get sellin' the house, 'specially with all the fixin' up that needs to be done. But I can take care of that, no problem. There's plenty there for you to buy yourself somethin' new—somethin' real nice—and cover all your troubles movin' too."

She clenched her teeth, her cheeks warm. Her fists tightened. "You...can't *buy* me," she said. She spat the words at him.

He withdrew the check but didn't return it to his pocket. "I'm offering to buy the *house*. The *property*. That's all."

"And who said it was for sale? Did you just *decide* that you were going to take it and that was that? Do you think you can take whatever you want?"

Harlan's mouth narrowed into a thin line. "Please don't make this difficult."

"Or what?"

Harlan glared at her, squinting, his eyes dark with anger. The expression lasted only a moment—a fleeting glimpse—before he caught himself and averted his eyes to the floor. He let out a low, humorless laugh. "Nothin', of course. But I still think you oughta give it some thought, Amanda Jean. It's what's best for you." Then he added, "For everyone."

"I asked you to call me Mandy," she said quietly, seething at the subtle implication. "And now I'm asking you to leave."

Harlan tilted his head to the side, as if examining her. He grinned.

Mandy couldn't recall ever wanting to punch someone in the face quite as much as she did right now. "I said get out," she repeated. Whether it was her anger or something else, something deeper, she didn't know, but she found herself holding back tears.

Harlan continued to stare at her, unmoving.

The anger grew within Mandy, to the point where it was almost uncontrollable.

"Get out of my house!"

She screamed it, the sound bursting out from deep inside of her. Her body shook. A single tear broke free and ran down her cheek. She thought she might hate him more now than she ever had. She hated that he'd done this. That he'd made her feel this way. Like she was trapped in this room with him.

This *horrible* room.

"You heard the lady."

It was Chris. He was in the hall, standing behind Harlan.

A wave of relief rushed over Mandy when she heard his voice. Knowing he was nearby. That she wasn't alone.

Harlan turned to face Chris and, in a genial tone, he said, "Oh, well, hello. I'm Amanda's uncle, Harlan Caul—."

"I don't give a shit," Chris said, cutting him off. "I only know she wants you gone."

Harlan stared at Chris for a moment, before smiling and nodding. "I was just leaving." He turned back to Mandy. "Think about it," he said, sliding the check under the casing of the door. He put on the baseball cap, turned, and moved past Chris in the hallway, walking with a slight limp. "Y'all take care now."

———

"So, it's true then?" Chris asked. He was seated across from Mandy at the kitchen table. "About your folks?"

"Yeah. I think so," Mandy whispered.

She was staring at her lap, at her hands cradling the folded check. They were still shaking, but she couldn't feel them. She was numb all over, detached from the world and from her own emotions. In her mind, she still pictured Harlan's smug smile.

Chris sighed. "It's obvious...you and your uncle have some *bad blood*."

Mandy nodded.

"You were...upset."

She nodded again.

"Do you want to talk more about it?"

Did she? What would she even say? Would she talk of all the times her uncles had tormented the family? Or the fight Harlan had once with her father? Or—

"No," she said. "He's just not a good guy."

"Alright."

"He offered to buy the house," she said. The words tumbled out and she regretted it immediately.

"What? Really?"

"Yeah," she said, sliding the check across the table to Chris.

Chris picked it up, unfolded it, and stared at it for a minute. "Wow."

"Yeah."

"Well, *that* is good news, right?"

"I turned him down," she whispered. Her voice, which had been so big a few minutes before now seemed miniscule. Insignificant.

Chris was staring at her, but she didn't want to look at him.

He scoffed. "Honey, I understand if you don't like the guy, but you don't have to *like* him to take his money." He paused, waiting for Mandy to respond, but when she didn't, he went on. "This house is…*so much worse* than we anticipated. We may not even have the funds to fix it like we planned. *You* don't want to be here. *The kids* don't want to be here. *No one* wants to be here."

"I'm sorry," she said. "I can't do it."

Chris sprung up, his chair scraping across the wood floor. He paced the kitchen, rubbing his face with his hands. After a moment, he stopped in front of the table, exhaled, and said, "I'm sorry, but I'm gonna need more than that."

"I can't… I can't let him…*buy* me."

"He wants to buy *the house*, Mandy!" he said. He was close to shouting. He waved the check in the air in front of him.

Mandy wasn't accustomed to Chris raising his voice. She didn't like it. Chris was an even-tempered man, and that was something she loved about him. She didn't like seeing him like this. For one, it meant he was far more stressed than he'd been letting on. But more, it seemed aggressive, and that had never been their dynamic.

He went on. "I'm… I don't even know what to say right now. I get standing on principle, but have you looked around? When was the last time you checked our bank accounts? Did you notice the guys in *hazmat* suits with the big pipes sucking *raw sewage* out of our basement? The septic situation *alone* is going to set us back thousands we didn't plan on. And that's only the beginning." He held up the check. "With this money, we could move back *home*, Mandy. So, I'm sorry, but I'm gonna need more from you than 'I can't.'"

She looked him in the eyes, teeth clenched. Defiant, as she had been with Harlan. But this new rush of anger was misplaced. Chris was right about deserving more of an answer. They'd uprooted their lives and he'd barely complained about it.

But how could she explain it to him? She didn't understand it herself.

He was *right!* They *should* take the money and run. This was a lifeline, and they should grab ahold of it with both hands. None of them wanted to be in Rosebury, least of all her. So how could she argue? How could she explain her hatred? The baffling defiance within her? She couldn't. There were no facts to be disputed, only feelings. Feelings she lacked the capacity to express.

Her eyes went to the faint red stain on the kitchen floor and lingered.

"I said…no, Christopher. And I can't explain why. But I need you to trust me. I need you to support me on this. He thinks he can have anything he wants, but…he can't have this."

Chris opened his mouth, as if to respond, but no words emerged. He turned and walked a few steps toward the front door, but pivoted and walked back. He took a deep breath and ran a hand through his hair. "This is a hard one." He struggled to find more words. "You… want my trust, but you don't act like you trust *me*. Not enough to let me in. We've been together over sixteen years, Mandy. *Sixteen years*, and it's like I'm still looking at your life through a keyhole. That hurts."

With that, he walked outside, letting the front door slam behind him.

Mandy reminded herself that they were both speaking from pain, more than anger. But she also realized that her silence—her reluctance, or *inability* to talk about her childhood in Rosebury—might drive a real wedge between them. Damage their relationship. But she didn't know what to do about it. Or where to start. And she worried that if she started, she might not be able to stop. That the memories might consume her.

Every time she tried to speak to him—about the poverty and neglect she'd faced, the abuse she'd suffered, how her uncles had terrorized her family at times—the words would catch in her throat and disappear, muffled by doubt and fear.

She *did* trust Chris. More than anyone in her entire life. But she wasn't obligated to share this part of herself with him, or *anyone*.

Trust didn't expunge fear.

She believed Chris had only the best intentions—to understand her, to partner with her in her healing, to face her challenges alongside her. But how could she let him in, when she feared the scar tissue was the only thing holding her together?

Chapter 9

Headlights on the Window, 1991

Amanda arrived home from school to find *The 700 Club* blaring on the television in the living room, with no one watching. She switched it off and called for her mother, but the house was silent.

Her father was at work, but she'd expected her mother to be home.

Amanda went down the hall to her parents' bedroom. The door was closed. Her mother might be napping. She knocked and waited a moment before pushing the door open. The lamps by the bed were on and the bed was unmade. Dresser drawers were left standing open, their contents disheveled. The box fan near the window was still running, but the room was empty.

Amanda switched off the lamps and fan.

She went to the kitchen and looked around to see if her mother had left a note, letting them know where she'd gone. But there was nothing on the refrigerator. Or dining room table—aside from an open bottle of milk, an empty bowl, and a spoon with dried crust around the edge.

No note.

She sniffed the milk and winced. It was spoiled from sitting out, though it might have been already. She'd known members of her family to drink sour milk if they were hungry enough—even herself once or twice, when it wasn't too far gone. Hunger made people desperate sometimes. Maybe her mother had been that hungry today. Or maybe she hadn't been lucid enough to tell the difference.

Amanda wasn't exactly upset that she was alone.

Her mother being away was better than her being sad. When she was sad, the whole house seemed heavier. With her gone, the house was lighter—quiet, calm. Her mother had many moods, and Amanda never quite knew which version of her she'd find when she opened the front door. It was like spinning a roulette wheel.

Sad Mama was the worst Mama.

Though it wasn't unusual for her mother to wander off, she *rarely* went without telling anyone. If she disappeared without warning, it usually meant that she was "in a mood." At least, that's what her mother called it. Her father was far more dismissive. He referred to it as "one of her states." And, when he was being less charitable, he'd say she was "on a tear," or that she'd "gotten a wild hair," or "gone 'round the bend."

If she *had* "gotten a wild hair," there was no telling when she might return, or what she might bring back with her.

Of late, many of her spur-of-the-moment trips had been to go gambling, most often at the Bingo Hall in Alcoa. Amanda could almost picture her at one of the long tables, cigarette in hand, cards laid out in front of her. If that was where she'd gone, she might not be back till morning. Amanda knew that firsthand, having been dragged along a handful of times. She'd sleep under the table at her feet in the Bingo Hall and wait for her to finish.

She went to the kitchen pantry. As usual, not much inside: two 6-packs of Mountain Dew, though one only had two cans left in its plastic rings; a large bag of marshmallows, opened and re-sealed with a clothespin; a box of Smacks, her father's cereal; three identical jars of dill pickles; an unopened bottle of hot sauce; a bag of sugar; and a bag of white bread, twisted shut, with only the heels left inside.

Most of the time, she'd find canned pork and beans. Or Campbell's soup, at least. But those weren't there today. She'd gotten pretty good at making meals out of next to nothing, but this was slim pickings.

Amanda shook the box of Smacks. Not much left. She probably shouldn't eat them. Her father wouldn't be very happy if he returned home from work and didn't have enough cereal to make a bowl. Since Amanda had already gotten scolded last week for swiping some of the Twinkies he kept in his work bag, she put the box back, deciding not to tempt fate again.

She unwrapped the marshmallows and put one in her mouth, but it was hard and stale, so she spit it right back out.

A search of the refrigerator didn't fare much better. It held four bottles of Bud Light, two cans of Mountain Dew, and some miscellaneous condiments.

One of Amanda's adopted cats, Moon Pie, passed between her feet, brushing up against each calf. She let out a loud, insistent meow.

"Are you hungry, Moonie? Join the club."

All Amanda wanted was something real, something hearty that would stick to her ribs. She'd started looking forward to school. Though the food in the cafeteria wasn't wonderful, at least it was something warm to eat that would fill her belly for a while, which was better than almost anything she got at home.

In six years, she'd be eligible for a driver's license. With that, she'd be able to get a job. And, with a job, she'd have her own money. She could buy herself food, *real* food, whatever kind she wanted. Six years seemed like forever when every day was hard. But it was something to look forward to. The faint promise of a small, precious bit of independence. The idea that someday she wouldn't be hungry.

Her stomach growled, as if on cue.

Down the road was a small grocery store called Petal & Stem General. They had a kitchen in the back, and sold sliders, three for a dollar. A few times in the past, Amanda had managed to scrounge up enough loose change from around the house to buy some for herself.

It was worth a try.

She went into the front room and removed the cushions from the couch. She found a quarter and a dime.

A good start!

Amanda replaced the cushions and moved to the recliner, her father's spot. Since he was often in his work clothes when he sat in it, she was optimistic. Though she found it unpleasant being so close to where her father sat (and farted), she was on a mission. She dug between the cushions, where she found two more quarters, a nickel, and three pennies.

Amanda counted the coins up. *Ninety-three cents.* She counted again to be sure. Yes, ninety-three. She was so close.

Kneeling, she checked under the recliner and the couch as well, but found no more money under either of them.

She went back to her parents' bedroom and checked her father's nightstand, where he often emptied his pockets when he got home. But today, nothing. She scanned the carpet, hoping to spot an over-looked coin, but no.

Seven cents. That's all she needed. Seven measly pennies. She had to be able to find that around here *somewhere*. She couldn't give up when she was only seven cents away from sliders!

Amanda skipped her brothers' rooms, knowing better than to enter without their permission. That would only lead to more problems.

She thought of another place she could check—the *basement*, by the washer and dryer. She'd had luck there before.

Amanda went to the basement door, switched on the light, and descended the creaky stairs. She wasted no time searching the ground near the washer and dryer.

After finding nothing, she almost left, but decided to check inside the machines.

Nothing in the washer.

But in the empty dryer was a single coin. It was small and dark. Amanda grabbed it and held it up to the light, sure it was only a penny. But she was wrong. It was a dirty, discolored dime. It was so tarnished, she had to check it twice to be sure.

The most beautiful, filthy little coin she had ever seen.

Amanda counted the money twice and ran back up the stairs, closing the door behind her. She was pleased with her victory.

Once outside, she jumped on her bike and began to ride down the street. She gripped the coins tight in her fist, headed for Petal & Stem.

When she arrived, no one was at the front counter. She dropped her coins on the Formica top, tapping her fingers, excited at the prospect of the greasy burgers, small though they may be.

As she waited, her eyes caught sight of a sign hanging behind the counter, and she grimaced. It read: NO CHECKS ALLOWED FROM DEBORAH HOLLOWAY. Her stomach sank and her cheeks got warm.

Amanda didn't know how many checks her mother had bounced, but it must've been quite a few to warrant a sign. She hated seeing her mother's name posted like that. It was *her* name too! Seeing it made her feel small. And guilty, as if her family's mistakes were hers as well, though she'd done nothing wrong, other than being born a Holloway.

Sam and Gertie, the older couple who owned the store, had always been kind to Amanda. Sam worked the counter most often. He always greeted her with a smile and treated her with respect, though he did raise an eyebrow any time her parents sent her to buy cigarettes.

Never enough food in the house. *Always* plenty of cigarettes.

As he approached, Sam said, "What can I do for you, little lady?"

Little lady. Amanda smiled.

She ordered the sliders and watched as he counted her change, dropping it into the cash register. She stepped to the side to wait, her mouth watering at the aroma of the burgers cooking.

After a few minutes, Sam emerged from the back and handed her a plain brown bag. "I threw some fries in for ya. Our secret." And he winked.

She appreciated how kind he was to her, despite her family's reputation. He treated her well and made her feel seen. Like she was her own person. Not *just* a Holloway. But Amanda.

The bag was warm in her hands, and the scent was intoxicating.

Her stomach growled.

She couldn't wait to eat. It would take too long to ride her bike back home. She wanted the burgers now, while they were hot. And while they were hers, and hers alone.

Amanda sat in the sun on the porch in front of Petal & Stem and opened the brown bag, ready to enjoy a meal she'd earned. The sliders were everything she needed in that moment—simple, warm, and satisfying. And though the fries were a bit undercooked, it didn't bother

her at all. They tasted like kindness, which was something she hungered for—sometimes more than food.

She was careful not to eat too fast, despite her hunger. This meal was hers, and she wanted to savor every bite.

———

As the sun set for the day, Amanda's mother still hadn't returned.

With both parents gone, that meant that she and her brothers would be alone in the house for the night. Though it was by no means the first time, it was never a situation she looked forward to. Her brothers often acted like children, and Amanda found herself feeling responsible for them and the house.

Travis returned home from hanging out with friends around 7PM and disappeared into his room, where he began blasting his music. Amanda kept to her room as well, lying on her bed with Moon Pie and Snickerdoodle, reading a book.

Shane was still out when she decided it was time to rest. She turned off her lights and lay in the dark, eyes closed, but not sleeping. The sound of Travis's music rumbled through the wall.

After a few hours, the music stopped. The house fell quiet.

Much quieter than usual.

Amanda had grown used to near-constant noise: her mother or father sitting in front of the television, her brothers blasting music or being raucous, friends and relatives coming in and out of the house at all hours, or the frequent drama that raised the volume.

This stillness was peaceful, but also somewhat disconcerting.

No noise meant no *distractions*.

She became aware of the small sounds around her, the ones normally smothered under a blanket of foreground noise. The chirping of crickets. The occasional rustle of some small animal moving through the bushes outside. The steady drip of the bathroom faucet. The refrigerator kicking on with a soft hum before settling back into silence. The groans and creaks of the old house settling around her.

Amanda took a moment to appreciate the unusual stillness, thankful that the evening had gone without incident. She'd almost drifted off when Shane came in through the back door, banging and stomping as if it were midday and he had the house to himself. He clattered around the kitchen for a few minutes, opening doors and clanging bowls, his footsteps heavy, but soon his noise faded too.

After that, it didn't take long for Amanda to slip off into sleep, surrounded by a rare, tranquil silence.

———

AMANDA JOLTED AWAKE, unsure of what had startled her.

Her heart was racing, her face flushed.

She blinked, her mind scrambling to make sense of where she was, what time it was, what was happening. It was the middle of the night, but why was her room so bright?

Then—the blare of a horn shattered the quiet.

Amanda shot upright, disoriented. It took her a moment to realize that the light flooding her room was coming from outside.

Headlights. Shining through her bedroom window.

Amanda sat frozen in her bed, gripping the blanket against her chest, and listened. An engine revved. Glass shattered. And over that noise, there was something else—*voices*, loud and slurred, stumbling over words.

"Come on out, Sissy!" one of the voices roared, followed by a wild laugh.

A second voice, louder and more menacing, growled, "Come on out here, Earl! Ain't no hidin' from the big bad wolves tonight! We're havin' a party and we need some favors!"

She recognized these voices.

It was her uncles—Harlan and Malcolm. They were outside, and from the sound of it, they were drunk.

The engine of their truck revved again, like someone preparing for a race.

"Or we'll huff and puff, and we'll blow this house right the fuck down!"

Amanda's heart hammered in her chest.

Her uncles were unpredictable when they got like this, liquored up and ornery. *Reckless*. And, even at her age, she knew that Harlan didn't make idle threats. If he said they were going to blow the house down, that was reason to be afraid.

This was by no means the first time they'd shown up to the house uninvited, but it *was* the first time both of her parents had been gone. And even *they* struggled to handle Harlan and Malcolm when they were drunk. Now it was just her and her brothers. What were *they* supposed to do? The thought filled her with dread.

The revving stopped and the truck idled, rumbling. She strained to hear if they were still talking. More glass shattered outside. Beer bottles breaking, she assumed.

Slowly, she slid off the bed and crouched under the windowsill, hidden from view. She held her breath as she pressed herself against the wall.

In the beam of the headlights, a shadow grew larger. Someone was coming closer.

And then—a rap of knuckles on her window.

The sound was loud enough to make her jump, but she stayed quiet, frozen in place.

Malcolm's voice followed, his volume lower now but still loud enough to be heard over the idling truck. "Amaaaaanda," he called. "Amaaaanda. Come on, darlin'. Let your uncles inside. We're just havin' a little ole fun." There was an edge to his voice that made Amanda sick.

She tried not to breathe. She clenched her fists, pressed herself tighter against the wall, and prayed he couldn't see her.

BANG! BANG! BANG! BANG!

A loud pounding at the front door.

It was mixed with the wild rattle of the door handle jiggling. Harlan's voice followed, shouting, "Debbie! Earl! Open up now, y'all!"

Each hit rattled the door, echoing through the house.

BANG! BANG! BANG! BANG!

A figure appeared in Amanda's doorway, and her breath hitched. But it was only Shane. He was crouched down, a troubled expression on his pale face. In his hand was one of their daddy's pistols. His knuckles were white around the grip.

Amanda didn't like the idea of Shane with a gun. It was only a bit more palatable than dealing with her uncles. But she understood he was only trying to protect them.

He gestured to her, his voice a forced whisper. "Go check the kitchen door."

Malcolm rapped at her window again, "Come on, girl," he taunted. "Let us in."

Shane gestured to her, but for the moment, she could only stare, motionless.

BANG! BANG! BANG! BANG! BANG! BANG! BANG! BANG!

The pounding on the front door grew louder, more insistent—then cut off.

"Now!" Shane whispered sharply.

Amanda gave a quick, furtive nod, and dropped to her hands and knees. She scurried across the bedroom floor, staying low, almost lizard-like. She tried to ignore the looming fear.

Once she passed the doorway and lunged into the hall, Amanda assumed she was in the clear. She scrambled to her feet and ran toward the kitchen. But as she turned the corner, panic seized her.

The back door was standing wide open.

She slid to a stop and stiffened, unsure what to do next. She was afraid that she was too late—that her uncle was already *inside the house.*

The door creaked in the faint breeze.

Her gaze darted around the kitchen, scanning the shadows. Her heart pounded so hard she thought it might burst.

Then—through the back door—she saw Harlan.

He was in the yard, just past the back porch. He wasn't inside. Not yet. Shane must've left the door open when he'd come in.

Harlan spotted Amanda and their eyes locked for a moment. His face twisted into a drunken snarl. Then they both lunged forward and began to race for the door.

Focus, she told herself. *Gotta get there first.*

Harlan stumbled on the porch steps, hindered by his inebriation. He tripped and fell to his knees.

Amanda reached the door, gripping the handle and slamming it shut. But her hands were shaking almost uncontrollably. She fumbled with the lock, her palms slick with sweat. Through the small window in the door, she saw Harlan climbing to his feet, steadying himself.

He started toward her again.

Focus on the lock, she told herself, taking a deep, labored breath.

He was almost to her when, finally, the lock slid into place.

His body slammed against the door with a thud, shaking it in its frame. The knob jumped and rattled. Harlan growled and cursed. As she backed away, she could see his face framed in the window, teeth bared in a sneer.

Amanda took another step back, her eyes locked on Harlan's. She didn't realize Shane was in the room with her until she bumped up against him. Startled, she jumped again. Shane put a hand on her arm, his expression stoic. Travis was right behind him.

The banging at the front door resumed.

Malcolm.

But this wasn't quite the same. It didn't sound like pounding anymore, but more like a dull thwack. Like the chipping of an axe.

Thwack, thwack, thwack.

The sound was like an ominous metronome, each rhythmic strike sending chills up Amanda's spine.

She couldn't handle it. Between Malcolm hacking away at the front door, and Harlan slamming his fists against the back door, shaking it in its frame, she wished she could disappear.

Shane stepped forward, positioning himself beside Amanda, squaring his shoulders to Harlan. He raised the gun in front of him, making sure that Harlan could see it.

Amanda gasped.

"Y'all need to go now," Shane said. His voice was shaking but his tone was firm. "Ain't nothin' here for ya tonight, Uncle Harlan. Ya need to take Uncle Malcolm and git."

Harlan hesitated, his gaze shifting between Shane's face and the gun. Back and forth.

Amanda held her breath. Seeing Shane step up brought both hope and fear in equal measure. Would it be enough? Or would it only serve to make Harlan angrier? She'd seen what her uncle could do to people who crossed him.

Thwack, thwack.

After a long moment of quiet deliberation, Harlan's sneer twisted into a slight, mocking smile. He leaned closer to the window, his eyes fixed on the children. Then he laughed. "Sleep tight, y'all," he said, his grin widening. "We'll see ya soon."

He turned and staggered away, disappearing from their view.

After a few moments, the thwacking sound stopped. Shane lowered the gun and exhaled, his shoulders sagging, the tension draining from his face.

Soon after, the truck engine revved up again. The tires squealed against the gravel, and it sped away.

They all stayed in the kitchen, looking at one another. Listening. None of them moved or spoke until the sound of the truck had faded into the distance, and an eerie silence settled over the house once more.

Chapter 10

Sleepwalking

"Do we get to go inside the house now?" Ethan asked, poking his head out of the hotel bathroom, his words muffled by toothpaste. He was already changed for bed, wearing a pair of red shorts and a faded Avengers t-shirt.

Mandy's grip tightened on her phone.

"I don't see why not," Chris replied while sitting on the hotel bed, flipping through channels on the television with the remote.

Mandy couldn't keep the kids out of the house forever. And since Chris had finished fixing the bathroom floor that afternoon, she'd run out of excuses.

"I'm excited!" Grace said. She'd gotten ready for bed early too, and was sitting on the bed next to Mandy, combing her doll's hair. "Do we get to pick our rooms tomorrow?" she asked, as if that was an exciting prospect.

Mandy placed a hand to her stomach. Her head was swimming and she was dizzy. She tried to focus on Grace's words, blinking away a sudden tiredness.

"Sure, honey," Chris said.

Though she'd tried to shake off a lingering unease from Harlan's visit, Mandy had been distracted and unfocused all day. And the thought of them making the move into the house—of the kids *staying overnight*—wasn't helping.

"I think the kids should take the first two rooms," Mandy said. "We can leave the third room for storage or an office."

Chris raised an eyebrow. "Does it really matter?" he said, his voice tired.

It does to me.

"Just my preference," she replied.

Chris shrugged.

Ever since their argument earlier that day, a chilly tension had settled between them. Mandy had tried to assist him in the bathroom, but between his silence and her lack of focus, she hadn't been much help.

They fought so seldom that Mandy wasn't sure how to fix it, and she hated that. Aside from Chris—and her children—she'd always felt alone in the world. She didn't want to be distant from him too. When they'd argue, a small joke or a kiss was often enough to break the ice afterwards, to ease the tension between them. But something about this seemed different, and it worried her.

The move had been hard on them both. It didn't help that they hadn't slept in the same bed since the trip began—Grace bunked with Mandy, while Ethan shared a bed with Chris. She loved to be held by him as she drifted off to sleep. She missed it.

Feeling loved. *Safe.*

If he put his arms around her, maybe everything would be right again.

"We met a kid today. Chase. He lives down the street," Ethan said, pulling Mandy from her thoughts. "He offered to show us around the neighborhood tomorrow after he goes to church."

Church? Is tomorrow Sunday? Already?

The days were blurring together.

"We'll probably need your help with house stuff tomorrow, bud," Chris said. "The movers brought our things today, so we'll need to start moving in."

Moving in. Moving in. Moving in.

The thought kept returning, nagging at her, tapping away at her brain like drops from a leaky faucet.

When the movers had arrived that afternoon, Mandy had stood motionless on the porch, watching as they dropped the storage pod next to the rented trailer. And it had hit her. *All* their belongings were here now. Everything from their life. Was *here*. In *Rosebury*. It wasn't theoretical anymore. It was real. And it couldn't be avoided.

They were *moving in.*

But what if it wasn't safe yet? For the kids. What if Mandy hadn't done enough to protect them? What if they found something she didn't want them to find—the image of bones in the yard flashed through her mind. Or what if Travis had left something behind—drug paraphernalia or pornography? It was even possible there were guns in the house. Or *worse.* They hadn't begun to discover what the house might be hiding. She hadn't even gone into…

And then she remembered.

The exterior door to the primary bathroom. She'd unlocked it earlier—before Harlan had showed up and derailed her day—and she'd never gone back to it. She was concerned, thinking of the door being left unlocked. What if someone had gotten inside while they were gone? She clenched her teeth and pushed the thought from her mind, assuring herself it would all be okay.

"Are we gonna sleep in our rooms tomorrow, too?" Grace asked.

"Not yet," Chris replied. "It's still gonna take some effort to get things squared away."

"Maybe we should plan to stay *here* one more night," Mandy said.

Chris exhaled, frowning. "We can't afford it," he said, his tone short, his words clipped. "Besides, I already packed up most of our things."

Mandy told herself to let it go, but her mouth didn't get the memo. "But…will it be clean enough for us to stay tomorrow?"

"If we put in the work," he said. "But we have tents in the truck. We can set them up inside and…*camp out.*"

"*Tents?* Really?" Mandy said, sharper than she'd intended. The thought of them setting up tents in that house—sleeping on the dusty floor—made her shoulders tight.

"Sure. Why not? I mean, we can't keep throwing money away on *luxuries*, Mandy. It's gonna run out."

Mandy bit her tongue. It was a jab, but he wasn't wrong. *She* was the one who was rejecting her uncle's money, and for reasons she couldn't explain.

"Camp inside the house?" Ethan asked, his face scrunched in incredulity.

"Yeah!" Chris smiled. "Why not? We'll make it fun."

Grace giggled.

The sound echoed, as if it were a million miles away. It was jarring to Mandy's current state of mind. Though she envied the ability of the kids to adapt, she wasn't liking *any* of it. But it was a battle she couldn't win, so she decided to be done arguing. At least for the night.

After a few minutes spent discussing what camping inside might look like—would they use sleeping bags, tell camp stories, eat s'mores —they all settled down, and Chris rented *Despicable Me 3* on the hotel pay-per-view.

The kids fell asleep within minutes of starting the movie. And Chris soon after. As they snoozed, Mandy lay in the dark, watching the screen, but the vivid colors and bright voices were far away. Her thoughts were elsewhere…

———

MANDY WAS IN THE HOUSE, in her parents' room, standing in front of her mother's antique mirror. But everything appeared the way it had when she was young.

She swayed back and forth, watching the reflection lag behind her movements, the edges of her vision blurring somewhat.

The reflection looked like Mandy, but it didn't *feel* like her. Her eyes were hooded, sleepy. Her blonde hair hung loose in front of her eyes, long enough to touch the top of her white dressing gown. Her skin was pale, and her face was free of make-up. She appeared tired, frail…*sick.*

The image in the mirror pulsed as if the glass was moving, alive.

Then she was pulled away, moving from the bedroom into the hallway. She drifted through the house as if on wires, suspended above the floor, lighter than air. *Floating.* Her head was clouded, fuzzy. The floor angled beneath her, disorienting. The house was quiet, but her head was full of vague whispers. She glided through the kitchen toward the back door. And though she didn't remember opening it, she was suddenly outside on the back porch.

It was nighttime, and the moon was bright. It painted the back yard in shades of blues and grays. At the edge of the yard, the trees shifted, their shadows moving under the moonlight. Mandy stared up at the cobalt sky, alive with blurry stars, and a wave of unbridled joy washed over her. It filled her up, but it was confusing, as if it were masking an indistinct, underlying heaviness.

A cool breeze moved over her face, and through her hair, but her skin still felt warm against the soft fabric of her gown, as if she was wrapped in a blanket.

She skipped down the back porch steps, her limbs light.

As her feet hit the ground, she began to dance through the yard, the dewy grass under her bare toes.

She reached down and lifted the bottom of her nightgown, moving it around her body as if it were a circle skirt. It billowed in cascading waves.

Moving to a rhythm she could feel but not hear, Mandy spun and turned and laughed. The sound of her voice echoed, loud and foreign, as though it belonged to someone else. Every spin went on forever.

And, as she twirled, nothing else mattered. The world outside shrunk away, inconsequential.

She loved this.

Being outside at night, surrounded by nature. The constant hum of the cicadas, The spying eyes of nightbirds. The sporadic, restless hooting of the barn owls. And, of course, the soft hypnotic glow of the fireflies.

Mandy had missed the fireflies.

She moved to them, pursuing their light, chasing them as she'd done so many times as a girl. She wanted to be in the middle of them. To dance with them.

As she followed them into the grove of trees at the back of the yard, their flitting patterns left remnants of light, trails that lingered like glowing threads. They stretched out in front of her, weaving in and out of the trees. She reached out to grab them, but the light slipped through her fingertips.

The world was moving slow around her, her every step taking an eternity, her body weighed down by a heaviness in her head. Her thoughts were thick and jumbled, but sometimes she'd get a sense that something was *inside* trying to pull her back. Some small voice—buried, but *urgent*—that she couldn't quite understand.

She kept following the fireflies as they encircled an oak tree—one of the larger ones—and began to ascend, twisting around its trunk in a glowing spiral.

"They're…going…up," she said to herself. Her voice dripped like honey—low, slow, and warm. She chuckled at the sound of it, the laughter bubbling up from inside of her, brash and strange. It echoed through the grove in slow motion, stretching out into an infinite loop, until it sounded like many others were laughing with her.

Mandy moved to the oak.

It loomed before her, tall and imposing, its branches outstretched like arms. Though she wasn't sure if it was beckoning her closer or warning her away.

She began to climb, following the light of the fireflies as if it was her guide, a pathway to a safe place. The bark under her hands was smooth—*lifeless*—as if it didn't belong to the world. She blinked against the fuzziness in her head. She was unsteady, but she reminded herself that she'd done this before. *So many times*. She could do it again now. She'd take her time. She'd be careful, deliberate.

Her ascent was slow, but soon she reached a fork in the tree, a place where she could relax a moment. Where she could sit and be comfortable while she watched the fireflies dance. An audience of one.

They were all around her, encircling the tree like a magical netting.

Mandy sighed. Her breath was loud in her ears.

As she went to reposition herself, she noticed a crag in the middle of the fork that had collected rainwater. Staring at the surface of the puddle, Mandy marveled, mouth agape. The fireflies appeared so beautiful in the reflection of the still water. She moved closer, leaning in to see them better. Her face was reflected in the water as well.

Except…it wasn't her face.

It was her *mother's* face. Her mother's eyes staring at her, unblinking. There was something vacant about her. Something sad. Haunting.

Mandy gasped in surprise, rearing back. The world angled as her foot slid, her body lurching backwards. She teetered at the edge of the tree for a long moment, flailing her arms, trying to fight the inevitable.

But then she began to fall.

She plummeted from the tree through the net of fireflies, the pull of gravity dragging her down. The descent sent her stomach lurching, constricted her throat. The wind roared past her ears.

Mama!

"Mandy!" someone shouted. It was Chris's voice. Faint. Muffled. Far away.

And then his hand was on the small of her back, slowing her fall.

Her body jerked to a stop.

He grabbed the fabric of her nightgown and began pulling her backwards, dragging her down again. She thrashed, grasping at nearby branches, but her fingers swept through open air.

"What are you doing?!" he screamed.

She landed with a jolt.

Not on wet earth. Not beneath the tree. Not splayed and hurting. Her feet were on concrete. The wind was gone, replaced by a near-complete stillness.

Her eyes flew open, and she lashed out, confused.

But Chris had her. He grabbed her hands and constrained her, pulling her in, holding her tight. He was trembling. And something terrible was in his eyes.

Panic.

"Mandy!" he said her name again through gritted teeth, "Stop! Stop, please."

She went motionless, but her heart continued to pound in her chest. Her face was covered in sweat. Her breathing was rapid and shallow.

Mandy whipped around, the world coming into focus.

They were standing on the balcony of the Briarwood Hotel.

"What…what is happening?" she whispered.

"You were…climbing up on the railing," Chris said, gasping.

Mandy glanced over at the wrought iron, trying to make sense of it, to piece it all together.

"I was dreaming," she said.

"You were sleepwalking?"

"No. I don't know. I haven't…I haven't ever done that."

Or have you?

"Jesus, Mandy…you're lucky Grace woke me up." Chris's voice cracked. His words came fast, running into each other. "I got you, but god, what if I hadn't gotten here in time?!"

She looked to the patio slider.

Her children stood in the doorway, their eyes wide. Full of fear. Sadness. *Confusion.*

She'd done this. Stirred up these emotions. She'd only ever wanted them to be safe. To *feel* safe. Now she'd played a part in taking that away from them.

"Oh my god," Mandy whispered. She felt like a child again. Small. Helpless. Not in control. "Goddamn this place."

Chris didn't let go of her. His fingers were digging into her arms from holding her so tight. "Jesus, Mandy," he repeated himself, his voice shaky. "I can't even imagine."

———

IN THE MORNING, they packed their bags and prepared to leave the hotel. Everyone was quieter than usual. There was worry on Grace's face.

"Mommy's okay, honey," Mandy said. "I just…I haven't been sleeping well. That's all."

They checked out of the hotel without saying much more to one another. As usual, Mandy drove the kids, following Chris in his truck.

After parking on the street on Stillwater Lane, Mandy sat in the car and stared at the house for a long while. She didn't want to go back inside. Every new discovery, each new bit of information, peeled back another layer of the past. Every new memory challenged her mental state. Threatened to wear her down. They'd only been here *two full days*, and she was already raw. How many more layers would she be able to unpeel before she unraveled?

"Mom, are you coming?" Grace stood by the open passenger side door.

"Yeah," Mandy said.

"I want to go inside."

Mandy nodded and forced a smile.

Gonna walk your kiddos right into the lion's den, ain't ya, Amanda Jean? Throw 'em right to the wolves.

Unable to put it off anymore, she got out of the car and joined her family, accompanying her children as they entered her childhood home for the first time.

As they stepped through the front door, they were met with the faint scent of mildew and old wood.

"It stinks in here," Grace said.

Ethan looked around and said, "Holy crap."

"Yeah, it's gonna take some work, bud," Chris said.

Ethan moved to the fireplace. Brushing his hand across the dusty mantle, he chuckled. "Yeah, you think?"

Grace went immediately to the pictures on the credenza and leaned in to look at them. "Who *are* all these people?"

"Relatives," Chris said. "*Distant* relatives."

Grace gave him a quizzical look. "From when? A hundred years ago?" she said, raising an eyebrow.

After brushing his dusty hands off on his pants, Ethan started down the hallway.

Mandy's pulse quickened. "Please stay out of the bedrooms for now…and the bathroom."

Chris moved close to her, resting a hand on her shoulder. In a hushed voice, he asked, "Where do you want them to go, Mandy? This is their house too, and we're gonna need…"

To protect them.

"…their help."

Mandy nodded, her heartrate quickening. "I know." She sighed. "I don't… I just worry."

"It's gonna be fine," he assured her. Then, in a normal voice, he said, "It's okay. You guys can explore a bit. But skip the basement and the bathroom for now. And…*be careful*, okay? Don't go digging in boxes or drawers. And don't touch anything if it looks dangerous."

Mandy moistened her lips, wiping the sweat from her brow. She rubbed her chest, suddenly short of breath.

"Are you okay?" Chris asked.

She didn't know how to answer.

"After last night, I mean?" he clarified.

Oh, that.

"I don't know what that was." She shook her head. Then added, "But, I'm fine."

Chris rubbed his neck with his hand. There was a weariness in his expression. Mandy realized he was frustrated, tired of hearing, *"I'm fine,"* when it was becoming quite clear she was not. But she didn't know what else to say.

From down the hallway, Grace said, "This door is locked."

Her parents' bedroom.

"Oh, I meant to tell you," Mandy said, happy to change the subject, "the house key worked in the outside lock for my parents' bathroom. I'll go open it up so we can see what we're dealing with."

Chris nodded.

Mandy crept past the basement through the kitchen to the back door.

Although it was early, the sky was overcast. Less hot than it had been, though the air was still. As she walked down the porch steps and across the back of the house, her footsteps sounded louder than normal, crunching through dry grass and weeds.

The key was still sitting in the lock to her parents' bathroom. Mandy put her hand on the doorknob, her thumb brushing the worn metal. She took a breath and then gave the door a push. It popped open with a small squeak.

No going back now, I reckon. Might as well do some more emotional damage.

Mandy stepped inside.

A rush of cold air moved past her face and arms.

She was hit with a fragrance she'd almost forgotten. The unmistakable mix of floral and citrus filled her nostrils. Her mother's favorite perfume. *Charlie Blue.*

The scent brought tears to her eyes.

It reminded her of the good times they'd had together. It wasn't all bad between them, not *always*. Her mother only wore perfume when she was happy. As she took the fragrance in now, Mandy remembered her mother's infectious giggle, and it made her smile.

How was it possible for a person to be two things at once? Her mother had danced with her in the living room, taught her how to put on makeup, and bought her a bike from a garage sale. She'd also let her go hungry, ignored abuse, and said horrible things to her that could never be unsaid. How could such different versions of the same person exist in one's memory?

The bathroom was dirty, but nowhere near as bad as the hallway bathroom. It was just old, uncared for, and in a state of natural disrepair.

It was smaller than she remembered, cramped even. The lighting was poor; a few dim bulbs hung over each of the two sinks. The linoleum floor was old and cracked, and the grout between the tiles had turned a deep black. Water stains spotted the walls and ceilings. And it reeked of mildew and cigarettes.

On one of the sinks, Mandy's mother's things remained as they'd been left. Some pill bottles. Cosmetics. A hairbrush still tangled with strands of her mother's hair.

It hit her then that the time to reconcile with her mother had passed. Any possibility of understanding, or of forgiveness, was now gone. When she'd left, she'd put this life behind her. And though she'd spoken to her parents from time to time, they hadn't played *any* role in her life in many years.

In that time, Mandy hadn't thought much about the reality of their age. Or their lifestyle. Sleepwalking past any notion of the finite.

Of the end and what that might look like. What it might *feel* like. But the end had come, regardless. Later than it might have, in a way. Later than she'd wished for, sometimes. And yet, still far sooner than she'd expected.

The other sink was her father's. On it, sat some mouthwash, a stand holding a toothbrush, and her father's razor, its blade dull from use and age.

Mandy remembered how tall he'd looked when she was young. She thought of how she'd sit cross-legged on his bed, watching him shave, his steady hands moving in an assured rhythm. How proud she'd been watching him get ready for work. The fragrance of his cologne. Her daddy, the train engineer. The man had always seemed carved from stone, invincible and everlasting.

Now he too was gone.

Was she…*missing them?* Was that what this was? Was that possible after everything they'd done to her? She'd spent so long distancing herself from them, resenting them, trying to forget. Was this *sorrow?* And…*regret?* For things left undone?

She stayed in the bathroom a moment, until she thought she was ready to enter her parents' room. When she finally pushed the bedroom door open, she realized it must not have been touched since they died. The full-size bed was unmade and misshapen from years under heavy bodies. On the sheets were stains, too faded for Mandy to identify—blood or vomit or urine or worse.

As she brushed aside a lingering cobweb and stepped into the room, something crunched underfoot—something plastic. Scattered on the nightstand, and on the floor as well, were empty pill bottles. So many of them.

The room was cluttered and chaotic. It'd always been this way, but it was worse now than she remembered. Things stacked upon things. Shoeboxes and newspapers and crossword puzzles. Empty food containers and garbage and other grime.

Mandy became aware of a new odor now, one that usurped the others.

Decay.

And with it, a realization that hit her square in the gut.

Her parents had *failed*.

They had failed her. And at some point in their lives, they'd failed themselves. Failed as human beings. Allowing their home to fall into squalor. Allowing themselves to live in filth.

A pang of guilt rose up within her.

Maybe, by leaving, she'd failed them too.

Chapter 11
What We Leave Behind

"I'm going to clean up my parents' bedroom before anyone else goes in," Mandy said. "I'll open the windows to air it out."

"Okay," Chris replied without looking up, keeping a steady rhythm as he sanded the baseboards in the hall.

"Speaking of airing things out," Mandy continued, "none of the windows have screens. I put it on the fixit list, but it may not be something we need to mess with."

"Yeah, okay." Chris nodded. He stood and gave her his attention, brushing the sweat from his forehead. "You need help?"

She hesitated. "No...I think I need to do it."

"Ah. You okay?"

Mandy smiled. "You know, you don't have to keep asking me that."

"But I'm gonna anyway."

She went to him and hugged him, holding on a little longer than usual. While the sleepwalking experience had been terrifying, she was glad to feel connected to him again.

After grabbing some cleaning spray, towels, and several large black garbage bags from the box of supplies that Chris had left near the front door, she headed down the hall to the primary bedroom. Before she went in, she stopped. The house was too quiet.

Then she realized why.

"Where are the kids? I thought they were excited to be in the house?"

"I guess you always want what you can't have," Chris said, shrugging. "The neighbor kid came by and wanted to show Ethan around. They took Grace with them."

"Oh, I'm sure Ethan loves *that*."

"I don't think he minds having a shadow. He looks out for her."
Protect them.

"And he's got his phone?" she asked.

"Of course."

GRACE FOLLOWED behind Ethan and his new friend. They were walking through the yard, heading away from the back patio toward the grove of trees at the rear. She often didn't speak much, but she was happy to listen. She found that when she was quiet, people often forgot about her and spoke their minds. She learned more that way.

Chase was a plain-looking kid. He was Ethan's age or close to it. Under his well-worn Titans baseball cap, he wore his dirty brown hair on the longish side. His black t-shirt said "Jelly Roll" and underneath the words was a picture of a skull wearing a crown. His jeans and sneakers were also well-traveled.

Grace was both fascinated and amused by his thick, Southern accent.

"Yeah, I guess Rosebury's alright," Chase said. "Lots of places to go. My dad takes me huntin' and fishin' up at the lake, sometimes. And some of the kids have dirt bikes, which is cool. Are you a gamer?"

"Uh, only, like, Minecraft. And Roblox," Ethan said.

"You should get on Fortnite. Or Call of Duty. A bunch of us play those ones."

"Oh, yeah…okay," Ethan said.

"So, ya haven't explored that much?" Chase asked.

Ethan shook his head, gesturing over his shoulder. "Only around our yard. We've just been here a couple of days."

"Bruh, this is *still* y'all's yard."

"Really?"

Grace smiled.

Chase pointed to the grove of oaks. "Uh huh, till somewhere in there. Up past the crick, I s'pose."

"We have a *creek?*" Ethan asked. He seemed surprised.

"Mom already told us that," Grace interjected, a hint of smug satisfaction in her voice.

"She did? When?"

"The other day," she said. "You weren't listening. As usual."

Chase laughed. "Dang, bruh. Your lil' sis called ya out."

Ethan shot Grace a look that was something between amusement and annoyance. "I listen. Shut up."

"So, ya haven't seen 'em yet?" Chase asked.

Ethan shrugged. "What is *them?*"

"We saw bones," Grace volunteered. "Ethan says it was a dinosaur."

Chase looked at her, his eyebrow raised, then at Ethan.

Ethan shook his head and rolled his eyes. "It was only…never mind. What is this *other* thing you're talking about?"

"They're right down over here. Y'all'll see."

They continued to walk through the yard. What had once been a lawn was now a patchwork of naturally growing things—crabgrass, wildflowers, dandelions, goldenrod, and other untamed growth.

As they entered the grove, the sunlight became muted by the thick canopy of the trees, with only a few narrow beams breaking through. The air was cooler here. Damp.

"Should we be going in here?" Grace asked.

Chase laughed. "This is still y'all's yard!"

"Well, that's just crazy," Grace said. She couldn't believe it. If what he said was true, they almost had their own forest! So many trees— giant oaks and maples. She heard a bullfrog croak, and birdsong. The wet, earthy scent was new to her. This was such a beautiful place to explore, she thought. She was already beginning to imagine the things she could do—climbing trees, building forts, playing in nature. That wasn't something she'd been able to do much back home.

She brushed her hand across the bark of an oak tree, its rough surface leaving her fingers dirty. It might've been their yard, but it was like stepping into another world.

"Heads up," Chase said, grabbing Ethan's sleeve.

Ethan—who had been distracted examining his new surroundings—stopped just short of a massive spider web.

It was strung between two trees, several feet across and almost as tall, its strands shimmering under faint sun beams. It was circular in shape, and intricate in construction, with evenly spaced radial threads all converging in the center. Thick strands of gossamer draped between the threads, forming uneven circles that started at the center and spiraled out in widening rings.

"It's a *writing spider web*," Chase said. "Cover your mouths." He covered his.

Ethan and Grace followed suit.

"And we're doing this…*why*, exactly?" Ethan asked, perplexed.

"My Mamaw always said that if ya smiled at a writing spider, it would write your name in its web," Chase said. "And that night you'd *die*."

Grace gasped behind her hand, her eyes getting big.

She spotted the spider sitting in the middle of the web. Its body was thick and yellow, patterned with black designs. Its legs were black and spindly with orange rings. Scattered around the web were several cocoons, bugs who'd found themselves ensnared.

"That's *silly*. That's not true," Ethan laughed. He took careful steps to avoid the web.

"Probably not," Chase said. "If y'all want to take a chance on it, be my guest."

None of them took their hands away until they'd moved on from the web.

"Y'all gotta be careful where you're walkin' out here," Chase said. "Snakes love hidin' under leaves and in the bushes. Step on a copperhead and you're in for it."

"Poisonous?" Ethan asked.

"*Very.*"

"Mom *told us* there'd be spiders and snakes," Grace said, her tone dripping with disgust. She frowned and shook her head at Chase's confirmation. If exploring the woods meant dodging various creatures, that might dampen her enthusiasm.

"Have to watch where you're going," Chase said. "And wear long pants and sleeves if y'all gonna be out here for a while. Check for ticks."

"Ticks, snakes, spiders out to murder you for smiling…sounds like a real blast," Ethan said, laughing. "Got any *killer raccoons?*"

Grace shook her head, scowling. These were *not* things she had to worry much about back home. "*Are* we going to be out here for a while?" she asked, pointing at the exposed skin above her ankle socks.

"You'll be fine," Ethan said. "But how far *are* we going?"

"They ain't far," Chase said.

They hadn't gone deep into the grove when they came upon the creek. Grace could hear the trickle of its flowing water before it came into view. The creek was shallow and clear. It meandered through the grove, following a well-worn bed of mud and stone. Its banks were uneven, lined with wild ferns, cattails, and blackberry brambles. In some spots, the width of the creek was narrow enough to traverse, but in others it was wide enough to make that impossible, at least without getting wet.

Chase led them to a small, wooden bridge where it was easy to cross. The bridge was old and weathered. They took turns crossing it. And as they did, the rotting wood groaned and creaked under their weight.

Grace peered down into the clear water. It was full of life. Colonies of tadpoles moved in clusters. And miniature fishes darted between the rocks kicking up tiny underwater dust clouds from the sandy bottom.

A dragonfly flew by, skimming the surface of the water and making it ripple.

Grace smiled.

Once they were over the bridge, Chase said, "A little bit farther."

As they moved on through the trees, Grace and Ethan marveled at the strange assortment of random junk that littered the yard—an upside-down red wagon, rusted and broken; the frame of a bicycle; a wooden rocking chair, splintered and lopsided, sitting slumped beneath a tree; a rotting horse saddle draped over a low-hanging branch. It was a treasure trove of relics—odd, eerie, and forgotten. But perhaps the strangest was the old yellow school bus. It was half-buried in the dirt, covered in weeds and vines, cobwebs hanging thick between its open windows.

Grace shuddered. She thought again of her name written in a spider's web. She knew it was only a story, but she didn't like it at all.

She and Ethan exchanged a look, an unspoken agreement between them. They'd be coming back to explore this when they had time.

Right past a cluster of trees, they came around an embankment and the dense canopy gave way to an open space, a natural clearing bathed in sunlight.

Chase stopped and pointed ahead of them. "There they are," he said.

Ethan froze. "What the hell?"

Grace squeezed between them, wanting to see as well. Her eyes followed Chase's pointing finger and she gasped, a shiver running down her spine.

In the middle of the clearing were headstones.

Five of them in total, lined up in a row.

The first two were similar, stone crosses. The third was a more traditional looking slab. All three appeared old. They were weathered and cracked, each of them slightly askew and obscured by tall weeds. The etched inscriptions were barely legible under layers of dirt and moss.

The last two stones were slabs as well, but they stood in stark contrast to the others. These were newer looking—*tidy*—with clean, polished surfaces. The etchings on them were clear and legible. The dirt in front of them appeared fresh. It was mismatched. Manicured.

"Are those…*real* graves?" Ethan asked, his voice almost a whisper.

"Reckon so," Chase said.

"*Whose?*"

"Your family, I guess."

Grace didn't like the sound of that.

Her family? Were these the people in those photos? If so, they suddenly felt far too real to her.

"Ya know…your grandparents or great-grandparents or…whatever," Chase said. He walked toward the graves, but Ethan and Grace stayed put. "It's no big deal, ya chickens. My daddy says it ain't the dead that'll hurt you. It's the living ya gotta look out for." He laughed, as if it were the punchline of a joke.

But Grace didn't think this was something to joke about.

She'd never been to a graveyard before, let alone one in her own back yard. She only knew them from Halloween and the movies. But she understood death. And though she hadn't experienced it herself, she understood it to be a somber thing, worthy of respect.

"Ain't this wild?" Chase asked, kicking at the weeds in front of one of the older graves.

Grace frowned.

Chase went on. "When my mama gets a cold chill, she always says, 'somebody walked over my grave.' Reckon I'm giving someone else chills right now?"

"What? That doesn't make any sense," Ethan said. "How would you be giving someone chills if they're *already dead?*"

"Like…in the past or somethin'?" Chase shrugged. "I don't know. I never thought about it too hard. I just thought it sounded kinda cool."

"I wonder who they were," Grace said, ignoring Chase's rambling.

As she stepped closer, she wasn't afraid, just a bit sad. She moved next to Chase and leaned down to examine the writing on the headstones. In order, the stones read: JAMES THOMAS "J.T." CAULDER, HELEN CAULDER, MALCOLM R. CAULDER, EARL HOLLOWAY, and DEBORAH MARIE HOLLOWAY.

"I don't know the first two," Chase said, "But I'm pretty sure that Malcolm was Travis's uncle, and the two new ones were Travis' folks."

"Who's Travis?" Ethan asked.

Chase shrugged. "The guy that lived in the house right before you. I didn't know him that good, but I guess he was a drug dealer."

"Jeez," Ethan said.

Grace put her hand on the tombstone of Helen Caulder, her fingers tracing the rough edges of the engraving. She held her hand against the cool surface for a moment. A wave of overwhelming grief welled up within her. It was like nothing she'd ever experienced before, as if some sorrow in the stone had seeped into her through her skin and huddled in her chest. She didn't know these people, but now it felt as though she'd lost something.

"I think this is a *sad place*," she said, after a long moment, her voice soft. "I think there's pain here that never left."

"Huh, well, I thought it was cool," Chase said, scratching at his neck, his voice quieter.

Ethan moved nearer to Grace. He glanced at Chase before leaning closer to his sister. "Are you…are you crying?" he asked quietly. He wasn't poking fun at her. He was surprised, concerned, and a bit *confused*.

She looked up at him. Her eyes were wet, but she smiled and shook her head no.

Ethan nodded. He glanced away from his sister to Chase and back. He didn't know how to react—she'd always been an upbeat little girl, and he wasn't used to seeing her cry—so he thought it might be best if he changed the subject somehow. Turning back to Chase, he pointed to the woods beyond the tombstones. "What's…what's that way?"

"More woods for a ways, until you get to the farms out near the high school," Chase replied. "Lots of sick paths for motorbiking though."

Ethan looked at his phone, noting the time. He locked eyes with Grace, seeking her unspoken approval, and she nodded. "I think we should start heading back now," he said.

As they left the clearing, Grace glanced back at the graves once more.

The sunlight was dimmer now, the shadows around the headstones deeper.

For a fleeting moment, she thought she saw a figure among them. But it was gone before she could focus. A blur of movement, perhaps? A trick of the light?

She lingered a moment, watching, waiting for something to move again, but only the stillness of the clearing remained.

———

MANDY CRANKED the handle on the bedroom window. She'd tried once before, but the handle had been stuck, so she'd given up. But now, the room was getting quite musty. And *rank*. She needed the air.

She had forgotten how aggravating opening these old things could be, turning and turning, like rolling down a window in an old car. The mechanism was not ideal if you were hoping to slip out through one, which she'd had to do on a number of occasions.

Like the time—

She cut off the thought before it could develop. It would be far too easy to get derailed by every little thing—to drift off into random childhood memories. Doing that would be a time-waster, if not downright problematic.

She was feeling positive about today, about what she was accomplishing. Every item she dumped into the black garbage bags was a small victory. Seeing the piles shrink was more satisfying than she'd anticipated.

The old newspapers, food containers, and other miscellaneous garbage had been the first to go. Getting rid of that layer had been helpful. Next had been the numerous, empty prescription bottles, which Mandy had been more than happy to dispose of.

Until they could get a dumpster delivered, they were putting all the trash on the right side of the house, near the work shed. An immense amount of refuse had already accumulated when they arrived, so she didn't have much guilt about adding to it. She told herself it would *all* be gone soon.

Mandy was breathing hard by the time she finished cranking the window open. She took a deep gulp of the fresh air from outside.

With the air circulating, she was able to remove the sheets from the bed. They were stained and worn. Foul smelling. She folded them up and dumped them in the garbage bag as well.

After a while, when Chris came to check in on her, she had him help her move the mattress and box spring out to the pile as well. They were old and filthy—quite unusable. Besides, they'd be moving their own bed in soon enough.

Bet ya can't wait to snuggle up in your parents' old room, huh? Takin' their place, just like you thought you might.

The little voice had only surfaced a few times today, but Mandy had been able to ignore it and focus on the task at hand.

Once the bed had been dealt with, she moved on to the night-stands. In her mother's, Mandy found several dog-eared romance novels, a heating pad, and her mother's jewelry box. This excited her at first. She was hopeful that perhaps Travis hadn't found it and picked through it, but that hope was quickly dashed. The jewelry box was empty.

In her father's nightstand was a jar of Vicks Vapo Rub, a bag of gummy bears that were rock hard, a handful of crossword puzzle magazines, and a gun safe. There was also a King James Bible. Mandy tilted her head and exhaled.

As if her father had even once cracked it open.

She opened the gun safe, but it too was empty.

Like a vulture picking a carcass.

Mandy moved on, going through her parents' dressers, separating the clothes into separate bags for trash and donations. Then their closet.

Every time she noticed things had been rifled through, she frowned. It felt invasive. And, though these weren't her things, she resented it.

Every so often, she paused to consider whether she should keep something, but was good about reminding herself to let things go. After all, if they hadn't been a part of her life for decades, she likely didn't need them now.

Under the bed, Mandy found file boxes, which she set aside to go through later.

There was also a small pistol.

Seeing it made her flinch.

Though she'd grown up around guns, she didn't like them. For a moment, she considered calling Chris in to handle it. Instead, she slid it out. She was careful, handling it by the metallic grip. She'd forgotten how heavy guns were. She wrapped it in towels and took it into the closet. Standing on an old chest, she placed it on the top shelf of the closet, where the kids wouldn't find it by accident.

She added it to the FIXIT list: PRIMARY BEDROOM, DEAL WITH GUN.

By early afternoon the room was much improved from where she'd started, and Mandy was satisfied. It was still a long way from "clean," but it was progress. It would be nice to have at least one room that was *almost* livable.

After stopping to pull a snack from the cooler, she went right back to it.

In the primary bathroom, she removed the mildewed shower curtain and the grungy, fuzzy cover from the toilet. She trashed the threadbare bathmats and dumped the bath towels into the bag set aside for donations. And she emptied everything from under her parents' sinks and from their medicine cabinets, junking almost all of it.

She hesitated to throw away her father's razor, her mother's cosmetics, and a few other items, but reminded herself again that she had no reason to keep these things. She did keep the Charlie Blue—her mother's perfume—taking a small whiff of it before setting it aside.

Inside her mother's medicine cabinet was a small key. It was an older key of an irregular shape. Mandy assumed it might unlock a cabinet or a curio box, even a safe, but she didn't remember ever seeing it before. She turned it over in her hand a few times, then slipped it into the pocket of her jeans.

But as she closed the medicine cabinet door, she gasped at the reflection in the bathroom mirror.

She spun around, her knees going weak.

She leaned against the sink to keep from falling.

Mandy couldn't make sense of what she was seeing.

The room had transformed.

In a flash, it had changed, and now it appeared as she remembered it from her childhood. The paint wasn't quite as aged and chipped. The plaster wasn't quite as cracked. The wallpaper appeared newer again, less yellowed from time.

"What the fuck?" she whispered to herself.

The items she'd taken outside were all back in their places. But the shower curtain appeared newer now, less mildewed. The bathmats weren't as frayed or stained.

Mandy turned and slowly pushed the bathroom door open. Her parents' room also looked as it did when she was a girl. The mattress was back in place, and the bed was made up, the bedding mussed. Pillows rested near the headboard. The indentations in the mattress were gone. As were the stains on the sheets.

The carpet wasn't as worn now, and many of the more obvious blemishes were gone.

The mustiness had faded somewhat, replaced by the sharp, fresh scent of cigarettes. The odor made Mandy tense up, and a thought of her father leaped into her mind. Him standing in front of her, belt in hand, a cigarette dangling from his lips, smoke curling into his eyes.

"Chris!" she called out. But he didn't respond. "Chris!"

You are having a delusion. A mental breakdown.

Mandy reached out and ran her fingers over the wallpaper.

It was real. Too real. But cold as ice.

She recoiled. *None* of this made sense.

She rubbed her eyes hard, blinking, willing the illusion away. But it didn't go anywhere. If it *was* a delusion, it was the most visceral one she'd ever experienced. Like she'd been transported back in time.

She stepped into the hall.

It too looked as it once had, many years ago. Even the hall bathroom appeared livable again. Not perfect—it had never been even *close* to perfect—but it was *intact.*

Mandy moved to the door of her old bedroom. She hesitated a moment, fearful of what she might find. That she might open the door and find her younger self waiting inside.

As she pushed the door open, she readied herself.

The bedroom was just as it existed in her memories.

No clutter. No moving boxes. Only the room she grew up in.

The bed was the same one her Aunt Lisa had given to her, another hand-me-down. At the foot of the bed was her toy box—the one she'd gotten from a garage sale and painted silver, adorning it with purple hearts and stars. A familiar box fan sat near the window.

On the dresser was her music box.

On the bookshelf, next to her books, was her Bible.

Mandy took a few tentative steps inside, mesmerized, like a tourist in time. In a strange way, seeing everything like this made her wistful. It was as if she was experiencing the past through her own rose-tinted recollections.

Then—a cat wandered out of the closet.

Mandy's heart swelled. Her lip began to tremble. The cat was orange with white splotches. She recognized it immediately. It was her adopted childhood cat, one of the two she'd rescued, still wearing the makeshift collar Mandy had fashioned years ago. The cat stopped in front of her and looked up with pale green eyes, its tongue protruding a bit.

"Snickerdoodle?" Mandy whispered, her voice shaky, her eyes full.

The two cats—Snickerdoodle and Moon Pie—had been her only steady companions throughout much of her childhood. They'd remained feral—or "barn cats," as her mama would say, even though they had no barn—but they were often in the house, joining Mandy in her room at night. She'd always thought they were protective of her, as she'd been protective of them.

You're losing your mind.

Mandy stepped forward and leaned down to pet him.

"Hi Snick," she said, her voice trembling.

But Snickerdoodle reeled back from her. And he hissed. His ears lay flat, and the hair on his back bristled. Mandy had seen him do this before, but never at *her*. Not once.

"It's me," she said. "It's Amanda."

Snickerdoodle crab-walked away from Mandy, his back arched, and hissed again.

Mandy started to panic. She remembered the times the cats had done this before. It was never good.

The cat swiped at the air, letting out a deep growl.

And a thought struck Mandy, sending a chill through her body.

Maybe…he's not hissing at me.

Dread washed over her.

The air behind her turned heavy. *Cold.*

Mandy whipped around, heart pounding, not knowing what she might find.

Someone was behind her.

She jumped, a startled yelp escaping her lips. Her hands shot up, ready to defend herself. The blood was rushing through her veins.

But it was only Chris, hands up, palms open in a non-threatening display. Surprise on his face.

"Jesus!" she panted.

"Who…were you talking to in here?" he asked.

Mandy glanced back, half expecting Snickerdoodle to still be behind her, back arched. She blinked hard, realizing the world had shifted around her once more. The cat was gone and in its place were stacks of moving boxes and various clutter.

The bedroom had reverted.

She realized that she was sweating, and her breath was loud and fast.

"Uh… I…"

She still had tears in her eyes.

"It's alright," Chris said.

He opened his arms and Mandy moved into his embrace. As his arms wrapped around her, she realized that she was shaking. *Hard.*

"What's going on with you, Mandy?" Chris asked, rubbing her back.

Mandy closed her eyes, sinking into him as her body continued to tremble.

"I honestly don't know," she said.

CHAPTER 12
THE THINGS PEOPLE SAY

MANDY SAT AT THE KITCHEN TABLE, STARING AT THE BACK DOOR. In front of her sat a can of Orange Fanta. The drink was warm, both from her nursing it and from the fact that the ice in the cooler was melting. A real refrigerator sat within the storage pod outside. Too bad it was more than likely buried.

Chris was vacuuming in the other room, and the generator was humming outside. She scratched at her arm. It was slick with perspiration.

It was already afternoon. The weekend was almost gone. And while the day had been productive at first, looking around now, it didn't feel like they'd gotten all that much accomplished. And they still didn't have electricity. Perhaps she could convince Chris they should spend one more night at the Briarwood Hotel.

The thought of not staying in the house was comforting.

The vacuuming stopped, and Chris appeared around the corner.

"How are you feeling?" he asked.

Still staring straight ahead, expressionless, Mandy nodded. She took another sip of her soda.

"How's the drink?" Chris asked.

Orange Fanta had always been one of her mother's favorites, right after Mountain Dew, but Mandy had never really cared for it. She wasn't sure why she had chosen it today. Or why she'd bought it at all.

"Warm," she replied. "And a little flat."

"Speaking of that, we should probably refresh our supplies before tonight."

Mandy looked up at him. "Shouldn't we stay one more night at the—"

"We'll be fine here," Chris cut her off, his tone gentle but firm. "You said you're okay, right?"

She nodded again, but her fingers tightened around the can.

"Great. If nothing is wrong, it's time we moved in. I have the generator going now. I picked up some gas to keep it running. I pulled the tents and sleeping bags out of the trailer. And the lanterns. We'll make it fun. Memorable. I promise."

Oh, what fun. Oh, how memorable.

"But…it's still so dirty in here," she argued.

"No dirtier than camping outside."

"Maybe we should do that."

"Do what?"

"Camp outside." She was grasping at straws.

Chris shook his head. "That would only be more work for us. We still have the rest of the afternoon to clean and cover anything that might be dangerous. Get the place in proper order. We're gonna be *fine*. But we *do* need more ice for the cooler. And more drinks. And snacks. I thought we could order pizza for dinner. Keep it simple."

She sighed. "So…I'm guessing you want me to go to the store?"

"Well, that's what I was thinking. Go out for a bit. Clear your head. I saw that the kids were back. Take 'em with you. Pick up some fun food for tonight. Let 'em choose what they want. Popcorn? S'mores? I made sure the fireplace is working." He smiled as if reassuring her. "The kids will have fun with it."

Mandy stared at him.

Great.

She knew that look. Chris had made up his mind. And worse, she couldn't think of any other objections to offer. So, she finished the last bit of soda and crushed the can, then pulled out her phone and opened her notes app.

"Okay," she said, half-heartedly. "What else do we need?"

———

MANDY DROVE the kids into town. Ethan sat up front this time, while Grace sat in the back. She sat in the middle and leaned forward as far as she could, straining against her seatbelt, wanting to be a part of the conversation.

"There were tombstones, Mom," Ethan said. "I mean, for real."

"Like for Halloween!" Grace interjected.

"Oh crap. I forgot to warn you about those," Mandy said. It was yet another thing she'd allowed her children to stumble across.

God, and Harlan just reminded you of it, too!

"You know," she said, scrambling to reassure them. "It's nothing to be scared of."

"I wasn't scared," Grace said. "I thought it was sad there."

"Well, sure, honey. Death can be sad, but…it happens to everyone."

"Mom, what happens after we die?" Ethan asked.

Mandy hadn't expected a trip to the store to turn into a deep conversation, but with kids, those always seemed to come when you least expected them. "Uh…I guess it depends on what you believe, honey. People believe a lot of different things."

"Like heaven?" Grace asked.

"Yeah. Like heaven. Or some people think that after you die, you come back and live another life. And other people believe that there's nothing at all—that you just blink out and are done."

"That's scary," Ethan said.

"Not to me. Was it scary to you before you were born?" Mandy asked.

Ethan shifted in his seat. "I guess not." He paused. "I don't remember."

"Exactly. So why should it be scary after?"

Ethan pondered it a moment. "Were the people in those graves our family? Chase said they were."

Chase? Oh right. The neighbor kid.

"Yeah, they were, but nobody you guys knew."

"Do you believe in ghosts, Mom?" Grace asked.

"No," Mandy said quickly. She gripped the steering wheel tighter, making eye contact with Grace in the rearview mirror. "No, I don't, honey. Why do you ask that?"

Grace's nose scrunched up. "I don't know," she said, shrugging. She settled back in her seat and stared out the window. "Just wondering."

MANDY PULLED a package of paper plates from the shelf and added it to her shopping cart, along with a package of red solo cups, a box of plastic utensils, marshmallows, graham crackers, and some Hershey bars.

She checked the list on her phone:

~~Silverware~~
~~Plates~~
~~Cups~~
AA and D Batteries
~~S'mores fixings~~
Granola Bars
Dried Fruit
Bottled Water
Juice Boxes
Soda

Batteries—she'd just passed those, hadn't she?

"Mommy, can I get this?" Grace asked, holding up a package of sour gummi worms.

Oh, it's Mommy now? She knows how to manipulate you. Little punk.

"If that's what you want. Like I told Ethan, you can each pick out two snacks for tonight. That's in addition to s'mores. Those are for everyone."

Grace studied the sour gummi worms as if considering whether they were good enough, then turned and went back to the candy section where Ethan was already weighing his options.

As Mandy rounded the corner, she almost collided with two young men who were moving fast in the other direction.

"Oh, 'scuse me, ma'am," one of them said. He raised a hand in a polite wave as an acknowledgment, but barely glanced in her direction.

Ma'am? Jesus. It wasn't that long ago that they would at least glance at your tits before dismissing you, even if they did think you were too old for them. Assholes, making me feel old.

Both men were in their mid-twenties and dressed for physical labor, wearing thick, dirtied jeans and well-worn work boots. One of them had a buzzed haircut and a messy goatee, and he was still wearing his mirrored sunglasses inside the store. The other had a younger, clean-shaven face and was wearing a bright orange UT Vols hat over shaggy blond hair.

Ugh, I did not miss that hideous orange. Can't escape it 'round here.

Mandy noticed both men were wearing matching lime green *Caulder Brothers Construction* t-shirts, and her stomach clenched.

Of course they would be from Harlan's company.

As she located the batteries, the two men made their way to the nearby beverage refrigerators, stopping in front of the beer section.

"You hear anything 'bout the new job?"

"You mean Caulder's old place?"

Mandy's ears perked up. She pretended to keep browsing the shelves in front of her but leaned in and listened close.

"Yeah. Bud or Coors Light?"

"Miller for me, but Coors'll do. I guess they turned him down. It's on hold for now."

"You tellin' me someone told Caulder no? Yeah, right." The man laughed. "That's a first."

"He's dead set on it though. Here, grab this." He passed the other man two twelve-packs of canned Miller Light.

"What's he want with that place? Ain't it a shithole."

"Big ole' shithole—can't see why anybody'd wanna live in that place! Who the hell knows? He's only fixin' to tear it down anyway, like the rest of 'em. But you know Caulder—he always gets what he wants in the end."

"Well, shit, he can have it."

The two men passed by Mandy again on their way to the checkout, each carrying two twelve-packs of beer.

Mandy lingered by the batteries, her mind racing. Harlan wanted to tear it down? But *why?* Why pay her all that money and then tear it down?

It didn't make any damn sense.

———

ONCE MANDY'S car was out of sight, Chris grabbed two Cokes from the cooler and headed next door to Cheryl's. As he climbed the steps to her front porch, he started to reconsider the visit. He didn't want to go behind Mandy's back. But he was desperate, and he assured himself that he had no other choice. If Mandy wasn't going to talk to him, he didn't know what else to do.

He knocked hard on the front door. He waited for almost a minute and was about to give up when he heard some rustling from inside.

Cheryl squinted as she answered the door. She seemed surprised by the brightness of the world outside. Her hair was mussed, her make-up uneven, and her plus-size pink "Swiftie" t-shirt was wrinkled and twisted.

Chris wondered if he'd woken her but decided not to ask. Instead, he said, "I'm sorry to bother you."

"Ya ain't no bother," Cheryl said, her voice cracking. "What can I do for ya?"

Chris held the Coke cans in front of him. "Not exactly homemade lemonade, but... Mandy and the kids are running an errand. I was wondering if you wouldn't mind talking for a minute."

"Naw, I don't mind. But I'm more of a Diet Coke gal, myself."

Chris chuckled. "More for me, then."

"Come on in," she said. "'Scuse the mess."

Chris stepped inside. The place was cluttered, but it wasn't dirty. Stacks of magazines and mail sat on the front table. In the front room, two mismatched couches sat next to a recliner. In front of one of the couches was a coffee table with a massive Bible on top. On the far wall was a fireplace. Above it, an enormous trout was mounted on a wooden plaque. Next to it was a gold-colored curio cabinet which housed an assortment of figurines, most of them Precious Moments. The television near the front window was on, playing Fox News.

Chris followed Cheryl into the kitchen. It was painted a baby blue with a wallpaper border featuring fanciful mice. Miscellaneous papers were spread across the dining table, and the kitchen sink was piled high with dishes.

"You can go on out back," Cheryl said. "We'll chat on the porch. You need ice for your Cokes?"

"Yes, please, if it's not a bother."

"Ain't no bother."

Chris stepped onto Cheryl's back porch. It was much nicer than theirs, but that wasn't a high bar to clear. It was covered and screened in. Like the house, it too was cluttered. He moved a stack of empty planting pots from one of the patio chairs, brushed away some loose potting soil from the cushion, and took a seat.

Cheryl appeared behind him, a glass of soda in one hand and a glass of ice in the other. She handed the ice to Chris, then moved a few gardening tools and a faded garden gnome from another chair. She pulled over a plastic side table with an ashtray. After she sat, she fished a pack of cigarettes from *somewhere* within her t-shirt.

Chris popped the top of a Coke and began to pour it over the ice. "Again, I'm sorry to bother you with this, and if you're at all uncomfortable talking to me, I completely understand."

"All depends on what it's 'bout," she said. She chuckled as she lit up a cigarette.

"It's about Mandy. She hasn't been herself since we got back here. And she won't talk to me about it, which is not really anything new—she's always been like that with me. Anything I know about her past,

I've had to pry out of her with a crowbar. But she's never wanted to talk about her life here in town or the house or her family. I never even met her parents, and I've known her almost twenty years."

Cheryl took a drag off the cigarette. Without exhaling, she rubbed at the corners of her eyes with the hand holding the butt and said, "Ain't surprised. Not one bit."

"You aren't?"

She blew smoke through her nostrils and tapped the cigarette against the ashtray. "Amanda? She didn't have it easy, no sir."

"Yeah, I figured. But she won't talk to me about any of it. She's stubborn. She thinks she has to do everything herself."

Cheryl chuckled. "That's 'cause she did."

"How do you mean?"

"Her parents—the *whole family*—they weren't too kind to her. Her daddy was always gone workin', and when he wasn't, he was, uh, a moody bastard. Violent at times. And her mama…well, she was off in outer space most often. She was like a child herself, at times. Some days she wouldn't get outta bed. Others she'd be bouncin' off the walls. Amanda's brothers were assholes—Travis more'n Shane. She… Well, they didn't *have* much, and they sure didn't *give* her much neither."

"She keeps having—hell, I don't know how to describe it. I think she's seeing things. *Flashbacks, maybe?* It's like she's experiencing something and I have to snap her out of it."

Cheryl chuckled again, taking another drag off the cigarette. "Well, that ain't nothin' new either."

"It isn't?"

She shook her head, pursed her lips, and narrowed her eyes. "She always saw things over there. They *all* did—the whole family. That house? That damn house is…*haunted.*"

Chris gave a short, harsh laugh, but swallowed it back. Cheryl wasn't smiling. "Haunted?" He hesitated, careful about choosing his words. "You mean…haunted…for real?"

"You ain't felt it?" she asked.

He shook his head.

"I 'spect you will," she said. "Even her daddy did, and that man didn't feel nothin'."

Chris put a hand to his temple. "What can you tell me about the...haunting?"

"Way too much. But they ain't my stories to tell. Best ask her about that part," Cheryl said, taking another long drag. "But I'll tell you this—*I* felt it too. Didn't much like bein' over there in that place."

Chris nodded and took a sip of his soda. "Is there anything else you think I should know?"

Cheryl leaned forward and stared off, either lost in thought or a memory. She dragged a nail across the cigarette filter, flicking at it. She sighed. "Let's just say none of that family ever had Amanda's best interests at heart. No little girl oughta live like she did. Far as I'm concerned, it's a wonder she ever got outta Rosebury." She hesitated, shaking her head. "Might be she shouldn't've come back."

"What do you mean by that—*live like she did?* Was there actual abuse? *Physical* abuse?" Chris asked. "Did they...beat her?"

She laughed dryly and shook her head, her mouth open. "Yeah, she got beat. But, honey, that was the least of it."

Chris's stomach tightened. "The *least* of it?" he repeated in a whisper.

Cheryl released a weary breath and stubbed out her cigarette, grinding it into the ashtray. "Now, I reckon that's 'bout all I got to say on it for now, if you don't mind."

CHAPTER 13
SLUT, 1994

AMANDA WASN'T USED TO MUCH FUSS OVER HER BIRTHDAYS—IF any at all. Most years, there was no party. Often, there were no gifts. On rare occasions, they had a meal at a local restaurant, which was considered a splurge—but only if her mother was focused that day.

When she was younger, her parents had forgotten her birthday altogether. Not only the day, but the date itself. It wasn't until her mother stumbled upon her birth certificate on accident that she realized Amanda was born on the 9th of September, not the 19th, as she had thought.

Simple mistake, right? Parents forgetting what day their daughter was born? Happens all the time.

It hurt, but Amanda took it in stride, as she always did.

That's why it was such a pleasant surprise when she was *acknowledged* on the day of her 13th birthday—a milestone birthday, the first of her teens—though it was not by her parents.

The romance with Bo Harper was a new one, and it was something Amanda cherished. He was kind to her and didn't seem to pay much attention to any of the rumors about her or her home life. He was a quiet boy. When he spoke, his voice was soft, and his tone was level. He never said anything mean to her. And he wasn't afraid to stand up for her either. It had happened a few times—small moments, to be sure—but enough to make her feel valued. Protected. She wasn't used to either of those things.

When she arrived at school that day, she was excited to find a birthday card in her locker. The front of the card read, "THE BIG 13!" and had an illustration of thirteen balloons held by a cartoon cat. Inside the card, the factory print read: "Hope you have a PAW-some birthday!" And underneath that, the handwritten inscription from Bo was, much like him, direct and to the point: "Happy Birthday, Amanda. Best wishes, Bo." And he had drawn a heart. On the back of the envelope, he'd written, "Can I C U after school by the flagpoll."

Amanda smiled at the misspelling. She smiled at the message. And she smiled at the thoughtful gesture. In fact, she didn't think she would stop smiling all day. And for the most part, she didn't. She couldn't wait to write about it in her journal later that evening—her best birthday ever.

She and Bo didn't have any classes together, and only encountered each other during the day on rare occasions, though she always looked for him. So, she was excited to see him after school and thank him for the card. She decided she'd hug him. Maybe a quick kiss on the cheek, if the mood was right.

They'd met over the summer at the Knox County Fair through mutual friends. Amanda had gone with a church group. Bo had been participating in the livestock competition with FFA, showing pigs.

Since meeting, the two had become close. They'd been taking it slow—holding hands and cuddling up together on the bleachers at the first high school football game of the season. But they'd also kissed each other on the cheek several times and once or twice on the mouth —a quick peck.

Amanda was enjoying the innocence of it all. In some ways, she was hoping the relationship would continue to move slow. Just as with a good meal, or a fancy dessert—she liked to savor every moment.

The school day dragged, but she didn't mind. In a way, she relished that too—the expectation, the anticipation of something pleasant.

After the last bell rang, she made her way to the flagpole. Bo was already there. She recognized him from a distance—his lanky frame, the way he stood with his shoulders somewhat slumped. He was wearing a denim jacket over a flannel shirt, and jeans over a pair of cowboy boots. When not hidden under a hat of some kind—cowboy or baseball—his scruffy hair hung loose over his eyes, and he seemed to peer out from underneath it.

Bo's eyes widened when he spotted Amanda, a smile spreading across his narrow face. She smiled back. She wanted to run up to him, give him a giant hug, and kiss his soft, thin lips. But she hesitated, afraid to presume too much, to *want* too much. Afraid that he'd pull away, though Bo had never been anything but kind and thoughtful.

Instead, she stopped a few feet from him and said, "You made my mornin' with that sweet card. Thank you."

"I have somethin' else for ya," he said.

She'd been so caught up looking at his sweet face that she hadn't spotted the small box he was holding, all wrapped in a bow. He offered it to her.

Grinning, she set her books down and took it from him. "Aw, ya didn't have to."

"I wanted to."

"Can I open it now?"

"Well, I'd sure like ya to." Bo wasn't effusive. His face stayed still when he spoke. His smile was understated, more of a kind smirk.

As Amanda pulled the ribbon loose and slipped the bow from the box, she said, "This might be the only present I get this year, so... thank you."

Right away, she regretted saying it. It sounded pitiful, and she didn't want him to look at her that way.

Amanda's stomach tightened.

"Well, that ain't right at all," Bo said, shaking his head.

He smiled at her, and just like that, all was okay again.

Amanda opened the lid to the box, and for a moment, all she could do was stare. Inside was a necklace. It was gold-tone and had a charm dangling from it—a half-moon. No one had ever gotten her anything like this. Something so lovely, so thoughtful. Words failed her.

"Oh my *gosh*. It's...it's *beautiful*."

"I hoped ya might like it."

She lifted the charm from the box and let the wrapping fall to the ground near her schoolbooks. "I love it!" Turning around, she unclasped the necklace and pulled her hair to the side. "Will you help me put it on?"

He took the ends of the necklace between his fingers. As he hooked it together, he said, "See, ya kinda remind me of the moon. You're bright, like the sun, but ya sorta keep it to yourself."

Amanda laughed, turning back to him. "Well, that sounds real sweet." She grinned. "Even if it don't make much sense."

"Well…maybe it don't. But it does to me."

She patted the charm against her top. "How's it look?"

"Looks just right on ya. Real pretty."

She loved when he looked at her. He treated her like she was important, and she adored that. Amanda wrapped her arms around his neck and kissed him full on the lips. It was the first time she'd done that in public, and she regretted it immediately. Had she overstepped?

But before she could pull away, Bo returned the kiss.

It wasn't much more than a long, sweet peck, but it made her cheeks flush and gave her butterflies.

When he offered to walk her home from school, she accepted. He carried her books so that she could hold his hand. Amanda found that charming and gentlemanly in an old-fashioned way, noteworthy given that he was only a thirteen-year-old boy.

They decided to take the long route. It was more scenic, and it also gave them more time to talk.

The sky was clear. Summer's heat still lingered, the air thick with humidity from recent storms, but hints of autumn were beginning to appear. The fields remained vibrant, with only the edges beginning to brown. And while the trees were still full, some of the leaves on the maples had begun to show hints of yellow and orange.

Amanda loved the smells this time of year. After the rain, the scent of cut grass and damp soil was sharp and fresh. She breathed in the aroma of wildflowers and marigolds as they walked along.

As they neared the local fields, the occasional sound of a rooster call or a cow mooing or a goat bleating would break through the continuous chirping of insects.

Their topics of conversation were trite and light. Bo wasn't much of a conversationalist, not really, but Amanda enjoyed any time they spent together. She liked to listen to his slow, lazy cadence, and the way the words dripped from his mouth.

They talked about school and their teachers, and about how each of them was adjusting to their classes. Amanda mentioned that Ethan Greene had broken his arm over the summer at Johnson Pond, where everyone went swimming, but Bo said he didn't know who that was. The OJ Simpson case came up, but neither of them knew too much about it, aside from the Bronco chase they'd seen on TV. Amanda asked Bo if he was getting ready for hunting season, and he said he was. He also mentioned that he was very upset about the Baseball strike and the season being ruined, but Amanda only shrugged, knowing nothing about it.

She kept looking down at the half-moon charm, playing with it, patting it, rubbing its smooth surface. The weight of it against her chest was comforting. Like it was just for her. Like she mattered.

As they reached her house, Amanda's steps slowed. A short, somewhat dilapidated school bus sat in their blacktop driveway.

"That, uh, your bus?" Bo asked.

She had no idea. Confused and a bit embarrassed, she gave an exasperated chuckle. "I dunno. Ain't never seen it before, but…maybe."

To Amanda's chagrin, it was all too common to return home and find unusual items at their house—cars, trucks, refrigerators, washing machines, and more—either sitting in the driveway or tucked on the side yard. It happened often when her mother was in one of her "moods."

As they got closer, Amanda saw that her father was standing in the threshold of the open front door. Though he was obscured by the screen somewhat, she could tell he was in his underwear, a loose white tank top and tighty-whities.

A wave of humiliation flooded her. She winced, her heart sinking. She wasn't comfortable kissing Bo goodbye if her father was watching, but worse, she was mortified that Bo might glimpse her father in his skivvies.

They stopped at the edge of the driveway.

Amanda nodded toward her father—still framed in the doorway—and said in a meek voice, "I best go." She patted her necklace again. "Thank ya for this. Thanks for makin' me happy on my birthday."

Bo nodded back, rubbing his fingers through his shaggy hair. He looked up at the front door and raised his hand. "Afternoon, Mr. Holloway."

Her father didn't look at him. He didn't say a word. He stepped back, retreating into the shadows of the house.

"I better get," Bo said, shifting his weight. "Got chores waitin'."

For a long, awkward moment, they stood facing each other. Amanda wanted to hug him, but she didn't. Though her father wasn't standing in the doorway now, she was still aware of his gaze. "See ya tomorrow," she said with a small smile.

"See ya, Amanda," Bo replied. He hesitated a moment, then walked off.

She watched him go. He ambled with an easy shuffle, cowboy boots scuffing the asphalt, hands buried deep in the pockets of his jeans.

Amanda patted the half-moon charm, and her momentary shame was replaced by a comfortable contentment.

She walked up to the house and opened the screen door. The moment she stepped inside, the stink of cigarettes struck her. The house was dark, heavy, almost oppressive—a stark contrast to the vivid brightness outside. The drapes on the front windows had been pulled shut. The TV was on in the living room, playing a rerun of *The Price is Right* with the sound muted.

And her father was there.

He was standing in front of the basement door, still wearing only his undershirt and underwear. He was staring at Amanda, anger in his eyes. She was quite familiar with that look.

Her mind raced, scrambling to find an answer. She tried to think of anything she might have done to provoke him. She'd been so good.

No messes. No missed school. She hadn't gone into their room. Hadn't talked back. What could it have been?

He was quick to anger, and the things that set him off were random and inconsistent. And though she couldn't think of a single thing she might have done, she knew it didn't matter.

She held on to a tiny sliver of hope—he wasn't wearing a belt. But more than anything, she felt sick, like something terrible was already in motion.

"Daddy?" she said, her voice small and uncertain. "Everything alright?"

"You little…*slut!*" he yelled, spitting the words at her like venom.

Amanda pivoted back to the doorway, glancing outside.

Was he talking about Bo? He couldn't have been.

"I didn't do nothin'. He ain't my boyfriend. He's only a friend. He walked me home 'cause it's my birthday." She talked quickly, desperate to defuse whatever had sparked her father's anger, hoping that an offhand reminder about her birthday might help—as if it might mean something to him.

For a moment, she thought her father might listen to her, but then he stepped forward, revealing something in his hand. She hadn't realized he'd been holding it. He raised it up, but it took a second for her brain to register what it was. A pink, spiral-bound book. A colorful unicorn sticker on the cover.

It was her journal.

Amanda's stomach dropped. Her face went numb. And she gasped. "That's…that's *mine*," she said, her voice no more than a hoarse whisper.

She'd only kept the journal a year or so, but she'd been writing in it almost every night. It had been calming. Therapeutic. Like whispering secrets to a steady friend. Now she felt betrayed. Exposed. Her most private confessions, ripped from her and defiled, twisted into something hurtful. Something shameful.

She'd hidden the journal between her box spring and bed frame, nestled into a small hollow space on the frame itself. And was convinced it would be safe. Convinced no one would ever find it, even if they had been looking. But why would anyone be looking?

"What's this supposed to be, huh?" he barked, shaking the journal in front of her. "You fuckin' *whore!*"

Amanda's mouth went dry. She didn't know if she'd ever seen her father this angry. Now she understood why.

A little over a year ago, two boys had followed her out of her middle school and cornered her in an alley. They had held her. They had grabbed at her. Fondled her. And they had touched her in places she'd never been touched before. And she had asked for none of it.

"Daddy, I—"

"*Tramp!* My only daughter…a tramp! A *slut!*"

Amanda didn't understand. She hadn't done anything wrong. *Or had she?*

She was the victim. *Wasn't she? Hadn't she been? Why was her father attacking her like this?*

The incident had plagued her. Wounded her. She'd needed to talk about it, even if only to a little pink, unicorn journal. But her words had been private, meant only for her relief and understanding. Now, they were being twisted and used against her. And she regretted ever writing it down.

"I didn't do nothin' wrong!" she protested. "Those boys—"

"Don't you lie to me! What did you do to lead them boys on, huh?" he shouted, taking another step toward her. "What did you say to them that made them think you wanted them to touch you like that?"

"NOTHIN'!" She screamed it, her whole body shaking, but already her voice was smaller. Her protest seemed like a shadow. Distant. Weak.

The doubts were creeping in.

The tears rolled down Amanda's cheeks, and she hated it. She didn't want to cry. More, she didn't want her father to know that he was capable of *making her cry*. That he had that power.

She clutched her schoolbooks to her chest. She wanted to say something else. Wanted to show him how unfair this was. Make him understand that she'd done nothing wrong. But his anger was making her unsure of herself.

She wanted to scream at him—*I HATE YOU*—to stand her

ground, to throw her books in protest. Her fingers dug into the covers of her books, her muscles tightening. Every part of her screamed for her to fight. To hurt him like he was hurting her. But she didn't. She held her tongue.

Instead, she turned and fled to her bedroom.

Amanda opened the door to the room and slipped inside, but before she could close the door, her father was there. He grabbed the edge of the door and forced it open. The doorknob slammed against the wall, cracking the surface.

Startled, Amanda dropped her books and gasped, eyes wide. He came at her. He appeared enormous to her, like a rampaging bull. A freight train. He shook the journal in front of him so hard it began to rip apart in his hand, loose pages fluttering to the ground to lie amidst her schoolbooks like leaves. "And you wrote it down?! Like some *pornographer?!* Like some *pervert!* Like some *slut!*"

He flung the book across her room, and it hit the wall by her closet with a thwack, coming apart at the spiral binding. The pages showered to the floor.

Amanda froze. Her muscles locked. She was like a rabbit caught in a snare, waiting for the killing blow.

"Daddy, please," she squeaked.

He was so much bigger than she was. He loomed above her, his eyes filled with rage.

He put his hands on her shoulders and shook her. Her head whipped back and forth on her spine. Then he lifted a hand and smacked her across the face.

The impact made a cracking sound, the flat of his fingers catching her cheek. The blow snapped her head to the side.

But he didn't stop. He grabbed her shoulders and shook her again. *"Dirty…slut!"*

As he reached toward her throat, his fingers snagged her new necklace, ripping it away.

Amanda cried out, grabbing for it, her vision clouded by tears. But, in doing so, she pushed away from him, and his hands came free of her shoulders.

This apparent evasion only angered him more.

As she reached for the necklace—the half-moon charm dangling between his thick fingers, a glint of light shining across its face—her father grabbed the top of her shirt with his other hand and twisted it into a ball. He flung the necklace aside, curled his hand into a fist, and pulled it back behind him.

Then—he slammed it into her face.

Amanda saw the blow coming just far enough in advance to anticipate the impact, but with no time to react.

His knuckles collided with her face, smashing against her mouth and jaw.

Her mouth was wet with blood.

The stinging in her face gave way to a deeper throb of pain.

The darkness began to envelop her, creeping in from the sides of her vision.

Her knees buckled.

The room tipped on its side.

And faded to black.

———

AMANDA'S EYES FLUTTERED OPEN.

The world was dim. The floor pressed hard against her body. Her limbs were heavy. Her face throbbed. And her bones ached—so much, it was hard to think of moving.

She was still in her bedroom. The window was dark now.

Her mother was leaning over her, wearing a red, cotton nightgown, waving a bottle of white vinegar in front of her face.

Amanda blinked several times. She tasted the blood in her mouth.

"Yeah, she's alright," her mother said. "Ain't nothin' broke?"

Amanda raised a shaky hand to her throbbing jaw. It stung to touch it. Her lips were stiff, cracked, caked in dried blood. Despite the pain, she moved her jaw, testing it, running her tongue over her teeth.

"Ain't nothin' broke?" her mother repeated, her tone dismissive and impatient.

Amanda tried to shake her head but winced at the sharp pain stabbing her between her eyes. "I don't think so," she whispered.

"No teeth, neither?"

"No."

Her mother exhaled. "You really got your daddy worked up. Best go apologize. And clean up this mess." She motioned around the room, to the carpet next to Amanda, the scattered schoolbooks on the floor, the mess of her diary across the room. Then her mother left the room, and Amanda heard the door to her parents' bedroom close.

She didn't move.

She sat on the floor another minute, continuing to rub her jaw.

Her father had beaten her before. He'd used a belt. He'd used a switch. He'd slapped her. He'd left welts. Even broken skin and drawn blood.

But he'd never done this.

Never punched her with a fist.

Never left her unconscious in a pool of her own blood.

She wanted to cry. But she didn't. The tears would only make it hurt more.

Amanda stood up. She was careful and took her time, using the bed for support. She blinked against the buzzing in her head, the needles behind her eyes.

Once on her feet, she looked down. The carpet where she'd fallen was saturated with her blood. A deep, wet stain at the center, its edges feathering out into fainter red tendrils. She wasn't sure how long she'd been unconscious, but the color of the blood had shifted from crimson to rust.

The news was playing on the TV in the front room. Amanda realized she should go in and get it over with.

She'd have to apologize to her father, though she still wasn't sure what she was supposed to be sorry for. She settled on "disrespect." It was vague, but deferential enough that she figured he would accept it.

As she walked into the hallway, she became dizzy and thought she might fall, so she steadied herself against the wall.

She took her time, shuffling into the family room step by step, making sure she wouldn't collapse. As she went, she prepared herself. To stand in front of him. The man who stole her private thoughts.

Called her names. Knocked her unconscious. Left her alone. Now she had to bow her head and thank him for it.

She only hoped her eyes wouldn't betray the hate she was feeling.

He was still in his underwear, reclining in the La-Z-Boy, watching the TV, his bare feet propped up.

But as she got closer, she heard him snore.

She stopped in front of him. His eyes were closed, and his mouth was hanging open. He was clutching the remote control against his chest with one hand.

She swallowed, staring at him. At her attacker.

Holding back her tears, Amanda whispered. "*Sorry for the disrespect.*" She made sure her voice was soft, too quiet to wake him.

Then, slowly, she made her way to the hall closet, gathered some cleaning supplies, and returned to her bedroom. In the corner, she found the necklace that her father had ripped from her neck, her only birthday gift—the chain was broken. She held it in her palm a moment staring at the pendant, a heaviness creeping into her chest, before dropping it into her jewelry box and closing the lid.

Amanda knelt and began to scrub the carpet.

Chapter 14

Reflections

As she drove back from the market, Mandy found herself lost in thought. She'd known all along that returning to Rosebury wouldn't be easy. Memories were *bound* to resurface. It would be nice, however, if at least a *few* of them weren't horrible.

"Don't forget to ask her," Grace whispered to Ethan from the back seat.

The whispering broke Mandy from her contemplation. "Ask me what?"

"We were wondering if we could play by the creek for a while this afternoon," Ethan said.

"Whaaa? *You* want to spend time *outdoors?*" Mandy teased. "No video games? No phone? It must be a *miracle.* Are you *feeling* okay?"

"Well…they need to charge."

"Ah, well, now it all makes sense." As she pulled the car up alongside the curb in front of 33 Stillwater Lane—a routine that had already become familiar—she asked, "Will you help me get the ice into the cooler first?"

"Uh huh."

It took Ethan and Mandy several minutes to move the cooler to the grass, drain the old water, drag it back to the carport, and then add the new drinks, food, and fresh ice. Grace was becoming impatient.

"Are you guys almost done?" she asked, pacing in the driveway.

"Go on, I can do the rest," Mandy said to Ethan, then added, "Take your phone. Be back before it gets dark. You should help your dad set up the tents. And watch out for your sister."

"He will!" Grace assured her, already on the move.

After they had gone, Mandy surveyed the car port. So much junk. So many memories. Too many.

———

GRACE RAN AHEAD OF ETHAN, but not by much. She had quickly fallen in love with their private forest but didn't want to appear *too* eager. Today, she was dressed better for exploring. Long sleeves. High socks. Sneakers.

No way are the ticks getting me today, she thought.

She kept one eye on the sun. It was already sinking. They wouldn't have much time to explore.

As they arrived at the creek, Ethan said, "Hey, let's check out that bus we saw the other day."

Grace shook her head. "We don't have time. I want to see the fish."

"But…Mom wants us to stay together," he said.

Grace hesitated, frowning.

"*You* wanted to see the bus too," he persisted.

"Fine," she muttered, folding her arms. She *did* want to see it, just not today.

They crossed the old foot bridge and set off in the direction of the school bus. It didn't take long to find.

It was clear the bus had been there a long time. It was smaller than a standard school bus. The roof was rounded off, not only on the sides of the vehicle, but on the front and back as well. The front windows were rounded, too, and resembled giant sunglasses. Grace was amused by the roundness of it. It reminded her of a bus she might've drawn when she was little.

Its yellow paint was almost gone on top, replaced by a ruddy gray rust. The same rust, mixed with a bright-green moss, obscured most of the front end of the bus and its hood, which was crumpled in from some long-ago accident. If the windows were its sunglasses, the moss on the hood was its moustache.

The idea that the bus had a face tickled Grace. It was smiley, but also sort of lonely. Like it had been forgotten and was waiting for someone to pay attention to it again.

Its front tires were buried halfway in the ground, and ferns and tall grass and other underbrush had grown in and around them. More rust marred the length of the bus, running in random patterns where water might have once flowed. The back half of the vehicle was covered by overgrowth—weeds and vines that had draped themselves around it, hugging it close. Thick cobwebs draped the windows. The front doors of the bus were open, but only somewhat, as they were lodged in the dirt.

"I wonder why it's out here," Grace said.

"Do you think we should go inside?" Ethan asked, raising his eyebrows.

Grace glanced at the cobwebs in the windows and wrinkled up her nose. "I don't think so."

"I'm just gonna…peek in," he said, rubbing his hands together. "Wait here, okay?"

Ethan approached the bus, stepping through the plants with care, avoiding patches of mud.

He picked up a stick and knocked down some of the spiderwebs that had grown between the bus's doors, before pulling at the doors, attempting to pry them open. Finally, he gave up trying to widen the gap. He hesitated and stepped back, as if reconsidering the idea. But then he darted in, squeezing through the small opening, disappearing inside.

Grace waited.

Despite the sound of rustling leaves and the steady buzz of the cicadas, the grove felt still. The air was warm and damp. It wasn't unpleasant, but it made her sticky. Her clothes clung to her skin.

Grace peered up into the canopy of the trees, which towered above her. The sun was almost blocked out by the fullness of their branches. It was peaceful here and she loved it, though she still would've preferred to be at the creek. In the distance was its faint trickle.

"Hey!"

The voice startled her. It wasn't Ethan.

Grace spun around.

A teenage boy stood about ten feet away, watching her.

He was older than Ethan, she thought, but not by much. Perhaps it was the toughness in his features that made him appear more mature —the dirt on his face, the dark circles under his eyes, the patchy tan. His hair was uneven—short in the front, long in the back, and matted all over. His clothes appeared unclean. The knees of his grimy jeans were ripped, and his sleeveless flannel shirt was marred with stains. His arms were lean and ropey.

"What're ya doin' here? You ain't s'posed to be here," he said, chewing on something.

"I *live* here," Grace said.

"Bullshit, ya don't," the boy said, stepping toward her. He spit something dark onto the ground near his worn boots, wiped his mouth with the back of his hand, and continued chewing.

"*Yes I do,*" Grace insisted. "We just moved here."

The boy's eyes narrowed. Then, slowly, he smiled. "How old are ya?"

Grace thought of all the times she'd been told not to talk to strangers, but this wasn't a stranger on the street. He was in *her yard!* She should be upset by his trespassing, she thought. But the lack of fences made it hard. She hesitated, choosing her words with care, "I'll be ten this year." She thought it might help to make herself sound older. She wondered if she should call out for Ethan.

The boy smiled again. "Ten's plenty old."

Grace swallowed. *For what?*

Her heart was racing. The boy hadn't done anything to threaten her, but she sensed something off about him. The way he moved, both arms at his side. The way he stared at her. She didn't like it.

He spat again. The dark wad hit the ground near her feet. Too close.

Grace winced. Spitting was bad manners. But spitting close to her like that…well, that was uncalled for.

"Do ya smoke?" he asked. He stepped closer again, chewing slow, his eyes on her.

Grace shook her head. *Did he mean cigarettes or something else?* She wished he would stop moving closer to her. She wanted to step back but fought the urge. She didn't want to appear afraid. Or worse, *rude.*

"Ya wanna smoke some weed with me?" the boy asked, grinning as if he had let her in on a secret.

"I'm…*only nine,*" Grace said, her voice thin. Maybe making herself sound older was the wrong strategy.

"And?"

Grace didn't know how to respond.

"Hey!" This time the voice was Ethan's. Grace exhaled, a wave of relief rushing over her.

The boy turned to look at Ethan, who was standing right outside the doors of the school bus.

"That's my sister," Ethan said, his voice firm and loud.

"Yeah? So what?" said the boy. His words weren't challenging, but his nonchalance was jarring.

Ethan's jaw clenched. "So…she's my *sister.* That's what."

His hands had curled into balls. Grace wondered if Ethan was aware he was doing it. She wondered if he meant to fight this boy.

The boy laughed. It was glib, dismissive. He spit on the ground again and snorted. He turned back to Grace, and asked, "Y'all really live here?"

Grace didn't say anything. At some point, her hands had started shaking. She hoped it wasn't noticeable.

"Well, I reckon I'll see ya again, then," the boy said. He stared at Grace a long moment before shifting his gaze back to Ethan. He exhaled, gave a small nod, and wandered off through the grove.

Ethan watched him until he was out of sight. Then he glanced at Grace and forced an awkward smile. "What a weirdo, right?"

Grace laughed, but it came out uneven. She looked at the dark lump on the ground near her feet and swallowed.

"Can we go look at the fish now?" she asked.

Ethan nodded, and they started back the way they'd come.

Grace was grateful that Ethan had shown up when he did and relieved the boy had left without any further incident, but the unease lingered. What she couldn't know then was that something just as unsettling was waiting for her at the creek.

———

With the kids gone, Mandy and Chris continued to clean the house, doing their best to ready it for their first overnight stay. Mandy tied her hair up and snapped on a pair of disposable gloves. No more daydreams. No more flights of fancy. No more distractions. They had work to do.

She and Chris were efficient together, slipping into a familiar rhythm. They had decided to focus on getting the family room and kitchen areas clean and ready, along with the primary bathroom. They would dump the clutter into the other rooms and close them off for the time being. Aside from Chris's portable radio playing 80's tunes and the sound of the generator humming outside, they worked in silence.

Mandy considered telling Chris what she'd overheard at the market, but since Harlan's offer was such a sore subject, she decided it was best to leave it alone.

She dragged two giant garbage bags full of random items into her old bedroom. The room was filling up fast and it wasn't very well organized. So, she took a moment to stuff loose items back into boxes and stack the boxes against the wall, making more space.

Mandy bent down to pick up a pair of dusty pink roller-skates. Had they been hers? They *must* have been, but she couldn't recall. They didn't seem familiar.

When she stood, she froze, struck by the reflection in the antique mirror.

It wasn't her.

A chill went through Mandy and her body shuddered.

She had never been this close to the little girl or seen her in this much detail. Her blonde hair was shoulder length, with straight bangs.

Her eyes were pale blue, and her skin was pallid. She was wearing the same white nightgown she had worn every single time Mandy had seen her.

Mandy's breath was fast. Unsteady. Too loud in her ears.

She moved, intending to step away, but the little girl in the reflection moved too, mirroring her movements.

You never should have come back here. Not to this town. And not to this house.

Mandy stepped closer to the mirror. The little girl stepped closer as well, in perfect synchronization. Mandy raised her hand. And the girl did too. Mandy opened her mouth and stuck out her tongue. The girl copied her exactly.

Mandy smiled, her teeth showing.

But the little girl didn't smile back.

Instead, she closed her mouth and her lips pressed together into a line. Her blue eyes widened, filling with terror. Her face began to quiver, her lips trembling. Her body began to shake. Her fists clenched together at her waist.

Then—she screamed.

It was a scream of pure agony, high and shrill. It ripped through the air, and Mandy winced, covering her ears with her palms. It was like glass in her skull.

The mirror shuddered in its frame. The walls of the room shook.

The little girl's irises vanished, her eyes swallowed by blackness. The skin around them began to wrinkle and wither. And the flesh sloughed away, sliding down her cheeks in wet, sagging ribbons, exposing raw muscle and sinew underneath.

Her mouth hung open. Her jaw unhinged, drooping down. Too long. It sagged, sliding, dripping from her skull like melting wax. The hole where her mouth had been grew impossibly large, until it tore open, revealing an endless black maw, a cavernous void echoing with the sound of anguish.

The scream tore through Mandy, tearing at her gut, making her nauseous. She wanted it to end. She needed it to stop. It had to.

But another sound was hidden deep within it. Another scream.

Coming from somewhere far away. From somewhere in the back yard. *Grace.*

Oh my god.

Mandy tore herself away from the mirror, as the sound of her daughter crying out rose in volume, gradually replacing the shriek of the little girl.

She bolted through the house, past Chris. And as she tore through the kitchen, a memory flashed—another time, another sprint toward the back door, praying she could reach it, lock it before *they* found their way inside.

Unlike that night, the door wasn't standing open. It was sealed up tight.

Mandy twisted the bolt on the new lock and yanked the handle. The door scraped and stalled, before flying open and slamming hard against the kitchen counter, as it always did. But she barely noticed it. She was already on the back porch.

The kids were in the yard. They were sprinting toward the house. Grace was holding her arm, screaming, "Mom! Mooooom!"

Mandy flew down the porch steps, hurrying to meet them. "What is it? What's wrong?"

Chris followed her outside, as Grace threw herself into Mandy's arms and held on tight.

"There was…someone…down there," Ethan said, huffing, struggling to say the words between labored breaths.

"Who?!"

"An old man," Grace gasped, her voice trembling.

"Wait—what?"

"He had a shotgun!" Ethan said, his hands on his hips as he steadied himself. "Grace saw him!"

"His beard was scruffy," Grace stammered. "And it looked like he was in his pajamas."

"Where!" Mandy demanded. "Where was he?"

"Down by the creek," Grace said, pointing. "He was…crazy. He said he lived here. He said we were on *his* property. Staying in *his* house. I thought he was going to shoot us!" She began to cry harder.

"I think he grabbed Grace!" Ethan said.

"What?! Let me see!" Mandy yanked Grace's sleeve back. There were three scratches on her right arm. The top layer of skin was scraped away, and the scratches were red, close to bleeding.

Could be from bushes. Brambles.

Or fingernails.

Mandy's cheeks went hot and her hands began to shake. She tore free from Grace and grabbed Ethan by the shoulders. "Is he still there?" she shouted.

"I…don't know."

Mandy was already running. Chris shouted after her, but she didn't stop, didn't slow, didn't even look back. "Stay with the kids!"

She headed straight toward the grove of trees at the back of the yard.

You sure you ain't bitin' off more than ya can chew? You don't know who's waitin' for ya. And here you are, runnin' off half-cocked, no weapon at all, no way to defend yourself.

Mandy's anger faltered a moment. A sliver of doubt crept in.

Just stay with the kids. Let Chris go instead. That's what a mama is supposed to do. Let the man handle it.

She clenched her jaw, grinding her teeth. And she broke into a full sprint, heading toward the trees.

She'd raced through this yard a thousand times as a girl. The space had seemed endless back then. Now it appeared so much smaller, but it was so much harder to cross.

As Mandy entered the grove, she slowed. "I know you're here!" she screamed, her tone strong. *Bold.* "*Who* are you and *why the fuck* are you on *my* land?" She came to a stop, her eyes darting, searching for the man. She listened, panting. The sound of cicadas. The soft whistling of a cardinal. The babbling of the shallow creek. "I know you're here, so come out!"

She stood still, scanning the landscape, watching for any hint of movement. She caught something out of the corner of her eye and whipped around fast, her pulse racing. But it was only a bird taking flight from a branch.

"You don't mess with my goddamn kids, you sonuvabitch!" Mandy screamed. But it didn't sound the way she wanted it too. Too small.

Too thin. The woods swallowed her words, and with it her fury, her fire, leaving only a toothless frustration behind.

She crept through the grove. She tried to be quiet, tried to steady her breath, but it was futile. She was too winded from the run. Leaves crunched underfoot, every step announcing her presence.

The creek. That's where Grace had seen him.

She neared the stream. How many days had she spent down here? Sometimes with friends, but most of the time all on her own. Wading through the water, playing in the mud, making up stories, skipping stones. Catching fish, crayfish, salamanders. This place had been hers once. But now something felt different. Felt wrong. Dangerous.

Mandy bent down and her fingers closed around a stick. She hadn't thought about it. It was second nature. Muscle memory.

She continued to scan the area. Listening. Waiting.

Perhaps the man had gone?

Or Grace imagined him.

Mandy knew *all too well* how easy it was to let your mind play tricks. Was it possible they were seeing the same things? Fabrications. *Phantoms.*

But, the scratches on her arm...

Mandy steadied herself.

She'd wait another minute, then she'd return to the house.

She tossed the stick into the stream. Ripples spread outward as it landed. But was there something else? A shape? A shadow? Mandy moved closer. She kneeled, squinting into the water.

At first, it was only her reflection.

But then—*no, it wasn't.* The image shifted. The mouth was wrong. The eyes, too narrow. It wasn't her face at all.

No, not again.

As she leaned in to get a better look, the water erupted.

A pale, blue-tinged hand shot up. The fingers clamped around Mandy's wrist, the chipped and grimy nails scraping against her skin. The cold hand tightened and wrenched her forward. She was already off balance. No way to resist. No way to stop the inevitable. Her body pitched forward. The world tilted.

And she fell, headfirst, into the water.

It wasn't possible. The stream was shallow. It had always been shallow. There was no way the water could be this deep. But she found herself pulled under. The water enveloped her, wrapping around her, stinging like ice.

Paralyzing.

She flailed, clawed at the liquid, but she was sinking. She tried to kick, to swim back up, but it was useless. She couldn't break free. The pull was too strong.

Dragging her down. *Deeper.*

Her muscles were tight. Limbs locked. Her lungs were on fire. The pressure. The weight of the water.

She was suffocating.

Drowning.

The water around her was disturbed and murky. She squeezed her eyes shut. And lightning flashed through her mind. Another time. Pressure like this. Weight. Stolen breath. But no, not water. Flesh. A hand. Rough. Smothering her. Smashing against her mouth. A body. Pressing down on hers. Pinning her in place. Holding her still.

Inescapable.

Shaking her head, she tried to scream, but the sound died in her throat, stifled by the water. A surge of bubbles escaped her lips, and liquid took its place, filling her mouth. Her lungs.

She thrashed. Kicked. *Desperate.*

Above her, the light danced on the surface, taunting her. It was so far from her, an almost impossible distance. She reached for it, but it only slipped farther away.

Her eyes stung and she closed them again. Another surge of electricity ran through her mind. A flash of images. Dirty hands clawing at the earth, fingers raw. A plastic gorilla, smiling a broad smile with big teeth, its eyes wide. A tree. Three interlocking circles carved into its bark. Branches, swaying against a gray sky. An oak. It was one of the larger ones near the creek. She knew the one. She'd played in it as a girl.

But these weren't things she remembered.

Her body shook, the coldness of the water leeching her strength.

She tried to scream again.

And again, that hand. Calloused. Covering her mouth, stifling any noise, pressing her lips hard against her teeth, pushing against the underside of her nose. Painful. Blood in her mouth. Body odor. Heavy panting. And a voice. A man. Whispering to her, hushing her. Her body ached.

For a moment, her eyes shot open. She needed air. *Right now.* Needed to surface. She was out of time.

I want to go.

Hands digging again. Her *hands,* but not her *memories.* Her point of view, but not her eyes. Fingertips raw, bloody, scraping at the dirt. Grit under her nails. Frantic. Digging—at the base of that oak.

You can't just leave, the whisper came in her ear.

Mandy opened her mouth again and...

The sound of her voice startled her—a resonant scream, bursting from her throat—and she gasped, sucking in a deep breath.

She was sitting as she had been, next to the burbling creek. And, except for the cold sweat beading her clammy skin, she was dry. The weight on her chest was gone. The fingers gripping her arm had vanished, though her hands still trembled.

Peering into the water, she searched for the woman's face, but there was nothing. Only the muddy creek bed of the gentle stream. A stick floating on the surface.

Mandy pulled herself to her feet and looked around.

Maybe it didn't really happen.

If only it were so easy.

Shaken, she started back toward the house. A few steps. But she stopped.

She could leave now. Forget all of this.

But the thought nagged at her.

You just gotta know, don't ya?

She turned back. Her stomach in knots, she returned to the creek, crossing the rickety wooden bridge. Would she even be able to find the tree again? It had been so long.

But Mandy did find it. With little effort. The same giant oak tree she'd seen in her mind. She approached it with a hint of caution.

Standing before it, it loomed taller than she remembered. Broader. The branches were so high.

And you used to climb it, all the time.

Mandy took a step closer. She placed her palm against the bark. It was rough, almost damp, and the deep grooves were like highways for the crawling fire ants. She moved around the tree, her eyes on the ground near its trunk.

Somehow, she already *knew* what she was going to find. She just didn't know if she wanted to.

She stopped.

At the base of the tree—half-buried in dirt, cracked and weathered, its color leached away by time—was a plastic gorilla toy.

Mandy kneeled and ran her fingers over its surface.

It was small and made of hard plastic, like something a child might have gotten from a gumball machine. It had been here a long time. *Years.* The gorilla's big eyes were still identifiable, locked open, unblinking. But the paint on its mouth had worn away long before, leaving only the faintest outline of its oversize teeth.

She realized she should be shocked to find it, but she wasn't.

Only troubled.

She looked up, letting her eyes follow an imaginary path from the gorilla straight up the trunk. And there, she saw another thing that should have surprised her: the same markings that she'd seen in her hallucination—three interlocked rings.

Chapter 15

The First Night in the House

The sun dipped low, framing the house in a fiery sunset. Its jagged outline was stark against the dying light. Leaves blew across the yard under a brisk breeze, the first hints of autumn rearing its head.

Chris was waiting for Mandy on the back porch, leaning against the wooden railing, his hands in the pockets of his jeans.

"So?" he asked.

"I…uh, I couldn't find anyone," she said.

As she got closer, Ethan and Grace appeared through the back kitchen door.

Mandy pointed at Ethan. "You were supposed to look out for her! You were supposed to look out for your sister! What the hell happened!?"

Protect them.

"He did, Mom," Grace objected. "He *was* looking out for me!"

"Hey, hey, it's not his fault," Chris said, stepping in and placing his hands on Mandy's shoulders. "Just take a minute, okay? Breathe. This is stressful for everyone."

"How's her arm?" Mandy asked.

"It's fine. Can't even see it. But I put on some disinfectant, anyway."

"I wish we could go back home," Ethan said.

"Yeah, well…ain't no goin' back now!" Mandy snapped. Her voice was sharp. "So, we best get used to it, all of us!" She pushed past Chris, moved past the kids, and went inside.

She stopped at the dining table, gripping the edge hard as she leaned against it, her nails biting into the wood. She shuddered.

It's not his fault. He's not them.

"I know, I know, shut up," she whispered, pressing her thumbs against her temples.

As she stood there, allowing herself to calm down, she heard Chris on the porch, reassuring the kids. "It's okay, guys. It's not about you. This has been very stressful for your Mom, okay? You know she loves you."

Her throat tightened. Her eyes filled with tears, but she wiped them away fast. They couldn't see her like this. Weak. Fragile. She didn't want that.

———

CHRIS WAS PLEASED that the two small pop-up tents fit in the house without making it feel too cramped. He set up the first tent near the front living room windows, a safe distance from the fireplace. The second tent went in between the two rooms, positioned so that its front flap faced the hallway, and the back of the tent faced the basement door. They would have to navigate around it, but it wasn't bad.

With the sun almost down, the light inside began to grow dim. Chris fired up two portable lanterns, switching their intensity from a harsh bright white to a softer warm hue. He placed one lantern by the tents, and the other in the middle of the dining room table. It cast a glow over their dinner of pre-packaged sandwiches and chips. As they ate together under lantern light, they discussed how the evening would go.

"I call the tent by the front window," Ethan said.

"Why?" Grace asked.

Ethan shrugged. "I like the color better."

Grace rolled her eyes, shaking her head.

"That should be fine," Chris replied.

"I want to share with Mom," Grace said. She sat next to Mandy, holding her hand while she ate her turkey sandwich. She'd been very attentive since her encounter with the old man by the creek.

Mandy released Grace's hand and stroked her hair. "Sure, we can do that, honey."

"Aw, but Dad farts," Ethan said, laughing. "Bad. He's gonna gas me to death." He pretended to choke and gag, crossing his eyes.

"Wow," Chris said. "Thanks, bud."

"*That's* why I want to sleep with *Mom*!" Grace said, joining in the laughter.

"Hey!" Chris said, feigning sadness. "You guys are gonna hurt your old man's feelings."

"*Y'all…*are gonna hurt your old man's feelings," Mandy corrected. "We gotta learn y'all to talk right! Ain't no way y'all fixin' to fit in 'round here if ya don't talk proper."

The kids laughed harder.

"Everyone talks so funny," Grace said, still giggling.

"Why don't you talk like that, Mom?" Ethan asked. "If you're from here."

Mandy took a moment to consider it. "Your mama tried real hard to get rid of that accent when she moved away from here."

"But it's sneaking back in," Chris said, still grinning.

His comment took Mandy off guard, and she grimaced. *Was* her accent creeping back? It made sense, she supposed, but she hadn't realized it.

Well, bless your heart. I reckon they can take the girl outta the South, but they sure as hell can't take the South outta the muthafuckin' girl.

After dinner, Chris started the fire—not only for the s'mores, but also in case it got too drafty overnight. He kneeled by the chimney and fed kindling to the embers, and soon a fire crackled to life.

Mandy slipped outside for a moment to herself, sneaking a

cigarette and breathing in the night air. When she came back inside, she poured herself a drink. A proper one.

With the fire going, the family prepared to make their s'mores. The kids got the fixings out of the grocery bags and laid them out on the dining room table. And Mandy retrieved the plates and napkins.

"Oh no!" she said. "I didn't get any skewers." She'd been thrown off seeing Harlan's employees at the market and the skewers had slipped her mind.

"Not a problem," Chris said. He disappeared out the front door and returned a few minutes later with four, thin, relatively straight branches he'd gathered from the oak trees. Each stick was around three feet long. Using his pocketknife, he stripped the bark from the first six inches or so of each and sharpened the ends to a point. Grabbing some sandpaper from his toolbox, he gave the tips a quick once-over, making sure there were no splinters.

"Voila! Nature's skewers," he said, carrying them to the fireplace. He held each stick over the flames and rotated them, charring the tips enough to burn off any sap. He glanced over at Mandy and smiled. "Sometimes fire's more cleansing than water.".

"I didn't realize you were so outdoorsy," Mandy said. "All these years, and you've been holdin' out on me."

Chris smiled, shaking his head, "Not so much these days. Just an old Scout trick. As long as you don't grab somethin' poisonous, you'll live to tell the tale."

"*You* were a Boy Scout?" Mandy said, surprised. "How did I never know this about you?"

Chris looked up at her, narrowing his eyes as he raised an eyebrow. He cleared his throat. "Do you *really* want to talk about the things we don't know about each other?"

"*Right*," Mandy said. She turned her attention back to the kids, helping them assemble tiny stacks of marshmallows and chocolate, sandwiched between graham crackers.

The s'mores disappeared fast, leaving only sticky fingers and laughter behind. Afterward, Ethan and Grace climbed inside the tent by the basement door together, where they ripped into the treats they'd chosen from the market and continued a fun evening.

Mandy poured herself a second drink.

Chris sat down inside his tent, the flap open. "Nothing like a sugar high right before bed."

"The days have been long. They've been crashin' out early and sleepin' hard,' Mandy said. "I don't think it'll be a problem."

"Not after a day like today, I bet," Chris said. "At least it appears she's not too scarred, huh? After the crazy guy in the creek?"

"Yeah," Mandy said, between sips. "Well…kids are resilient."

"Is that what you needed to be as a kid? Resilient?"

Mandy stared. She blinked but said nothing.

Chris gave a small nod, taking the hint. Before the silence stretched on too long, he said, "Grace mentioned something about an old school bus down in the yard."

Mandy chuckled. "Holy cow. I forgot about that goddamn bus. My mama brought it home one day when she'd gotten a wild hair. The thing had been in an accident. I don't think it even ran. My brothers ended up towing it back past the creek and dumpin' it. Like they were gonna deal with it later." Mandy shook her head, thinking of it. "Who knows why Mama wanted it…or what she thought she was gonna do with it. She was probably off her meds. Or on *one too many*."

"The kids also mentioned a graveyard, where some of your family is buried?"

"Haven't you even walked the property yet?"

"Haven't had any time," Chris said with a shrug

Mandy nodded, sighed. "Yeah, that's true too. Morbid, huh?"

Chris nodded. "I read somewhere that old family plots like that used to be pretty common." He thought about it a moment. "I don't think it's that morbid. Sorta nice for people who want their loved ones nearby. Not for me, though. I don't care where I'm buried. Who gives a shit what happens after you're gone? The livin'—that's the stuff that matters."

Mandy smiled at him and took another sip, finishing her drink. She stared off. "Once, when I was a little girl, we had this awful storm. The roof was leakin' and the wind was howlin'. And it was rainin' so hard. It wouldn't stop."

The image of the little girl sitting at the edge of her bed flashed through her mind.

She hesitated before continuing. "I don't know if he was messin' with us or not, but…my daddy told us the rain was so bad it might wash through the graves, dig up the bodies, and carry them away. It really bothered me. I thought about that every time it rained hard after that."

Chris patted the sleeping bag next to him. Mandy set her glass down on the credenza, crossed the room, and climbed into the tent beside him, tucking herself under his arm.

"What are we doing here?" she said, staring at the silhouettes of her children, giggling in the adjacent tent.

"I have no idea. But I love you. And we'll get through it."

She inhaled, almost content for a moment. "I love you too."

Less than an hour later, the kids started to tire, and their laughter faded. Chris let the fire burn down to embers, and Ethan joined him in his tent by the window.

"Here," Chris said, handing Mandy a flashlight. "I'm going to turn the lanterns off to save the batteries. But keep this in your tent in case you need anything in the night."

Mandy took it, kissed him goodnight, and slipped into the tent by the basement door. Grace was already asleep inside, so she moved with care, trying not to wake her.

———

MANDY WAS IN THE GRAVEYARD. The rain came down hard, soaking through her clothes and shoes, drenching her socks. She cowered beneath an oak tree, shivering, shrinking from the icy, piercing drops.

She clung to the tree trunk, bracing against the fierce wind. Above her, the trees whipped and danced under its force.

Lightning struck nearby—a blinding flash illuminating the tombstones. The water surged over them, a growing stream carving a path in the earth.

Thunder cracked, shaking the ground. One of the tombstones dipped, then collapsed, sinking into the flooded earth beneath it.

Mandy screamed. But she couldn't hear herself over the sound of the howling wind.

Another tombstone teetered and fell.

A woman's body floated to the surface of the water, unshrouded, drifting free of its grave. The mounting current seized it and it began to glide away, pulled downstream. Horrified, Mandy tried to turn away, but she couldn't. She didn't want to be shown the detail. Didn't want to know *who* had been unearthed. The limbs of the body jerked, lifeless. The water seized them, twisting them like a macabre puppeteer.

Another tombstone gave way, collapsing, disappearing under the water. And another body surfaced.

The dead were rising.

Mandy ran—stumbling, clawing her way through the underbrush, the wind shoving her back. The rain lashed against her in unrelenting sheets, each drop biting into her skin. Her feet slipped in the slick mud, and she fell. She felt herself being pulled toward the rising river. She clawed at the mud, grasping at roots, shrubs—*anything* that would stop her from sliding away. She pulled herself up. Ran again. An impossible battle. Relentless.

She slipped again and went down hard.

Her face smacked the surface of a freezing puddle, hands sinking into the wet earth. Her wet hair was in her eyes.

The tree was right in front of her. *The* tree. Three circles carved into its trunk. The water was lapping at its base. The toy gorilla surfaced, rising with the water as the tree's roots eroded.

As Mandy struggled to rise again, the tree began to give way. Cracking. Teetering.

Lightning split the sky. The tree creaked and leaned forward, falling toward her.

Mandy jumped. The massive tree crashed down right behind her, shaking the earth, flinging her forward. The thunder rolled in accompaniment.

Every time she fell it was harder to rise, but she pushed herself on through the rain, running as fast as she could across the yard. The house was ahead of her, its power out, its form almost indistinguishable from the dark sky above it.

And as she neared, she saw Ethan and Grace standing on the porch, waiting for her. They stood, motionless, like statues, untouched by the wind and rain.

Mandy screamed for them, but the storm swallowed her voice.

The house groaned. Wood splintered. Glass shattered. The roof buckled. And began to collapse.

She shouted for them to move. But they were still.

Mandy could only watch as the house folded in around them, wrapping them in its arms, crumpling in upon itself.

Mandy screamed again. Called their names. Begged them to run. Told them she loved them.

They didn't move. Didn't blink. They stared straight ahead as the house fell around them, sucking them in, swallowing them whole.

Keeping them forever.

———

Mandy shot upright, her heart racing.

Just a dream. Only a dream. Where was she? Had she screamed out loud?

She glanced down next to her. Grace was still sound asleep in her sleeping bag.

The tent. The house. They were still in the house. Only a dream.

Mandy pressed a hand to her chest and listened to her breathing.

In. And out. In. And out.

Control your breath. Be intentional. Slower. Each time. Calm.

Calm yourself.

But then came another sound. Creeping footsteps. Floorboards creaking under someone's weight.

Mandy leaned down next to Grace and continued to listen.

Someone was moving. Inside the house. She was certain of it. Moving toward them. One step. Then another. She listened to them, trying to pinpoint the sound. Was it Chris? Ethan? Had they gotten up to use the bathroom in the middle of the night? Were they trying to be quiet?

No.

The sound wasn't coming from the hallway. Not upstairs. *Below.*

The basement.

Someone was coming up the basement stairs. The creaking stairs. Someone had gotten into the basement *somehow.*

Mandy tried to stay calm. She put a hand near Grace's mouth and nudged her awake. When Grace opened her eyes, Mandy shook her head and placed a finger to Grace's lips. Grace nodded. She understood.

Mandy placed her hand in front of her own pursed lips. *Quiet.* Grace nodded again.

The sound of the footsteps was getting closer.

Mandy reached up and, ever so slowly, she unzipped the flap of the tent. She moved cautiously, making herself small. Like when she was a girl, and afraid—just like that. Once the zipper was open enough, they both climbed out of the tent.

Once free of it, Mandy crouched down and stared back at the basement door. She motioned for Grace to move over by the hall, and glanced around in the dark for anything that might be used as a weapon. The fireplace poker was not far away. She went to it and picked it up, careful not to make any noise. Then returned to stand in front of the tent again, facing the basement door. She held the poker like a sword.

The creaking pressed on. Slow. Deliberate.

"Chris," she shout-whispered. "Chris!"

The creaking stopped.

The movement forward ceased. But she could tell that—whomever it was—they were right behind the basement door now.

Mandy waited. Listened.

But there was nothing but silence. A long, torturous silence.

Then something else. From the basement. A mechanical whirring sound. Distant. Faint. The sound of…the *washing machine?*

Mandy cocked her head. The sound of the washing machine stopped. And the house was silent again. Deep. Almost unnatural.

She waited. And the feeling of someone being with them in the house—a presence behind the door—dissipated. It thinned, dissolving away, until she doubted it had ever been there at all.

She let the tension slip, allowing herself to soften. She took a deep breath in.

Then, from behind her—a *giggle*.

She turned, expecting to see Grace. But Grace was no longer standing at the front of the hall.

Mandy squinted into the thick, oppressive darkness, willing her eyes to adjust. And finally, she began to make something out. The light pink of Grace's pajamas. And something else…

A white nightgown.

The little girl.

Grace was being led down the hallway, walking hand in hand with the little girl.

Mandy felt chills rush over her body, crawling up her neck. She turned back to the tent and reached inside, frantic. She searched in the dark for the flashlight. When she found it, she whipped back around, flicking it on. Only to glimpse Grace at the end of the hall.

She smiled at Mandy.

Then she disappeared, the little girl's hand pulling her into the primary bedroom.

The door slammed shut.

"Grace!" Mandy screamed.

She tried to run.

But she couldn't move. It was as if the hallway had stretched. A corridor with no end. And Mandy was trapped in place. A fly in a web. And time seemed to stall. She tried with all her might, but the more she wanted to run, the further away the door seemed to get.

Then—just like that—everything was normal again. The hallway returned to its actual size, and Mandy ran down the length of it as fast as she could, the beam of her flashlight bouncing in front of her, the fire poker in her other hand, wielded like a cudgel.

As she reached the primary bedroom, she didn't think. She didn't consider what was on the other side. She ripped the door open, ready to fight for her daughter, ready to kill if necessary, to keep her safe.

Protect them.

But behind the door was only Grace.

She was sitting on the floor in her pajamas, cross-legged, facing the back wall.

"Grace!" Mandy gasped, her breath catching in her throat.

Grace looked up at her and smiled.

"You don't have to be afraid, Mom. She won't hurt you."

Chapter 16
Digging Down

Mandy blinked awake. The canvas walls of the tent glowed in the soft morning light. She didn't know what time she'd finally gotten back to sleep, but she was still tired. Her mouth was dry. Her teeth were fuzzy. Her neck ached—both from sleeping in the tent and from the stress of what she'd experienced.

She patted the sleeping bag where Grace had been, but it was empty. Mandy listened. She could hear her small voice somewhere outside, seeping through the walls, through the canvas of the tent. Ethan's voice as well, thin but ready to deepen any day. And the hum of Chris's baritone. *All* of them.

Mandy caught the aroma of something pleasant—*bacon*.

She slipped out of her sleeping bag and nudged the tent flap open. Standing, she stretched her sore muscles and yawned. For a moment, her gaze lingered on the basement door behind the tent, the warnings not to enter.

Contamination.

Mandy stared at the sign, her heartbeat ticking up for a moment. The thoughts were persistent. Someone standing behind the door. Her, gripping the fireplace poker.

She huffed. And she caught another odor. Her breath. She needed mouthwash or toothpaste, and she needed it bad.

As she wandered through the kitchen to the open back door, she thought she heard the crackle of a hotplate. She stopped in front of the screen door and looked outside.

On the back porch, under a beautiful open sky, a sunrise as his backdrop, was Chris, a spatula in hand. He stood, somewhat hunched, over a portable grill which he'd balanced on a stack of three concrete blocks. Sitting next to the blocks was a portable propane tank. On the hotplate, a smattering of bacon and eggs was sizzling away. A makeshift kitchen.

Ethan waited nearby, watching him cook. "You really went all in on the camping thing," Ethan said, looking at the food.

"Why not?" Chris said with a grin. "If we're gonna do it..." He let the thought hang.

Grace sat on the porch steps, holding a blanket, still wiping the sleep from her eyes.

Seeing them like this—happy in this moment, the majesty of the oak trees in the distance behind them—Mandy experienced a fleeting sensation. It was something almost like hope. Something she hadn't felt in a while.

This place don't want you, girl. No happy endings. Not for Holloways. Never were. Never will be.

"I'm makin' pancakes too, if you want some," Chris said.

Grace perked up. "I love pancakes!"

"Yes, please," Ethan said. "No eggs for me. I'll just take the bacon and the pancakes."

"Whatever you guys want. Gotta build up that strength if you're gonna help Mom and me work on the house today."

"Wait—for real?" Ethan said, his shoulders slumping.

Grace dropped her chin into her hands in an exaggerated pout. "Serious?"

"Super-duper serious," Chris said, chuckling.

"Ahh...*shoot*," Grace whined.

Mandy stepped onto the porch, the screen door creaking shut behind her.

"Hey, there she is! Sleeping beauty," Chris said, smiling at her, staring a bit too long.

"Well, bacon *is* the best alarm clock." Mandy wasn't sure if Chris was teasing or prodding, checking for something deeper. How much had Grace told him about the events in the middle of the night? She wiped at her eyes, grimacing at the morning light.

"Ah, see…you know all my tricks," Chris replied.

"Mom, did you know we had to work today?" Ethan asked.

"Of course I did. Did you two *freeloaders* think you were gonna play the whole time while we worked?" Mandy laughed. "C'mon, it won't be bad."

"All day?" Ethan protested.

"Maybe not *all* day," Chris said, most of his attention still focused on the hotplate.

"At least a few hours," Mandy added.

Good job, Mom. Drag 'em right back into that house again. Mother of the year. Guess the apple didn't fall far from the tree.

Grace got up from the porch steps and stood next to Mandy. She slipped her hand into her mother's and held it tight. Mandy wasn't sure if Grace was seeking comfort or giving it.

They ate at the dining table while Chris ran through his plan for the day: "The front rooms are gonna be *your* bedrooms."

"Cool," Ethan said.

"Right, cool. So, you guys need to help Mom clear the junk out so we can move your stuff in. Make piles—stuff we want to keep and garbage. We can store stuff in the work shed for the time being. Trash goes on the side yard. Mom will supervise."

"Speaking of that, we should call for a trash pickup soon," Mandy said.

"Agreed."

"And what are *you* gonna work on, Daddy?" Grace asked with a cheeky smile.

Chris chuckled. "*I* am gonna *keep* workin' on the electrical, honey." He turned back to Mandy. "Gotta get the power back on."

"Yeah, we don't want to spend too many nights…tent camping,"

Mandy said. The words caught in her throat and a tightness spread across her chest.

No more nights like last night. Please.

"Oh, it wasn't that bad, was it?" Chris asked, ruffling Grace's hair. She giggled.

Mandy forced a polite smile. Of course not. They'd slept right through it.

"I had fun," Grace said.

Mandy studied Grace's face—her effortless smile, innocent laughter, and unironic joy. *She had genuine fun last night, didn't she? How?*

Chris kept talking—to himself, it seemed—about wiring, the hallway bathroom, not having a garage. "I wish we could get into the basement," he said. "We need the space."

Basement.

The word vibrated in her ears and Mandy drifted away.

She thought of the creaking sounds she'd heard in the night. Of the footsteps. Someone coming up from the basement. Of the little girl in the mirror, screaming her piercing scream while her face melted away. Of Grace sitting cross-legged on the floor in the dark. And of the creek. Staring into the dark water and seeing a face reflected. The horrifying sensation of being pulled down. *Deeper.* The images—flashes of events she didn't remember. Pain. A violent suffocation, her lungs aching for air. The tree, with its markings. Hands scraping through the mud. The toy gorilla she knew she'd find, half-buried, vacant eyes staring up from the soil. A witness to whatever had transpired there.

She grimaced, shifting in her seat.

"Mandy?" Chris's voice cut through her thoughts. "Are you listening?"

She snapped back into the moment.

"Of course," Mandy lied, averting her gaze. "I just didn't sleep well. I feel…scattered."

After breakfast, despite their objections, Ethan and Grace began sorting through the junk in their respective rooms. Mandy supervised, managing them, going through the drawers and boxes ahead of them, making sure there was nothing inappropriate or dangerous inside.

Together, they sorted the clutter, placing any obvious garbage into large, black bags.

"Can we store stuff in *here?*" Ethan asked, cracking the door to the third room—Shane's old room, which had first been Mandy's.

"No, not in there." Mandy stepped past him, pulling the door shut. Her fingers lingered on the knob. "Not yet, okay?"

Ethan shrugged.

Carrying two full bags, Mandy made a trip to the growing junk pile on the side of the house. Before heading back, she saw that the door to the tool shed was ajar. Had it been like that before? She wasn't sure. She went to the shed and examined the door latch. It was old, but functional.

Mandy reminded herself they needed to pick up some new padlocks. She'd add it to the list.

Before she closed the door, she peeked her head in. The shed smelled as old as it appeared—a stale mix of dirt, wood, and rust. And underneath it, something else. Faint. Like rot.

Cobwebs clung to the corners and covered the old push mower. The rickety wooden shelves were lined with supplies: mason jars filled with nails and screws, coffee cans stuffed with bolts and washers, spare car parts, old bottles of turpentine and arsenic, gate hinges, and rusted tools—hammers, wrenches, screwdrivers, and saws.

Mandy was sort of surprised that Travis had left so many tools behind. Of course, none of these were new, but *some* of them were old enough that they could be antiques.

A few of the longer tools leaned against the wall of the shed—hoes and rakes and pitchforks. Near the front of the shed were a spade and a shovel—dull with rust, but serviceable.

Her gaze lingered.

Digging tools.

The image of the tree returned—vivid in its detail. A towering oak. A marking on its side. A marker in the earth at its base in the shape of a small gorilla. Hands scraping. Fingers raw.

Digging.

And then the thought hit her—*something* was buried under that tree. Something was down there waiting to be discovered. Underground.

Bless your heart, sugar. You're so far off the trail, I reckon you couldn't find the barn if the Good Lord himself was pointin' the way.

Mandy reached into the shed, her fingers hovering over the handle of the shovel, her mind churning. She waited for the impulse to pass. But it didn't. It only sank in deeper. The pull of it was undeniable. Her fingers twitched.

Oh sure, you go on now. March on over and tell Chris you're fixin' to dig up the yard. He'll think the cheese done slid right off your cracker. But don't you fret, none. He's gonna see it soon enough, either way. Gonna realize he never shoulda hitched his wagon to ya. 'Cause you're back home now, darlin'. Ain't no hidin' who you are no more. Never was. This was always waitin' for you.

"Fuck off," Mandy said aloud.

She picked up the tools and began to walk down the yard toward the grove.

———

She walked with purpose, retracing a path she'd walked a thousand times before, her footsteps heavy. As she crossed the creek, the flowing water glistened under the morning sun. For a moment, she pictured herself there as a girl, barefoot, knees muddy, hunting for tadpoles with a plastic cup or fishing with nothing more than a stick and line. This grove was her home away from home. Her retreat. Her *sanctuary*.

Aside from the single time, the day before, when she'd stormed in, looking for the man who'd frightened her children, Mandy had resisted coming to this place since returning home.

Being here now, she realized why—it felt too much like it used to.

Continuing on, the trees began to grow thick, and soon she arrived at the one she was bound for—*the* tree. As she stood before it—its branches looming above her, swaying in the breeze—it was like she was a girl again.

Mandy stepped to the trunk and traced the three carvings with her fingertips, overlapping circles, two on top and one on the bottom. She studied the shape a moment, setting the tools down at the base of the tree.

She began to wander further into the grove. She didn't realize where she was headed until she got there, until she came upon the clearing. The line of headstones.

This was another thing she'd avoided since returning.

She'd side-stepped the kids' questions. Shoved the thought aside whenever it began to creep in. But now she was here, crossing the small clearing. No more delays. No more excuses.

Her stomach ached as she approached her parents' graves.

The headstones were plain. Simple. Unassuming. They stood silent and gray, pristine in condition, in contrast to the other stones which were weathered and timeworn.

Mandy stood in between them for a minute or more, silent. She read the words inscribed on the stones. She read them over several times. *Loving Mother—Faithful Spouse. Loving Father—Dutiful Son.*

She nodded.

Should she do something? Say something?

She hesitated before she spoke.

"I'm sorry you're gone. And I'm sorry that I wasn't here toward the end." Her voice cracked, and a hard knot tightened in her throat.

The quiet pressed in again, thick and unmoving, and Mandy took a step back.

She thought she was finished. That she would leave it at that and get on with the task at hand.

Polite words. Expected words.

She took a shaky breath. And something inside of her broke.

New words bubbled to the surface. They were pouring out of her mouth before she could even think to stop them.

"You know what...*no.*" Her voice quavered with a seething anger. "That's horseshit. I'm *not* sorry. Because you *weren't* good parents. You never gave me *anything.* And I didn't ask you for much. Only to give a shit about me every once in a while. But ya never did. You never *believed* in me, and you never gave me anything to believe in. Never made me feel like you cared. And that's all I ever wanted." She hesitated, then added. "So…no, I'm not sorry. Not really. Just fucking *sad.*"

The clearing was silent, except for a hushed whisper of wind through the trees, the rustling of leaves.

But the voice sneered back inside of her, bitter and harsh.

You always thought you were better than us. Better than this place. Your home. Your family.

"I never thought I was better. I only wanted to matter!"

Wah. Wah. Wah. Looks like little Amanda wants attention again.

Mandy huffed, shaking her head. "Ever since I got the news 'bout you dyin', I keep *feeling* things. And I think to myself, what is this? Am I *missin'* them? Am I *sad* that they're gone? But I don't think so. I think I'm sad that I'm *not* sad! I'm sad that I don't care about my *parents* enough to mourn them. That I missed out on having a family. Christ, you have fucking *grandchildren* that you never even met! It wasn't like you didn't know they existed. So…no, I'm not sorry that I left. I'm not sorry I wasn't here at the end. You didn't earn it. You didn't earn me being here."

And yet, here you are, right back in Rosebury, same as us.

Her hands clenched at her sides, her fingers digging into her palms. "Yeah," she sighed. The word scraped its way out. She swallowed against the ache in her throat. "I guess you were right about that." She let out a short, bitter laugh. "*You win.*"

———

MANDY STOOD in front of the tree, staring at the symbol, a shovel in one hand and the small, faded gorilla toy in the other.

What do ya think you're going to find here? Do ya think you're some sort of psychic now or something? Remember that saying? People will do anything, no matter how absurd, to avoid facing their own souls. Well…THIS is absurd, honey pie.

Mandy tossed the toy aside, then pressed the shovel into the earth at the base of the tree trunk. The soil was dense, thick with foliage and stubborn roots. The shovel was rusted, and its wooden handle was splintered and graying, but she trusted it would do the job. She stepped down on its ledge and leaned her weight onto the handle.

The ground gave way under her.

She drove the shovel into the earth again and again, dumping clumps of damp dirt behind her in the underbrush. Insects skittered out of the disturbed ground—tiny, dark shapes vanishing into the brush. After a few inches, she had to stop digging and switch to the spade to chop at a knot of roots with its flat edge.

Sweat began to bead along her brow as she dug, and her breathing grew shallow.

Switching back to the shovel, she continued to dig, pressing down harder. The scent of earth and moss filled her nose.

It went like that for a while. Digging. Then switching to the spade to chop through stubborn roots or to dislodge a random rock. Back and forth.

This is stupid, Amanda Jean.

She gritted her teeth and doubled her pace, stabbing at the earth with a focused intensity.

Clunk.

The blade of the shovel hit something new.

Son of a bitch.

Her heart began to race.

She thrust the shovel down again.

Clunk. Clunk.

A hollow sound. Not a rock. Not a root.

"Stupid, my ass," she whispered.

Mandy dug with a renewed urgency, until the item began to take shape. A rectangle, covered in an odd, uneven texture.

She stepped into the hole and kneeled. She brushed away the remaining dirt from its top and corners, to reveal a burlap-wrapped bundle, bound with a length of twine. The burlap was old—frayed and brittle—and its coarse fibers began to crumble as soon as she began pulling the package from the ground.

Mandy set the shovel aside and sat down on a nearby rock, where she began to unwrap the bundle with trembling hands.

The remaining burlap fell away, unveiling a wooden box. It was almost six inches tall, almost a foot across, and only somewhat less deep. It was weathered from time spent underground, and the edges were cracked and black with rot.

The box was weighty in her hands.

She traced a finger along the grain. There had once been words on the top, but they hadn't survived the elements enough to be legible.

On the front was a simple latch, rusted over. With some effort, she was able to get it to move.

Inside were two items.

The first was a thin, cloth, case-bound book. The cover was worn and scuffed, but the book itself didn't look wet or mildewed—the outer box seemed to have succeeded in protecting it. Embossed on the cover in gold leaf was the word DIARY.

Mandy pulled it from the box and flipped through it quickly. The pages of the book were thin and yellowed from time, but the hand-writing was legible.

The other item in the box was a small, rusted, yellow metal container. It reminded Mandy of a cash box. Its lid was latched shut. She picked it up, letting the outer box fall to the ground between her feet. The metal was cold. The latch, locked.

A box within a box, she thought.

Mandy turned her attention back to the diary. She opened it. On the inside cover was a calendar for the year, and on the first page, it read: PERSONAL DIARY, 1964. At the bottom of the page, in smaller letters, it read: PUBLISHED ANNUALLY BY LITTLE WORDS PRESS.

She flipped to the next page, which was meant for the owner's personal details—name, address, telephone, and who to notify in case of an illness or injury—but it had been left blank.

Mandy flipped forward to the middle of the book, picking a page at random. The handwriting was lovely, looping and delicate. And yet, somewhat juvenile in appearance. Her fingers traced over the faded ink, and she began to read:

Mary Beth was at church this morning, and I swear, all she talks about now is boys. She's gone completely boy crazy. It's all she goes on about. I don't see what's the fuss. Folks keep saying I'll under-stand soon enough, but it's hard to imagine. Most of the boys around here don't even smell right, like they don't bother to wash up. It's strange to think Mama and Daddy started courting when they were only a little bit older than me.

Speaking of Daddy, he was real cross with me today for not getting my chores done. He threatened to fetch the switch. But even though he didn't, he said some mighty cruel things. He can be downright mean sometimes, but I count my blessings. I know he's a lot worse with Malcolm and Harlan.

Mandy gasped. Her vision blurred.

This was her mother's diary.

She took a slow, unsteady breath, letting the weight of it sink in. Then she closed the book and clutched it to her chest.

Chapter 17
In a Mood, 1988

Amanda woke up that Saturday morning to the sound of her mother singing. Not nearby, but somewhere in the house. It was the Christian hymn "How Great Thou Art," and she was singing at the top of her lungs.

Amanda stretched. Her favorite doll—a hand-me-down from her Aunt Lisa—was tucked under her arm, its blonde hair messy and tangled. There wasn't much light yet, only the soft amber glow of a sunrise peeking through the window. She wondered how early it was.

The Fourth of July was coming on Monday. And it seemed like the whole town had been setting off random fireworks on Friday night. Listening to the sporadic bursts and explosions always worried her. She hadn't slept well, fearing something might go wrong—that an errant firework would start a fire or that someone would end up hurt.

The hymn ended and the vacuum cleaner started up.

Over the noise, her mother began singing the song "Islands in the Stream." She performed both parts of the duet, starting first in a lower octave, mimicking Kenny Rogers, and switching to a higher part of her register when it was Dolly Parton's turn. Her mother didn't have a good singing voice—quite the opposite in fact—but she certainly gave it her all.

Amanda knew what this was.

Her mother was "in a mood."

What that meant for the day was anyone's guess.

Yawning, Amanda crawled out of bed and straightened her pajamas. She tottered out into the hall, her doll still under her arm.

Seeing her mother cleaning was a rare thing. She was dancing around the living room in her nightgown, pushing the vacuum cleaner with one hand, holding a cigarette and a Mountain Dew in the other. From time to time, she'd take a drag from the cigarette, sip from the can, and continue singing into it as if it were a microphone.

When she had energy like this, her mother's moods could go either way. She could be productive. Or chaotic. And sometimes, frightening. Amanda was pleased to see that her energy was positive today. *Good-natured.*

Her mother spotted Amanda standing in the hall and switched the vacuum off. She turned and began singing louder, a broad smile on her face. "Sing it with me, Amanda Bear!" she said between verses.

"I can't!" Amanda giggled. "I don't know the words."

"Well, poo on you then," her mother said. "But hey, good mornin', sunshine! You ready to get this day started?"

"It's so early," Amanda said.

Her mother scoffed. "Gotta get goin'! Lots to do!"

"Where's Daddy at?"

"Workin'. He won't be back 'til tomorrow. And you know what they say, don't ya? When the cat's away, the mice'll play." She gave Amanda a playful wink. "That's you and me, Amanda Bear. We're the *mice.*"

Amanda giggled again.

It was hard not to like her mother when she was like this—calling her nicknames, singing, playing around. It didn't happen often. And it likely wouldn't last too long. A part of Amanda already dreaded that part of it, knowing her mother's mood might shift at any time, and with little warning.

"Go on now, get dressed," her mother said.

"For what?"

"For the day, silly! For mischief!" Her mother laughed. She walked over to the dining room table and picked up a slip of paper, holding it up in front of her by the corners, giving a little tug at each side that made the paper snap. It was a paycheck. "Daddy makes the bacon. Mama eats it up."

Most of the time, her parents were tight with money. Days like this could end up being a rare gift, resulting in food—delicious food, *fun* food—and sometimes other surprises too. That was reason enough to motivate Amanda to change her clothes. Her father would be none too happy about it, but that wasn't Amanda's concern. Not right now.

She went to her bedroom and slipped out of her PJs into a loose-fitting t-shirt and a pair of pants that used to belong to her brother Shane. They were too big for her, so she pinned them at the waist with a couple of safety pins to keep them from sliding down and embarrassing her. After she was dressed, she went into the bathroom and brushed her hair, enough to smooth out the worst of the tangles.

By the time she was ready, the sun was peeking over the trees in the back yard, turning the sky a soft pink. She hoped her mother's mood would last long enough for the stores to open.

Her mother was sitting at the dining room table, a cigarette smoldering in the ashtray in front of her. She'd changed as well and was now wearing capri pants and a white blouse. Her hair was pinned up in a haphazard bun. She was flipping through the ads in the PennySaver, humming a tune Amanda didn't know, tapping her feet on the wood floor.

The scent of Charlie Blue was in the air, her mother's favorite perfume.

"All ready?" her mother asked, glancing up at Amanda.

"Right now?"

"Sure, right now. I'm hungry as a tick on a dry dog. How 'bout you?"

Amanda laughed, nodding. "Waffles?"

"Waffles sound right to me."

"Are the boys comin'?" Amanda asked, hoping the answer would be no.

"Nah, we'll let 'em sleep. They was out runnin' the roads with their friends 'til all hours. 'Sides, this here's girl time."

Girl time.

Amanda smiled. She liked that idea a lot.

Just the two of them.

———

AMANDA SAT in the booth across from her mother, watching as she cut an enormous bite of waffle and stuffed it into her mouth, syrup and butter pooling on her plate. She ate with unnecessary urgency, making small noises of pleasure as she chewed.

The overhead speakers in Rose's Diner were playing a varied mix of music. Her mother was bopping along to every song—wiggling in her seat, tapping her feet, patting the Formica tabletop with her fingertips, and hitting the plate with her fork for emphasis. First it was "Blueberry Hill," then "Jack and Diane," and now it was "Forever and Ever, Amen."

Her mother scooped up a bite of grits. The waitress—an older woman with her hair in a high bun, wearing pink kitsch cat-eye glasses —stopped by to refill her coffee. Before walking off, she asked Amanda, "You like that waffle, sugah?"

Amanda nodded. She'd chosen the blackberry preserves instead of maple syrup, and she was not regretting it. She took a bite of her bacon.

"Enjoying girl's day so far?" her mother asked. She pulled a handful of creamers from the dish next to the ashtray and added them to her coffee.

Amanda nodded. "Did Mamaw ever take *you* out to eat like this?"

Her mother's brow furrowed as she thought it over. She picked up the cigarette from the ashtray and inhaled. "Nah, not really. She was busy raisin' the three of us after Daddy up and left. We didn't have two nickels to rub together most days."

Amanda thought about it and asked. "Are *we* poor, Mama?"

"We get by, I reckon," her mother said. Then she grinned, flicking ashes into the tray. "But we ain't poor today, are we?"

Amanda wasn't sure about that. She'd seen the consequences of her mother's actions too many times. Instead of answering, she pushed a piece of waffle into her mouth. After swallowing, she asked, "What was *your* Daddy like? Before he went missin'?"

"My daddy, hmm. He was a…*strict* man, I 'spose," she said, hesitating. "He…"

Amanda saw her mother's expression falter. Had she asked the wrong thing? She bit her lip, panicking. She didn't want her mother to become morose. Couldn't risk her mood shifting. She changed the subject as fast as possible.

"I love this song!" Amanda said.

It was "Billie Jean" by Michael Jackson. Amanda bobbed her head to the rhythm, making silly expressions. And after a moment, her mother's face softened, and she joined in.

When the song finished, her mother went back to eating, alternating bites of waffles, bites of grits, drinking her coffee, and smoking her cigarette.

Amanda kept a careful eye on her for a few minutes, hopeful that she hadn't derailed the day by accident. When she was content that she hadn't, she kept eating, shoveling forkfuls of waffle and bacon into her mouth until she was so full she was almost uncomfortable. She didn't want the meal to end, but she couldn't eat anymore.

After leaving the diner, they drove to the East Towne Mall in Knoxville, about fifteen minutes away from Rosebury. When they arrived, the mall hadn't opened yet, so they sat in the car and listened to country music on the radio while they played "I spy."

Most of the time, her mother felt like a stranger. Sometimes, a zombie. At times, a monster. Today, she was a friend. A sister, even. And Amanda soaked it up. All of it. She tried to savor every second, knowing it might all vanish in an instant. That if she blinked, it might be gone.

When the mall opened, she followed her mother from store to store as she tried on clothes and bought random items—a candle here, a blouse there. As they passed the kids' section at JCPenney, Amanda stopped and admired a t-shirt with playful cats on the front. They reminded her of the feral cats that often roamed their yard. She stroked the fabric. It was soft beneath her fingers.

"You want it?"

Amanda looked up, startled. She hadn't realized her mother was behind her, watching her. She studied her mother's expression, trying to see if she meant it. Sometimes her mother offered things with no intention of following through.

Wary, Amanda nodded.

Her mother thumbed through the rack, checking sizes. She pulled one out and held it up to Amanda. "Might be a *touch* big on ya, but you'll grow into it."

Amanda was surprised and thrilled when her mother took the shirt, along with a few other items, to the cash wrap. She wished she could put it on right away—to make it real before the moment lapsed. Before her mother changed her mind. *No takebacks.*

But the surprises didn't stop there. As they left JCPenney, her mother suggested that Amanda needed a lunch box for when school started again. They searched for one as they continued to shop, and soon Amanda spotted a Hello Kitty lunch box that she fell in love with on the spot. She thought she'd seen one like it at school. A real, proper lunch box—like something a normal kid might have.

Her mother bought it without hesitation.

It was early afternoon when they left the mall. Her mother said it was time for lunch. Amanda was still so stuffed from breakfast, she wasn't sure she *could* eat, but there was no way she was going to turn down the opportunity.

On their drive home, her mother steered the car into a Sonic Drive-in. Amanda loved this one because the servers came out to the cars on roller-skates. Her mother told her she could have whatever she wanted, so Amanda ordered a Coney Dog, a Cherry Limeade, and a hot-fudge sundae. Though she hadn't thought she was hungry enough for another meal, she ate it all.

When they got home, Amanda and her mother carried their bags inside and put them on the dining room table. Her brothers weren't there, so the house was empty. Amanda asked for her new shirt, and her mother rummaged through the bags to find it.

Amanda went to her room and put it on immediately, then went to her mother's room and stood in front of her antique mirror to examine herself. The shirt *was* a bit large, but she loved it anyway. It was soft. It smelled new. And most of all, she had picked it out herself —it was no hand-me-down. It was *hers*.

Her mother's energy hadn't faded. She bounced around the house for hours—digging through her wardrobe, changing her clothes, cleaning the kitchen, singing. Amanda took some time to herself in her room, listening to it all from a distance.

By early evening, she assumed the day was winding down, but soon her mother appeared in the doorway and asked, "Y'hungry?"

Amanda was not *at all* hungry.

"How 'bout a hotdog and a dill pickle?"

A hotdog sounded horrible. She'd eaten a giant one for lunch. But the dill pickle sounded tasty and refreshing. And if saying yes meant her mother's mood might last a while longer, that's what she'd do.

"Sounds alright," Amanda said.

"Well, c'mon then, let's get movin'!"

———

THEY WERE in the car for almost half an hour when they came up on an interstate sign that read: "ALCOA, NEXT EXIT."

Summer days were long. The sun was still in the sky when they arrived in Alcoa, but it was nearly Amanda's bedtime.

The parking lot was deep and had begun to fill up with a random assortment of cars and trucks. The building was sizable, symmetrical, and nondescript, with two giant doors at the front—it reminded Amanda of a barn. Mounted above the doors in bold block letters was the word "BINGO."

Amanda didn't understand why they were here. She'd heard her mother mention bingo before—"*playing bingo*"—but she'd always assumed it was a game, like *Monopoly* or *Sorry!* But all the people here were grown-ups—most of them old women. She doubted they were going inside to play a board game.

Amanda hurried to keep up with her mother as she weaved

through the crowded lot toward the building. The giant front doors stood wide open.

In the lobby, people mingled, their chatter already loud and growing in volume. The place reeked of cigarette smoke. The walls were covered in wood paneling, and the floors were scuffed linoleum. Two oversized cork bulletin boards hung on the paneling, decorated in red, white, and blue in honor of the upcoming holiday. Several oversized calendars were pinned to the boards, along with announcements and church event flyers. Several people were milling nearby to take a peek.

Amanda stood beside her mother as she waited in line near the entrance.

Several of the other people waiting seemed to know one another. A few of them made comments to Amanda, telling her she was pretty, asking her if she was ready to play bingo, joking she must be a "night owl," etcetera. One of them commented on her cat shirt, which she appreciated.

At the front of the line, several folding tables stood in a row. They looked like the ones at Amanda's school—brown metal tables with faux wood tops, cracked in places, exposing particle board underneath. At the tables, a few older women sold bingo cards. Her mother purchased several, but Amanda still wasn't sure what that meant.

Around the corner was another line, shorter than the first. People were waiting in front of a counter, behind which was a small room. Above the open window, a hand drawn sign read: DRINKS AND SNACKS.

"What ya want?" her mother asked. "Hot dog? Pickle? Fries?"

"Can I have a pickle and fries…and a drink?" Amanda asked.

Many of the people were laughing, joking, teasing each other about losing streaks, asking about family. Old men in baseball caps. Old women in bright floral blouses and slacks. Amanda appreciated the sense of community. She didn't experience that often—except at church, but there it always felt stiff, like people were only going through the motions. Here, the comradery seemed easy, natural.

But her mother kept to herself. She didn't seem interested in any of it.

Her mother handed Amanda a cardboard box with the food inside —a hot dog in a paper sleeve, a dill pickle wrapped in butcher paper, a cupful of fries, a Coke for Amanda, and a Mountain Dew for her.

Carrying the box, Amanda followed her mother into the room.

It was like an auditorium, filled with rows of folding tables and stackable black chairs. Amanda figured there must've been ten tables per row, at least, going four or five rows deep. The bright overhead fluorescent lights made the beige cinderblock walls appear yellow. The smoke was visible in the air, hanging thick, despite the fans mounted along the walls. At the front was a head table, on which was a metal cage filled with numbered balls. Various red, white, and blue decorations hung around the room, and a "HAPPY INDEPENDENCE DAY" banner hung above the front table.

The tables were beginning to fill up, but her mother snaked her way through the crowd to claim a spot she liked. Amanda followed. Once there, Amanda climbed up on a black chair next to her mother. Her feet didn't touch the ground.

Her mother laid the bingo cards out on the table in front of her. She grabbed the hot dog out of the cardboard box, took a bite off the end, and began to go through her handbag. She pulled out what looked to be a marker or highlighter, and a rabbit's foot keychain.

She handed the rabbit's foot to Amanda. "Rub on this for Mama. For luck."

Amanda wasn't sure about that, but she rubbed the rabbit's foot a few times before setting it on the table to keep an eye on it. She pulled the pickle from the cardboard box and set it next to the keychain, then began to munch on some French fries.

Her stomach hurt, but not in the usual way. Perhaps she'd eaten *too much* for a change. That would be new.

A man and woman—not quite as old as most of the crowd—went to the front of the room. The woman picked up a microphone and announced over the scratchy P.A. that the first game was about to begin. The man went to the metal cage and inspected it. He cranked the handle on the side, making sure it spun freely.

Amanda unwrapped her pickle and took a bite. It was delicious— maybe the best thing she'd had all day, and that was saying something.

She thought that alone might make the journey to the bingo hall worthwhile. The fries, however, were cold and flavorless.

During the first part of the first bingo game, Amanda was captivated by the process. She watched the man spin the cage and select a ball and listened as the woman read the letter/number combinations in her thick, slow drawl, sometimes tossing in a joke to keep the crowd engaged.

She was amused by the occasional complaints from people in the crowd—*"Too fast!"*—and fascinated by how her mother and others responded to each new bingo call in their own way. Some people had a method for how they marked their cards, perhaps even a superstition. Her mother went down the line of cards in front of her, marking them with her thick pen, which she called a *dauber*.

However, by the end of the first game, Amanda was bored. Her pickle was long gone. So were the fries and drink. She played with the rabbit's foot and wondered how long they might be here.

When a woman called "Bingo!," Amanda was relieved. She thought that was the end. But it was only a break. Another game would start soon.

During the break, her mother bought more bingo cards, and got herself a cup of complimentary coffee from a table in the lobby, but this time she didn't offer to buy Amanda anything. She was too anxious to return to the table and set up for the next game.

Amanda was exhausted. This was *way* past her bedtime.

Toward the end of the third game, she noted the intensity and focus in her mother's eyes and realized it might be a while before this was over. She tugged at her mother's shirt sleeve and asked if she could go sleep in the car.

"Nah," she said. "Just curl up right here, under the table."

That didn't sound at all appealing to Amanda. The room was warm and smokey, and the floors appeared grimy.

The woman kept calling letters and numbers. The metal cage spun. The crowd chattered, calling out at random moments. And Amanda's eyelids got heavier and heavier. Soon, she couldn't fight it anymore. She climbed under the table. Resting her cheek on her arm and holding the rabbit's foot in her hand, she found a shallow and uncomfortable sleep.

When her mother woke her, the bingo hall was beginning to empty. The remaining attendees were packing up to leave, and the staff moved about, stacking chairs and wiping down the tables. Amanda had no idea how long they'd been there, but she was relieved that they were going home at last, where there was a real bed.

Groggy and disoriented, she didn't think about the rabbit's foot she'd taken under the table. And by the time they left, it was long forgotten.

————

WHEN AMANDA WOKE, the sun was already shining through her bedroom window. She didn't remember arriving home. As she pulled back the covers, she realized she hadn't changed into her pajamas. She was still wearing her clothes from yesterday, including her cat shirt. Though the night had ended in a tedious blur, she was still grateful for the day she'd gotten to spend with her mother.

The house was quiet for a Sunday morning. Most of the time, her mother was insistent upon them going to church with her. Had they stayed out too late? Had her mother overslept?

Amanda wandered into the kitchen, but no one was there. Both of her brothers' doors were closed. *That* was no surprise. Unless they were getting up early for a specific reason—hunting or fishing or school— they slept as late as they were allowed.

But her parents' bedroom door was closed as well. When her father was away for work, her mother usually slept with the door cracked.

She knocked quietly.

There was no response.

"Mama?" she called. She knocked again.

After a moment, her mother answered from behind the door. "What?" Her tone was low and monotone, and there was little life to her voice.

Amanda pushed the door open. The room was dark. The blinds were drawn. Her mother was sitting at the end of the unmade bed, hands in her lap, shoulders slumped forward. She was staring at the wall, her face pale.

"You alright, Mama?" Amanda asked, holding onto the edge of the door. "You feelin' sick?"

Her mother turned to her slowly, her face blank. "I'm fine. What do you want?" The words dropped from her mouth, lifeless.

"It's Sunday. I thought we was goin' to church."

Her mother stared at her, slack jawed, eyes glossy. "Does it look like I'm goin' to church?"

Amanda shook her head.

"Maybe ya aint' so dumb after all, then," her mother said. Then she turned back to face the wall.

"Mama?" Amanda said in a small voice.

"Get out now, please," her mother said, emotionless.

Amanda hesitated. Seeing her mother decline so fast was worrying. Yesterday, she'd been so alive. Vibrant. Fun. Last night, she'd been focused and intense. Now, she was barely a shell of herself.

"I said…get out," her mother repeated.

Amanda closed the door, leaving her mother in the dark. Alone. Then she went back to her room and crawled under the covers.

———

AMANDA WAS PLAYING by herself in her room. She didn't realize her father had gotten home until she heard him yelling. Her mother was screaming back at him.

"Ya can't go off and buy all this shit, Debbie! We can't afford it!" he yelled.

"We can afford it just fine! If you can afford to take out other women!"

Amanda went to her door and listened. Her father was going through the shopping bags they'd left on the dining room table.

"I ain't got no other women, you nutter! When the hell would I have time? I'm too busy makin' money for you to piss away on crap!"

"You're a liar, Earl! I know!"

"All this stuff is goin' back, ya hear me, ya crazy bitch? All of it!!"

Amanda's heart started to thud. She glanced down at her shirt, the soft fabric, the bright colors. Thought of her Hello Kitty lunch box. He was going to take them away.

"I hate you!" her mother screamed.

"Hush your mouth, Debbie! I'm sick to death of yer nonsense!"

As the arguing continued, Amanda left the door and sat on the edge of her bed, wondering how everything had gone from wonderful to horrible so fast. She didn't want him to take her shirt. She loved it. *How* could she keep him from it? What if she hid it somewhere? No, they'd make her find it. And probably punish her for hiding it from them.

Amanda dug her fingers into her thighs.

Think. Think.

She had an idea.

Frantic, she raced to her toy box. She dug inside until she found what she was looking for: one loose orange crayon. She took her t-shirt off and laid it on the top of her dresser. Taking care, she colored in one of the cats.

No. That wasn't enough.

It was still too nice. It didn't even look drawn on. The store might take it back without noticing. As much as it pained her, she needed to go further.

She hesitated.

She pushed her tongue against her lower lip in concentration, then pressed the crayon down so hard it almost snapped in half. She dragged the orange outside the lines in one spot, just far enough, just dark enough, just *ugly* enough that no store would ever accept it.

Nothing more happened that day. Amanda stayed out of their way, as she so often did. And her parents kept to themselves as well.

A few days later, her mother took away her Hello Kitty lunch box, telling her it needed to be returned. She asked for the shirt too.

Amanda hesitated before pulling it out. She pointed to the crayon marks.

The moment she saw them, her mother's face twisted in anger. "What the hell is wrong with you? How could ya do something so stupid?" she screamed.

Amanda expected more. She expected a beating. She was ready for one. But it didn't come.

In the end, Amanda was allowed to keep the shirt.

She only wore it around the house since it was marred. But she saw it as a small victory. The shirt was still hers. And she'd spent a day with her mother when she was in a rare, good mood, eating food, singing, laughing.

The memory was hers too.

Chapter 18

Long Shadows

Chris tossed another rotten board onto the growing pile in the side yard and wiped his brow with the back of his glove. He stretched. His shoulders ached, and his knees were stiff. This work was wearing on him, and there was no end in sight. It was the kind of work that reminded him he wasn't as young as he used to be. He rolled his shoulders. After removing his gloves, he rubbed the back of his neck. His skin radiated heat.

He wandered over to the electrical box mounted on the side of the house. He'd spent some time that morning charting circuits, tracing wires, doing repairs. They'd have power again soon—*some*, at least. But despite all his effort, the house still was far from habitable.

His eyes drifted to the grove of trees at the far end of the yard. The kids had said Mandy went that way almost an hour ago. He hadn't gone after her, assuming she needed alone time—perhaps to visit her parents' graves.

Their relationship had always been built on trust. They'd often described their partnership as two individuals who were stronger together. They'd always respected each other's space, never prying unless invited. But his frustration with her distractedness was growing.

He glanced again at the grove.

Her distractedness…*and* her mental state.

The day hadn't gone to plan, and he was way behind. His attention had been focused on specific and necessary tasks. Without Mandy around, little else had gotten accomplished. The kids had become aimless. He considered giving them work to do, but without supervision, he didn't think it was worth the effort. One thing was clear—he couldn't do this alone, no matter how hard he tried.

Now, the kids were poking around the junk pile, more interested in goofing around—normal and understandable, but not helpful. Ethan was lingering near the tool shed.

"Don't go in there, okay, bud?" Chris called out. "There's sharp stuff. And who knows what else."

"Dad, can we go play?" Grace asked, her voice lacking its usual brightness.

"Your mom should be back soon, and we need to get stuff done today."

"Well, can we go inside?" Grace asked.

Chris shrugged, already turning back to the electrical box. "Yeah, go ahead. But stay away from where I'm working and don't touch the tools. And I know it's taped off, but stay out of the basement. It's still not safe."

Grace didn't hesitate. She took off toward the house, followed close behind by a much less enthusiastic Ethan.

"Come on, let me hear you say it!" Chris shouted.

"We understand," Grace called back without turning around.

"Let me hear you say it, bud," Chris repeated, directing it at Ethan.

Ethan huffed. "No work areas. No tools. No basement."

Chris nodded. "Good man."

As the kids disappeared inside, Chris glanced back at the grove and checked his watch. He'd give Mandy another fifteen minutes. Twenty, perhaps. Then he'd go find her.

———

GRACE LED Ethan down the hallway. The echoing of their footsteps on the uneven wooden floorboards was amplified by the emptiness of the house. Without their mother around, the house was different, she thought. Emptier. Less tense. It was sort of exciting to have it to themselves for a while.

Under their mother's supervision, they'd spent the morning clearing and organizing the two rooms closest to the front door—the ones that would be theirs. Whatever mystique those rooms might have held was gone now. Now they were only a chore.

Grace passed by the bathroom, where her father had set up his toolbox and portable lights. She opened the door to the primary bedroom, the only room that was almost completely empty. Dad said they'd be able to start moving furniture in soon.

Grace glanced at the carpet and smiled, remembering how she'd sat cross-legged with her new friend in the night. She thought she caught a whiff of the little girl's shampoo.

"Let's check out *this* room," Ethan said from behind her. He'd stopped in the hallway, and was motioning to the third room, the one their mother had asked them to stay out of.

"Mom said not to," Grace reminded him, eyeing the door. She didn't like the idea of breaking the rules.

Ethan shrugged. "Yeah, well…you've seen how *weird* Mom's been acting."

"Ethan!"

"Oh, come on! She has! Don't tell me you haven't noticed."

Grace hesitated, trying to gauge the sincerity in Ethan's face, then nodded. She didn't like admitting it, but their mother had indeed been different since they'd arrived at the house. She was distracted. And there was a nervousness about her—an agitation that Grace could sense, but not understand.

"Besides…she's not here right now," Ethan added. He pushed the door to the bedroom open and stepped inside. "I only want to take a look."

Grace shifted from foot to foot before following him, pausing at the threshold.

This room felt *different.*

It was in better shape than some of the others. She could tell it had once been bright and cheerful, but the color had faded over time, and the floral wallpaper was now peeling away in long, thin strips.

The front window was bare, its glass smudged and dirty, and although the overgrown plants out front blocked most of the sunlight, a few stubborn beams broke through. Grace could see dust motes floating through their light.

The furniture was sparse. A bunk bed stood against one wall, the bottom mattress missing, a stack of random boxes sitting on the box spring. A mismatched, ramshackle dresser stood against the opposite wall, its surface cluttered with old junk and a broken lamp. Various crates and packing boxes littered the floor near the bed and the closet. And an old rocking horse stood off to the side, parked in the corner, coated in dust, its paint chipped and faded, its blank wooden eyes staring ahead. It appeared as if it was waiting for them.

She took a cautious step inside.

"See?" Ethan said, gesturing. "Just a room."

A coldness ran through Grace's body. It started in her fingertips and toes—faint at first—then crawled up her limbs to her spine where it settled at the base of her neck.

She drifted toward the bunk bed, drawn by a faint sound—something beneath the silence, tickling her ear. She crouched down near the bed, leaning in, straining to listen.

There was a voice. No—*voices.* They seemed to come from everywhere and nowhere at once.

Whispering.

But Grace couldn't understand what they were saying. What they meant. Their words were fragmented, tangled in noise.

Psssst… Beee…. Huuunhhh… Nnnnaa… Waaaah… Sssss…

"*Hello?*" Grace whispered. "What is it? What are you saying?"

Ethan moved to stand beside her. "Grace? Who are you talking to?" he asked, his voice small, subdued, as though he was afraid to speak any louder.

The whispers persisted, an incoherent chorus that continued to grow. Grace found herself whispering back in the same rhythm, repeating the sounds, matching the tone, hoping it would help her understand. It felt right. *Natural.* Like speaking to a pet in its native tongue.

"What are you doing?" Ethan asked, putting a hand on her shoulder, his voice shaky. "You're freaking me out!"

But he sounded far away. Grace was focused on the words, straining to glean any meaning behind them as they grew louder still, coiling around her like creeping ivy.

And then—buried within the rising cacophony—there were words she understood.

Riiiiight be…hiiiind yoooou… they hissed.

Grace whipped around, her eyes searching the room—her brother, the closet—but there was nothing. *No one.* She thought of the little girl and wondered if the voices were talking about *her.*

"It's okay," she whispered, trying to reassure them. "You don't have to be scared of her."

But the voices began to grow more frantic. To overlap one another. She wasn't sure if they were women or men, young or old. But they sounded urgent. Fearful.

Once more, behind the noise, the words repeated: *Behind you…*

She spun around again. This time the room darkened, growing colder. A chill wrapped around her like icy fingers. And she saw it— the long, dark shadow of a man, stretching across the wall of the already dim room. The figure grew, elongating, as if it were creeping closer. She stared up into the distorting shadow as it spread up the wall and onto the ceiling.

"*He was hiding,*" she muttered. The words slipped from her lips before she understood them. Her breath hung in the air, frigid and visible, coming in short, shallow gasps. Her feet were locked in place. "*In the closet. In the dark.*" Her voice was almost imperceptible.

The shadow loomed over her, stretching wider. It was oppressive— leeching the color from her cheeks, the joy from her heart, draping the room in darkness. The whispers were swirling all around her, filling her ears with an anxious dread.

And she understood their fear.

Her brother's voice pierced through the din. Faint and thin, but sharp—as if he was yelling from a great distance. "Grace!" he shouted, the sound echoing like it was emanating from a deep well. "Graaaace!"

The whispers ceased.

A moment of utter stillness.

One last icy breath lingered in the air before evaporating. The darkness receded, the shadow ebbing away...and it vanished. As if it had never been.

The room had returned to normal.

Grace blinked, and saw that Ethan was standing next to her, his face pale, his eyes wide. He was repeating her name, his voice thick with fear.

"We need to go," she said. She grabbed his hand and pulled him toward the doorway. He didn't protest.

"Are you okay?" he asked, as they stepped into the hallway. He glanced back into the room. "What...what *happened?*"

Grace turned and closed the door behind them, her hand lingering on the doorknob for a moment before she let go and backed away.

"What *was* that, Grace?" Ethan asked, a slight tremor in his voice. "Are you...alright?"

Grace nodded, though her gaze was still fixed on the door. "Mom was right," she said finally. "We shouldn't go in there. The shadow man is scary."

———

"You disappeared on us," Chris said, his attempt at a light tone undercut by a frustration that wasn't easy to hide.

Mandy set the grimy box on the dining room table. "Yeah...uh, sorry about that," she said, her voice distant. Her clothes were soiled. Dried mud streaked her wrists. Dirt clung to her nails.

"Can I...ask where you were?"

Mandy didn't answer immediately. "I got to feelin' like I oughtta visit my folks."

Chris nodded, scratching his upper lip. "I figured that might've been where you went. But you could have said something. We were right in the middle of work."

"I'm sorry," she said.

"What's up with the box?"

"Somethin' of my mama's." She shifted, uncomfortable in her skin. "Why so many questions? I said I was sorry, Chris. *I'm sorry.*"

Chris sighed. "I don't know, Mandy. Maybe because you disappeared for hours when we were supposed to be working. I'm busting my ass fixing up a house that we *could* sell—but *you won't*. And I'm doing it *alone.*"

"I know, I know. I don't mean for it to feel that way. I found my mama's diary…" She hesitated. "I…found her diary and I thought I should go visit her."

"To be honest…it seems like you're keeping things from me," Chris said. "That's a new feeling. I knew you had things in your past that you didn't want to talk about. That's fine. But I never thought you were *excluding* me from things. Because this *isn't* the past anymore. It's affecting us. *Right now.*"

"I'm fine, Chris. I only needed to—"

"*No,*" he interrupted, stepping closer, his voice dropping. "No, you're not. And you can't keep saying you are, because it's *bullshit.* You vanish for hours. You can't focus. You wander around like…like you're looking for something you can't find. You haven't spoken much to any of us all day. You are *not* here. You are *not* present. You're like a *ghost* of yourself."

Mandy flinched, as if the words had weight, as if they'd bruised her.

A silence stretched between them. She stared down at the box, her jaw tightening. She exhaled and nodded, her shoulders slumping. It was as if she was powering down, her energy draining away.

"I'm really sorry," she mumbled. "I guess I have more feelings about all this than I thought I would. Thinkin' of Mama and Daddy. The way they're sayin' it all happened. All I can ask is that you're patient with me."

Chris exhaled. "I do get it. It is…a lot. And I'm *trying* to be patient and make space for you to work through it. But the reality is that our bank account is not gonna wait for you, babe. It's dwindling fast. So, if you're not gonna sell the house to your uncle—for *whatever* reason that is—you need to understand that the clock is ticking, and we need all hands on deck."

Mandy nodded, her face blank.

Chris leaned against the sink. He looked as if he wanted to say more but didn't. After a moment, he suggested, "Why don't you clean up and take a drive? Head into town. We need some more ice. Grab some groceries, drinks. Pick us up some dinner. Clear your head. Come back to us in a better space. We all need you here, okay?"

"Alright."

———

MANDY SLAMMED her fist against the steering wheel as the car rattled down the narrow road toward town. She took a deep drag from the cigarette, the air from the open car windows whipping at her hair.

You lied to him. Told your fella that you found the diary first, then went to the grave. You lie slicker than a greased possum on a tin roof!

And if she'd told him the truth? Would he understand? He couldn't. How could she explain what was going on in her head? The voices. The images—the little girl, the reflections. And now this? *Digging in the yard.* Chasing a vision, like a crazy person.

She'd run away from this place, built a new life, put Rosebury behind her. She thought she'd distanced herself from the chaos. The nastiness. Hatefulness. Lies.

But now it was pulling her back in.

And it didn't even take a week.

She thought about her parents' deaths—the possibility they weren't accidental. She pictured the skeleton of the dog. The smiling toy gorilla. The decaying house. The creaking stairs. A diary buried in dirt. Her uncle's sneer.

And under it all, a sickening notion had slithered in—*this* was her real life.

That everything she'd created away from here was only a façade —a dream she was being dragged from, kicking and screaming. A fantasy she'd clung to that was always destined to crumble. To expose her as a secret pretender. The imposter she'd always feared she was.

Undeserving of any of it.

Fool thing, thinkin' ya could pull this off, Amanda Jean. Ya can take the girl outta the South, but—

"Stop! Just *fucking* stop!"

Mandy tapped the cigarette against the top of her open soda can, a makeshift ashtray. She drove past familiar landmarks, some with new paint and updated signage: the gas station, the junkyard, storefronts she remembered from her childhood. But, despite the town's attempts at improvements, under any gloss and modernization Rosebury remained the same declining town she always knew.

Same as you, darlin'. Like puttin' lipstick on a pig. Dress her up all you want, but a hog's still a hog.

Mandy cranked the radio up and started singing along at high volume, hoping the noise might drown out her thoughts.

———

The market's parking lot was small. She pulled into a spot near the ice machine by the entrance.

Do NOT forget the ice, she reminded herself. She repeated it in her mind several times. She told herself she should put it in her phone but ignored her own advice.

As she opened the door to the market, a bell above her jingled, a throwback to be sure. A blast of cool air hit her as she entered. Mandy grabbed a basket. She'd made no list, had no plan, so she began to wander the aisles, tossing groceries into the basket at random: a box of crackers, a few bags of potato chips, a bag of apples, beef jerky, a package of Gatorade.

As she rounded the corner to the refrigerated section, she almost collided with a tall, slender man wearing a dark polo shirt and khaki pants. As she staggered to the side to avoid him, she spotted the Knox County Sheriff emblem on his chest.

"Whoa!" the man said.

"Sorry…so sorry," Mandy said with a small wave, avoiding eye contact.

"Wait—Amanda?" His voice was deep.

Mandy blinked and took a step back. The man's eyes were familiar in a way that was comforting.

"Bo?" she said, his name returning to her in an instant.

She was certain it was him, but the last time she'd seen him was in high school. It was hard to reconcile the baby-faced teen she remembered with the man standing in front of her. He was still slim, but softer around the middle. His face was still narrow, his mouth still thin, but his cheeks were fuller now. The lines on his forehead and around his mouth had deepened. His eyes were the same—soft, kind, *understanding*—except for the dark circles beneath them.

"Heard through the grapevine you'd come back to town," he said, his cadence slow and measured, his accent as thick as she remembered. "Didn't 'spect to run into you." He shifted his weight. "Didn't know if you'd wanna see me."

Mandy had a twinge of guilt. She hadn't thought about seeing him. Truth be told, she hadn't thought of him in years.

"No, it's *great* to see you. It's been a…long time," she said. His scent was the same—clean but tinged with sweat. It was a scent she hadn't thought about in forever, but it was familiar in a way that scratched at her memory. A silence settled between them—full of old, unspoken things. It stretched out long enough to make her restless, so she said, "You're a cop now, huh?" She chuckled. "Makes sense, I guess. You always did want to do the right thing."

"S'pose so," Bo said. He nodded, his cheeks flushing. "Hey, I wanted to tell you…I'm real sorry 'bout your folks."

"Thanks." She forced a shrug, as if it was a casual topic. "Guess it was their time."

"'Spose so," Bo's gaze dipped for a moment. Something flickered behind his eyes—hesitation. Or *doubt*. Right as Mandy spotted it, it was gone. "Y'all stayin' around long?" he asked.

"Only until we get the house…" She waved a hand, her voice trailing off before she could finish the thought. The truth was, she didn't know anymore. How long it would take. If their stay would be temporary. Or if her family—her *sanity*—would survive the process.

"Yeah, I get it," he said. "Renovations are rough." He pulled a wallet from his pocket, retrieving a business card from next to his badge. "If you ever need anything…this is where you can find me." He tapped the number at the bottom.

For a moment, as she took the card, she felt the roughness of his fingertips, and she was back in middle school, sitting with Bo in front of the Dairy Freeze after the football game, sharing a milkshake, their hands entwined, whispering about the lives they wanted to live.

"Thank you," she replied, running her thumb along the edge of the card before tucking it into her back pocket.

"It was nice seein' you, Amanda," he said, nodding once, as if he wanted to say more.

"Likewise."

As Bo turned to walk away, a sudden desperation seized Mandy. Before she could reconsider, the word was already out of her mouth. "Bo?"

He glanced back over his shoulder with a slight smirk, his eyebrows raised.

Mandy's stomach tightened. She hadn't thought this through. Should she keep going? She pushed herself to say the words before she had time to overthink. Before she lost her nerve.

"What do you know about my parents' deaths?" She was surprised. The question sounded calmer than she'd expected.

Bo's expression shifted. He started to speak, but stopped, his mouth pressing into a thin line. Perhaps it was disappointment in the subject matter. Or maybe it was something else. His brow furrowed, as if he were considering his words. "I know what you're gettin' at. Reckon I heard the same things you did 'bout what happened."

"Yes. That. *What happened?*" she asked, her voice calm but firm.

Bo took a deliberate breath. "I checked. Wanted to see for myself. But beyond the official story, ain't much more I can say about it."

Mandy swallowed hard and looked him in the eye. "But you would tell me if you knew something?"

He hesitated before nodding. "I'd tell you. If I knew somethin'.

But I *don't*. Folks are gonna talk. *Always*. But talk is talk." His expression tightened, his eyes narrowing. "I do know that Travis was stayin' with 'em." He hesitated. Exhaling, he added, "And, for what it's worth, he's the one that called it in."

"*Travis?*" Mandy glanced down at the floor, her thoughts jumbled, trying to process what Bo had said. What he'd insinuated. Her hands began to tremble. When she spoke again, her voice was softer. "Ya think he had something to do with it?"

Bo was stoic, his face unreadable. He stared off across the store, but it didn't seem like he was looking at anything at all. "I didn't say that." He took a beat. "But I think you might wanna talk to him 'bout that night."

Mandy exhaled. "We don't exactly have much of a relationship."

"Yeah, I can't imagine ya would."

"Why do you say that?" she asked.

"'Cause you had enough self-respect to get yourself outta that house. Outta this town. Travis…well, let's just say he took a different road."

Mandy frowned. Bo was dancing around something, weighing his words, and she didn't understand why.

Bo continued. "It's a messy damn thing, is all I'm sayin'. Your family…cast a long shadow over all of ya kids." He exhaled, shaking his head. "Maybe they still do."

Mandy nodded to be polite, but she'd already moved on in her head. These weren't answers, not really. And it was clear he wasn't going to tell her anything else. "It was good seeing you, Bo."

"Yeah," he replied, giving her a small, tight smile. "Ya look good. Keep on takin' care of yourself. And don't go stirrin' up trouble."

He turned and moved toward the exit.

Mandy watched as he walked away, before turning back to her shopping. Her thoughts were scattered. Bo's words kept replaying in her mind.

Travis was stayin' with 'em…he's the one that called it in.

Mandy shifted the basket to her other hand. Her fingers were stiff from gripping the handle too hard.

Her head was buzzing. Black spots flickered in her vision. She stopped in the aisle, blinking hard. She grabbed ahold of the shelf and took several deep breaths, hoping it might help. It didn't. The air was thick. The fluorescent lights pulsed overhead. Too bright. The market didn't feel cool anymore.

She cut her trip short, hurrying to pay for the items she'd gathered and go, unsure if she'd gotten anything they needed.

She was already halfway home when it hit her—she'd forgotten the ice.

CHAPTER 19
TRAPPED, 1993

AMANDA DIDN'T SEE THE TWO OLDER BOYS FOLLOW HER OUT OF
school. If she had, she wouldn't have turned into the alley, the fenced-
in stretch that separated her middle school from the back yards of the
surrounding homes.

She wasn't used to drawing the attention of boys. Or girls. Or
anyone, really.

Between her ill-fitting, hand-me-down clothes and plain appearance, Amanda felt invisible at school most of the time. But she didn't
mind invisibility. It was better than ridicule. And it seemed like the
only times she ever did receive attention was when rumors were going
around about her family.

*Did you hear that Deborah Holloway stole a school bus? Did you
know that the Holloway boys are selling dope? Did you hear that Harlan
Caulder stabbed someone in a bar fight? Did you hear that everyone in the
Holloway house got lice?*

All of those were true.

And when enough rumors about you and your family were true, it
didn't matter when one was false.

I heard that Shane Holloway ran over someone! I heard that the

Holloway family are all nudists! I heard that Amanda Holloway makes out with her brother!

Amanda found it best to keep her head down and ignore it all as much as possible. That was the way to survive. She didn't care about the people in school, and they didn't care about her. So, why bother trying?

By the time she got to middle school, her brothers had already established a reputation and the Holloway name was well known. Amanda had little chance of living that reputation down, no matter that she had done nothing to earn it. Even the teachers didn't hide their disdain for her family, and that meant Amanda as well. One teacher told her straight to her face that she'd amount to nothing. And though it had pissed her off, Amanda couldn't help but fear the woman might be right.

A shoe scuffed behind her.

"Where ya goin'?" called one of the boys.

Amanda jerked her head up, becoming aware of their presence. She spun around instinctively, but wished she hadn't. It would've been better to ignore them, she thought. It was two high school boys. She didn't recognize either of them. They were following her. Her heart began to race. Her fingers tightened around her schoolbooks.

"Hey, Holloway girl! Where ya off to in such a hurry?" said the lanky one. He was wearing a John Deere baseball cap and a white *Alabama* t-shirt with the sleeves cut off. A long-sleeve flannel was tied around the top of his jeans.

"Yeah, c'mon now," said the other boy. He was thicker with a round face. Perhaps the younger of the two. His hair was spiked on top and long in the back, and he was dressed in a plain black t-shirt and jeans. "We only wanna talk to ya."

Amanda kept walking, her eyes on the ground. She picked up her pace and clutched her books even tighter, her sweaty palms slick against the covers. She didn't know if she should respond or not. The boys continued to call after her. Giving in, she called back, choosing her words with care: "I gotta be gettin' home. My mama's waitin' on me."

Maybe that would be enough. Maybe they would stop following

her and leave her alone, knowing that someone was expecting her. But that hope evaporated with every footstep on the pavement behind her, every whisper. She didn't turn around again, afraid that any glance might seem too much like interest.

There were homes just on the other side of the fence. She *could* call out, *try* to catch someone's attention, but it was unlikely anyone would hear her. In the alley, she was alone with them. *Trapped.*

Then—fingers clamped around her arm, hard. They yanked her back, spinning her around. In an instant, she was face to face with the lanky boy. He was taller than she'd thought.

"Why ya actin' like a rude bitch?" he snarled. He was so close she caught the scent of cigarettes on his breath, thick and invasive.

"I ain't," she muttered, trying not to make eye contact.

"*Must* be a rude bitch if ya won't stop to talk." He sneered. "Ain't that right, Duck?"

"I think so, Donnie," the thicker boy replied. He was close behind her. She could feel him, but not see him.

"I…gotta get home." Amanda choked the words out. "I ain't meanin' to be rude."

Donnie scoffed, licking his teeth under closed lips. "Why would ya wanna go home for, Holloway? Ain't your family crazy? You oughta hang out with us instead." He reached out and dragged his fingers down her cheek. His touch was rough, clumsy—unwelcome. His hands reeked of tobacco and motor oil. Amanda suppressed a gag. She stiffened, her skin crawling, her stomach turning. His fingers clamped under her chin, pulling her closer. "I want ya to *look* at me," he demanded.

Amanda did look, eyes squinted, jaw set. Her fear was tangled up with her fury. She wanted to scream at him, to spit in his face. He had no right to keep her like this. But she did nothing. Said nothing. She thought again of calling for help, but she didn't. Calling out might only make things worse.

"Ya got pretty eyes for a retarded girl," Donnie said, chuckling. "Duck, didn't you say she was a retard?"

"Naw, I think she's just a touch dim, like the rest of her inbred family."

"Yup," Donnie said, laughing. He was still cradling her jaw in his palm. "I think you're gonna hang out here with us for a while," he said. His grip tightened until her jaw ached. Still smirking, he leaned in to kiss her.

Amanda jerked back, but Duck was still behind her, his body against hers, unyielding. He grabbed her, restraining her arms. Her schoolbooks slipped from her grasp, tumbling to the ground.

Donnie pressed his lips against hers.

Amanda drove her knee up, aiming for his groin. But he was too close. Her leg was pinned between them, *useless*. A jolt of fear ran through her.

Then—his face crashed into hers, smothering her. His mouth engulfed her mouth, lips crushing lips—hot, wet, suffocating. He forced his tongue inside. His rank breath was in her nose. Her stomach lurched. She tried to scream, but his mouth swallowed the sound.

She recoiled, twisting, but Duck was behind her—a wall of flesh, holding her tight.

Donnie's hands raced over her body—clawing, groping, fumbling, tearing at her clothes. His fingers dug into her skin—greedy and controlling.

She struggled, twisting, trying to evade him.

His tongue moved over her cheek and down her neck, and he bit her. *Hard*. A warning.

Amanda yelped. Her neck was wet under the pain. She was unsure if it was blood or only his saliva.

Then he shoved his hand down the front of her loose jeans. His rough fingers fumbled with her underwear, yanking them aside. Violating her. She writhed but had nowhere to go.

Nothing she could do.

Hot tears streaked her face. She squeezed her eyes shut and wished she would disappear.

She'd ride it out, she thought. It couldn't take long, *right?* Surely, her father's beatings had been worse. She told herself the best thing to do was keep quiet. Let it happen. Endure it. Let them finish.

Don't make them angry.

But suddenly—Donnie was gone. His hands on her skin, his body on hers, his breath on her face. All of it—ripped away in an instant.

She opened her eyes to see him on the ground in front of her, holding his nose, blood seeping between his fingers.

Another pair of hands. Grabbing her. Not to hold her down, but to pull her free. Her head was spinning. Her knees went weak. She stumbled forward, almost tripping over Donnie's legs.

When she turned, there he was.

Her brother. Travis.

His left hand was wrapped up in the collar of Duck's black tee, and his right was pulled back behind him. In a quick motion, his fist cracked against Duck's face. There was a sharp crunch. Then another punch. Harder. Meaner. Duck crumpled, landing hard on his tailbone in a heap. He sat on the ground, dazed, legs splayed in front of him, his chin already streaked with blood.

Donnie was on his hands and knees, trying to stand. When Travis noticed, he moved fast. He turned his body to Donnie, wound up, and kicked him in the face. Donnie's head snapped back and his body went limp as it hit the ground, landing on its side with a thud. Travis reared back and kicked him again, driving his foot into Donnie's ribs. Donnie's body shook from the impact, but otherwise remained motionless. His eyes were closed, and a small pool of blood was gathering near his injured mouth.

Amanda watched the shocking violence, but it seemed far away, like something out of a movie. She was detached from it, unable to process.

Travis waited, his breathing normal, his fists still curled and ready. He was almost eager for Donnie to move again, but the boy was unconscious. Travis turned back to Duck. He was still on the ground, sitting upright, though he'd slumped like a marionette whose strings had been cut.

"You want more?" Travis shouted.

Duck shook his head, moving slowly. He placed a hand on his mouth. When he pulled it away, it was covered in blood. His tongue ran over his teeth.

"Didn't think so," Travis huffed. He walked over to where Donnie lay unconscious on the ground and leaned over him. "You don't *fuck* with the Holloways, shitbird!" he bellowed, spittle flying. He reached down over Donnie's bloodied face, snatched his baseball cap, and put it on. "This here's mine now."

Amanda hated the violence, but she was relieved seeing the two boys on the ground.

For the first time, Amanda understood what it was like to have a big brother. To have family on her side. She glanced at the two boys on the ground, her relief intertwined with pride and disgust. She wasn't sure what any of it meant.

As Travis turned back to her, his demeanor shifted. The tension in his body disappeared, as if he hadn't just beaten two other people bloody. As if he hadn't saved Amanda from their assault. From whatever *else* they might have had planned.

No reflection. No remorse. Moving on with the day.

Then, with barely a glance in her direction, he said, "Come on, Sissy. Need ya for somethin'."

And that was it.

Without waiting for her, he began to walk away.

For a moment, Amanda stood frozen. Confused. Her jaw was sore. Her skin felt grimy. She needed a moment. To catch up. To make sense of what had happened. To try and understand. But her brother was already getting further away. So, with shaking hands, she bent down and gathered her schoolbooks.

Then she turned and followed.

———

Travis and Amanda walked along in silence. Amanda struggled to keep up with her brother's pace.

Her legs were weak, her hands still shaking.

She was glad that Travis had arrived when he did. The two of them were family, but they'd never been friends. Even on their best days, their relationship had been tenuous. She did her best to avoid him for fear of his volatility, and now she was strangely grateful for it.

She wanted to say something—to *thank him?*

But Travis wasn't behaving like anything was wrong. He wasn't waiting for her to catch up. He wasn't even looking at her. Just walking, and humming. Like nothing had happened.

Amanda didn't know where they were going. She wished they were headed home where she could shower and crawl into bed, but she didn't protest. She figured she owed him for saving her from those boys, whether he thought it was a big deal or not.

Soon, they arrived at a house she didn't recognize. Travis walked through the yard and straight into the back, where an old trailer was parked, nestled among a small group of trees.

Amanda glanced around, anxious. What if the homeowner spotted them? Or what if they had a dog? She was on edge. She didn't want to be here.

"Don't be squirrely," Travis muttered. "It's Wade's house. We're alright."

She didn't know Wade, but she knew his name. He was one of her brother's friends.

The trailer was decent size, rounded at the back. It was two-tone, red along the bottom and white on top. Both colors were scuffed and faded. It had a single door and two windows, one at the front and a cracked one at the rear that was covered from the inside by ripped cardboard and cereal boxes.

It was clear the trailer had been sitting in that spot a long time. The tires were flat and half-buried in dried mud. The trailer hitch— propped on a jack resting on a plank of wood—was rusted over.

Travis squatted near the trailer's tire, pointing underneath with his thumb. "I need ya to crawl under this thing and fetch somethin' for me."

"What is it?" Amanda asked, holding her books against her chest. She eyed the cobwebs stretched between the trailer and the tire.

"Don't matter what," Travis said.

Amanda winced. She didn't want to do this.

Weeds had grown up under the trailer. The metal along the bottom edge hung low, looking sharp and jagged in places. Spiders and other bugs had likely made their home underneath—and who knows what else.

"Can't *you* do it?" she asked.

Travis sighed. "D'you reckon I'd waste my damn time comin' to find you if I could?"

Ah, so that was it. That was why he'd been in the alley. Not to save her. Not because he was looking out for her. Because he needed her. For *this*.

"Don't it move?" Amanda asked, looking up at the trailer.

"Naw, this beast don't budge," Travis chuckled. "C'mon now, get a move on. Won't take but a minute. In and out, lickety-split."

Amanda sighed. This was probably the last thing she wanted to do right now. But she set her books on the ground and moved closer to the trailer, crouching down.

It was dark. Where the trailer was parked, amongst the trees, almost no light reached the underside.

"What am I lookin' for?" she asked.

"Baggie," he said.

She looked up at him, scowling. "A baggie? Like…*drugs*?"

"Hell, does it matter? Ain't none of your business anyway. Just get under and find it. That'll be that."

She took a deep breath and moved a bit closer, sizing up the narrow space between the trailer and the ground, trying to decide how to go about it. Did she have to get down on her stomach? In the dirt? She couldn't think of another way. "I don't even see it. Where is it?"

"I dunno. I threw it in here by the tire."

She glanced under, squinting. "Why'd you throw it down here?"

"Jesus! How many questions ya got?" Travis snapped. Then he softened. "I was out here…uh, with Wade, when a sheriff pulled up in the driveway. Wade and I 'bout shit ourselves." He chuckled. "Turns out, cop was only here to talk to Wade's daddy about somethin' or other. Now ya know. Happy? Can you just fuckin' do it already?"

Amanda realized she couldn't stall any longer, not without making Travis angry. As much as she didn't want to, she got down on her stomach and began to shimmy under.

She sniffed. *Gasoline.* She wondered if the trailer was leaking it. And if it was safe for her to breathe.

Cobwebs brushed her face, clinging to her hair. Though she didn't mind spiders, she didn't want them *on* her either. She tried not to think about it.

She hadn't gotten a foot under the trailer when she understood why Travis had come to find her—there was *no way* he would've fit. It was tight, even for her small frame.

Amanda tried to glance up, hoping to spot the baggie, but the back of her head banged against the underside of the trailer hard. She winced, and wondered if she might be bleeding. But she couldn't maneuver her arms enough to check. She tried to look up again—taking more care this time—and thought she spotted it ahead of her, only a bit further in.

She tried not to think about how tight it was. How the space felt like it was getting smaller, closing in on her. How her arms were pinned. Thinking about it made her anxious. How would she back out?

Her breathing was shallow.

The sense of being constricted made her think about before. Being held against her will. Pinned. Stuck. A boy's mouth covering hers, stinking of cigarettes and halitosis, his tongue forcing its way into her mouth, his hands on her body, touching her in places she didn't want to be touched. She thought about wanting to scream, and not feeling like she could.

Her pulse began to throb in her neck and jaw.

In that moment, she wanted out. *Needed* out.

Amanda took a deep breath and focused.

Find the baggie first.

Whatever was happening inside of her—this new panic, this mounting anxiety—was something she could ride out, just as she had before.

She pulled herself forward a few more inches and began reaching out into the weeds, searching blindly.

A drop of liquid hit her cheek and rolled down toward her mouth. She shuddered. She didn't want to think about what it might be. But it stunk, as if it was rotten.

Her fingertips grazed something. She strained to reach further, praying she wouldn't have to go any deeper.

Another drop of something hit her neck.

Need to go.

And then—*yes!*—there was *something.* Not grass. Not dirt. Something artificial. Plastic. She stretched and clawed at it with the tips of her fingers, pulling it closer, bit by bit, until she was able to wrap her hand around it.

"I think I got it!" she called out.

Travis answered, his voice muffled as if calling from far away, "Ya *think?*"

"I can't *see* under here! C'mon…*please* pull me out!"

A long pause.

"Please!" she called again. "I need your help!"

In the darkness, the trailer creaked above her.

She started to panic. She wanted to cry out. *Why wasn't she moving? Why wasn't he helping?*

"Travis?"

Still nothing. Was he still there? Or had he gone away? Abandoned her?

She tried to back out by herself, but she couldn't. It was too tight. She was stuck. A bead of sweat rolled down her temple.

The moment stretched on for an eternity.

In silence. Unable to move.

Maybe she'd be stuck under the trailer forever.

Then—his hands were around her ankles. As she started sliding backward, she said a little prayer and held her breath.

Thank God. Almost out.

A piece of jagged metal on the trailer began to dig into her thigh through her jeans.

"Slower!" she shouted. "Pull me straight back!"

Almost, she told herself. *Almost out.*

She prayed she really *had* located the baggie. She didn't want to do this again. *Not now. Not ever.*

Amanda breathed a sigh of relief when she saw daylight, as if a weight had been removed. As she emerged, she gasped, taking fresh air into her lungs, gulping it down. She was thankful to see the baggie clenched in her hand.

As soon as she was able, she scrambled to her feet. The front of her clothes was a mess. She touched her head. There was blood on her fingertips.

"Give it," Travis said, holding out his hand.

She started to hand it over, but hesitated. A strange urgency had come into Travis's eyes—like nothing mattered except for the damn baggie.

He snatched it from her and stuffed it into his back pocket. He pointed at her face and said, "You got something on your cheek."

Of course. Whatever filth had dripped onto her skin. She wiped at her face with her sleeve, and grimaced when she saw the greenish brown stain it left behind.

When she looked up, Travis was already gone.

———

As Amanda approached the front door of her house, raised voices were coming from inside. It sounded like her father and Travis were arguing. Yelling. But she couldn't make out the words.

For a moment, she considered turning around and walking in the other direction, finding somewhere else to be until things settled down —the creek, the market, *anywhere* but here. But depending on her father's mood, coming in late might only make things worse for her.

Instead, she slipped in the front door quietly, ducked around the corner into the hall, and snuck into her room, closing the door almost all the way, just shy of it clicking.

She listened in as they argued, her anxiety rising.

Why was there always so much fighting?

"This ain't nothin' new, Travis!" her father shouted. "You know the rules! Ain't no drugs in this house!"

"Well, that's fine, 'cause I don't got any!" Travis yelled back, matching his father's volume and intensity.

"Don't you lie to me! I talked to Wade Guthrie's daddy!"

"So?"

"He caught Wade with pot, and Wade said he got it from you!"

"I already told you, I ain't got no *damn drugs!*"

"Turn out your pockets and show me."

There was a long silence. A dangerous silence. Amanda held her breath. She imagined what Travis was thinking—could he talk his way out of this, or was it already too late?

Then he shouted, "To hell with this! I'm outta here!"

"Where d'ya think you're goin'? We ain't done talkin'!"

There was the sound of a scuffle.

Amanda's mounting anxiety surged into full-blown panic. She pulled the door open a bit more and peeked out into the living room.

Her father and Travis were grappling, her father's hands twisting in the collar of Travis's t-shirt, stretching it out of shape. Travis was shoving him back, one hand on her father's arm, the other on his face.

"Get off me!" Travis yelled, breaking free and raising his fists. "You don't give a shit 'bout nothin' 'round here 'cept ridin' my ass!"

"This is my house, goddammit!" her father yelled back, jabbing a finger at Travis. "You best show me some goddamn respect if you're livin' here! I ain't gonna have no damn drug addict under my roof!"

"Well, I guess ya best talk to Mama!" Travis snapped.

Amanda winced. This was not going to end well.

A tense silence followed as Travis's words hung in the air. Without warning, her father lunged forward and took a swing. He cursed, but the word was swallowed by his rage. His fist connected with Travis's jaw, and Travis's head snapped to the side. Travis swung back in a wide arc, his fist wrapping around her father's head, hitting him in the ear.

For a moment, the living room became a blur of flailing limbs.

No more words. Only the raw sound of a struggle—labored grunts, the thud of fists meeting flesh, a gasp of pain, the squeak of shoes sliding on wooden floors.

Travis pushed her father back hard.

Her father stumbled, tripping over his own feet, and went crashing into the credenza. Pictures tumbled, and one hit the floor. The frame cracked, and glass shattered.

"Ya don't put your hands on me *no more!*" Travis spat, his voice shaking with rage. "Or I'll kill you, old man. I swear to God."

He turned and stormed from the house, slamming the front door behind him.

Amanda slipped back into her room. She climbed onto her bed, crawled under the covers, and clutched a pillow, waiting—*hoping*—that the violence was over. That her father's temper had run out of steam.

She was dirty, both from being underneath the trailer and from what the boys had done to her.

The scent of Donnie's breath lingered in her memory. The roughness of his hands against her skin. The pressure of his oppressive mouth. She touched her neck, remembering that he'd bitten her, wondering if he'd broken the skin, left a mark.

She pulled back the mattress, retrieved her journal from its hiding place, and began to write about the day, attempting to process everything she was feeling.

She didn't know about Travis. She'd gone from being grateful to him for rescuing her to despising him for using her. Now—thinking about how little he understood himself, how volatile he was, how desperate he'd been to snatch the baggie from her—she felt a combination of pity…and *fear*. He wasn't just acting out. He wasn't only a confused teenager. He was lost. He was angry. And he was *dangerous*. And sooner or later, he was going to make someone suffer.

CHAPTER 20

SHANE

Mandy's night had been restless. At first, she'd been lying awake, listening to the sounds of the house and the world outside, wishing for sleep. But when she'd nodded off, she'd had nightmares again.

Storms. Violence. Travis. *Childhood.*

She'd awakened before the others, only to discover that her bare feet were dirty, caked with dried mud. The only explanation she could think of was that she'd been sleepwalking again. She'd gotten up quietly and cleaned herself before anyone else could see. She didn't want to worry any of them, but most of all Chris. He was already doing plenty of that.

Now she sat at the dining table, coffee cup in hand, staring out the back door, which stood open except for the screen.

The nightmares weren't new, but they'd intensified since she'd returned.

Dreaming of Rosebury had never stopped for Mandy. Not in college. Or California. They'd continued after she met Chris. And after the birth of her children.

Not every night, but often enough.

Some of them had been actual memories, played out in her mind's eye. But most had been hazy. Scattered recollections without much form. Feeling afraid. Being pursued. The sense of being trapped within the house. Powerless to escape.

Now, her dreams were intense again. Vivid. And *haunting*.

Being away from Rosebury had been like being away from the source of a transmission. She still picked up the signal on occasion, but it had been weak, garbled, buried beneath static. Being back meant the transmission was once again strong, intense, and horrifyingly clear.

The last four days had been a whirlwind—both mentally and emotionally. She'd returned to town assuming her parents had died of natural causes. She'd been shaken by the possibility that their deaths actually could've been some sort of ghastly murder-suicide, an idea she didn't want to believe. And now—after a brief run-in with Bo Harper at the market—another unsettling possibility had surfaced. That somehow, Travis might have had a hand in it.

Mandy couldn't stop thinking about it. The thought tormented her. Perhaps it was because she didn't want the other possibility to be true. Or perhaps it was because she still had so much contempt for Travis—it was easy to believe the worst of him because the worst was all he'd ever shown her.

As she took another sip of her coffee, she watched Grace trot up the back porch steps. She was carrying a moving box labeled "MAST. BED." The box was so big in her arms it was almost comical, but Grace was carrying it without any effort. Mandy assumed it must be the bedding.

With the kids' help, Chris had begun moving their things from the storage unit into their bedroom. Though working around furniture might make repairs a bit more difficult, they both agreed that continuing to sleep in tents was not tenable. They couldn't keep starting the day stiff and sore.

Mandy felt almost hungover from the uneven sleep.

She wanted a cigarette.

You know damn well Travis coulda done it. He ain't never cared 'bout nobody but his own damn self.

"But why?" Mandy asked herself, under her breath.

Do ya need a reason? He might've thought he'd get the house. Or he was sick to death of Mama and her crazy. Or maybe they just went at it one time too many.

This wasn't blind rage, Mandy thought. *It was cold. Deliberate.*

And who's to say it can't be both?

Mandy pondered it, sipping her drink, hoping the caffeine might jolt her awake. Get her moving.

Ethan followed behind Grace up the steps, carrying a box that looked much heavier. Then Chris, carrying pieces of their bed frame. He smiled at her, but she thought she glimpsed disappointment in his eyes.

She should be helping, but she was numb. Glazed over. Zombie-like.

You know who might have somethin' to say 'bout it?

"*Not* Travis," Mandy whispered, making sure Chris was out of earshot.

Nah, not him. Somebody else.

She sighed.

Shane lived less than an hour away, but Mandy hadn't told him she was back in town. She hadn't even told him she was planning to come home. They'd spoken on the phone a few minutes the day she'd learned about her parents' deaths, and again when he called to ask if she wanted to be included in the funeral—such as it was. She'd told him no.

Go visit him. Listen to what he says. Go in person. Ask him questions and see how he reacts. You know him. You can tell if he's bein' truthful.

"I need to be *here*," she insisted, trying to convince herself.

Mandy eyed the dirty lockbox, still sitting on the dining room table. She'd been too tired to read any more of her mother's diary last night. She was eager to return to it, but anxious about what she might discover.

Helping Chris with the house *needed* to be her top priority. She *knew that*. She needed to keep reminding herself. Why did it seem to be falling further and further down her list?

'Cause ya got an itch to scratch. Ain't no way you're lettin' it be 'til you get yourself some answers.

Mandy did her best to shake off the distracting thoughts, determined to be of use. She downed her coffee and got to work helping.

She assembled the bed frame while Chris brought in the nightstands. Together, they moved their box spring and mattress into the bedroom, struggling to maneuver them down the narrow hall and through the doorway. Mandy's parents' bed had been full size, so the bedroom felt quite a bit smaller with their queen-sized bed in place.

She'd missed this bed.

When Mandy pulled the sheets from the box, they were a bit musty from their trip cross-country, so she shook them and aired them before she put them on the bed. She wished she had a way to wash them, but the laundry was off limits until the basement was clear.

The basement.

Mandy's stomach soured at the thought of going down there. But she'd deal with it when the time came.

After that, they carried in a dresser. That meant they wouldn't have to live out of suitcases anymore, which was a relief. Between that and her bed, Mandy almost found herself looking forward to sleeping in the house that night.

Almost.

They completed setting up the primary bedroom before noon.

No sooner had they finished than there was a knock on the front door. It was Ethan's new friend Chase asking if Ethan could hang out for a while. Mandy saw it as a good opportunity to propose a break. Chris was hesitant to lose momentum—and perhaps a bit irked by the suggestion—but he agreed to it.

Ethan went with Chase. Grace wasn't invited this time.

"While we're stopped...I think I might drive over and visit my brother, Shane, for a bit," Mandy said. She made it sound casual and not premeditated. "I haven't seen him in a few years. I thought I should say hi, since I'm back."

"You wanna go *right now?*" Chris asked, looking at the time on his phone.

"I won't be gone long."

Chris sighed, not bothering to hide his frustration. "We finally get going again and now everybody wants to stop."

"I can help you, Daddy," Grace offered.

Chris smiled at her. "Thanks, sweetie." He thought about it for a moment.

Mandy fidgeted with the hem of her t-shirt.

"I *could* use some help with the electrical," Chris said.

"That sounds dangerous," Mandy said.

Chris exhaled, making no effort to hide his annoyance. "Do you *really* think I'd put her in danger, Mandy? I'm only going to have her tell me when lights come on or off over the walkie-talkie." He turned to Grace. "You up for that?"

"Okey dokey."

Mandy grabbed her keys.

Best git while the gittin' is good.

ETHAN WALKED ALONGSIDE CHASE, who let out a hearty laugh about something. Ethan still wasn't used to his accent and hadn't quite caught what he'd said, but chuckled anyway.

Chase glanced back at Ethan with a grin. "So, what's better —Tennessee or Cali?"

Ethan shrugged. "It's just...*different* here. Nothing wrong with it, but I lived in California my whole life."

"Yeah, well, we ain't got beaches. And no yoga, or whatever else y'all got out there." Chase laughed again. "Ain't got no celebrities, neither. 'Less you count the time Daddy swears he met Conway Twitty."

"Who's...Conway Twitty?" Ethan asked.

Chase shrugged. "Country singer. From back when my Daddy was young."

"I'm not really into country music," Ethan said.

Chase chuckled. "Well, you're probably gonna hate it here."

"Awesome. So, where we goin'?"

"Wade's. Couple of guys hangin' out."

"Who's Wade?"

"'Nother kid. Lives nearby."

They turned off the road onto an overgrown path that ran between a few of the houses—a shortcut. When they arrived at Wade's a few minutes later, Chase bypassed the house and headed to the back. With some hesitation, Ethan followed. He wasn't accustomed to walking into people's yards.

Behind the house, a few kids were hanging out in a standalone two-car garage. An older, nondescript white pickup truck was parked on one side. The other side was lined with tool chests. On the back wall, more tools hung on a pegboard next to a large confederate flag.

Ethan thought the boys looked older than him and Chase.

A skinny, pale blond kid in a red Ford shirt sat on the truck's tailgate.

Two other boys sat in blue fold-out camping chairs, a small cooler in between them. Each held a can. Ethan wondered if it was beer.

The dark-haired, freckled kid wore a white t-shirt with an eagle on it.

Ethan recognized the other boy by his lop-sided, messy looking haircut—it was the kid he and Grace had run into down by the abandoned school bus. He didn't look quite as dirty today, but his clothes were still shabby—if the holey jeans and sleeveless flannel weren't the same ones from the other day, they were damn close.

Chase introduced Ethan to everyone as the new kid. He mentioned that Ethan was living in Travis Holloway's place, and the boys all exchanged looks and nodded.

Wade, the dark-haired boy, let out an "Ahhh."

The skinny, blond kid was Wade's cousin J.J.

The other boy—whom Ethan encountered in the grove—was Hunter.

Ethan nodded in their direction, and they all nodded back.

Hunter studied Ethan a moment before saying, "Wait—I seen this guy before."

"Oh yeah?" Chase said. "Where?"

"Back behind Travis's place," Hunter said. "With his lil sister."

"You were back behind Travis's place with his sister, huh?" Wade joked, and the others laughed in approval and whistled.

Ethan tensed. "Well, she's nine, so…" He shrugged.

Hunter snorted. "Yeah…for *now*. Won't be long though."

Ethan's cheeks went hot. He knew he was being baited and it was best to let it go. But he didn't want to. He tried to think of a comeback, but he was never that quick on his feet under pressure. After a long pause, all he could come up with was: "If you're…into little girls, I guess."

Hunter gave a dry laugh, still eyeing him. "Y'know what they say —if there's grass on the field, play ball!"

The boys erupted in raucous laughter.

Wade added, "Old 'nough to sit at the table, old 'nough to eat."

Then Chase chimed in, saying, "If she's old 'nough to bleed, she's old 'nough to breed."

Ethan was disappointed Chase had joined in. He did his best to keep a neutral expression, but a frown slipped through. He wasn't sure if Hunter had spotted it.

J.J. piped up: "If she can buy her own ticket, she's ready to ride."

Again, laughter.

"Yeah," Ethan said, forcing a chuckle, "but she's…*just a kid* right now."

Hunter leaned forward in his camping chair. "Hey now, don't get your panties all bunched up, man. We're only fuckin' around." He took a sip from his can. "Where'd y'all move from?"

"California." Chase answered before Ethan.

"Ahh." Hunter grinned. The boys snickered. "Well, that tracks. Cain't be soft if yer gonna make it in Rosebury."

"Yeah, alright," Ethan said. "Sure."

"Y'all want a beer?" Wade asked, opening the cooler next to his chair.

Chase took one, but Ethan waved it off. "Nah, I need to help my dad with the house today. He'd kill me if he smelled beer on my breath." He wondered why he hadn't just said he didn't want one. That he wasn't interested.

"So, you're fixin' up Travis's place?" Hunter asked.

"I guess so," Ethan said. "Didn't know the guy."

"Hmm," Hunter said, nodding. "He could hold his own."

"Well, he sure was a shitty housekeeper," Ethan said.

J.J. hopped down from the tailgate of the truck, grabbed a beer from the cooler, and smirked. "Prob'ly too busy fuckin', I bet."

Hunter and J.J. bumped fists, and the boys laughed again.

Ethan glanced at Chase. He was laughing right along with them. Ethan tried to picture his dad laughing like this with *his* friends. Being crude. Making jokes about women. *Girls.* He couldn't.

He didn't think this was his idea of fun. Didn't know if he was going to fit in here. Or if he wanted to. Perhaps he'd meet *other* kids his age, ones he could better relate to. *Perhaps.*

In an obvious gesture, he glanced at his watch, and said, "Well, I gotta get back and help my dad, but good meeting... uh, *y'all.*"

"We just got here," Chase said, popping the tab on his can.

"You stay," Ethan said. "I can find my way back."

As Ethan turned to walk away, Hunter said, "Tell your lil' sis I said hey."

Ethan glanced back over his shoulder, making sure that Hunter saw that it didn't bother him. "Sure...if she even remembers who ya are." He felt sort of good about that one. And if it *wasn't* great, at least it was quick.

Hunter narrowed his eyes, then nodded like he didn't care either way.

Ethan didn't know if Hunter was mature for his age or if he was older than the rest of them. But he didn't like him. And he didn't want to be around him.

As he walked away, the boys murmured behind him and laughed. Ethan couldn't make out what they had said.

———

MANDY CONSIDERED CALLING AHEAD but decided not to. Instead, she found an address she'd saved from a Christmas card, plugged it into her car's navigation, and drove the forty-nine minutes, hoping for the best.

When she arrived at the house she thought was her brother's, she stopped the car in front and let it idle. Her stomach twisted, and for a moment, she considered driving back to Rosebury, abandoning the idea altogether.

But then, with a determined breath, she switched off the engine, pushed her way out of the car, and walked up to the front door, taking long and purposeful steps.

He ain't gonna wanna see you. Ain't no one wants you back here, Amanda Jean.

She rapped on the front door with her knuckles and waited.

After a moment, the door opened, and her brother appeared from within. His face was rounder than when she'd last seen him. His hair was darker and there was less of it than she remembered; what remained was hidden under a red baseball cap. The dark stubble on his chin was flecked with white. His UT Volunteers shirt, once bright orange, was now a faded pumpkin color, the screen-printed logo worn and cracked.

He smiled, and she was reminded how much he looked like their mother. And how much Ethan looked like them both.

"Lil Bit?" he said. He smiled. "What're ya doin' here? Come on in."

Mandy followed him inside. She stopped in the entryway as he went to turn off the television in the other room, where the news was blaring. His home was small but clean. She was glad to see that.

A crucifix hung by the door, beside a placard that read "Bless This Mess."

She scanned the entry table. A bowl of loose change. A pocketknife. And two framed photographs: one of Shane and his ex-wife with their children, and another of Shane on a boat holding up a big fish.

On a coat rack nearby was an orange vest and a hard hat.

After muting the television, Shane invited her into the kitchen. She noticed his limp as he moved down the hall. She took a seat at the table, and he offered her a beverage.

"Nah, I'm alright. I had a Coke on the way up. Hey, why you limpin'? You okay?"

Shane pulled out a chair from the table and sat down, kicking his leg out in front of him, then smacking his thigh with his palm. "Stepped wrong comin' offa ladder. Broke my foot. Damn thing just ain't never healed right. Which reminds me," he said, reaching for a small wooden box in the middle of the table and a book of matches nearby. "Time for my medicine." He opened the lid of the box and pulled out a half-smoked joint. He struck a match, lit it, and inhaled. He took the smoke deep into his lungs and held it. As he did, he extended his hand, offering the joint to Mandy. "You want some?" he sputtered.

"No thanks," she replied. "But I'll take a ciggy if you got one."

Shane exhaled. He reached into his back pocket and retrieved a half-empty pack of USA Golds. He tossed it on the table in front of her and pulled the ashtray between them.

"Thought you quit," he said.

Mandy lit the cigarette, nodding. "I quit a lotta things."

She tossed the matchbook back on the table next to the ashtray and paused to examine it. The cover advertised the *Red Rooster Tavern*, a dive bar that had been in town since she was a girl. Leaning against the bar's logo was a cartoon rooster. He was wearing sunglasses and drinking from a beer stein. Something about it—the logo, the mascot—had always bothered her. She'd found the rooster unsettling. Though he appeared like something from a child's cartoon, something about him was too adult. The sly smile on his face. The beer in his hand.

It reminded her of…*something*.

It made her skin crawl. A small wave of nausea swept through her.

She ignored it and turned her attention back to her brother.

They exchanged pleasantries for a few minutes. Shane asked about her relationship and her kids. Mandy answered in the vague manner he expected and asked about his kids in return. It was the sort of small talk that she tried to avoid, but today she was grateful for any excuse to delay the *real* conversation. And she *was* pleased to hear that Shane was doing well.

"I see Sharon's still in the picture by the door. How's that going? Y'all gettin' along?" she asked.

"Aw, hell, who knows," he laughed. "Reckon she's been 'round more since we split than when we was married. I love her. But she gets on my last nerve."

Mandy told him about how she and Chris had found themselves out of work, and about their plan to fix up the house and sell it. She also told him about the horrible condition they'd found it in, and how she was worried they'd bitten off more than they could chew. She decided to leave out the other things—the whispers, the visions, the dreams…seeing the little girl. No reason to bring it up if it wasn't necessary.

"Travis did a number on the place, huh?" Shane asked, shaking his head.

"That's kind of an understatement."

"Don't surprise me none," he said. "Might've been desperate for a fix at the time. He'd been livin' off Mama and Daddy for…oh, a while."

"He still messin' with that junk?"

Shane nodded. "He's been strugglin', that's for sure."

"Figures he was still livin' with them. Mama never could say no to him."

"That's the truth," he said. "Never had a problem tellin' *me* no. *Or you*, neither."

Mandy took another drag and let her shoulders relax. It had been a long time since she'd talked like this, with someone who understood. But now that they'd brought up Travis, she couldn't avoid the reason she'd come. "Shane, what d'ya know 'bout the night they died?"

"Not much. I wasn't there. Why ya askin'?"

She took a drag of her cigarette, contemplating how to phrase the question. "I guess… I'm hearin' it might not've been entirely…*natural*. Their deaths, I mean. I heard it might've been Mama did it."

She studied his face for any reaction, but there wasn't any.

"Yep," he said, giving a small nod. "Heard that, too."

"You didn't say anything to me. What do you think about it?"

He chuckled and looked her in the eye, a smirk in his expression. "Bit, I gave up bein' surprised by anything to do with our family a long, long time ago."

"Yeah, I 'spose so."

"Mama was like she *always* was. We're talkin' 'bout the same woman who buried Daddy's boots in the yard to cast some kinda 'witchy' spell, make sure he wasn't messin' 'round on her."

"I remember that." She smiled, but she didn't know if it was actually a good memory, or if enough time had passed to soften its edges. She didn't remember thinking it was amusing at the time.

"She wasn't right, Bit. Never was. And I reckon she didn't much care to be. She held on to her *crazy* same as Daddy held on to his *mean*. Do you remember how he used to scare the neighbor kids off the property with that shotgun?"

"I do. He was a scary sonuvabitch." Mandy took another drag. "Do you think it's possible… Lord, how do I ask this…"

"Do I think Travis had a hand in it?"

The quickness of his response took her by surprise. "Yeah."

He shook his head, exhaling smoke. "I caught that one floatin' 'round too. And I ain't got no idea. On one hand, we both know Travis. His temper. His mood swings. On the other, folks've said plenty of shit 'bout the both of us, and most of it ain't never been true. So, why you here askin' *me* about *him*?"

"The two of us…we don't talk. Ain't much to say anymore."

"Well, if folks was sayin' stuff 'bout me, and you was thinkin' 'bout believin' it, I reckon I'd wanna hear it from you straight."

"Yeah," she said. "Yeah, I 'spose you're right. I just don't think I wanna…see him."

"Well, I reckon I understand *that* better'n most," Shane said, coughing into his fist. He got up, hobbled over to the kitchen counter, and rummaged in a drawer, pulling out a pen and paper. He opened his phone and squinted at it, then jotted something down on the page. "If you change your mind, here's where he is. Or *was*, last I knew. Reckon he's still there."

He returned to the table and sat again, handing her the paper. Mandy took it and folded it in half. "Maybe."

Shane leaned in, his expression intense and unreadable in a way that reminded Mandy of their father. "You gotta remember somethin'," he said.

"Yeah?"

"It mighta seemed like Travis got all Mama's soft spots, but maybe she knew somethin' you didn't."

"Which was?"

"That he was never gonna be strong as you."

Mandy hesitated, unsure of what to say. She didn't know what she expected from Shane, but it wasn't that.

He continued looking at her. "Mind if I ask ya somethin?"

She nodded.

"Why do ya *care* what happened?"

Mandy blinked, caught off guard. At first, she was confused—even offended—by the question. "They're our *parents*, Shane."

"Sure they are. And ya left 'em behind some time ago. And I ain't sayin' you were wrong for goin'. And I ain't sayin' you were wrong for *stayin'* gone. But it does make me wonder why any of it matters to ya now."

Mandy considered the question, struggling to come up with an answer, but none came. She deflected. "Hell, you got out as fast as I did. *Faster.* Soon as you could go, all we saw was *taillights.*"

"And you feel some kinda way 'bout that?"

She considered it. "No. Shit...no, I don't. I understood why you left. Still do."

"I hope so," Shane said, then added, "Can I ask something else?"

"Go on."

"Why d'ya reckon Mama and Daddy left you the house?"

Mandy huffed. "Lord, I have no idea. I've asked myself that more times than you can imagine. I can't make sense of it. There was no note, no explanation."

He smiled. "*Musta* been a reason."

"And what reason is that?"

"Hell if I know," he said, raising his eyebrows and chuckling. "But they got you back home, didn't they? Shit...maybe that's all it was."

"Maybe."

"Or there's more to it." His tone turned solemn. "Reckon that's somethin' you'll have to figure out for yourself."

Mandy nodded, stubbing out her cigarette. "Well, I best be headin' back."

"Alright, then," he said, standing up to walk her out.

"Thanks for seein' me without warnin'."

"You look good, Lil Bit. It was real nice seein' you."

Mandy drove home in silence with the windows down, a warm wind hitting her face. She thought of Travis—the one she'd feared at times, the one she'd loathed at times, the one she'd walked on eggshells around, careful not to do anything that might set him off. And Shane's words kept circling in her mind: *he was never gonna be strong as you.*

CHAPTER 21
THE SLEEPOVER, 1992

"WHAT IS THAT?" CHERYL ASKED.

"It's a Ouija board, duh," Amanda said, placing the box on the bed between them. "Ain't ya ever played with a Ouija board before?"

Cheryl shook her head and frowned, continuing to brush her hair. "Ain't that supposed to be, like…evil? You know, sorta…against God?"

Amanda rolled her eyes. "They sell it at K-Mart, don't they? They wouldn't be sellin' *evil* at K-Mart. My mama brought it home. It's for talkin' to ghosts."

"Yeah, well…that *definitely* sounds evil. I don't think I wanna mess 'round with that."

Amanda sighed, her disappointment unmistakable. "Well, what else are we gonna do? We gotta keep busy if we're gonna stay up 'til midnight."

Cheryl shrugged. "We could listen to music."

"Travis don't want us messin' 'round in his room," she said, hoping Cheryl wouldn't ask about Shane's room. She might not understand that she didn't go in there. She let out a quiet breath when Cheryl moved off the subject.

"I brought my mama's VHS of *The Goonies*," Cheryl said. "Wanna watch that?"

"My daddy is already watchin' the TV."

Cheryl frowned. "We could prank-call someone. We could tell Sheila Dean she won a radio contest. I *hate* that girl. She's so *mean*."

Amanda shook her head. "Can't be on the phone. Railroad might call for Daddy. 'Sides, ain't there that thing where folks can call back now?"

"Uh…we could do makeovers," Cheryl said, getting up from the bed to rummage through her backpack. She produced a few cosmetics. "I can do your makeup. Your hair. We can get dressed up."

Amanda scrunched up her face. "We're already in PJs. 'Sides, my folks would throw a fit if they caught me wearin' makeup."

"Well, *you* think of somethin'!" Cheryl huffed, throwing up her hands.

"We can tell ghost stories. Or play Bloody Mary. Or—"

"Those're even *worse!*" Cheryl interrupted, looking horrified. "Ain't you got any *other* board games we can play?"

Amanda thought about it. "No, not really. We used to have *Uno*, but it's gone missin'. Got *Operation*, but it don't have no tweezers. I know *Hungry Hungry Hippos* and *Candy Land* are in the basement, but those are sort of…"

"For little kids?"

"Yeah," Amanda said. They sat in silence for a moment, thinking. Amanda half-heartedly added, "I think Daddy's got some playing cards here somewhere."

Cheryl sighed. "Fine! Tell me how you play…Ooh-ee-jah?"

Amanda grinned. She considered correcting Cheryl's pronunciation but wasn't about to jeopardize her win. Instead, she jumped up from the bed and went to the dresser where she lit her candle with a match from a matchbook she kept nearby. The flame took a moment to catch, then flickered to life. Amanda flipped off the light switch by her bedroom door that controlled the lamp near her bed.

"Why does it have to be in the dark?" Cheryl asked.

"Spookier."

Cheryl groaned, hesitating before climbing onto the bed. "I'm already regrettin' sayin' yes to this."

Amanda ignored her. She pulled the Ouija board and the planchette from the box and set them on the bed.

"Okay, so here's how it goes. We sit across from each other in front of the board. And we both put our fingers on this little triangle thingy. Ya barely touch it—like this, real gentle—so it can move 'round. And we ask it questions—like 'Is anyone there?' or 'What's your name?' Stuff like that." She leaned in closer and in a hushed and excited whisper, she warned, "But you can't mess around or laugh, or it won't work. And don't ask nothin' creepy, like how you're gonna die. And if it moves, don't freak out, alright?"

"I *really* don't like this," Cheryl whined. "I'm tellin' ya right now, I might quit."

"That's fine," Amanda said, "but if ya quit, we *have to* say goodbye at the end, or the spirit can stay 'round."

"*Great.*"

"I mean it. You gotta be serious, okay?"

"*Alright, fine*, I said!"

The girls settled in, cross-legged on the bed, the board between them. Amanda put the planchette on the board and rested her fingertips on top. She glanced at Cheryl. Though she was wary, she also appeared fascinated. She placed her fingertips on the planchette as well.

"You want to go first?" Amanda asked.

Cheryl licked her lips. "Just…ask it *anything?*"

Amanda nodded.

Cheryl adjusted her hands and exhaled. "Does Jesse Rayburn think I'm cute?"

Nothing happened.

Amanda giggled.

"*You said* we had to take it *serious!*" Cheryl protested.

"Okay, okay, but…Jesse Rayburn?"

"What? He's sweet," Cheryl said. "I wanna know, okay?"

"Fine. Serious now. For real. Ask it again."

"Does Jesse Rayburn think I'm cute?" Cheryl repeated.

Still nothing.

Except for the soft droning of the box fan, the room was silent and still. Cheryl sighed and smiled, chuckling under her breath.

"Hmm. Maybe we should ask it something...*easier*," Amanda said. "Like...uh, is anyone here?"

Another long moment of waiting.

The candle flickered. And the planchette twitched.

It was almost imperceptible. But it was enough to make Cheryl gasp. Both girls held their breath and stared at the board, eyes wide.

"That was just us movin' it, right?" Cheryl asked in a whisper.

"I didn't do *nothin',*" Amanda said. "Go on, ask it somethin' else."

Cheryl nodded, her eyes uncertain. "Um...okay. Who is this?"

The planchette began to glide across the board and Cheryl made a small, unintentional noise in her throat. Slowly, it moved over the letters: "Y-L-L-I-S." The girls announced each letter as it went.

The planchette stopped.

Cheryl let out a little laugh, both from relief and perhaps a bit of disappointment. "That don't spell nothin' but nonsense."

Amanda was beginning to get frustrated. She leaned forward and repeated the question in earnest. "Who is this?"

The planchette moved over the board once more, sliding over numbers that also didn't make much sense: "1-0-0."

Cheryl rolled her eyes, relaxing. "Well, that don't help none."

"Let me try one more time." Amanda stared down at the board, her face somber. "If you are *here with us* now, *who are you?*"

There was a pause, and the planchette started to move again. Faster now. It was racing around the board, and Amanda's pulse raced with it.

It began to spell: "S-H-A-"

Cheryl fell quiet, but Amanda continued to read each letter aloud. Her fingertips began to feel sweaty against the planchette.

It continued: "D-O-W-M-A-N."

"Shadowman," Amanda whispered, a chill running up her spine.

The planchette stopped and was still again, as if waiting. Cheryl appeared anxious, but she didn't remove her hands. Amanda made eye contact, seeking her approval to continue. Cheryl nodded.

Amanda took a breath and said, "What is...a *shadowman?*"

The planchette was still a moment, then it began to slide again. It moved to the letters E, V, I, and came to a stop on the L.

"*Evil*," Cheryl whispered, her voice trembling. "I told you. I told you. I don't like this at all, 'Manda."

"Do ya wanna stop?" Amanda asked. "It just started answerin' us."

Cheryl sighed, swallowing hard. There was an audible gulp that reminded Amanda of a cartoon character. Cheryl asked, "Is the shadowman in the house with us now?"

The planchette slid again. It moved slow at first, picking up speed as it went, tracing over the letters: "F-O-R-E-V-E-R."

The air in the room turned heavy. A coldness spread over Amanda, and her pulse quickened. Her mouth had become very dry. When she spoke, her voice shook and cracked, as if the words didn't want to come out at all, "Why…are you here with us?"

"L-I-T-T-L-E-"

"Little?" Cheryl questioned.

But the planchette continued to move: "G-I-R-L."

The girls stared at each other, clearly spooked by the answer.

"Do you think we oughta stop?" Amanda asked.

"Maybe," Cheryl said, biting her lip. But without waiting, she asked, "Do you mean one of *us?*"

The planchette darted to the word "NO" at the bottom of the board.

"Then who is the little girl?" Amanda asked, her voice quieter, urgent.

The planchette slid, and the board replied: "D-E-A-D"

Cheryl's face went pale.

"I think we should stop now," Amanda said. "I think we should say goodbye."

But before they could do anything, the planchette moved again.

It circled around and landed back on the D, slid to the O, the N, and finally the T. Then it returned to the D and began to spell it all again: "D-O-N-T" The planchette continued spelling the word in repetition, faster and faster, until the board itself began to wobble on the bed.

The candle sputtered, and their shadows stretched across the bedspread and onto the wall. The girls locked eyes, the fright within them clear.

Amanda thought about lifting her hand from the planchette, but that idea frightened her too. The planchette seemed to be warning her against it: "D-O-N-T-D-O-N-T-D-O-N-T-D-O-N-T-D-O—"

Suddenly, the board lurched under their fingertips, as if pulled by some unseen force. Then it flew—planchette and all—hurling itself across the room. It slammed into the wall with a thud and fell crashing to the floor.

"*Why did you do that?!*" Cheryl screamed, tears at the corners of her eyes.

"How would *I* do that? I had my fingers on the triangle, same as you!"

Shaking, Cheryl got to her knees on the bed and pointed at Amanda. "It ain't funny, 'Manda! I told ya I didn't want to do it! I told ya it was bad! I told ya!"

"I swear, I didn't have nothin' to do with it! I swear!"

Without warning, a loud pounding rattled Amanda's window. *BANG! BANG! BANG! BANG!*

Both girls jumped. Cheryl screamed.

Amanda reared back, almost falling off the bed. Her heart was pounding. When she was able to focus through her fright, she spied Travis's face pressed up against the bedroom window. He was sneering, laughing like a maniac. His breath fogged the glass.

She scrambled off the bed. "Not funny, Travis!" she yelled.

He continued laughing as he backed away from the window, his face disappearing into the darkness outside.

As Amanda's pulse returned to normal, she saw that Cheryl was still on the bed. She was lying on her side, her face scrunched up, her cheeks wet with tears.

"I'm *sorry*," Amanda said.

Cheryl shook her head and began to chuckle, laughing at herself through her tears. "I ain't *never* messin' with that thing *ever again*! Not for a million bucks."

"Promise I ain't ever gonna ask ya to."

"So much for not sellin' evil at K-Mart," she said.

Amanda laughed.

"I think… I think I mighta peed myself a little," Cheryl confessed, ashamed.

Amanda moved to her dresser and retrieved some pajama bottoms, the ones with Tweety Bird on them. She handed them to Cheryl. "Change into these and wash up your undies in the bathroom. No one will know."

Cheryl nodded, taking the pajamas. "Thanks." She changed before opening the bedroom door and heading for the bathroom.

Amanda heard Travis talking to her out in the hall.

"So, you guys were scared, huh?" he said.

"Yeah, you got us, alright," Cheryl replied, laughing it off with mock bravado.

Amanda stared at the Ouija board on the ground.

A dark, heavy feeling settled in her gut. One she couldn't shake. She thought of some of the words it had said—*EVIL* and *FOREVER* and *DEAD*—and how it had flown from the bed all on its own, crashing into her wall.

She didn't want to touch it, but she didn't want it in her room anymore, either. Perhaps it was her imagination, but as she picked up the board and planchette with shaking hands and tucked them back into the box, she thought they seemed heavier than before.

And another thought crept in. One that made her sick to her stomach.

They never got to tell it goodbye.

———

Amanda jerked awake. She was confused and disoriented. The candle she'd lit had burned out and the room was now pitch black. She realized she must've fallen asleep on the bed while waiting for Cheryl to return from the bathroom.

Had Cheryl even come back? She wasn't lying next to her.

Amanda glanced around the room, her eyes adjusting to the dark. She spotted Cheryl sitting at the end of the bed, facing the door. She wasn't wearing Amanda's Tweety Bird pajamas anymore. She'd changed into a nightgown.

And she was crying.

Amanda worried that she'd done Cheryl wrong by making her play with the Ouija board. It was clear that it had frightened her on a deep level. It was affecting her still, making her sad. Amanda sighed. This was her fault.

Cheryl continued to cry, her hands covering her face, her sobs quiet but audible.

Mournful.

Amanda moved down the bed and sat behind her. Hearing her like this hurt Amanda's heart. She placed a hand on Cheryl's back. Her friend's body heaved as she sobbed. "*I'm so sorry,*" Amanda whispered. "We never should've done that. I sure hope you ain't mad at me."

She scooted a bit closer, wrapped her arms around her from behind, and rested her cheek against Cheryl's back. As Cheryl continued to sob, Amanda held her, rubbing her arms from time to time, doing her best to comfort her.

Cheryl's nightgown was cold against her face. And the scent of the fabric was familiar, but Amanda couldn't place it. It was...*old.* Like some of her Mamaw's clothes.

In the dim light of the room, Snickerdoodle wandered out from the closet. Amanda didn't realize he was in there, though it was a spot where he often curled up and nodded off. As he approached the bed and the girls, he began to growl.

"Shhh," Amanda whispered.

The hair on Snickerdoodle's back rose and he started to hiss and spit, clawing at the air in front of him.

"Hush, Snick."

He bared his teeth and growled again, a long, deep, guttural snarl. He almost never behaved this way, and it upset her that he was acting up when her friend was already in pain.

Cheryl continued crying, but something about it was...*off.* It was still soft, muffled, but it was repetitive now. *Distorted*—like a record playing back a bit too slow.

The door to her bedroom opened.

Two people stood in the doorway. Their dark outlines were framed by the bright hall light. They flicked the light switch. As Amanda's bedside lamp turned on, illuminating the room, she realized who it was: Travis…and *Cheryl.*

"What are ya doin'?" Cheryl asked.

Dread rushed over Amanda.

She pulled away from the person she'd been embracing on the bed—the crying girl she'd been comforting, the one she'd assumed was Cheryl—but there was no longer anyone there.

She'd been hugging *nothing but air.*

Snickerdoodle's growling subsided. He sat down on her carpet and started to groom himself, as if nothing had happened.

But, for Amanda, the creeping dread remained, now tinged with embarrassment. "Uh…nothin'," Amanda muttered, her voice shaky. "You alright?"

Cheryl gave an uneasy nod. "Yeah, fine." She glanced back at Travis as she moved into Amanda's room. "Well…uh, 'night."

As Cheryl closed the door behind her, Amanda tried to pretend that nothing was wrong. But she knew what she'd seen. She'd heard her tears. Felt her nightgown against her skin. The body under her embrace.

She thought of the Ouija board, and to one message, in particular: *LITTLE GIRL.*

CHAPTER 22
WHISPERS

"WHERE ARE YOU RIGHT NOW?" CHRIS ASKED, LEANING AGAINST the frame of the primary bedroom door.

Mandy looked up.

"You're somewhere else," he said. "I was wondering where."

Mandy realized she must've been staring at the same crack in the drywall for a long while, lost in thought.

"Sorry," Mandy replied. "I was thinking about a sleepover I had once."

"Sleepover, huh?" Chris raised an eyebrow. "Wait—how old are we talkin'? I don't want to make any inappropriate comments."

"*Way* too young," Mandy said, chuckling.

Chris grimaced, clenching his teeth and pulling at the collar of his t-shirt in mock chagrin. "Yikes! Forget I said anything!"

"I had no idea you were such a lecherous old man." Mandy laughed.

"Hey, you said sleepover! Too many '80s movies, I guess—pillow fights, that sorta thing. *Nevermind*—I retract my statement."

Chris removed his jeans and laid them across the foot of the bed, before going into the bathroom. Mandy could tell he'd been moving slower the last few days.

She scanned the bedroom. She wasn't used to seeing it uncluttered like this. It was strange being in it, reclining on *their* bed, with *their* lamps on *their* side tables next to *their* phone chargers. It was odd to experience so much of her present in a place made up almost entirely of her past.

Her eyes returned to the mar in the wall.

Travis had punched it, making that crack when he was in his early twenties. She couldn't remember what he'd been mad about. But she remembered the yelling. She remembered the sharp crunch of the drywall under his fist. And she remembered he'd scared their mother that night.

This house had many wounds. And many of them had been inflicted by Travis. Was it possible he'd done it? Inflicted the *ultimate* wound?

She tried to picture him. She hadn't seen him in so long. As with Shane, he would be close to fifty now. But when she thought of him, she pictured him as a teenager. Grinning in the night, his face pressed against her bedroom window. Laughing.

Chris leaned out of the bathroom, toothbrush in hand. "You want to tell me about the sleepover?"

"Not much to tell. Only…*memories*."

When he was finished brushing his teeth, Chris joined her in bed. He pulled the sheets back and climbed in, groaning.

"Long day?" she asked.

"Every day, it seems. But today went well. I got a lot done. We have power, at least in the main rooms—bedroom, bathroom, kitchen. And the stove is working, which will be nice. Now we need to find the fridge and move it inside, so we can stop living out of a damn cooler."

Mandy's cheeks flushed. "You've been working so hard. I'm sorry for being distracted."

Chris placed his hand over hers. "Your visit with Shane didn't help?"

"Might've made it worse."

Chris exhaled slowly. "I need to know. What is it gonna take to get you back to normal?"

"I don't want you to be upset with me, Christopher," Mandy said.

"I just… I need to figure out what happened with my folks. It's all I can think about."

"Okay. So, what does that mean?"

Mandy hesitated. The warmth of Chris's hand on hers was comforting at first, then a little claustrophobic. "As much as I don't want to, I think I need to go see Travis. I need to look him in the eye and ask if he had anything to do with it."

Chris nodded, quiet a moment. He took his hand away and dropped it in his lap. "I'm gonna use my words here. I'm having a hard time with this. I'm struggling with…feeling *abandoned* by you. And I—"

"Chris, I—"

"Please…" he said. "Please let me finish." He swallowed hard. "I realize this has been hard for you. I also realize you're going through something that I don't *really* understand. A lot of unresolved…*shit.* And, as much as I *want* to understand. As much as I wish you'd *talk* to me about it, I realize that's likely not gonna happen. And I'm not gonna try and force you. But I *am* asking for you to make a deal with me. Okay?"

Mandy knew these words weren't off-the-cuff. He'd been thinking a lot about this, rehearsing it. She nodded and listened, doing her best not to tense up.

Chris continued: "You go and talk to your brother. Do what you need to do. Get it *all* out of your system. Then, I need you to promise me—whatever you discover, you're gonna let it go. Promise me you'll accept this was a sad, tragic situation. Because it's the only way you can start healing from this and move forward. And I need you. I need you to be here with me. Not just because it's a lot of work. I need to have my partner back. I need to know we're in this *together.*"

Mandy took a moment to contemplate his words, and said, "That's fair."

Suddenly, she wished his hand was back on top of hers.

Chris continued, "But, for the record…"

Mandy braced herself.

"I think you're getting a little…*obsessed.* And I don't think it's very healthy."

She nodded, chuckling under her beath. "Consider it on the record."

"Okay," he said. "I'm sure you're tired of me asking, but…are you okay?"

She thought about it. "No. Not really."

"I didn't think so."

"There's a lot of shit bubbling up—shit I thought was behind me. I'm sorry."

"You don't have to be sorry, Mandy," he said. "But we can't afford for it to derail us. Not right now. I hope you understand where I'm coming from."

"I do."

"How else can I support you?" he asked.

"Just love me."

"I do." He put his hand on hers again and pulled her in for a long hug.

Mandy sighed.

When they were done, Chris gave her a soft kiss on the forehead and asked, "Did you say goodnight to the kids already?"

"I did, but I'm not sure they noticed. They were excited to have the tents to themselves."

Mandy didn't love the idea of the kids sleeping out in the family room alone. She kept thinking of Grace disappearing down the hall, pulled by the little girl. But she tried not to dwell on it.

Chris reached over and turned off the lamp. "You gonna be okay sleeping in this room tonight? On top of everything else?"

"Probably not," she grumbled. "But it's better than a tent."

She'd been trying not to think too much about it. She'd often not even been allowed to enter this room as a child. It was the room where her parents had lived nearly their whole lives. And the room where they had died.

Little Amanda Jean thinks she's hot shit now, don't she? Queen of the castle? Ruler of the roost? Sleepin' in her Mama and Daddy's room?

Mandy glanced at her mother's diary on the nightstand. Waiting for her. She'd hoped to start reading it, but her thoughts were too scattered, her eyes too tired.

It would have to wait.

As she put her head on the pillow, she thought she caught the faint whiff of Charlie Blue.

———

GRACE AND ETHAN took a long time getting to sleep. They'd left their tent flaps open so they could talk to each other. They made jokes and giggled.

Ethan fell asleep first, a faint snore escaping his lips.

Grace lay on her sleeping bag, peering out the opening of the tent into the hallway, listening to the house settle.

And to the whispers.

Many houses had whispers. But this house was noisy.

Sometimes, they would become loud enough to stand out, to break through the normal clamor. But most of the time, they were easy to tune out. She needed to be quiet and focus to really understand them.

She often found them pleasant.

Even when she was by herself, she wasn't alone. She was *never* alone.

In a strange way, that was comforting to her.

Tonight, she listened past the sound of her brother snoozing, the sound of chirping insects outside, and the groaning of the old house. She listened to the whispers and tried to make out the words.

Money.

Someone was talking about money.

No! I won't!

The whispers faded.

Grace got up and crept to the kitchen, where she got a bottle of water from the cooler. She unscrewed the cap and took a swig. As the water ran down her throat, the kitchen grew cold. She sensed a wall of it behind her, like ice against her back.

When she turned, they were there. She wasn't surprised to see them.

A young man and a woman.

Their energy was chaotic. It was breaking through. Distorted images. Whispers through static.

Anger. Frustration. Exhaustion.

Grace squinted at them, leaning in, trying to understand.

The man was in pain. But the woman wouldn't help him. Her face was tired.

The woman turned and left the kitchen, storming down the hall. The man hurried after her, staying close behind.

Grace followed them.

So much pain in him. So much fear in her.

Grace took a sip of her water.

As they turned into the primary bedroom, the nightlight in the hall dipped to black.

Curious, Grace thought.

She stopped at the bedroom door. Her parents were asleep. They couldn't hear the arguing. They weren't stirred by the noise.

The woman was standing her ground. Unsympathetic. The young man was becoming more aggressive, more insistent. He *needed* this.

Bitch!

It made Grace want to cry.

The man was becoming scary. Not to Grace. But she could feel the fear. It was exhausting.

He screamed and the energy from it flowed past Grace, moving her hair back.

The wall broke near the bedroom door.

And the young man and woman disappeared.

But a darkness lingered behind. It was something Grace hadn't experienced before. It hovered over her, surrounded by a thousand tiny whispers.

The shadow man?

She hoped not. But something about this *was* different. *Heavy.*

She stepped closer to the wall, running her fingers over the jagged crack. The paint had peeled around the edges.

Then—"*Grace!*" The sound of her mother's voice cut through the din.

The lamp switched on near the bed, and the dark sensation was gone, as if it had evaporated. The whispers vanished. And the sounds of the house returned to normal.

———

MANDY'S SLEEP WAS RESTLESS, shallow. At times, she would teeter on the edge of a deep sleep, but she was unable to push herself over. Her mind was too busy. She feared she might sleepwalk again.

As she laid in the dark, shifting from side to side, she began to hear whispers. Soft, unintelligible mumblings. The byproduct of a noisy brain, she told herself. They were distracting. A nuisance. They wouldn't stop.

Her eyelids flickered open.

Someone was in her bedroom doorway.

Her eyes went wide.

Pink. Pajamas. *Grace.*

And someone else.

Some*thing* else.

Something *wrong*. Too tall. Too dark.

It was there, standing behind Grace, looming above her. At first, only a shape. A dark presence. A smear of black in an already dark room.

Then—it shifted.

Mandy gasped, sitting up quickly.

As her eyes adjusted, a figure began to take shape.

Massive. Bestial. It stood on two legs but seemed more like a giant ram or ox. Horns curled. An elongated skull, and thin jaw. Long teeth.

It was either in robes, this thing, or it was amorphous. It was hard to tell against the dark.

Mandy fumbled for the lamp. Her fingers found the switch.

"Grace!" she shouted, switching the light on.

But the thing was no longer there.

Mandy leaped up.

Grace was standing with her hand on the wall, her fingers against the crack. She turned to face Mandy, surprised but not frightened.

Chris's lamp clicked on. "What's going on?" His voice was groggy but anxious.

Mandy ran across the room, passing by Grace. She darted into the hall, looking for the intruder, but she found no one. When she returned, she kneeled and put her arms around Grace, examining her. Her head. Her neck. Her arms.

"What were you doing?" Mandy snapped.

"I…was following the people," she said in a soft, almost apologetic voice.

"What people?" Mandy shouted. "What are you talking about?"

"Hey," Chris said. "It's okay. Calm down."

Ethan appeared in the doorway.

Mandy pointed at him. "You go back to bed!"

Ethan wavered.

"The people arguing," Grace murmured, close to tears.

Mandy stood and put her hands to Grace's face, exhaling. "*You can't do that!*"

"What did she do?" Ethan asked.

Mandy didn't know how to respond. Her heart was pounding.

"I'd like to know too," Chris said. "What's going on right now?"

Grace looked up at Mandy, tears welling in her eyes. "I'm sorry. I didn't mean to scare you, Mommy." Grace touched the crack in the wall one last time before she turned and disappeared past Ethan down the hall.

Mandy glanced at the others. Chris was staring at her, his mouth open. Ethan appeared frightened…or was it angry?

Her hands were still shaking, her pulse still racing—*too much adrenaline!* Her mind was still clouded, confused.

She was beginning to realize—had she *overreacted?* Was that all this was? She'd *seen it*—hadn't she? It had seemed so real, but now she was doubting if *anything had been there at all.*

Ethan turned and walked off.

Mandy's eyes sought Chris's, hoping to find reassurance. Instead, she only found uncertainty. He was looking back at her, waiting for an explanation. He didn't say a word.

She told herself she should go apologize to Grace. But after a moment, she heard Ethan down the hall, comforting her. Doing her job for her.

Raising themselves. Just like you had to do. Jesus Christ, Amanda Jean! Ya best pull your shit together.

Mandy sat on the edge of the bed, trying to slow her breathing.

What were these emotions that had her twisted up? Sadness? Embarrassment? *Shame?*

Even after Chris turned off his lamp, Mandy continued to sit in the dark for a long time—trying to calm down, trying to make sense of what was happening to her—all while staring at the crack in the wall. Somehow, it appeared deeper than it had before.

———

MANDY WOKE EARLY, though she wasn't sure if she had actually slept at all. She got up before sunrise and showered. While getting ready for the day, she paused to look at herself in the mirror. Her face looked different now. Older. Wearier.

Since the stove was working, she decided to make breakfast, hoping bacon and waffles might serve as a peace offering.

Once she started cooking, the others filed in, one by one. Chris first. Then Grace. And finally Ethan.

It was quiet around the breakfast table. Stilted.

Grace didn't seem wounded, but Mandy knew she should talk to her. Apologize for overreacting. She'd have to find the right time.

Eating like this reminded her of her childhood. The morning after a blow up. No one speaking. Everyone acting as if nothing had happened.

She didn't like it.

Chris was the one to break the silence, asking, "Whereabouts are you going today?"

"It's 'bout an hour, I 'spose," Mandy said.

"Gonna drop in?"

"I thought so. I figure it might be best if he doesn't realize I'm comin'."

Chris nodded, taking a sip of coffee. "When are you leaving?"

Mandy glanced at her watch, wiped her mouth, and stood up from the table. "I guess I should get movin'. I wanna stop by and see Cheryl for a minute 'fore I go." She gathered the dirty dishes and put them in the sink. "I'll wash those up when I get back."

"Be safe, okay?" Chris said.

Mandy nodded and told the kids goodbye, kissing them on the tops of their heads.

But she left without apologizing to Grace.

———

CHRIS WATCHED her go and sighed. He was hoping for more from her. For an apology. For explanations. Every time he expected her to communicate like *he did*, he ended up disappointed. He almost went after her, but he didn't have it in him.

After Mandy left, Ethan excused himself to take a shower. And Chris was left with Grace. A long but comfortable silence stretched between them. Chris took another sip of coffee and stared down into his mug.

Grace was still munching on waffles and sipping milk from a plastic cup. She was quiet, but otherwise appeared normal.

"So..." Chris said, unsure of his next words. "You said...you were *following* people last night?"

Grace nodded.

"Who were you...following?"

Grace used her napkin to wipe the syrup from her fingers. "I see things sometimes."

Chris nodded. "Things like...*ghosts?*"

Grace shrugged.

Chris ran a hand through his hair and pushed back in his seat. "I don't actually believe in ghosts."

"That's okay."

"Do *you* believe in them?" he asked.

She took another bite of waffle and shrugged again. "I hear things. See them sometimes. I don't know what to call them."

"What do you...*see?*"

Grace put her fork down and her eyes narrowed. She appeared to be giving it thought. "People, sometimes. *Whispering.* Sometimes I can listen to what they're saying. Sometimes I only feel them."

"Feel them?"

"Yeah, like…sometimes it gets cold and I know they're nearby. And sometimes I can tell when they're upset. Or sad. Or *angry.*"

Chris's jaw twitched, and his eyes darted to the hallway. The word *angry* lingered in his mind. He took a breath and asked, "When does this happen? Are you sleeping?"

Grace smiled. "No, *those* are dreams. That's different. Most of the time, I have to be quiet and pay attention. Sometimes not. They don't always stay long."

"So, is it like…imaginary friends?"

She chuckled. "No. I'm too old for that."

Chris nodded again. "My dad…he saw things too. Well, more like, he *felt* things. One time, he took me hunting. I was a kid, around your age. We were staying in a campground with some of his buddies. In the middle of the night, when I'm dead asleep, he wakes me up and tells me we have to go. I don't understand, but he's my dad, so I get up and we pack up and we leave. Just like that. He never told me why. Then we find out later from his friends that a huge tree crashed on our campsite. Right where we were sleeping. Would've *killed* us."

Grace was listening, focused on his words, staring up at him with an earnest expression on her face.

"Is that kinda what it's like?" Chris asked.

Grace smiled. "No. But that's pretty cool."

———

THEY SAT down on her back porch. As Cheryl lit a cigarette, she told Mandy she'd been in the middle of "a program," but that it "wasn't important." Mandy suspected that meant it actually *was*. She considered offering to come back later but decided to ignore the passive-aggression and press on.

"I've been doing some thinkin' 'bout my folks," Mandy said.

"What kinda thinkin'?" Cheryl offered Mandy a cigarette.

Though Mandy knew she should decline it, she didn't. "I ran into Bo Harper the other day," she said as she lit it.

"Oh yeah, good ole Bo," Cheryl said, her tone wistful. "He's a sheriff now."

"Yeah, I saw that."

Cheryl took a drag and coughed—a thick, full cough. "Always liked that boy."

"We were talkin' 'bout my parents, and he said somethin' that got me thinkin'. What're *your* feelings 'bout Travis?"

Cheryl chuckled. "Well, now, *that* boy I never took to quite as well."

Mandy pulled the smoke into her lungs and held it a moment before releasing it. "Do you… What are…" She fumbled her words, searching for a delicate way to ask what she wanted to ask. "Do you think Travis could've had something to do with my folks dyin'?"

Cheryl gave no reaction at all but took another puff of the cigarette. "Travis ain't *never* been no good, Amanda. You know that."

"Yeah, but…do you think he's capable of somethin' like that? It's been a while since I've been around here. Around *him*."

"He ain't no good. That's all I know. Always getting' in some kinda trouble. Your folks had to bail him outta jail more times than I can count. He was even sellin' weed to some of the young kids 'round here. And then—" Cheryl cut herself off mid-thought. "Well, like I said, he ain't a good person."

Mandy's eyes narrowed. "You stopped yourself. What were you goin' to say?"

Cheryl took another deep drag from her cigarette and stared off into the back yard. "You might not remember this," she said, after a moment, "but one time I spent the night at your house—it was the night we did the Oo-ee-gee board."

Mandy stifled a smile. There was something sad yet comforting about Cheryl's lack of growth. "I was just thinkin' 'bout that night."

Cheryl winced a little, hesitating. "I went to change my clothes and you fell asleep on the bed."

Mandy nodded.

"Your brother—" she stopped short, taking another pull off the cigarette.

"Did Travis do somethin' to you, Cheryl?"

She sighed. "I told him no. Told him I was too young for all that makin' out stuff. But he wouldn't let up on me."

There was a knot in Mandy's stomach. "What did he do?"

"Don't worry, he didn't *rape* me or nothin'. But he locked himself in the bathroom with me. And he wouldn't let me leave. I told him I didn't wanna do nothin'. Told him I didn't wanna be touched. Or kissed. But he put his hands on me anyway. Put his mouth on me. Put his tongue in my mouth. I remember his breath stank, like moldy beer and corn chips."

"Jesus Christ, Cheryl. He *assaulted* you."

"Naw. Like I said, it weren't no rape or nothin'."

Mandy stared at Cheryl. She didn't push back.

"Your daddy musta knew we was in there, 'cause he knocked real loud on the bathroom door. Travis stopped, got all scared, like a little boy." Cheryl forced a laugh. "I guess I'm bein' silly. Makin' a big deal outta nothin'."

Mandy sighed. "You ain't makin' a big deal. Not one bit. It wasn't right, and I'm sorry it happened."

"But...if I'm being truthful, somethin' in his eyes that night scared me, like I was lucky your daddy showed up when he did. After that, I started steerin' clear of Travis, best I could. *Always.* So, if you're askin' me if I think he's capable of murder? Hell, I dunno. But Travis is always lookin' out for Travis, and I don't reckon he cares much 'bout anyone else. Even your folks."

CHAPTER 23
TRAVIS

With trembling hands, Mandy checked the paper Shane had given her one more time, doing her best to decipher his chicken scratch. She wanted to make sure the house number was correct before knocking.

The house didn't look any different from the others on the street, but the small, brunette woman who answered the door was wearing scrubs. The top was white with black and orange cartoon cats, while the bottoms were wine colored. Both colors clashed against her bright red Ked sneakers. Her hair was pulled back into a ponytail, and the glasses she was wearing were too big for her small, round face.

The woman appeared surprised that someone was on the porch, but she wasn't unpleasant. "Can I help you?"

"Uh…I *may* not be in the right place. I was lookin' for my brother. His name is Travis Holloway."

The woman nodded. "You're in the right place, but we have set hours for family visits."

Mandy's eyes narrowed. "Is this… I'm sorry, what is this place?"

"It's a sober living home."

"Oh." It was the only thing Mandy could think to say. Her thoughts were drifting. She didn't know if she was more surprised to discover that the house was a facility, or that Travis was a patient. She wondered if he'd come here of his own volition.

"Is it possible for you to come back at four this afternoon?" the woman asked.

"I would've called. I didn't realize…" Mandy glanced at her watch, thinking of the conversation she'd had with Chris the night before. "It took me about an hour to get here, so I probably can't come back *today*, but…"

The woman smiled, and gave a small, sympathetic laugh. She glanced off to the side for a moment before turning back to Mandy. "It's okay. We can make an exception. A few minutes. This *one time*, okay?"

"I don't want to put y'all out, I'm gonna—"

"It's fine. Come on in."

Mandy nodded and stepped inside. She'd never visited a sober living home before and had no idea what to expect, but she was somewhat surprised that it looked like any old house.

In front of her was a living room and behind that was a kitchen. A young blonde woman wearing sweatpants was sitting on the couch holding a magazine; she glanced up at Mandy then went back to reading. The décor of the home was dated, but did not appear unusual in any way, except for the oversized calendar attached to the front of the refrigerator in the kitchen. Coffee and lemon-scented disinfectant were in the air.

To Mandy's left was a hallway, lined with doors, not too dissimilar to the one at 33 Stillwater Lane.

To her right was a staircase, and next to that was a den that had been converted into an office. A second woman in scrubs sat at a desk behind a computer. As they made eye contact, she smiled at Mandy, and said "I'm sure it'll be good for Travis to talk to family."

The woman in the red Keds led Mandy down the hall, stopping in front of the second door on the left. That would've been Travis's room at Stillwater Lane, as well.

She knocked and waited.

"Yeah?" came the raspy male voice from within.

The woman gestured for Mandy to wait before slipping inside. As the door closed, voices drifted from within, too muffled for Mandy to understand. After a brief exchange, the woman reappeared, stepping into the hallway. She left the door cracked.

"Go on in," she said.

Mandy nodded.

As she pushed the door open, she found herself short of breath. She hadn't talked to Travis in many years, let alone seen him in person. It was as if she were a child again, ten years old, entering his room with permission, but uncertain of which version of him she would find. She half expected the walls to be lined with Iron Maiden posters. Instead, the room was clean and bright, with minimal décor—a bed and a nightstand, a folding chair, and a dresser. Nothing to indicate any sort of personality. No knickknacks or photos.

Travis was sitting on the edge of the twin bed, framed against the light of the window behind him.

At first, the light made it hard for her to make out the details of his face, but as he leaned forward, she did her best to hide her shock.

Though Travis was only five years older than Mandy, his appearance made it seem like fifteen. He was as lean as she'd ever seen him. His face was gaunt, his eyes were rimmed with dark circles, and his unshaven jawline was covered in red blemishes. His hair was cut short and arched up on the sides, receding and thin. The skin on his face and arms was rough and wrinkled, and thin like crepe paper—the bones were sharp underneath. Both the white t-shirt and blue pajama bottoms were too large—they hung on his narrow frame like a scarecrow.

Mandy stopped inside the doorway and took him in, her stomach clenched, her palms sweaty, her breathing shallow. She wasn't certain what she was experiencing—disgust, disdain…or was it *pity?*

"Hey, Sissy," he said, making no movement from his place on the bed. His voice was so raspy now. Speaking sounded like it might be painful for him, as if the words had to drag themselves over broken glass to escape.

Mandy glanced around the room. "Homey," she said.

"No, it ain't," he replied, rubbing his left arm, avoiding direct eye contact. "But it could be worse, I reckon."

"Whose idea was this?"

"Well…you're *here*, ain't ya? I figure *he* musta told ya."

"Shane's paying for this?"

He nodded. "After Mama and Daddy… After the bank come… Well, I went to him and asked for a place to stay, but he's smarter than that, I 'spose." Travis laughed. "Reckon this is Shane's idea of *tough love*." He glanced at Mandy, his eyes red and tired. "Better'n Daddy's, huh?"

The room was quiet. The only noise was the television out in the living room.

Mandy regarded him. "Are you, uh…*serious* about this? Are you really tryin'? Or is this just for now?"

Travis's jaw tightened, and his breathing became heavy. His fingers curled into the fabric of his pajama bottoms, and his knee began to twitch. "Don't you come in here judgin' me. Don't you fuckin' judge me. You don't know shit 'bout this."

Mandy raised her hands to show him she hadn't come to fight. "Alright, that's fair. Maybe I don't. But we both grew up in the same house. We both had the same mama. I know what this road looks like and I know it don't lead nowhere."

Travis stared at the floor and allowed his breathing to return to normal. "Ya got a cigarette?"

"I gave it up," Mandy lied.

He rubbed his arm again. "Alright."

"Trav, I came here because I need to ask you something—"

"You remember when you was a girl? You'd sit up on your bed and I'd sit down at the end with all them stuffed animals of yours, and put on them puppet shows?"

She smiled, surprised by the memory. "I do remember that, yeah. I was *real* little."

"You used to laugh so hard. Thought you were gonna laugh yourself clean off the bed."

"I did laugh, yeah. That was the fun part. But do you remember how you'd always end them shows?"

Travis shrugged, still only taking furtive glances at her. "Don't reckon I do."

"You'd always end the puppet show by makin' my stuffed animals kill each other."

A flicker of something ran across his face—recognition perhaps. It was only visible for a moment and then he squashed it. "Don't 'member that."

"It's true," Mandy said, folding her arms across her chest. "It *never* stopped at the laughin', did it? That is one of my *few* good memories with you, and you still had to fuck it up by makin' me cry."

"Ya was always too sensitive," Travis said. His voice was flat and devoid of emotion. It felt like a choice.

"Course I was sensitive, dumbass. I was a girl. Fendin' for myself."

Travis stopped rubbing his arm long enough to pass his hand over his face and eyes, then continued with the motion. "We was all in the same boat."

"Yeah. But we coulda helped each other. Coulda had each other's backs. Instead, all the shit rolled downhill. You were my *big brother*, Trav."

Travis looked her in the eye, perhaps for the first time since she'd come into the room. "What the hell are ya complainin' about? You got out, didn't ya?"

"We do what it takes to survive," Mandy said. "For me, that was leavin'. Ever since, I've been tryin to focus on what's next—on the *future*—and not think about home, about the past. I'd grown sorta numb to all of it, like all my memories weren't even real. Like it was someone else's life. But now I'm back, and I'm realizin' it *was* real. *All* of it. All this *shit* keeps bubblin' up, and that numbness is startin' to turn to somethin' else. Anger, I think."

"Well, at least ya got out," Travis sniped. His fingers gripped his leg, digging in. "*You* got out. *Shane* got out. And y'all didn't give a damn *I* was never goin' *nowhere*."

"It…it wasn't about leavin' anyone *behind*, Trav. You coulda gone too."

He huffed.

"I'm sorry if you felt abandoned."

"Oh, yeah?" Travis said, his body stiffening, his volume growing. "Are ya sorry, Sissy? Are ya really?"

There was a quick knock at the door before it opened. The woman in the red Keds peeked her head in. "Everything alright?"

Travis nodded, though his body language was tense and restless. "Yeah. We're fine."

"You sure? If this visit's a little much for right now, we can always do it another time."

"Nah, it's okay," he said. "I just… I need to focus up. I'll do my countin'."

The woman acknowledged him and gave Mandy a slight smile before leaving the room and closing the door again.

Travis shut his eyes and started counting under his breath, his body still shaking, his fingers twitching with every number.

Mandy watched him. This was new to her—this careful way he had of holding himself together. As was the sense that he was so close to breaking apart.

After waiting a moment, she lowered her voice almost to a whisper and said, "I really *was* only tryin' to survive. I couldn't stay in that place no more."

He opened his eyes. "Outta nowhere, you was *gone*. And I was left behind. All alone with Mama and Daddy."

"I didn't know what else to do. Except to *go*."

Travis couldn't stop his fidgeting, first rubbing his arm, then his leg, then his face, and back to his arm. He was back to staring at the floor, but his gaze darted back and forth, as if following an invisible tennis match.

Mandy had never seen him quite like this. So unfocused. So fractured. Was it the illness— years and years spent altered, buried under the haze of the drugs—or was it the treatment?

Whatever it was, it meant he was less aggressive than she remembered, and for that she was thankful.

"Trav, what happened to Mama and Daddy?"

He looked up at her again. His brow furrowed and he let out a sharp laugh. "Jesus, you too?" The laughter died in his throat and his shoulders drooped. He shook his head. "I dunno nothin' 'bout it—I told the cops the same thing. And I don't like folks thinkin' I did somethin' to 'em."

Mandy thought she'd recognize the truth when she saw him react, but as she studied his face, she was unsure of what she was seeing. *Was it guilt?* Something in his wide, hollowed out eyes felt more like sadness. Exhaustion.

"Well, I'm here askin' you direct, ain't I?" she pressed. "I ain't assumin' nothin'. I just need to know. I need to hear it right from you."

Travis nodded and his eyes fluttered a moment before staring back at the floor. He took a shaky breath. "Mama…she kept slidin' downhill. She was still takin' them pills, but she started forgettin' things. More and more things. Forgettin' people, even. Daddy, sometimes. Me too. She started sayin' all kinds'a crazy things. Hard to tell what was real and what was…*nonsense*."

"So, you *do* think it was Mama that done it?"

"I dunno," he muttered, his voice thin, its edges worn down.

Mandy moved the folding chair closer to the bed and sat. "Please…tell me what you know, so I can understand."

Travis thought about it a moment. His eyes flicked back and forth again. He took his time, as if sorting through what he should say. How much. Where to start. "Mama said some stuff 'bout Uncle Harlan. It got Daddy all worked up."

"Harlan? What kinda stuff?"

Travis pressed his fingers to his temple, as if the conversation was hurting his head. "Like I said, she was talkin' crazy. Said stuff about Grandpa hurtin' them—her and Harlan and Malcolm. And about Harlan hurtin' her too. And…" He stopped.

"Go on." Mandy urged.

Travis winced, his eyes narrowing. Mandy reached over and put her hand on his knee. At once, his jitters subsided a bit. He placed a shaky hand on top of hers, patted it, then went right back to rubbing his arm.

In a soft, uncertain voice, he continued, "She said… Said somethin' 'bout Harlan bein' scared of gettin' caught."

"Caught for doin' what?"

"I dunno."

"What else, Trav?"

He looked her in the eye again. "She said somethin' 'bout him…maybe…*hurtin' you.*"

"Hurtin' *me?*" That didn't make any sense.

Travis opened his mouth but shut it again. He shook his head.

"What does it mean, Trav?" Mandy pushed.

"I got no idea." Travis's jitters were back now. "Daddy heard her say it. Toward the end, she got *real* loud. Hard *not* to hear her. But whatever she was ramblin' on 'bout…it got him awful mad."

"Mad at her?"

"A bit, I reckon. Just…*mad.* Ya know how Daddy was. He called up Harlan and started hollerin'."

"What did he say?"

"Couldn't make it out. Only lasted a minute, and he slammed the phone down. Next thing I know, Uncle Harlan's truck's pullin' up outside."

Mandy's chest tightened. "Are you tellin' me…that Harlan was *there?* In the house the day our folks died?"

Travis sucked in air, closing his eyes. "Shit, does it matter?" His leg shook as his foot tapped.

"Yeah, it *does* matter."

He swallowed, and after a moment, he whispered, "Yeah. He was there."

"Jesus Christ, Trav. Did you tell the police about this?"

Travis shook his head. "Didn't think to, at the time. Wasn't…*thinkin' straight.*"

"What happened after he arrived?" she asked.

"I dunno. I left soon as he showed up. I didn't wanna be 'round if Daddy was angry."

For a moment, Mandy thought Travis looked like a boy. She thought of Cheryl saying the same thing about him the night he'd trapped her in the bathroom. Scared, like a little boy.

She continued to push. "But you saw Mama and Daddy when you got home?"

He shook his head. "No. Got back late. They was already in bed. The TV was goin' in their room though."

"And you didn't check on 'em?"

"Not till later. Why would I?"

"Well, why'd you check on 'em later?" Mandy asked.

"Daddy always falls asleep with the TV goin', but he flips it off when he gets up to pee. I couldn't sleep real good, and that TV was blarin' all night. Went in to turn it off, and I knew somethin' weren't right." Travis looked at her again. It seemed to take all his effort to hold her gaze, but he did. "*I didn't hurt 'em*, 'Manda. I swear. I didn't hurt our folks."

There was another quick knock at the door, and the woman in the red Keds peeked in again. "We got a group activity in five minutes or so, and we're gonna need Travis for that. I'm sorry to cut the visit short, but if y'all can wrap it up for now, I'm sure you can pick it up another time."

Mandy gave her a slight nod and the woman left, closing the door once more.

Travis stared back at the floor and his shoulders slumped.

A hundred questions battled for space in Mandy's mind. *Was he telling her the truth? Had her mother been speaking nonsense? Or had her grandfather hurt her mother and her uncles? Had Harlan hurt her mother too, somehow, and had her father confronted Harlan about it that day? And, above all, was Harlan somehow involved in her parents' deaths?*

She scrutinized Travis, studying his face. His eyes were glassy. His jittering had subsided. He seemed weary, *broken*. And more than that, he looked scared. She believed he was being truthful, but she'd always wanted to believe the best about him. About everyone. One thing was certain—she wouldn't find any more answers here today.

Still, she needed to press him on one last thing. "What do you think Mama meant when she said Uncle Harlan hurt me?"

Travis was silent a moment. He sighed. "Mighta been babblin' is all. But Uncle Harlan…he ain't a good man, 'Manda. I'm sorry if I weren't neither. You said it right—I was your big brother, and I shoulda… I shoulda done *better* for you." His eyes glistened in the light of the room. Mandy couldn't recall ever seeing her brother cry before. "I shoulda protected you."

Protect them.

Mandy drew a deep breath, letting it all sink in.

She recognized the significance of this, of an *apology*. Something she'd always wanted. And now, she wished the words meant more. She wished she could feel them. She wanted to muster the maturity and grace to forgive him. To embrace him. But no words would ever undo the past. No words would erase the terror she'd experienced as a girl. *Because* of him. All the awful things he'd done.

She searched his face, looking for the brother she'd needed once. But he was a stranger to her now, a man slowly withering away, being eaten alive by his own ghosts.

She was sorry for him. Sorry for his pain, for his suffering. But it was no longer her burden to bear. He was not her responsibility.

This feeling—a coldness, an indifference, a *numbness*—bothered her. It wasn't the way she'd ever wanted to be. She wished she could rise above it. She wanted to love him. But she was afraid the time for that was gone.

Perhaps *understanding* was all she could muster now.

She patted his leg. "Like I said…we were all tryin' to survive."

Mandy stood and pushed the chair back into place. She thought she should say more, but none of the words she considered were right. None of them were honest.

"I hope this works for you," she said, gesturing around the room. "I hope you get well."

She turned and started toward the door. As she opened it, an earnestness came into Travis's voice, and he said, "I think I'm really gonna do it this time, Sissy. I think… I think this is the one."

Mandy gave a little nod and smiled. It was a small, sympathetic smile. But in her heart, there was nothing but doubt. She'd heard words like these her whole life. How *this* time it would be better. How *this* time it would be different. How *this time*, things would *finally* be good.

She left the room and closed the door behind her.

———

CHRIS STRADDLED the top rungs of the ladder, inspecting the roofline at the back of the house. He was distracted, thinking about Mandy.

Wondering how her crusade was going. Hoping it would all be over soon.

The voice behind him startled him and made him jump. He'd been so lost in thought, he hadn't realized anyone else was there.

"Hope I ain't catchin' ya at a bad time." The drawl was deep and rough.

Chris steadied himself on the ladder and glanced over his shoulder. It was Mandy's uncle, Harlan. The one who'd offered to buy the property. The one Chris had helped usher from the house only a few days prior. Now, he was standing in their back yard, hands on his hips, fingers gripping the belt of his jeans. He was squinting up at Chris from under his gray HARLAN BROTHERS baseball cap.

Harlan spat tobacco on the ground near his boots and wiped his mouth with the sleeve of his flannel.

Chris gripped the ladder. He realized how exposed he was, perched up high, with no one around except a man Mandy didn't trust or care for. He shifted his weight and moved to climb down. "Never seems to be a good time these days. What can I do for you?"

"Wanted to have a quick word. Make sure your gal—my lovely *niece*—told ya about my offer to buy this place. Offer's more than fair, if I say so myself."

When Chris's foot stepped off the bottom rung of the ladder, he exhaled with relief. He picked up a rag resting on his toolbox and wiped the dirt from his hands. "She did."

"And what do *you* think? Seems like a no-brainer to me. Don't make much sense for you to keep spendin' time and money fixin' up an old place like this when me and my boys can take care of it."

"Well…she says she doesn't want to sell."

Harlan studied him, chewing. He smiled, his lip curling. "Well… now *we're* talkin' man to man, ain't we? No need for emotions muckin' up a decent negotiation."

Chris chuckled. "Well…Mandy and I are a *team*. And the house belongs to her, legally. And…as I said, she doesn't want to sell at this time."

Harlan adjusted his hat and scratched at his hairline. "I reckon it's natural for Amanda Jean to have some…*sentimental* feelin's about this place. But that's all they are—feelin's. And feelin's pass. Sometimes it's best to leave the past behind, don't ya think?"

Chris cleared his throat. "Look, I'll, uh…tell Mandy that you stopped by to repeat your offer. And I'll ask if she's changed her mind. How 'bout that?"

"Why don't you do more than that, friend. Why don't you convince your gal to see the sense in it. Get her to look at this thing the right way, so we can keep things nice and friendly."

Chris's cheeks flushed. He clenched his jaw and eyed the handle to the claw hammer sticking out of his toolbox. "Well, that sounds an awful lot like a *threat* to me."

"Aww, hell no," Harlan said with a laugh that started strong and faded into a smile that was more like a sneer. "You misunderstand me, son. I ain't threatenin' violence. I ain't even a violent man. 'Sides, if I ever wanted violence done, I got folks who'd see to that *for* me."

Again, a sense of vulnerability seized Chris. He scanned the yard, his eyes darting back and forth, searching for any sign of Harlan's "folks."

Harlan raised his hands, palms open. "Ain't nobody here but me today. This is still a peaceful negotiation. But I think you oughta talk it over with your lady. Think it over, the both of you. See if y'all don't decide it's best to change your mind, after all. Then you can scamper on back to California. Leave the past in the past, where it belongs. Don't that sound better?"

Chris's heart was racing. "I think Mandy already gave you an answer, but we'll let you know if we change our mind."

"And, uh…that's that?" Harlan asked, his eyes narrowing.

"Yup. That's that."

"Alright then," Harlan said. He spat tobacco on the ground, before tipping his baseball cap with a faint smile. He ambled off toward the front yard, whistling a song the Chris didn't recognize, slow and out-of-tune.

CHAPTER 24
THE DIARY

MANDY ARRIVED HOME FROM HER VISIT WITH ENOUGH TIME TO assist Chris for a few hours before it was time for dinner. She cooked up some hot dogs she'd picked up at the grocery store, and they all ate together.

The meal was brief, with minimal conversation. Mandy didn't have much of an appetite. And she was grateful that Chris hadn't asked about her day. She wasn't ready to talk about it. Grace was quiet, perhaps reflecting Mandy's energy. She thought Ethan was still miffed at her from the night before.

After dinner, the kids retreated to the tents and hung out together.

Mandy located the vodka and quickly washed out a large, plastic cup. She considered adding a mixer but poured it straight over ice instead.

After the day I've had, why not? she thought.

Chris was already on the back porch with a beer, so she joined him. They sat with their drinks and watched the sky turn dark. After a few minutes, Chris told her about Harlan's unexpected visit.

"Jesus," Mandy whispered, her fingers tightening around her cup. That was the last thing she wanted to hear after her conversation with Travis.

"Yeah, it was super fun," Chris said.

"I *know* we need to talk about it. I know it's important," she said. "But I'm drained after…*today*. Can we revisit this in the morning?"

"That's fine. As long as you're actually going to talk to me."

Mandy exhaled, fidgeting with her fingers. She wished she had a cigarette.

Inside, Grace giggled.

"I really wish the kids weren't sleeping in those tents again." Mandy said.

"They're fine, Mandy. They're having fun with it."

"Yeah, well… I just don't want a repeat of last night."

Chris turned to her, raising an eyebrow. "Then don't repeat it."

———

THE COMFORTER HAD BEEN MUCH TOO hot for Mandy, so they'd pulled it down. But even without it, the room was stifling, so Chris had brought back in one of her parents' box fans and set it up near the bedroom window.

Now they lay in bed, chatting every so often, while Chris scrolled on his phone. Its screen was the only light in the dark room.

Mandy couldn't stop thinking about Travis.

And Harlan.

She wanted Chris's opinion, but dreaded what he might say. She told herself to wait and sleep on it. But it was no use. It was eating at her.

"I want to talk to you," she said.

"Oh?" Chris set his phone down. "For that, you have my full attention."

As he listened, Mandy told him about her visit with Travis. She left out most of the details—the sober living home, the physical state of her brother, the arguments—and focused on the bit about Harlan being in the house the day her parents had died.

When she finished, Chris was quiet and still. It was too dark for Mandy to read his expression, so she waited. She found the silence excruciating and had to stop herself from filling it.

After a moment, Chris sighed. "I'm very worried about you. I think being back here is messing with your head."

Immediately, a heat came into her cheeks, but Mandy bit her tongue.

This is what you get for communicating!

"They weren't *your* parents." Her voice was tight and choked, like a hushed shout forced through clenched teeth.

"Honey…they were *barely* yours."

She couldn't even speak. Her hands began to shake. She turned away from him, lying on her side in silence, seething.

"I'm sorry," he said. "That was colder than I meant it to be."

Mandy didn't respond, but her mind was busy.

How fucking dare you! she thought. *You want me to talk to you and when I do, you're like this? Insensitive! Disrespectful! Of me AND of my folks!*

Her emotions built—shifting between sadness, anger, and confusion—before withering, strangled by an even more horrifying idea: *He's right.*

Finally, in a small voice, she choked out, "I don't understand why. I just…*need* to know."

Chris exhaled and started rubbing Mandy's back. His hand was warm.

"I hear you," he said. "I'm sorry."

They both fell silent.

They lay next to each other in the darkness, the box fan whirring, his hand on her, until he nodded off.

Mandy listened to the sound of his breathing. Her mind kept turning. She was unable to quiet her thoughts. Thoughts of Harlan. Travis. Her parents. The little girl. The dark thing she'd seen the night before. And thoughts of her children, asleep in tents in the other room.

She listened for them but heard nothing. She considered checking on them but resisted.

Many times, she would begin to nod off, only to jerk back awake again.

It was some time before she found sleep.

———

When Mandy opened her eyes, she was standing in the hallway of the house.

There were voices, but they were muffled, as if they were speaking underwater.

As the sound came into focus, she heard Hank Williams playing on a tinny radio—"Lost Highway." Someone was whistling along.

As she began to walk down the hall toward the kitchen—toward the sounds—the walls of the hallway began to pulsate, as if they were breathing.

The lights flickered off and on.

She turned the corner.

Her father was there, sitting at the dining room table, looking just as she remembered him as a child.

On the table in front of him was a tarnished pocket-watch, open, gears exposed. Her father was holding a small screwdriver and was working on the pocket-watch, stone faced and focused, whistling.

The song slowed, then sped up again.

The lights blinked off, then on.

And Mandy realized that her mother was there as well.

Standing at the sink. In front of a running faucet.

As Mandy came closer, she could see that her mother was peeling potatoes. The damp, scraping sound of the potato peeler was repetitive, loud and sharp in Mandy's ears.

Shhkkk. Shhkkk. Shhkkk.

"Mama?" Mandy whispered.

Her mother jerked around to face her, her jaw slack, her eyes dull and black.

She didn't stop peeling.

Shhkkk. Shhkkk.

"Are you bein' nosy again, Amanda Bear?" she asked, her voice low and lifeless. "Stickin' your nose where it don't belong?"

The sound of the peeler continued, a rhythmic, wet, ripping sound.

Shhkkk. Shhkkk. Shhkkk.

Mandy noticed that the potatoes in the sink were gray—old and rotting.

But they began to turn bright red. And Mandy realized that, in addition to the skin of the potatoes, her mother was peeling away chunks of her own flesh.

Shhkkk. Shhkkk. Shhkkk. Shhkkk.

Her mother continued to stare at Mandy—expressionless, unblinking.

She seemed unaware that her hands were getting bloodier—more raw—with every swipe of the peeler. Her skin was falling away in sheets, landing in the basin of the sink.

Mandy wanted to scream for her to stop, but no sound would come.

She stepped forward, but her mother smiled and shook her head slowly.

"You don't fix nothin' by lookin' too close," she muttered.

Shhkkk. Shhkkk.

Then another sound: *Tick Tick Tick Tick*

The two sounds began to converge.

And, as Mandy backed away from her mother, the ticking began to take over. It was suddenly loud. As if it was right behind her, all around her, pounding in her ears.

She whipped around to find herself face to face with her father. He was towering over her now, so close it was suffocating. He stared down at her, his expression stern. His breath was hot on her face, smelling of tobacco.

The space around Mandy seemed to shrink. She was tiny next to him.

Powerless.

"Daddy!" she gasped.

But her father didn't say anything. He thrust the ticking pocket-watch toward her, almost hitting her in the face. Off balance, she fell backward, landing hard on the floor.

He moved to stand above her.

"Ain't got no use for this no more. Not where I am," he said. "It's all yours now."

Her father began to laugh, his eyes stretched wide, almost unnatural. He held his hand up in a fist, letting the pocket-watch dangle in front of him.

Tick Tick Tick Tick

He pulled his hand back, and, with a sneer, he threw the pocket-watch at her face as hard as he could. She flinched, squeezing her eyes shut, pulling her hands up to guard herself against the blow.

But it never came.

When she opened her eyes again, the symbol was in front of her: three circles, interlocked.

She was outside now, in the grove of trees in the back yard, right past the creek.

Facing the oak.

And her mother was in front of her, kneeling in the mud, hovering over a hole she'd finished digging with her bare hands.

She stood and turned, wiping her grimy fingers across her apron. Her hair was disheveled. Her face was streaked with dirty tears.

When she saw Mandy, she chuckled under her breath. "Gotta bury it. Won't get out that way," she said. Her teeth were gray and rotting. "Bury it, Amanda Bear, or it buries *you*."

"Mama, no," Mandy whispered.

"It's all ready for *you* now," her mother said.

She lurched forward, grabbed Mandy's arm, and began dragging her toward the hole. Mandy dug her heels in and tried to pull away, but before she could, the roots of the tree began to move. Like living tendrils, they slithered toward her, wrapping themselves around her wrists and ankles. Mandy's feet slid through the mud as the roots pulled her forward.

And she fell into the hole.

She plummeted, as if from a great distance, her stomach lurching, the air rushing past her. She slammed into the muddy earth with a sickening thud.

She turned, writhing, struggling to pull herself free, but it was no use. The roots had her. And every time she moved, they tightened, constricting her more and more.

Her mother stood above her, right outside the hole, watching her sink.

Then her mother knelt and began to fill the hole again, scraping handfuls of mud in on top of Mandy. Pulling at the earth in a frenzy.

The soil began to cover her. Blanketing her body. Burying her alive.

The rain of dirt stung her face. Clung to her hair.

Her lungs burned from its weight.

It began to obscure her vision.

Mandy squinted through it. At her mother. Face twisted into something that looked like hunger. Working in a frantic fury. Trying to fill the hole.

Mandy tried to scream, but she couldn't.

Her mouth was full of dirt.

———

MANDY WOKE UP, startled and sweating.

It took a few seconds for her to realize where she was. Still in Rosebury. Still in her childhood home. Sleeping in her parents' old room, with Chris asleep beside her, a small snore punctuating each of his long breaths.

The sheets were soaked through with sweat. She kicked them off and lay in her underwear for a long while. She checked her feet to make sure they weren't covered in mud, but they weren't, only beaded perspiration.

She couldn't stop thinking of how odd and uncomfortable it was to be sleeping in her parents' room. To be dreaming of them in the place where they used to dream.

After tossing and turning for almost half an hour, Mandy got up and used the bathroom. As she washed up, she glanced at her reflection again. The stranger in the glass—older and more tired—was beginning to appear familiar. She never thought she looked much like her mother, but maybe she did a bit now.

Mandy walked down the hall to check on the kids in their tents. They were both sound asleep. She went to the kitchen. Trying to be quiet, she fumbled in the dark, looking for the plastic cup she'd used before. Once she found it, she poured herself another generous slug of vodka.

After slamming it back, she returned to the bedroom, where she did her best to fall back to sleep. But it was no use. The sounds of the house kept her awake. The box fan droning near the window. The insects outside. Chris snoozing.

Mandy glanced at her phone, charging on the nightstand near the lamp.

3:33 A.M.

Shit.

Next to it was her mother's diary.

She sighed. Might as well read some of it, she figured. Maybe it would distract her from the noise inside her head. Maybe it would even tire her out.

She pulled her phone from the charger and turned the flashlight on, then laid the phone across her sternum, under her chin. Having been with Chris for almost two decades, she knew that he was a deep sleeper, and she wasn't concerned about waking him. She probably could've turned on the lamp, and still not bothered him.

Mandy held the diary up. The old leather cover was worn and brittle beneath her fingers.

As she opened it, the scent of old paper filled her nostrils. The pages were stiff from age. And from being buried under the earth for who knows how long.

Taking care, she began to flip through it. She stopped a few pages in and picked an entry at random. It was dated "March 3, 1964." Mandy did the math in her head and figured that her mother must've been nine years old at the time she'd written it.

Examining her mother's handwriting, she was surprised at how legible and graceful it was for a girl that age.

She began to read the entry.

MARCH 3, 1964

 We had a spelling bee in class today. I did well, except I misspelled the word library. I left out the r in the middle. Mrs.

Collins said I did good though. That made me happy. Pa came home grumpy again last night. He got mad at Harlan and me because we were squabbling and sent all of us to bed early with no supper. Ma said he's working hard for us, and we shouldn't be ungrateful.

Mandy flipped a few more pages in and chose another entry.

MARCH 16

I got a book from the library. After school, I went down to the creek and sat on the bridge to read for a while. The book is about a girl named Betsy who moves away to the city and makes new friends. I can't wait until I'm old enough to move away from Rosebury and live someplace new. Harlan makes fun of me for reading when I don't have to, but I don't care what he thinks. He ain't very smart. Before dinner, Ma made me sweep the front porch.

Mandy never knew her mother liked to read. Or that she too had been made fun of for it. She also never had any clue that her mother once dreamed of leaving Rosebury, as she'd never given Mandy any indication that she'd been unhappy living here. She was born here. She died here. Mandy assumed she was happy with that situation.

She chose another entry.

APRIL 12, 1964

It was Harlan's 12th birthday today. It was raining when we woke up. We went to church. I wore my pink dress, the fluffy one that Ma likes, but Harlan and Mal said I looked like a wad of chewed bubblegum. Hurt my feelings. Pa got mad at Malcolm for talking during the sermon, and Mal said it was my fault for getting him in trouble, but I don't see how.

Since it was raining, Ma let Harlan make a fort out of blankets for his birthday, but he wouldn't let me in unless I gave him some of my Bazooka Joes, and I didn't want to. Mal said I was too fat to fit anyway, but I don't think I am. Mal treats me like he's my big brother, but he ain't. I'm almost a full year older than him. He follows Harlan around and does whatever he says, most of the time. I played jacks by myself instead.

Mandy skimmed a few more entries. There was a mention of school ending, of having gone swimming at Johnson Pond, of wanting to watch *Mary Poppins*, and miscellaneous talk of jump rope and church friends. Most of it was light enough—the musings of a young girl. But when Mandy came across the entry for JUNE 15, 1964, she saw it started with the words: "Pa came home drunk..."

She knew next to nothing about her grandfather. He was gone long before she was born, and her mother almost never spoke of him, let alone in much detail. The writing on the entry was scrawled, rushed almost, as if her mother had been afraid of being caught.

JUNE 15, 1964

Pa came home drunk again last night and in a mood. Mad he lost money on a card game. We all tried to stay out of his way, but he cornered Harlan by the back door and hit him hard enough to knock him to the ground. Ma screamed at Pa to stop, but he told her to shut up and go back to cooking. I hid in my room and waited until it got quiet again.

Mandy clenched the edge of the diary. Her heartbeat spiked up. This reminded her so much of her own childhood. She didn't realize it had been that way for her mother as well.

She continued to skim the entries, stopping when a word or phrase caught her eye.

JULY 1

Malcolm's been getting in fights. I don't know if he starts them or not, but Pa says he's useless. Harlan told Malcolm it ain't his fault, but yesterday, Pa whipped Malcolm so hard he screamed, then he made him chop wood till it was dark.

Mandy continued to peruse the diary, and the tone of the writing began to shift. It was more agitated, hurried.

JULY 21

Pa beat Harlan because he forgot to take the trash out. He said it was to teach him a lesson. I saw Harlan cry. I went to his room and told him it was gonna be okay, but he got angry at me. He pushed me out of his room and hurt my wrist. I feel all alone sometimes. I don't like it when Pa's home.

Mandy continued reading, selecting pertinent passages. The handwriting became tighter as she went along, and the ink was darker on the page, as if the pen had been pressed too hard against the paper.

AUGUST 15, 1964

Lately, Pa seems more cruel than usual. He's been taking the belt to us almost every night. Harlan and Malcolm get it worst. He always comes up with reasons for the beatings, but I think he likes to see us hurt. Ma tried to stop him yesterday, but he smacked her across the mouth and pushed her down on the floor. Made her mouth bleed. He called her names and told her to stay out of it.

I dread coming home every day. I don't want to be here anymore, but Harlan says I can't go. He says it'll be worse if I try to leave and Pa finds me. He says he'll protect Malcolm and me, but I don't know about that. He says he ain't afraid of Pa, and he's getting old enough to stand up to him. That scares me too.

Mandy's stomach knotted as she read of her grandfather's abuse. She read on, scanning entry after entry, seeing more and more mentions of beatings. Of scoldings. Of name calling and torment.

She felt heavier with each word, but she was compelled to continue reading. It was a part of her mother's life she'd never known anything about. A part that had shaped her mother and her uncles, both.

Though she'd lived through similar herself—and wasn't surprised by much—this made her heart ache.

She'd never really forgiven her mother for contributing to her own torment as a child—or for turning a blind eye, at least. Now she realized that abuse was something her mother had been surrounded by since she was young.

It didn't excuse her mother's own actions. It didn't exonerate her from her role. But it did help Mandy understand her in a way she never had before.

As far as her uncles went, she'd always thought of Harlan and Malcolm as monsters, and she still did. But now she could see the *other* monster hiding in their shadows.

She continued flipping through pages and pages of horrible recollections. Until she came across the final entry. The remaining pages of the book were left blank.

As she read it, chills started to run down her spine. Her hands began to shake as she held the book in front of her.

OCTOBER 4

I don't know if I should be writing this down. I don't have anyone to talk to. I don't think I will ever speak of it again.

Yesterday was Saturday. Harlan and Malcolm were fishing in the creek. Ma asked me to let them know that supper was almost ready, so they could start wrapping up and heading back. Malcolm went up to the house right away, but Harlan kept me back. He said he wanted to show me something. I didn't want to stay with him, but he was firm on it.

I followed him to one of the big oak trees out past the bridge, and he showed me that someone had put a strange marking on it. Three circles. I asked him what it was and he said he didn't know, but it looked like a brand, like they use for cattle. I told him it was interesting, and I started to leave, but he stopped me. He told me he'd always look out for me because he was my brother and he loved me. He asked if I believed him and I said yes. He gave me a hug. But he didn't stop. He started to kiss me. First on the cheek and then on the mouth.

I told him I didn't like it and that I wanted to go back to the house, but he wouldn't let me. He held me down and kissed me again. He used his tongue. He tasted like cigarettes. He said it was okay because we loved each other. But I don't think it was. I told him again that I wanted to leave. I tried to yell for help, but he put his hand over my mouth. I couldn't breathe. I thought I might suffocate. I started crying real hard. I thought it might get him to stop, but it didn't. He touched my body. He got on top of me. He was heavy. I don't remember what happened after that.

I am confused and scared. I don't want to be in this house no more. I don't even want to be alive. I feel dirty even after taking a bath. I think I must have done something terrible for this to have happened.

I tried to talk to Ma, but she didn't believe me. She told me not to make things up. I can't stop crying, but I don't want her to see, because she gets mad. I don't want Pa to see neither.

I think it was a mistake to write this down. All of it. I think I will burn this book when I'm done writing this. Goodbye.

Mandy closed the book.

With trembling hands, she set it back on the nightstand, and turned off the light on her phone. She wiped the tears away from her eyes and from her cheeks, and she lay in the dark, staring at the ceiling, feeling as if she might be ill.

The house was hot and still, but she couldn't stop shivering.

She felt small and helpless again.

The past was a beast she'd had to contend with her whole life. But reading her mother's diary made it seem like a tangible thing—living and breathing. A feral creature that had clawed its way out of the earth and slithered back into her space. A monster sitting with her in the dark, ready to bite through her sutures and stab at her scar tissue.

It was a brutal reminder that some wounds never fully heal.

You wanted to dig, Amanda Jean. Now you know things you can't unknow.

CHAPTER 25
THE CAULDERS, 1989

IT WAS EARLY EVENING AND AMANDA LAY ON HER BACK ON Travis's bedroom floor, listening to his stereo. The large cups of the headphones swallowed her tiny ears, immersing her in the music of Led Zeppelin.

She held the "Houses of the Holy" album up, folding it out to see the entire image—numerous, diminutive, towheaded girls, their bottoms exposed, cavorting on a rocky terrain. It amused her. The nudity was innocent enough, but she wondered if her parents would approve.

Travis probably wouldn't show it to them. He'd been more secretive about his records ever since he made the mistake of showing their father Poison's "Look What the Cat Dragged In."

At first, their father had been intrigued, remarking that the four women on the album cover were quite beautiful. "*Sexy*" was the word he'd used. When Shane told him that the members of Poison were actually *men*, their father had become angry. He'd broken the record over his knee, pacing and cursing about how "them fuckin' fags" were ruinin' America. And he'd lectured Travis about not being lured in by such *vile wickedness*.

Of course, it had been "*sexy*" when he'd thought they were women.

Amanda wondered if that incident was why Travis had no pictures of girls on his walls, only rock bands—Metallica, Judas Priest, Slayer. But Iron Maiden was his favorite.

Iron Maiden stickers adorned the frame of his bed. A patch was sewn onto the lapel of Travis's favorite denim jacket. And an oversize Iron Maiden poster hung from the ceiling, featuring their zombie-like mascot, Eddie.

Travis had found the poster discarded behind a local record store, and while it wasn't in the best shape—frayed at the edges, torn in spots, and sun-bleached—it was still a prized possession.

Travis allowed Amanda to listen to his records, as long as she didn't scratch them. In addition to Metallica, Guns N' Roses, Dio, Iron Maiden, and others, he also had a box of miscellaneous albums he'd picked up at a garage sale for next to nothing.

The box included a decent assortment of Led Zeppelin, David Bowie, Pink Floyd, and Jimi Hendrix. *Those* were the ones Amanda preferred, though she appreciated it all. She looked forward to having a music collection of her own one day.

With Travis gone for the evening, Amanda stayed in his room, listening to albums for the better part of two hours. As she removed the needle from Pink Floyd's "Dark Side of the Moon," she heard arguing, even through the thick headphones.

She pulled the headphones off and listened.

It was her parents. Their voices were raised. Nothing new about that.

But there were other voices as well.

Her uncles.

Amanda tensed. She crept to the door and cracked it open, crouching low. They were in the kitchen.

"Jesus Christ, Earl," Harlan barked. "You live in *my daddy's house.* That don't count for nothin'?"

"Fuckin-A right," Malcolm added.

Amanda could tell right away that her uncles had been drinking. It wasn't unusual for them to show up unannounced—either on their way to or from a bar—worked up over some crazy notion.

Her father had likely been drinking too. It was a safe bet when he wasn't working.

The combination of all of them, liquored up and unreasonable, was never a good thing.

"Mama left the house to *us*, Harlan," Amanda's mother said, her voice curt. "Ya didn't stick *around* to take care of her after Daddy went missin', did ya?"

"Just 'cause ya got hitched young and moved yer husband in don't mean shit," Malcolm said. "We need *our part*."

"That's what I'm sayin', Debbie. You need to make it right," Harlan said. "Hell, all we're askin' for is a bit of a loan."

"We already gave you a *goddamn* loan!" her father shouted.

"I wasn't talkin' to you, jackass!" Harlan shouted back, his words slurred. "I was talkin' to my sister."

Her father huffed. "Well, this is *my* house too now. And I'd like you both to get the fuck out of it, thank ya very much."

Harlan sneered. "You think ya got the stones to put me out?"

There was a long silence. Amanda wondered if they might leave without incident. She hoped they would.

But then came a commotion.

Amanda knew the sound all too well—a scuffle.

Her mother shouted, "No, Harlan—Jesus! *Just go!*"

Glass shattered.

Amanda rushed out of Travis's room and peeked around the corner into the kitchen.

Harlan had her father pushed up against the kitchen counter. The front of her father's white t-shirt was balled up in Harlan's hands, and her father's hands were pushing back against Harlan's face. Shards of broken glass covered the floor, crunching under Harlan's boots.

Malcolm stood by the dining table watching them grapple. He held Amanda's mother by the arm, keeping her from interfering.

"Knock it off!" her mother shouted. "Y'all are grown men!"

Her father grunted and shoved hard beneath Harlan's jaw. Harlan stumbled backwards, colliding with the refrigerator.

"Get the hell outta my house!" her father screamed, pointing at the front door. His face was red. His t-shirt was ripped at the collar.

Harlan wiped his neck and glanced at his fingers—they were smeared with blood. "*Your* house, huh?" Harlan sniggered. "Hell, Earl, you ain't fit to piss in the yard, much less claim the deed."

"Get out! Now!" her father shouted again.

Amanda's stomach was in knots. But what could *she* do? Nothing at all.

"I want our *damn money!*" Harlan shouted, strands of spittle flying from his mouth.

"Ain't a dime comin' yer way! Y'all hear me?" her father yelled.

Amanda clenched her teeth as Harlan reached into his pocket and pulled out a pocketknife. He flipped it open, the small blade glistening in the soft light of the kitchen.

The blood rushed to Amanda's head. She wanted to call out, but the fear had her paralyzed.

"Come on now, Harlan," her mother said, her tone changing from combative to conciliatory. "Please. Don't go doin' nothin' crazy now."

She started to step forward, but Malcolm yanked her back. "Ain't nobody crazy here," he said. "We just want what we came fer, that's all."

"Damn straight," Harlan said. "We know you got the money, Earl. And we asked all polite like. We just need a little loan. Reckon that's the *least* ya can do."

Her father was still red in the face, his teeth bared, his breaths heaving. "And I done told ya once. If you're so dim ya didn't catch it the first time, let me tell ya 'gain." He pointed his finger in Harlan's face. "You can go straight to hell, Caulder."

Her mother gasped—a weak, fearful sound that made Amanda's heart sink.

Harlan stared at her father and wiped his neck again.

He shifted his gaze to her mother. "I still can't believe ya married this piece of shit, Deb."

Her father's bloodshot eyes narrowed, and he yelled at Harlan again, "Get outta my house!" He stepped forward and grabbed Harlan by the upper arm.

Amanda squeaked out the only thing her tight throat and dry mouth would allow—the tiniest *no* ever.

He shoved Harlan toward the front door.

But Harlan dug his heels in, scuffing the floor.

Then he turned and grabbed her father.

People always said Harlan had unusual strength for a thin man, but watching him manhandle her father—controlling his arms, pushing him back—was terrifying. Harlan's hand clamped around his throat and squeezed. Her father's eyes bulged.

And in a blur of movement—too fast for Amanda to process —Harlan thrust his arm forward, driving the knife into her father's gut.

As the blade pierced his flesh, it made a sickening *shink*. Like slicing into a pumpkin at Halloween.

For a moment, the room fell silent.

Then her mother cried out, "Earl!"

Amanda screamed.

At the edge of the kitchen, still holding her father, Harlan turned and looked at Amanda, noticing her for the first time. His face was still twisted, his eyes full of rage. But then he softened…and he *smiled*.

Somehow, that was worse.

Her father slumped to his knees, sliding onto the kitchen floor. He was holding his stomach, his hands covered in blood. "Motherfucker," he said with a frail defiance. "Son…of a bitch." He groaned, voice shaking. "You…you stabbed me…goddamn you."

Harlan turned back to her father, glancing down at the bloody pocketknife in his hand. Then he leaned over, placed a hand on her father's shoulder, and pulled on his t-shirt, using it like a cloth to wipe the blade clean.

He folded the knife up and slid it back into his pocket.

"I hope this sets ya straight. Next time, ya best listen," Harlan slurred. "Let's git, Mal."

Malcolm released his hold on Amanda's mother and fell in behind Harlan.

Her mother ran to her father, crumpled and moaning on the floor. She leaned over him, wrapping her arms around his back, pressing her face into him. "Earl! Earl! Earl!" she cried.

Harlan turned back to Amanda again.

And, in a soft, almost pleasant voice, he said, "Evenin' y'all."

The brothers walked out the front door, the screen slamming behind them as they left.

"C'mon, help me up," her father said. "We need to go to the hospital."

Her mother gripped his hand, helping him into one of the kitchen chairs.

"We gotta stop the bleedin' first," her mother said. She turned to Amanda. "Go fetch some wet rags, towels…*gauze.*"

Amanda hesitated, her mind racing, then hurried down the hall to the cabinet.

She wasn't sure if they *had* gauze. With shaking hands, she fumbled through the meager medical supplies. Bandages. Antiseptic. Aspirin. *No gauze.* Instead, she grabbed several hand towels and some of the larger bandages. Before returning, she wet the towels in the bathroom sink.

Amanda stood by as her mother mopped up the blood around the wound in her father's abdomen, but she tried not to see too much detail. She was already nauseated, but this wasn't the time to be sick.

"Hold it on the wound," her mother said, pressing a towel down over the cut. She picked up her father's hand and placed it over the wet towel.

They lifted him, one of them under each arm. Amanda smelled the sweat on him, the alcohol on his breath. Would that make the bleeding worse? She'd read that somewhere, hadn't she?

Supporting him, they shuffled outside and down the front steps, easing him into the car. Amanda stood on the lawn watching as her mother drove away with her father, headed to the hospital in town.

The house was a mess.

The floor was covered in blood. There were bloody shoeprints leading to the front door. Sticky, red handprints on the walls.

Amanda picked up the broken glass in the kitchen. And she did her best to clean the blood, despite it making her gag. When she was done, she took the rags down to the laundry in the basement. She looked at them in her hands, white rags turned red. They were ruined, she thought. The blood would never come out.

She set them on top of the washer and went back upstairs, returning the unused bandages to the hallway cabinet.

As she stood at the end of the hall, putting them away, organizing them so they'd be easier to find next time, there was a noise behind her.

An urgent, whispered *scream.*

Distant. Yet close enough to make her skin crawl.

She whipped around.

A bright light hovered at the end of the hall, about three feet above the floor. It was almost painful to look at it. Like the beam of a flashlight shining right into her eyes.

Then it moved toward her.

It came at her fast, bouncing, whipping from side to side.

Before she could move—before she even *thought* about it—the light passed through her. The force of it blew her hair back. And her skin went cold.

Amanda became dizzy. She stumbled back, thinking she might throw up.

And blackness overtook her.

She woke to her brothers standing over her, calling her name. They'd come home not long after the stabbing and found her passed out on the carpet at the entrance to her parents' bedroom.

Amanda told them that the incident had made her lightheaded. That was all.

Her mother and father returned later that evening. Her father appeared to be okay. He was bandaged, medicated, and *groggy*—he passed out on the couch in front of the television the moment he sat down.

When Amanda told her mother what had happened after they left, her mother dismissed it, assuring Amanda she'd only fainted. That it was from the shock of seeing her father stabbed.

But Amanda had felt it.

Something had passed through her. And she knew it was real.

———

While recuperating from his stomach wound, her father took over Shane's room, and Shane bunked with Travis, an arrangement none of them were happy about.

Amanda's mother insisted it would be better for her father—Shane's bed was lower, and the hall bathroom would be easier for him to use. But Amanda suspected her mother didn't want to share space with him when he was in pain and grumpy. On his best days, Amanda's father was difficult. When he was in pain, he was almost intolerable.

Amanda did her best to avoid him as well.

When she was home, she tried to stay outside as much as possible. That worked well, until the day she didn't hear him call for her. That made him angry. Amanda knew that she'd been fortunate he was in pain and somewhat incapacitated; otherwise, she was sure he would've taken the belt to her. After that, she stayed close to the house, where she would hear him.

Amanda thought he liked the attention, as scant as it was. He made the most out of being laid up, fishing for sympathy, groaning and moaning and bellyaching.

And though his health improved, his bad attitude remained. Before long, he was able to hobble around the house, wincing and sighing with every step.

Amanda adapted, teaching herself how to manage him. She found it was best to remain out of sight, and to come as fast as possible whenever he called. She also realized that when he fussed, it was best just to listen and nod—he wasn't looking for a conversation.

When it was only the two of them in the house, it was like she was on a seesaw—he'd move to one side and she'd move to the other, back and forth.

One afternoon, Amanda was sketching at the dining room table when her father bellowed. She scurried down the hall, pausing to take a breath before cracking the door to Shane's room. After what had happened with the dolls last Easter, she hated being in this room—even for a minute. She did her best to provide whatever her father needed, and then got out as fast as possible.

"Did ya call, Daddy?"

The room was dark, the shades drawn. Her father was lying on Shane's bottom bunk in his underclothes. His enormous body was draped over the twin bed like it was a toy, one foot on the floor, the other dangling over the end of the bed.

"I need some water," he groaned.

"Okay. Anything else?" Asking was polite, but she also found it saved her time. Fewer trips.

"Not right now."

Amanda shut the door and hurried back to the kitchen, where she filled a glass with tap water. Dreading re-entering Shane's room, she opened the door slowly and tiptoed across the carpet. Perhaps—on a subconscious level—she was trying to make as little contact with the floor as possible.

A rickety TV table sat next to the bed. On it was a box of tissues, a half-empty bottle of pain meds, and a pulp western novel called *Lonestar*, a monthly series her father liked to read; Amanda found it amusing that the covers always featured an Asian man fighting, and an attractive woman, half undressed.

She pushed the clutter aside and set the glass down.

Her father never said thank you. It was rare he even managed a grunt. But Amanda was content with that. Keeping the conversation to a minimum meant less time spent in this room.

She tiptoed back out and eased the door shut. She went back to the dining room, returning to her drawings, losing herself in her thoughts.

Half an hour later, her father screamed.

Amanda froze, gripping her pencil.

Her father wasn't one to scream. He'd gotten stabbed in their kitchen, and he hadn't cried out. Hadn't made much noise at all. Now, he was *shrieking*—full throated, blood curdling.

Amanda had no idea what to do.

After a long moment, she forced herself to her feet, moved across the kitchen, and started towards Shane's room. Was her father's scream from anger? Pain? *Terror?* She wasn't eager to find out.

Shaking, she pushed the door open. A rush of cold air swept past her.

Her father was still on the bed.

In fact, he seemed *pinned* to it.

His body thrashed and twisted. His legs kicked out. His arms flailed in the air above him, fists clenched, as if engaged in a struggle, fighting an unseen enemy.

For a moment, Amanda thought he was having a nightmare, lashing out in his sleep. But his eyes were wide open. And she saw something in them she'd never seen before—*terror*.

What could she do? She was only eight. He was a full-grown man. If she got too close, one of his frantic fists might hit her.

"What's happenin'?" she whispered.

As the words left her lips, her father's struggle stopped. His scream cut off and he bolted upright, leaping from the bed—nimble despite his injury. He rushed for the door. Amanda jumped aside as he lumbered past her, brushing against the doorframe. He ran into the living room and stopped, wild-eyed, gasping, confused. He bent over, panting, trying to catch his breath, his hands gripping the pale skin of his thighs. He was drenched in sweat.

"What the…*goddamn hell*…was that?" he wheezed.

Amanda shut the door to Shane's room. It made her feel better to have it closed. As if she was…*containing something*. Whatever it was. Trapping it.

"Are you alright?" she asked, following her father into the living room.

"*Lord Jesus*, protect us."

Amanda wasn't used to her father calling on Jesus. That alone was unsettling.

"Daddy, what happened?"

"Something…had me," he gasped. "Something *strong*. Like a damn bull on me."

"What…what was it?"

He shook his head, still panting. "I don't… *I don't know*."

Amanda saw that blood had seeped through his white tank top where his wound was. She pointed at it. Her father glanced down but he only acted put out by the red stain, as if it were a distraction, a minor inconvenience. He waved it away, still fighting for breath.

"It was…*on top of me!* Sittin' on my chest. Holdin' me down. Thrashin' on me, like it aimed to beat the life outta me."

"What was?" Amanda asked. "I don't understand."

"It wouldn't let go of me," he muttered. His voice was only a whisper. "It felt angry. *Evil.*"

A shiver coursed through Amanda, raising bumps on her arms.

"Like some kinda demon."

Chapter 26

Opening the Basement

"First off, the good news," the man from the septic company said.

It was the same thin, bearded man Chris had interacted with before. The nametag on his blue overalls said *Randy*, but he'd never introduced himself. He wasn't wearing his safety vest today, or his hard hat, only a regular baseball cap and thin safety glasses. He was holding a clipboard and a pen with gloved hands.

"I'll take *any* good news you want to give me," Chris replied with a chuckle.

"First, only part of the basement got hit, which saved y'all from a bigger mess. Second, a lotta the stuff was up on shelves or tables, or stacked on other boxes, so a good bit of it made it through alright.

"We disinfected the whole room and had the fans and dehumidifiers goin' all week to dry it out. Per the agreement, anything that came into direct contact with sewage or had visible contamination, or showed signs of mold, well, that stuff had to go. We pulled all of it out —mostly things sittin' on the floor or lower shelves."

Behind Randy, the other members of his crew had peeled the tape from the basement door and were busy removing the equipment from the basement and hauling it back to the truck.

"I understand," Chris said, smiling and nodding as the men passed by.

"Now, this part's important," Randy continued. "Y'all'll need to look over everything else yourselves. Anythin' with mold, odor, or signs of contamination needs to get cleaned or tossed. I've got a list here of the stuff most likely affected, like paper, and porous items like wood. Clothes'll need a thorough wash with detergent. The cardboard boxes should probably go. It's up to y'all to decide if somethin's worth cleanin' or replacin'."

"Okay, gotcha."

Randy scribbled something on the clipboard, then flipped it around to show Chris. He offered him the pen.

"Here's your invoice. We take cash, check, or credit. Heads up, though, there's a 5% card fee."

Chris was prepared and pulled the checkbook from his back pocket. "That ain't cheap." He signed the invoice, using the clipboard to make out the check.

"No, it sure ain't," Randy said. "But you *might* be able to file it with insurance, dependin' on your policy."

As he handed over the check, Chris sighed. He doubted that was going to be a possibility.

Randy secured the check on the clipboard and handed Chris a copy of the invoice in return. "Now, I hate to add bad news, but this is gonna have to be the last time we do any work for y'all."

Chris frowned. "What…you mean, like, ever?"

"Uh…yeah." Randy appeared a bit sheepish. "That's right."

"Why?"

"I can't say," Randy said, fumbling with the clipboard. "But it ain't personal, okay?"

"*You can't say?* I don't under—" And then it dawned on him. "Wait —does this have something to do with—"

"I just can't say," Randy repeated, cutting him off. His eyes said, *Please don't push this.*

Chris nodded, sighing. "Okay. I get it."

Randy shrugged and gave a slight smile, a sort of silent apology.

"Wish y'all the best. Take care now." He turned and walked out the front door.

———

Mandy heard Chris talking with the men from the septic company in the front room. She sat on the edge of the bed, staring down at the diary on the nightstand, as if the book itself was responsible for her state of mind, rather than the words written within it.

She couldn't stop thinking of the things her mother had confessed within its pages.

Mandy picked up her jeans from the floor and pulled the business card from one of the pockets. She sat back down and held the card between her fingers, staring at the phone number, thinking it through.

Chris is right, ya know. You're obsessed, Amanda Jean. Your folks ain't even tryin' and they're pullin' you back in. Deeper and deeper you go.

She unplugged her phone from the charger and began to dial, but she stopped and put the phone back down.

Ridiculous. Unnecessary. What good can come of it?

She steadied herself, then picked up the phone again, and dialed. Her finger hovered over the call button, taut. She pressed it before doubt could take hold again. After a few rings, he answered.

"Harper," he said.

"Bo? It's Mandy…uh, Amanda."

There was a beat and he said, "Well, now, look at that. Real nice to hear from ya."

"Is this a bad time?"

"Not for you, it ain't."

She hesitated. She was having trouble saying the words. She felt silly verbalizing it. *This was a mistake.*

"You still there? Everything alright?" he asked, his voice low and calm.

She decided to say it. She spoke quickly, before she could lose her nerve. "After I ran into you the other day, I couldn't stop thinking about what you said. So, I went and saw Travis."

"Oh yeah? And…how'd that go?"

"I asked him about our folks," she said. "And I don't think he had anything to do with it."

"Alright."

"But he told me something else. He said my uncle Harlan was in the house that day too. Did you know that?"

There was silence on the other end of the phone.

It was long enough that Mandy decided to fill the void. "So…no thoughts on that?" she asked.

He paused. After a faint intake of breath, he said, "None jumpin' out at me right now, no."

"Okay." She shook her head.

"Amanda…what are ya hopin' to find here?"

Mandy rubbed her eyes—they were sore, almost *raw*. She considered hanging up the phone but didn't. "I don't know—the truth? Does anyone care about that anymore? 'Cause it sure feels like my uncle's got everyone in this town scared of him. Like y'all are trapped under his boot."

Bo sighed. "What is it you'd like me to do?"

"Aside from your job, you mean?"

"I'm not a detective, Amanda."

"Is *anyone* around here?"

Again, he didn't respond.

"I'm sorry," she went on. "I… I'm frustrated."

"And I wanna help. I'm not the enemy," Bo said. "But ya gotta ask yourself if this is a thread you wanna keep pullin' at."

It seemed like a warning, but was it about Harlan or her state of mind?

She considered it. Maybe she *shouldn't* continue—what was she going to do with the truth when and if she found it?

After a moment, she said, "Yeah, I do."

"What can I do to help?"

"I don't know." She paused. "You have access to police reports?"

He sighed. "Yeah."

"Can you pull up any involving Harlan and Mama? Or him at this address? Or with my family?"

"And then what?"

"Just…share them with me?"

He took another deep, slow, thoughtful breath. "I'll see what I can dig up. But I'll need a couple of hours. Can you meet me later?"

"What time? Where?"

———

Mandy picked up the diary from the nightstand, hurrying out of the bedroom, but she stopped short.

She wasn't expecting to see the basement door standing open.

She gasped. The breath caught in her throat and her stomach tightened. Her pulse began to race.

She told herself the reaction was silly. Reminded herself to take a breath.

But her hands started to shake.

Why was it standing open?

Mandy closed her eyes and focused on her breathing.

In. And out.

"Well, *that* could've gone better," Chris said. His voice startled her, sudden against the tense silence. She did her best not to jump.

When she opened her eyes, she focused on Chris and tried to ignore the basement door behind him, though she could feel it looming. Chris's expression was dispirited.

"Uh oh," she said, trying to steady her voice. "Worse than expected?"

"Better, actually," he said, holding the invoice in front of him. "They said it wasn't as bad as it could've been. But the guy said their company won't work with us anymore in the future."

"What?" Mandy's eyes narrowed. "Did they say *why?*"

"No. But I think we both have an idea."

"I certainly do," she said through gritted teeth.

"Your uncle warned me something like this would happen. He said we needed to sell while everything was '*still friendly.*'" Chris added finger quotes for emphasis.

Mandy scoffed. *Still friendly—what a joke.*

"I asked him if he was threatening me," Chris said. "But he said he wasn't a violent man."

Wasn't a violent man! She could feel the heat coming back into her cheeks. At least rage was better than fear, she thought.

"He *really* wants the house, Mandy. And, yeah…I don't appreciate being threatened any more than you do. But your uncle seems ready to do whatever it's gonna take to get us *out of here*. I don't know about you, but that scares the shit out of me."

"Fucking—*cocksucker!*" Mandy shouted at the air. She began to pace around the living room, around the tents, her body shaking, her fists tightening into balls. "They gave this goddamn house *to me!* Fuckin' asshole!"

Chris's voice was calm—almost maddeningly reasonable—like he was explaining something to a child. It made her want to scream. "I realize it's a bitter pill to swallow, but I think we need to—"

"NO!" She turned back to him. "You *say* you love me. And you *say* you trust me. Well, if that's true, you have to drop this subject *right now*, because I *cannot* sell to that man! Not ever! *I will not!*"

"*If that's true?* Jesus, Mandy, I have been by your side through thick and thin. I've kept vows you never even let me take!"

Mandy flinched.

Chris continued. "But now, our family might be in *real danger!* So, my patience and understanding are running dry. And I don't know what to do anymore! So, tell me!" His voice broke, raw, pleading. "Tell me what to do!"

Mandy stopped moving, unable to find the right words. Her heart was thudding. She stared at the open basement door. The darkness of it seemed to be mocking her, like a wide-open mouth, laughing, ready to swallow her whole.

She hated it so much.

For a moment, she considered handing the diary to Chris and letting him read. It would tell him everything he wanted to know. But she couldn't. She didn't want him learning about any of it. The reality of life here—the life she'd lived before him. The world she'd known. The people who'd shaped her. She didn't want him to see these parts of her—the ones she'd taken care to hide away, and the ones she'd ignored, denied, and buried for so many years.

"I need air," she said.

Chris sighed, his shoulders slumping.

Mandy went out the front door, crossed the front yard, and got into her car.

As she drove away, she resisted the urge to look back.

———

As Grace moved through the house, she noticed that the doorway to the basement was open. That was new. She went to it and peered in. The stairs were weathered. They led to a landing. The lights were on, but they were weak, little match for the darkness below.

Grace called down. "Hello?"

"I'm down here," her father called back.

"Can I come down?" she asked.

"Yeah, but…be careful on the stairs. They're old."

Grace started down, taking her time. Step by step. They creaked, even under her small frame.

As she reached the landing, she sniffed. The basement stunk. It was stale, like spoiled milk.

When she reached the bottom, she stopped and looked around. It was dark—the few hanging lights didn't do much. But she could see that the basement was big—almost the size of the living room, dining room, and kitchen combined. Near the stairs was a laundry area—a washer and dryer and a clothes rack with miscellaneous hangers. On the far side of the room was a long, narrow window, positioned near the ceiling.

The rest of the room was a cluttered mess. Full of storage racks and tables. Overflowing with a mishmash of packing boxes, bins, and assorted junk.

The lower shelves had all been emptied during the septic clean-up, and what remained was a jumble, with no rhyme or reason: piles of old clothes, stacks and stacks of papers, old books, greeting cards, and yellowed newspapers. Among the rest of the clutter, Grace spotted a stack of board games, an assortment of plates, a broken bicycle, a record player, and an old computer monitor.

In one corner were several fishing poles, a large bird cage, a plastic Christmas tree, and a wooden sign that read "Sweet Tea Served Here." A garden gnome statue sat nearby, its paint nearly gone. The outline of a tailor's dummy caught her by surprise, and she jumped before realizing what it was.

In the middle of it all was her father, sweat beading on his forehead. He was moving fast, trying to make sense of it all, to impose some sort of order on the chaos, but he appeared frustrated. And exhausted—like his heart wasn't in it anymore.

"Hi sweetie," he said when he saw her. "I was hoping we'd be able to move stuff down here, but it looks like we're gonna have a lot of work to do first. I guess I shouldn't be surprised, huh?"

He made his way over to her, navigating his way through the mess. Once clear, he wiped his hands together and brushed his shirt and pants. Dust filled the air and he coughed.

"I don't want you and your brother messing with any of this crap, okay?" he said. His voice was firm, but he was distant, still scanning the mess like it was a puzzle to be solved.

Grace nodded.

"I'm serious. It may not be safe. We're gonna have to go through it all and see if any of it can be cleaned and salvaged…if we even want to keep any of it."

After following her father back up the stairs, conscious of each step, Grace ran to find Ethan. There was a new area for them to explore.

"Be careful of the stairs," she cautioned, echoing her father's words. "They're very old."

They went down into the basement together.

After warning Ethan they shouldn't touch anything, they began to look around. But not a minute had gone by before Ethan was thumbing through the board games.

"I *said* we're not supposed to touch anything," Grace stressed.

Ethan shrugged. "They're only games. How could they hurt us?"

He pulled one of them from the pile and brushed the dust from the box.

"What is it?" Grace asked.

Ethan held it up so she could see.

She squinted, reading the front, sounding it out. "What is Ouija?"

———

Mandy remembered having waffles with her mother in this diner, once upon a time. Back when the place had been called *Rose's*. Now, she sat in a booth across from her childhood boyfriend, waiting for him to speak.

He'd set his hat on the seat of the booth when he came in, revealing hair that was damp with sweat, flattened to his scalp.

His eyes, as ever, were kind. But also furtive. Mandy wasn't sure what it was, but she thought he appeared uneasy. Perhaps he had news. Or perhaps it was because of their shared past.

Either way, it made her anxious.

"The department has been upgradin' a lot of the older cases from paper to digital," he explained, "but anything before the early 90s is usually only digitized when there's a particular need, like if we reopen a cold case, somethin' like that. Anything before that is stored in cabinets in the records room or stuffed in boxes in a storage room. And, as you might imagine, recordkeeping from that far back was spotty as is. So…"

"So…you didn't find anything."

"About your mama and Harlan?" Bo shook his head. "No, I'm sorry. I didn't."

Mandy was disappointed, but not surprised.

"However," he said. "I did find a few…*other* things."

She leaned in.

Bo pulled a folded paper from his jacket pocket and unfolded it. He laid it on the tabletop, smoothing the creases with his fingertips far longer than was necessary, like he was stalling.

"There were a handful of…*reports* from the early to mid-90s. Your uncles causing trouble. A couple about them showing up at your house. But then…" He paused. "Then there's this." He patted the paper.

Mandy's stomach tightened. "What is it?"

"I found… There *was* a police report in 1990 about an assault at your house involving your uncle. But it was withdrawn."

"Really? Harlan and Mama?"

Bo shook his head. His voice was soft, almost apologetic. "Harlan and *you*."

Mandy winced. "What?" She shook her head, heat creeping up her neck. "That doesn't—there must be a mistake. *I don't understand.*"

"You don't have any idea what it's about?"

She searched her memory, but there was nothing. "No."

"Well, that's all I got. Couldn't find no other details."

"I never filed a police report. There was no assault. Harlan was scary, sure, but… I don't understand this at all."

"I'm sorry," he said. "I know this ain't what you were hopin' for."

Bo reached across the table and placed his hand over hers.

Mandy quickly pulled her hand back, and a pang of guilt followed. "I'm sorry," she said.

"Nope. Shouldn't have done that."

"It's okay." She pressed a hand to her face, her head swimming. "I'm just confused. I don't know what to think. It's like reality glitched on me."

———

ETHAN SET the board up on the dining room table. He couldn't find any instructions, so he looked them up on his phone and read them aloud to Grace.

Though the idea of the Ouija board creeped him out a bit, Ethan was a natural skeptic like his father. He didn't give much weight to things like this. Plus, it was still the middle of the afternoon. With sunlight streaming through the kitchen window, it was much easier to be bold.

Grace didn't seem scared either. But she almost never did. He admired that about her.

"Ready to try it?" he asked.

Grace nodded, placing her fingers on the planchette. Ethan did as well.

"Are you nervous about this at all?" he asked.

Grace shrugged. "Seems kinda silly."

The planchette jerked beneath their fingers. Grace's eyes shot open. Ethan held his breath. They watched as it slid from letter to letter.

"N-O-T-F-U-N-N-Y"

"Not funny," Ethan whispered.

Grace looked up at him, disbelief on her face.

"I guess it didn't like you calling it silly," he said.

"Okay, but *who* didn't?"

Ethan shook his head. "I guess we should ask it. Is someone here with us?"

With no hesitation, the planchette moved again. "M-A-Y-B-E"

Ethan's jaw clenched.

Grace smiled. "Who is this?" she asked.

The planchette sat still on the board.

"Who are you?" Grace asked again.

Still no movement.

Grace's smile disappeared and her brow furrowed. "Okay. So, what do we do now?"

"I'll ask it something else," Ethan said. He was still a moment. He thought of what was on his mind the most. "Is mom going to be like this forever?"

The planchette eased into action.

"N-O-N-S-E-N-S-E"

"Okay," Ethan said, taking a relieved sigh. "Sort of a *weird* answer, but I'll take it. Do you have anything you want to ask?"

"Maybe it'll only answer *you*," Grace said. "Maybe it's a sexist ghost."

Ethan chuckled. "Try again."

Grace stared at the planchette, concentrating. "Ah. Who is the little girl?"

After a short pause, the planchette slid over the surface of the board.

"A-N-Y-O-N-E"

"Anyone?" Grace asked, her face scrunched.

"Does that make sense to you?" Ethan asked.

Grace shrugged. Then she asked, "Is the little girl dead?"

Ethan didn't like that question at all. But the planchette began responding the moment the words left Grace's mouth.

"I-N-T-H-E-D-A-R-K"

Grace's lips pressed together and her eyes narrowed. "Well…*that's* horrible."

Ethan's hand trembled against the planchette. This was skirting the edge of his comfort zone, but he was too curious to stop. "*Where* is the dark?" he asked.

Without hesitation, the planchette moved.

"I-N-T-H-E-H-O-U-S-E"

Ethan felt his skin crawl. He hadn't experienced anything strange since they'd been in Rosebury, nor had he seen the little girl. But Grace said she had, and he had no reason to doubt her. Now it was like the board was telling them that she was here, *somewhere* in the house, in the dark.

Before he could voice his apprehension, Grace asked another question. "Who is the shadow man?"

Another question Ethan didn't care for.

The planchette sat still a beat, then twitched and began to slide again.

"M-E-A-N-O-N-E"

"Mean…one," Grace whispered, nodding in agreement. "Yeah, he is."

"Should we be afraid?" Ethan asked.

As the planchette started to slide, he heard the front door open. He read the letters aloud as they came.

"T-A-K-E-I-T"

"What the hell!? *NO!*" It was their mother's voice, shrill and loud. Shaking. Furious. She rushed into the kitchen. "Don't!"

The planchette jolted beneath their fingers, sliding faster: "S-E-R-I-O-U-S"

"*Stop* that right now! That thing is—*evil!*"

Ethan tried to concentrate, keeping his focus on the board. But the planchette was ripped away. Their mother snatched the board from between them and hurled both pieces across the kitchen. They crashed against the wall, the sound echoing through the room.

Ethan flinched. He'd never seen his mother act like this before. Rage twisted her face. Her body shook. Her fists were clenched. Across the table, Grace shrank back, hands up, her eyes brimming with tears.

"I told you a *hundred* times I didn't want you going into the *goddamn* basement!" their mother continued, screaming at full volume. "Did you think I was joking around! Do you think I tell you things to fucking hear myself talk!?" She was out of breath. Her hands were shaking. After a moment, she steadied herself. "Get out," she said, her voice shifting from anger to disappointment. "Go outside. Go play outside. Go away. Both of you. Now."

Grace sniffled. Ethan grabbed her hand and pulled her toward the back door, keeping himself between her and their mother.

Chapter 27

Faces in the Dark

"What the hell was that?" Chris charged into the kitchen, looking from Mandy to the Ouija board and planchette lying near the wall.

Mandy had nothing to say in her defense. She was trembling. She couldn't look at him.

"Do you think that was okay?" He gestured to the board. "To scream at them like that? To throw their game across the room?"

"It's not a game," she whispered.

"I don't give a shit what it is. It's not okay. You and I agreed before we ever had Ethan that we wouldn't be those kinds of parents, and we never have."

Mandy felt nauseated. She grabbed her left shoulder with her right hand and buried her face in the crook of her arm. "I know."

Chris pulled a hand through his hair and walked over to the kitchen counter. He leaned over the sink, taking deep breaths, his shoulders heaving. He lowered his voice, almost to a whisper. "I don't even know what to say anymore. I really don't. I realize you haven't been yourself since your parents died. But it's gotten so much worse since we arrived here. And I've been trying so hard to be understanding, but it's hard…because you *do not* let me in."

"I know."

He turned back to her, folding his arms. He stayed where he was, next to the sink, a good eight feet away from her.

"I understood that there were parts of your life you were…*never* gonna share with me. I knew that. I accepted it. And you've always been a good partner—and a good mom too. But I also realized, sorta early on, that you were never gonna be *that kinda* mom. The warm and fuzzy kind. The share your feelings kind. You were a bit better with Grace, but you've always been so standoffish with Ethan, ever since he was a little boy, like you were afraid to know him. Like you were scared of him. And all he's ever done is want your approval. Your *love*.

"But I figured…hey, there are two of us, right? We both have strengths and weaknesses. We can complement each other. *I* can pick up the slack. *I* can be the warm and fuzzy one. But Jesus, Mandy, you're acting like a total stranger now. And it seems like there's always something more important than us."

"That's not true," she whispered.

"Please, let me finish."

She nodded and continued staring at the floor, feeling small.

"I understand that you're wrestling with old ghosts. But you're not supposed to be fighting us *too*. *We're your team*. We're *not* your enemies."

"I understand that."

"We've been here—what, a week? And how many of those days have you been *here*? How many hours have you spent with your children? And even when you *are* here, you aren't. Not *really*. You're a million miles away. Inside your own head. You're like a shadow of yourself. A shell. And when you look at us, it's like you're looking right through us."

"I'm…sorry," Mandy said.

"I'm not asking you to be *sorry*, I'm asking you to be *here*. That's all I have been asking. But every day you find a reason not to. And I don't know whether you're searching for something…or running from something."

She didn't say anything. Just took it in.

"Today, for example," Chris said, "where did you go?"

Mandy's body tensed. She wasn't expecting this question and she wasn't prepared to respond. "I met with…a friend."

Chris hesitated, studying her face. "A friend?"

"A friend that works in the sheriff's office. I ran into him at the store a few days ago."

Chris nodded. "A man? Someone from your past? And you didn't think it was worth mentioning? Wouldn't be an old boyfriend, would it?"

Mandy was silent.

She wanted to say something that would make him understand. But, as usual, she didn't have the words. At the very least, she wanted to look at him, but she couldn't lift her gaze from the floor.

Chris huffed again, shaking his head. "You're getting lost in the past. In all this unresolved *bullshit*."

They were both quiet. The house was still.

Finally, Chris said, "Well, do you want to know what happened while you were gone?"

It was a rhetorical question. She knew that and she let it hang.

"I followed up with the electricians I'd reached out to. And guess what? They aren't gonna work with us either. Neither of them. Wanna take a wild guess as to why?"

Mandy held her breath.

"We're *screwed*. Dead in the water. And what do you think's gonna happen when we try to sell this place to someone *other* than your uncle?" He sighed. "You might think you're grasping for an oar, but it's an *anchor*. And it's going to pull us all down. But you don't care."

"That's not true. It's not fair," she said, gritting her teeth, holding back tears.

"Isn't it, Mandy?" Chris said, his volume ramping up again. "You don't want to be here. Yet, we have an opportunity to be done with it —to *leave*—and you won't take it. And if we stay, we're between a rock and a hard place. *We already are!* But it doesn't seem to matter. And it doesn't change your answer, does it?"

He paused, giving her a chance to reply.

Inside she was screaming at herself: *Just fucking tell him why!*

But she remained silent.

"That's what I thought," he said.

He was quiet until the silence became oppressive.

He exhaled. "I hate this. I never wanted our relationship to be like this. But I'm gonna have to ask you to make a choice. You either need to agree to sell this place and allow us to start over…or you need to stay here and figure out this shit on your own. But it's not safe for your family to stay here anymore. So, I'm asking you…this house or *us*."

A tear rolled down Mandy's cheek. She continued to hug herself tight, staring at nothing on the floor. She wanted to scream, to break down, but all she could do was close her eyes and try to remember to breathe.

"That's what I thought," Chris said, his voice cracking. "I'm gonna move my stuff into another room." After a moment, he dropped his arms and moved to the back door. Before he stepped outside, he turned back to her. "I don't want it to be like this."

And then he was gone.

I don't want this either.

———

CHRIS SEARCHED for the kids outside, both on the side yard near the shed and in the front. He circled around the other side of the house near the trailers but found no one. They must have gone deep into the yard, into the grove, he figured. He began to walk that direction. He'd been so consumed with the overwhelming amount of work the house required, he hadn't ventured into the yard yet. He hoped it wouldn't be too hard to find them.

It wasn't.

Grace was sitting on a ramshackle bridge that ran over the small, trickling brook. Her feet were dangling. Ethan was standing next to her, pulling the petals from a flower and watching them float down into the water.

"Hey guys," Chris said.

They appeared surprised to see him in the yard.

Grace's face was slick with tears, but she smiled. "Is Mom okay?" she asked.

Chris couldn't help but admire her empathy.

He strolled over to the foot of the bridge and leaned against the old wooden railing, careful to avoid the thick mud that ran along the creek's edge. "Your mom...she is going through something right now. She's not mad at you guys."

"Seemed pretty mad," Ethan said. Another petal floated down.

"Well, you're not wrong," Chris said, "She *is* mad. But...not at you."

Grace tilted her head. "What's she mad about?"

"That's complicated," Chris said. "I don't really understand it. I don't think *she* even understands it either. She's...got a lot of feelings right now."

"And being mad is easier?" Ethan asked.

Chris smiled and nodded.

"Well, she scared us," Ethan said. "She scared Grace."

"I know. And I'm sorry." Chris glanced around at the grove. "So, this is where you two have been spending all your time, huh?"

"A lot of it, yeah," Ethan said.

"It's nice."

"There's a lot more," Grace said, pointing. "Lots of trees and paths, and the bus, and the tombstones."

"Oh, yeah," Chris said. "The tombstones. And you guys don't get scared being out here all by yourselves? No more old men with shotguns?"

"It's not scary," Grace said. "He hasn't come back. And the little girl doesn't like it here."

"Little girl?"

Ethan shook his head and rolled his eyes slightly, as if to say, *Don't encourage her.*

"Yeah," Grace said, after a moment. "It makes her sad."

"Is this one of those...?" Chris asked, leaving the question open ended.

She nodded.

"Well…alright," Chris said. He changed the subject. "Listen, after tonight, we may move back to the hotel for a bit. Is that okay?"

Both of them appeared surprised, and uncertain. Ethan nodded.

"With Mom?" Grace asked.

She was quick. She always had been.

Chris was careful with his words. "Mom might stay in the house by herself, just for a bit. Try to figure out what's making her so sad."

"Do you think that'll help?" Ethan asked.

Chris shrugged. "I don't know, bud."

Ethan pulled another petal from the flower. "I hope so." He let the petal drop, and it fluttered down, landing on the surface of the creek, sending small ripples out in the water.

———

At some point during the afternoon, Chris had made up Shane's old room—the one Mandy both hated and feared. If she'd realized he was going to do it, she would've talked him out of it. Or tried to. But now it was done. Now, she thought mentioning it would only add to his perception that she was growing more unhinged. And she had to admit, the longer she was here in Rosebury—the more she learned and the deeper she sank into the morass—the more she was inclined to agree with him.

She stayed silent as he told the kids goodnight, then disappeared into a room she couldn't stand. She winced as he closed the door.

Mandy had been quiet around the kids the rest of the day. She kept telling herself she needed to apologize, but she hadn't. She didn't know how to go about telling her own children she was wrong. And that she was ashamed. She didn't know how to start a conversation like that. Instead, she wandered into the living room, made sure that they were ready for bed, and wished them goodnight, ignoring the elephant in the room altogether.

As she walked back down the hall toward the primary bedroom, the house became cold. And she heard whispers all around her. The walls began to breathe—just as they had in her dream. It was as if the house were alive, predatory, and she was trapped inside of it, wasting away in its belly.

She couldn't discern what was real anymore.

Mandy climbed into bed and closed her eyes, pulling the covers over her head, trying to muffle the sound. But it was far too hot to stay under them for long. When she emerged, she was thankful to see that the house had returned to normal. The walls were still. The whispers were gone.

She changed into a tank top and shorts and lay on top of the sheets, listening to the box fan hum. Her mind wouldn't stop. She kept replaying the conversation with Chris, the episode with her kids and the Ouija board, the passage from her mother's diary, the visit from her uncle. On and on. Her brain was a crowded subway car—thoughts bumping into each other, no room to breathe. As one would exit, two more would push their way inside. Too many. Too much.

She turned onto one side. Then the other.

And the hours began to tick away.

In the middle of the night, the house grew still, and the air turned heavy. Something was amiss. Mandy told herself it was only nerves, a product of her overstimulated thoughts, but something had shifted. The blackness became unnerving. She began to see images in the shadows, movement where there was only stillness. Her mind conjured faces in the dark.

And a dread began to creep in.

She sat up in bed, peering around the room.

You are losing your mind, Amanda Jean. Losing your mind. Losing your family. Losing everything. But you were never meant to have it all in the first place.

Mandy got up and went to the bathroom.

The lights flickered before coming on full, and she was reminded of her recent dream once more. The walls breathing, the lights fluttering, ready to blink out. After running the faucet, she splashed water on her face, and glanced in the mirror.

You can't run from blood, girl. The crazy's always in ya.

She flicked the light off and returned to the bedroom. Everything was darker after feeding her eyes a bit of light. She glanced at the bed, which had been of little comfort to her so far. The covers were still pulled back and the sheets looked undisturbed. Like it was waiting for her to return.

Just go next door and tell Chris you're sorry, she thought. *Wake the kids. Get out of here. Together.*

But she didn't.

Something inside her held fast, as if it was impossible. Having those conversations seemed physically painful. No matter how desirable it was to think of driving away from this place, as a family, and seeing the house get smaller and smaller in the rearview mirror.

Instead, she distracted herself. Told herself she was thirsty, that a drink of water was all she needed. After that, she could go to sleep.

Mandy walked through the house, trying not to run into any walls or make any noise that might wake Ethan or Grace.

She stopped in the living room and stood near the two tents where the kids were sleeping. The moonlight coming in through the front window cast the room in an eerie blue light. And for a moment, it almost appeared as if the tents were set up outside under the stars, as they should be. Not here. In this house. In this dirty place where she'd brought them to live.

As she entered the kitchen, her mind flashed to her father, sitting at the dining room table, tinkering with a stopwatch. Her mother at the sink, potato peeler in hand.

Finding her way to the cooler wasn't as difficult as she feared it might be. The moonlight seeping through the window coverings helped. As she opened the lid, she realized she'd been so preoccupied, she hadn't made a trip to the store to refresh the supplies and buy more ice.

Mandy pulled one of the bottles out of the water. Its label was soggy, sliding away. She unscrewed the top and took a sip.

Before returning to bed, she took a moment and drank her water, surveying the kitchen. A cockroach ran by her bare feet, scurrying across the wood floor that was still stained with her father's blood.

Infested, she thought. *Just like it always was.*

She took another sip, trying her best to shake off the unease that had taken hold of her. But it wasn't working. Something was off—more than usual. But she couldn't figure out what it was. Couldn't put her finger on it.

She went to the back door and checked that it was locked. She thought of her uncle's face peering through the window.

Next, she went to the basement door and made sure it was locked as well. As she placed her hand on the doorknob, there was a moment she swore she heard the creaking of the basement steps. It took her breath away, the idea that someone might be there, waiting on the other side of the door.

It was then—standing in front of the basement, straining to listen —that Mandy realized what didn't feel right.

The silence.

There were no sounds tonight.

No crickets. No cicadas. No owls. No random barking dogs.

Only stillness.

A chill ran through her. She couldn't remember a single time when there was no background noise in this house.

She took her hand away from the basement door and stepped back, pushing the thought from her mind.

Taking care to be as quiet as possible, Mandy went to the front door and checked that lock as well. She didn't want anyone to get inside.

She went back down the hall, stopping in front of the door to her childhood bedroom. There was no reason to go in. None. But before she could think better of it, she pushed the door open and stepped inside, looking around the dark room.

The window coverings in this room were doing a better job of keeping out the moonlight. She had to strain to see. Although the kids had spent a lot of time clearing out the unwanted junk, the room was still quite cluttered.

Mandy thought again of the night she and Cheryl had played with the Ouija board, the incident with her children still fresh in her mind. She thought of the headlights on the window, of crawling from the room on her hands and knees. And her eyes sought out the stain on the floor, where she'd laid, knocked unconscious, her face bleeding.

She moved to the antique mirror, now covered once more. Though she knew she shouldn't, she found that she couldn't stop herself. She pulled the painter's cloth away. At first, she strained to see her reflection in the dark, letting her eyes adjust.

She stared at her face—a face that had begun to appear foreign to her over the past few months, and even more so in the last week. And as she gazed at the image, it began to soften, shifting into something more familiar, something more like her. But it wasn't her at all. Not the person she saw in the mirror every day.

It was her childhood self.

Though unsettled, Mandy was also fascinated. She recalled a concept from a college psychology course called Mirror-Self Misidentification, a delusion where one perceives their reflection as someone else, often a younger version of themselves. But her intellectual curiosity was overshadowed by a far more unsettling thought.

Losing. Your. Mind.

Then the reflection—the little girl version of her—began to cry. Soft at first, then harder.

Mandy watched. At first with a cold fascination, as if it were just another hallucination, one more strange and unsettling experience.

But then the weight of it settled.

This was *her*. Crying. Desperate.

Mandy began to feel it too.

Little Amanda's pain. Her sorrow. Her shame and grief.

Mandy had kept this version of herself at arm's length for so long, it almost didn't feel like the same person. And while a part of her wished she could hold Little Amanda, comfort her, wipe her tears away, she also understood that this version of her—no matter how real it might seem—didn't exist anymore.

It was trapped in the mirror now. It existed only in photographs. In memories. Lost to time. Glimpsed only in rare, fleeting moments.

Little Amanda continued to cry, to *sob*, her body shaking. Her tears grew heavier, her anguish more potent. Helpless, Mandy watched as the girl's shoulders heaved and her nose ran, mixing with her tears, the kind of grief normally reserved for privacy.

Then something inside Little Amanda shifted. Sadness into anger. And she began scratching at her forearms. Slowly at first. Then faster. And harder. Her fingernails dug into her soft skin until it became raw. She kept clawing, even after she'd started to bleed.

"No," Mandy whispered.

She moved closer to the antique mirror, holding the edges of the frame, watching as the younger version of herself tore at her own flesh. Tears came into Mandy's eyes now.

"No," she repeated, a bit louder, as if the image would hear her, as if there was anything she could do to change this.

Little Amanda stopped clawing and became still.

She wasn't crying now. Her face was expressionless, her eyes lifeless.

A wave of nausea swept through Mandy. She shook her head, biting at her wet lips, tears dripping down her face.

"No," she said again in a hushed tone. And she realized she wasn't speaking to the girl in the mirror. Not anymore. She was talking to herself, fighting against the emotions that were bubbling up within her.

Little Amanda stayed still, blood running down her arms.

Then Mandy saw something move behind her—a shadowy form, emerging from the darkness.

Mandy gasped, whipping around—but nothing was in the room with her. This was all playing out in the mirror.

She turned back and watched in horror as the shadowy figure moved closer to the child, placing its long black fingers on her shoulder, leaning in close.

The figure was immense. Billowy. Long teeth. Empty sockets. Curved horns blending into the darkness. It hovered over Little Amanda, wrapping around her, a dark and nebulous wraith.

"No," Mandy whispered again.

She caught a whiff of stale cigarettes. Felt the hot breath on her neck, near her ear.

She jerked around again, her heart pounding, hands shaking, but she was still very much alone.

As much as she didn't want to—as much as she wished she couldn't—Mandy turned back to the mirror once more.

The shadowy figure wrapped Little Amanda up in its arms. A haunting melody and the sound of jingling keys rose unbidden in Mandy's mind. And she realized, suddenly and with terrible certainty, that she knew what this was.

Who this was.

That, in some way, she had always known.

The realization struck her like a blow, leaving her gasping. Disgust and revulsion coiled within her—so intense she thought she might throw up, as if her body wanted to expel the truth. To purge it.

But as quickly as the nausea came, it was replaced by anger.

Her hands tightened into fists. "You son of a bitch!" she yelled.

Before she could stop herself, she drew her arm back and punched the mirror as hard as she could. Her knuckles crashed into the glass. The image splintered. For a moment—a brief, almost infinitesimal flicker in time—the mirror held, an interwoven spiderweb of cracks and fissures. The reflection fractured, splitting into infinite, distorted copies of the same scene. For only a moment. Then the glass gave way, and the mirror shattered, raining jagged shards onto the floor.

Her knuckles throbbed, but she barely noticed the pain.

Mandy fell to her knees and began to sob.

She pressed her hands to her face and allowed the tears to flow, unchecked. Her body shook as the sobs tore through her, and she didn't fight it. The emotions poured out, raw and primal. They had been stored up for far too long, buried deep within her, and now they were clawing their way free.

She held herself and made no effort to stop the tears, though she worried she might wake the others.

Minutes passed before Mandy began to calm. Her tears slowed and her breath steadied, though it still came in short, catching bursts.

She opened her eyes and looked around at the broken glass littering the floor. Some of the shards were quite large, jagged. Others were mere slivers. But they reflected the same broken and distorted image of her—damaged, exhausted, grieving.

"Mom?" Ethan's voice broke the silence, startling her.

She jumped, wiping the tears from her face, but it did little to mask the state she was in.

"Are you okay?" he asked in a whisper.

"I'm fine honey. I'm fine," she lied, her voice quavering.

Mandy glanced up at him. He was standing in the doorway of her childhood bedroom. She wondered if he'd ever seen her cry before.

"You're hurt," Ethan said, pointing at her hand. "You're bleeding."

Mandy followed his gaze, noticing the blood for the first time—a deep gash across her knuckles. "Oh…" she said weakly, placing her other hand over it to restrict the bleeding.

"I'll get a bandage," Ethan said. He disappeared before she could stop him. When he returned, he was carrying a small first aid kit. Careful to avoid the glass, he knelt beside her, took her injured hand in his, and began to care for her. He disinfected the wound and wrapped her hand in gauze. His movements were steady, his brow furrowed in concentration, his touch gentle but assured—as if caring for her came as naturally as breathing.

Mandy's anguish began to recede, replaced by something else—a quiet awe at the boy kneeling before her. She observed him, so focused and gentle—mature beyond his years—and wondered what she had done to deserve a son like this. She hadn't earned it. She'd kept him at arm's length, horrified by the prospect of replicating the sins of her parents. And yet here he was, quietly mending her in the dark.

Despite how much Ethan resembled the men in her family— despite all of her fears of him following in their footsteps—in this moment, all she could see was Chris.

Tears welled in her eyes again.

"I'm so sorry I woke you, honey," she whispered.

"I was awake," Ethan said. "Grace woke me."

Mandy frowned. "Is she… Is everything okay?"

"Yeah," Ethan nodded, continuing to attend to her hand. "She's okay now. I got her to go back to sleep."

"What was wrong?"

"She had a nightmare," Ethan said. He finished the bandage before looking up at her. "She was worried about you. She said you were in pain."

Mandy stared at him, fighting to hide fresh tears. She'd tried so hard to hide the past, to shield her children from her demons, to keep them from experiencing the same sort of suffering, from bearing the same sort of weight. But Grace had still sensed her pain, even in her sleep.

Finding no words, Mandy pulled Ethan in close and held him tight.

Chapter 28

The Woman in the Tree, 1991

Amanda preferred the nights when her father and brothers were gone. Since Shane had gotten a job at Little Caesars, that had happened more often. And she figured they would happen even more when Travis got his driver's license—that was less than a year away.

Though she wouldn't describe her mother as a calming presence, the house was still far less frenzied when it was only the two of them. She'd hoped they would spend some time together that night, but her mother had gone to bed early, leaving Amanda to her own devices. She was disappointed, but not at all surprised.

She always found ways to entertain herself. She attempted to dress Moon Pie up in clothes taken from her dolls. And though the cat had been patient at first, it wasn't long until she decided she'd had enough. Now, Amanda lay on her stomach on the carpet of her room, her legs under the bed, doodling on a drawing pad.

She was sketching a princess when she heard a child's voice outside her door—*a girl's voice.*

"I didn't mean to. I didn't mean to break it," the voice said in an anxious tone. "Aw jeez, Pa's gonna be real mad."

Amanda frowned, tilting her head.

Nobody was supposed to be in the house except for her and her mother. She got up from her drawings and opened the door to her room, but no one was in the hall. The door to her mother's bedroom was standing open, and the lamp was on. When she went to it and peeked in, the bed was unmade but no one was inside.

The voice came again—from the kitchen this time.

Amanda hurried down the hallway. As she turned the corner, the kitchen door banged against the counter. Beyond the doorway, the same small voice echoed outside, growing fainter, the words indistinct.

She darted to the kitchen door and peered out into the night.

There, she saw her mother, skipping through the yard toward the grove of trees, her white nightgown flowing in the breeze, glowing blue under the moonlight.

Somehow, the childlike voice belonged to her mother. She was still murmuring to herself, a string of words that made little sense.

Amanda called out, "Mama, where ya goin'?"

But her mother didn't seem to hear her. She giggled as she danced her way through the yard, grabbing the hem of her nightgown and twirling.

Amanda had never seen her mother behave this way before. Like a *child*. It scared her. Where was she going? What if she got hurt? As much as she didn't want to, Amanda knew she had to follow.

She went to the "junk drawer" in the kitchen. She was relieved to find a flashlight, and more relieved that it worked. Without even putting on shoes or changing from her pajamas, Amanda ran out into the yard.

The night air was thick with humidity, and the hum of the cicadas seemed louder than usual. Amanda followed as her mother neared the creek.

Fireflies hovered over the water in clusters. Even through her distress, the beauty of them never ceased to stun her. They were like tiny constellations, their soft greenish-yellow lights flickering among the branches of the trees or drifting near the ground, only to float up and away in slow arcs.

Her mother crossed the bridge over the stream, giggling in the darkness.

Amanda almost caught up to her, when her toes caught a root that was hidden in the shadows. She stumbled, throwing her hands out to brace her fall. The flashlight spiraled away into the undergrowth. She went down hard, but the damp ground eased her landing.

She lay still a moment, her toes throbbing, the soft earth cool against her chest and arms. She knew she was lucky not to have landed on a rock, but she could feel the grime on her face and hands. In her hair. Her pajamas, no doubt, were covered in mud.

By the time she'd righted herself and retrieved the flashlight, Amanda could no longer see her mother. She swept the beam of the flashlight through the grove, calling out. Her nerves were already frayed, and the fall had only made it worse. Her hands trembled. Her palms were slick with sweat, and she almost dropped the light again.

What if she couldn't find her mother?

She did her best to listen past the sound of her own shaky breathing, trying to hear her—or at least, the creepy voice she'd been using. She tried to block out the sounds of the night—the cicadas, the crickets, the soft wind rustling through the leaves.

At last, there was something else. Another noise.

A small giggle. A childlike voice. "*They're going up!*"

Amanda bolted toward the sound. She ran full out, ignoring the pain in her toes and the feel of the rocks, twigs, and roots under her bare feet.

Then she spotted it again—the unmistakable glow of her mother's white nightgown. But something was wrong. She wasn't on the ground anymore.

Amanda gasped. *No!* Her mother was already halfway up the trunk of a large oak tree, and she was climbing higher.

Amanda ran to the base of the tree. "Mama! Come back down! Mama, you're gonna fall!"

She wasn't sure if her mother was answering her or only talking to herself, but she said, "I'm gonna be safe up here. Cain't nobody git me up here." Her words had a lyrical quality, like a nursery rhyme.

Amanda peered up through the branches. Beyond her mother, the fireflies glowed, a radiant halo.

Her mother was barefoot, her hair disheveled, her nightgown

uneven. She climbed with a strange assurance, yet she was unsteady—reaching for branches with confidence, only to miss. She'd teeter as if she was going to fall, only to right herself and try again.

Amanda breathed a sigh of relief when her mother reached a fork in the branches and stopped. There, she hugged the tree, mumbling to herself. "Won't find me up here, no sir."

"Stay there, Mama!" Amanda called. She glanced around, trying to decide what she should do next. Should she follow her up? And then what? How could she hope to bring her back down?

At that moment, her mother leaned out, almost as if reaching to grab something Amanda couldn't see. She wobbled and almost slipped from her perch. Her leg kicked out as she caught herself, regaining her balance. She hugged the tree again and continued to mutter in a hushed voice.

Amanda didn't know *what* to do. Her mother might fall. She might hurt herself. She might *die.* This was far too much for a ten-year-old. She needed help.

"Stay right there, alright?" she shouted up at her mother. "I'm gonna… *I'll be right back!*"

In an unsure voice, her mother whispered, "Alright."

As Amanda ran back toward the house, she thought about how wrong this was. *She* was the child. Her mother was the *adult.* Her mother was supposed to be looking out for her. *Not* the other way around.

What should she do? Who should she call?

She had no way to reach her father, and even if she could, he was away on a train somewhere. Shane was at work. Travis was…who knows where. For a moment, she thought of her uncles, but there was no way she was going to involve them. Her aunt was too far.

A neighbor, maybe? Maybe Cheryl's folks could help? Or they could call someone who would?

Did firefighters rescue *people* from trees?

She ran to Cheryl's as fast as her feet could move. The house was dark and the porch light was out, but she pounded on the front door anyway. She wasn't sure what time it was—nine o'clock? Later? She hoped they were still awake.

Amanda waited on the porch, catching her breath, hoping someone would answer. After a minute, as she was about to leave, the front door cracked open. Cheryl's father squinted at her through the gap, his eyes heavy with sleep.

"Amanda? What's going on? It's *very* late, honey—we were already in bed."

Through labored breaths, Amanda explained what had happened. But he didn't act like he understood the seriousness of the situation. He appeared less concerned and more *inconvenienced*.

"I'm afraid I can't help you. I have a bad back." He sighed. "Do you want me to call someone?"

Her desperation rising, Amanda blurted out the first thing that came to mind, "Call Little Caesars. Ask for my brother, Shane. Tell him he needs to come right away. Tell him it's an emergency." She thought if she reiterated how grave the situation was, it might help get her point across.

"Okay, honey. I'll do that. You go on back and watch her till he gets here."

Amanda turned and ran back toward the grove, praying he'd follow through. She wasn't confident. She'd learned that adults didn't always make good on what they'd promised.

Her feet had taken quite a beating. She hurried, but this time she was a bit more careful watching her step. As she arrived back at the tree, she was relieved to find that her mother had remained in the same position, her cheek still resting against the tree's trunk.

"I'm gettin' help, Mama," Amanda called.

Now, something about her mother seemed sad. Had she been crying? Her face appeared streaked, though it may have been a trick of the light. Her mother held on to the branch, hugging it as if it were a person. "Don't let him get me," she whimpered.

"Who?" Amanda asked.

"Don't let 'im take the switch to me. Didn't mean to."

It hurt Amanda to see her mother like this—fragile, afraid, *lost*. But it was better than her moving about, all confused and chaotic.

Higgledy-piggledy.

Her mother remained like that—sad, fearful, and nearly immobile —for what felt like an eternity.

Then, out of nowhere, she began to laugh.

It was a loud, wild, maniacal laugh.

She let go of the branch and began moving again, exploring the tree, gripping one limb and another, repositioning herself over and over again. "I'm the queen of the tree." She giggled. "I can touch the sky."

Then, to Amanda's horror, her mother looked up and started to climb higher.

"No! No, Mama, don't do that!"

Her heart pounded.

She glanced toward the house. For a moment, she thought she saw a light through the trees, cutting through the darkness. Was it a flashlight? Headlights? Or only wishful thinking? She hoped her brother would come soon. She was worried there was no time to spare.

Amanda's head snapped back and forth, torn between her mother and the help she prayed would come soon.

Then—a flashlight. The beam bobbed through the trees, moving toward her.

A figure approached. No—*two!*

Her brother had arrived, and he'd brought help!

But as the shadows came closer and began to take shape, she realized it could *not* be Shane. Neither of the figures were tall enough. And both were far too thin.

As they lowered the beam, Amanda caught a glimpse of their faces in the moonlight. The first was Cheryl.

The other—her uncle Harlan.

Amanda's breath hitched.

She had never felt so torn. The relief and dread wrestled within her. Help had finally arrived, but why did it have to be *him?*

As Harlan got closer, he said, "Shane said y'all got some trouble with yer mama."

"Yeah," Amanda whispered. "Why didn't he come?"

"Cain't leave work." Harlan pushed his ball cap back. "Where is she?"

Amanda pointed up in the tree.

Cheryl's mouth fell open as she spotted Amanda's mother, high above the ground. "Holy cow," she whispered.

Seeing her, Harlan let out a short, dismissive chuckle. "Figures." He turned to Cheryl. "Welp, ya done showed me. Best git on back to yer daddy now."

Cheryl nodded but hesitated, locking eyes with Amanda for a long moment.

Amanda wished she would stay.

But Harlan just stared at her. And after a moment, she turned and walked off, leaving them alone in the grove.

Harlan turned back, stepping closer to the base of the tree. Clearing his throat, he shouted, "Debi, it's time to come down now!"

When Amanda's mother heard his voice, she started to panic. Her head moved back and forth, and she began wringing her hands. "No, no, no, no, no," she muttered, frightened. "I didn't mean to make that mess. Don't tell Pa. You *cain't* tell Pa."

"Oh, I'll be tellin' him for sure, if ya don't git yer ass down!" Harlan growled. "Right now!"

Amanda didn't understand why he was being stern with her. She needed their help, and he was bringing nothing but anger and condescension.

"Don't be mad. Cain't...*cain't* be mad," her mother continued to stammer.

She let go and covered her face with both her hands. And Amanda gasped, certain her mother was going to fall.

But Harlan called out again, "Don't you let go of that tree. You best come down here *right now*, or else I'm gonna be *real* mad. And *I'm* gonna punish you. You don't want that, do ya?"

Her mother reached out and grabbed the branch again. She looked sheepish. Her eyes darted around, as if she were guilty of some crime. There was a fear in her eyes that was new to Amanda.

But after a moment, she began to make her way down.

Harlan moved closer to the tree, positioning himself underneath her. And when she got closer to the ground, he reached up and put his hand on her back, guiding her down.

Once she was clear, Harlan scooped her up, cradling her in his arms like a tired child. He carried her, heading back toward the house through the trees.

Amanda followed along behind them, listening to her mother mutter, a rambling string of nonsense, with an occasional cogent thought slipping through.

The back door stood open. Harlan asked Amanda to open the screen door as well. Once inside, he carried her mother down the hall.

Amanda stood in the doorway of her bedroom, as Harlan lay her mother down on the bed. He glanced over his shoulder at Amanda and nodded. "Ya mama ain't never been…quite right." He pulled the covers over her legs and nudged the glass of water on the nightstand closer to her. Then he jabbed a finger at her and barked, "I best not catch you outta bed again tonight, Debi. Ya hear me?"

Her mother nodded, a childlike innocence buried inside her fearful expression.

Harlan turned back to Amanda, and his demeanor shifted. He grinned at her—a broad, warm smile. Amanda couldn't recall if she'd ever seen him grin like that before.

"Law, look at you. You're covered in mud," he said. "Ya shouldn't be walkin' 'round the house in them dirty clothes."

Amanda glanced down at her pajamas. She was, indeed, covered in dirt and mud, some of it still damp.

"Get on down to the basement and put them old rags in the wash, 'fore ya track more mud for yer mama to clean. I'll bring ya down a change of clothes."

Amanda didn't see why the clothes had to be washed right away, but she didn't question it. She didn't want to upset her uncle or foul his mood. So, she went to the basement. After turning the lights on, she descended the stairs to the laundry area. She stripped off her dirty pajamas and dumped them in the opening at the top of the machine.

As she reached over the machine to retrieve the liquid detergent, a stain on the wall caught her eye. It was shaped like a fish. She hadn't ever noticed it before. It amused her.

Amanda measured out the detergent and added it to the washer. She leaned over and turned the dial, starting the cycle.

She turned to head back up the stairs, but stopped. Her uncle was standing on the landing. He stepped down the rickety staircase slowly, the stairs groaning under his weight, creaking with each boot step.

He said he'd bring a change of clothes, but he didn't have anything in his hands. She suddenly felt very shy and awkward standing there in nothing but her panties.

"Ya got the wash goin' all by yourself?" he asked, reaching the bottom step.

She nodded. "I do my own washin' all the time."

"Look at you. Why, yer almost all grown up now." He moved past her, so close it was uncomfortable, his shirt sleeve brushing her naked shoulder. Then he stopped and leaned against the dryer. He pulled a cigarette from behind his ear, opened a matchbook, and lit up.

He tossed the matchbook onto the washer, and it landed near Amanda. It said: *Red Rooster Tavern*. A picture of a cartoon rooster was on the cover—he was wearing sunglasses and drinking a beer from a frosty mug.

Harlan took a deep drag from the cigarette and exhaled the smoke. A moment of silence hung between them, except for the sound of the washing machine running.

Harlan looked at her, his eyes narrowing, sizing her up, scrutinizing her.

Amanda didn't like the way he was looking at her. She wanted to ask about the clothes. But she didn't.

He dug into the pocket of his jeans, rooting around, jingling his keys. He pulled out a red checkered handkerchief. "Ya got mud all over yer face, Amanda Jean. Lemme fix that."

Harlan crouched down close to her and placed a calloused hand on her bare shoulder. Then he began to wipe at her face with the handkerchief. The cloth was rough against her skin, grating, and it stunk of tar and grime. Harlan's face was so close, the scent of the stale cigarettes on his breath made her wince.

He wiped too long, until her face was almost raw. When he stopped, he didn't remove his hand from her shoulder right away. Harlan grinned at her again, his yellowed teeth flashing. "Now...ain't that much better?"

She nodded.

As he released her and stood back up, Amanda decided it was well past time for her to go and get dressed. But as she turned to go, Harlan called out, "Whoa, now. Where ya goin?"

Amanda stopped at the foot of the stairs and turned back to him. "I'm gonna get dressed now."

Harlan chuckled, dismissively, shaking his head. "We're washin' them clothes up right now."

"I just thought—"

He cut her off, his tone somewhat indignant. "Whatcha worried 'bout bein' in your skivvies 'round me for? I'm *kin*."

Amanda shivered, despite the warm summer night.

"I'm bein' friendly, now. Helpin'," Harlan said, his eyes locked on hers, his voice low and terse. "You can't be impolite to someone like that. *You can't just leave.*"

Amanda stood at the foot of the stairs a moment, then nodded and took a step closer. "I'm sorry," she said.

"Well, there ya go. Apology accepted. Now we can get back to bein' friendly." Harlan chuckled and glanced around the basement. "Your folks…they sure are packrats, ain't they?"

Amanda didn't know that word. But she nodded.

He strolled over to one of the nearby tables that was covered in miscellaneous junk and began thumbing through it. He picked up a doll and held it up to show Amanda. It was a porcelain harlequin, black on one side and white on the other, with a row of light blue pom poms adorning its chest. Its smooth, white face appeared made up, bright lips and eye shadow, tiny clownish accents on its cheeks and eyelids. A white cone-shaped hat sat on its head.

"This yours?" he asked.

"It was Mama's," Amanda whispered.

Harlan nodded and put the doll back on the pile. "I guess that makes sense. You're too big for dollies now, I bet."

The harlequin slid from the table. It landed on the floor with its back against a cardboard box. But Harlan ignored it. He found a music box and opened it. A tiny ballet dancer sprung up from inside as a soft tinkling melody began to play. *Music Box Dancer.*

"That's nice, doncha think?" he said.

Amanda nodded again, her hands crossed in front of her, fingers intertwined.

"I bet that one's yours," Harlan said.

Another nod.

Harlan stepped to the song, as if dancing along. His steps were awkward, his rhythm off. He kept glancing at Amanda, as if to see if she was entertained.

Amanda did her best to smile—she couldn't risk making him angry—but all she wanted was to go upstairs.

"Why doncha come dance with yer Uncle Harlan," he said, extending his hand.

She didn't want to. But she stepped forward and put her hand in his.

The tune on the music box ended and immediately started again.

Harlan held her hand and began to move. This was him dancing—dipping, bending at the knees, no grace in his movements, no rhythm in his step. He watched her, waiting for her to join in. His gaze crawled over her.

Amanda's heart began to race.

They moved around each other in a slow, awkward circle, and Amanda did her best to keep her distance. Still holding her hand, Harlan raised his arm above her head and began to turn her around in small circles.

When his arm came down again, she was facing away from him, and his arm was now wrapped around her midriff.

The music box tune stopped—and started again.

The washing machine droned on, a steady hum.

Harlan let go of her hand but didn't step back. He lingered close behind her. Too close. His fingers brushed her bare shoulders, his hot breath was against her neck. The stench of cigarettes hung in the air.

She took a deep breath and held it, telling herself that none of this was real. That it was all a bad dream. And it would be over soon. Any moment now, she'd wake up in her bed, her cats curled at her feet.

She focused on the delicate notes of the music box, allowing its soft melody to drown out the murmurs of his voice, the faint metallic jingling of his keys.

Her eyes fixed on the porcelain doll. She poured her attention into it, memorizing every detail. The thin, red lips. The white cone hat. Blue pom-poms running down its chest—there were *four* of them.

She stared into its painted face until the world around her faded away. Until nothing else existed. And the harlequin stared back, unblinking, its dark eyes glinting in the dim light, its painted tears mirroring her own.

CHAPTER 29
OLD GHOSTS

MANDY SAT ON THE EDGE OF HER BED AND FACED THE WINDOW, watching the black night shift to indigo, and then to crimson. She hadn't been able to sleep—even after promising Ethan she would try. But she doubted that was the primary cause of her weariness, or of the ache sitting in her chest, throbbing in the marrow of her bones. She did not think it was fatigue that caused her hands to tremble.

The house was quiet. It had been still since she'd broken the mirror, as if it were waiting for something. For the sun to rise, perhaps. Or for her family to stir. Or maybe it was waiting for Mandy to do something—anything at all—to break the silence. It pressed down on her, smothering her.

But she wasn't ready to speak to it.

She wasn't ready to move.

Wasn't ready for a new day.

It was like she'd crossed over into an alternate timeline. Things were different now. *Worse*, somehow. That was hard for her to comprehend.

She wasn't quite ready to accept this new world. To step into this new life. To make it real.

Not just yet.

The bedroom window, with its shifting colors, was almost like an abstract painting. She found herself lost in it, staring until the colors blurred, until she wasn't seeing anything at all. And every shift in color was bringing her closer to a dawn. It was coming, whether she was ready or not.

Her eyes were dry now. Her anger had gone.

Only the ache remained.

Her body was heavy against the mattress. Her hands were like weights in her lap, where her phone was resting in her palm.

Chris and the kids would be up soon.

Mandy thought of her mother. How she would lock herself away in this very room, in the dark, with nothing but her pills and her pain. How she would sleep, either oblivious or simply unwilling to face the fact that she was needed. By Mandy. And her brothers. That they'd longed for a parent to be present and to guide them. To love them.

Mandy felt a bit more empathy for her now. She understood feeling like you couldn't face the world. But in her isolation, her mother had failed them. Mandy couldn't—no, she *wouldn't*—let herself do the same.

Ya already have, darlin'.

Mandy closed her eyes and took a deep, fortifying breath.

With some effort, she lifted the phone and stared at it. She had already punched in the number and hit dial, only to hang up before it could ring through. She'd done it several times over the course of the last few hours. No one was likely to answer before sunrise. Perhaps that was worse. Would she leave a message? Leave it to chance?

Her intellect told her to wait until she was sure she could speak to him. Her gut told her she couldn't wait. She had something to say. Something she *needed* to say. If she was going to be forced to live in this reality, she was going to do it on her terms.

She stared at the recent numbers. Her finger lingered over the one at the top. Unlike the others, there was no name, only digits.

What are you waiting for? she asked herself. *Get it out. Get it done with.*

But what if he laughs? What if he denies it? Or worse—what if he doesn't? What if he throws it right in my face? Makes me feel small all over again?

Her finger hovered over the screen, trembling.

She pressed down on the number and listened as the phone began to ring.

A sick feeling poured through her. She didn't know if she would be able to speak.

But she didn't hang up.

After a few rings, the call went to voicemail. A robotic voice approximated a young woman: "Hello and thank you for calling *Caulder Brothers Construction*. No one is in the office to take your call at this time. Press 1 for a directory. Press 2 for—"

Mandy pressed 1 before the message could continue. The robotic voice began to list extensions. She selected her uncle's name and waited. She expected his voicemail, and was surprised to hear his voice: "Hello?"

Mandy held her breath.

She thought about hanging up. The urge was almost overwhelming. But she didn't.

When she started to speak, she was surprised that her voice sounded normal. Calm, steady. Assured. Even a bit forceful. But she was feeling none of those things.

"This is Mandy. I have something I need to say," she said. She paused and waited.

There was silence, except his breathing. After a long moment, he replied, "Go on, then."

Mandy licked her lips and swallowed against the dryness in her throat. "I need you to understand something. I want to make it clear. I'm not selling you this house. I won't be bullied by you. I know what you did now. Do you understand? I know *everything*. So, unless you want me to come forward and muck up this bullshit reputation you've built as some sort of upstanding member of the community, I suggest you back off. Of me, and my family."

A long silence.

"I need to know that you heard me, Harlan. And that you understand what I'm saying."

The silence continued a moment longer. Then he grumbled and cleared his throat. "You always were a drama queen. Just like yer mama."

She realized he was trying to bait her. But she waited, saying nothing, and let the silence continue.

After a long, tense, moment, Harlan said, "Yeah. I hear ya."

"Good," Mandy whispered. "Now…I don't ever want to talk to you again. I don't want to see you. I don't want to *smell you*. I don't want to know *anything about you*. You got that?" Her voice was trembling now, but her words were clear and precise, every syllable enunciated.

Another long silence.

He inhaled, as if about to say something. But Mandy didn't wait for it—she hung up the phone.

Her hand fell into her lap, as she took several deep, uneven breaths. Her stomach clenched, nausea creeping in. Her face was hot, wet with perspiration.

She'd done it.

But what *had* she done?

She wanted to believe that she'd won. That calling Harlan and demonstrating her resolve—her *strength* in the face of everything—was enough. But she knew better. She'd seen Harlan go up against many people over the years and she couldn't recall ever seeing him back down. Ever seeing him lose. Not in the long run. Sometimes he'd beaten them with charm. Most times with brute force. But he'd always won.

Mandy looked back at the bedroom window. The reds had faded to pinks now, and the pinks were softening to white. She closed her eyes and nodded, commending herself for taking some sort of control, allowing herself the victory for now.

The air shifted. The house was finished waiting.

Or perhaps it was only her.

There was movement in the living room. The kids were stirring. Or Chris.

It was time.

Time to get up from the bed. To go to her children. To try again to make her partner understand her. Time to figure out how to go about living in this new reality.

———

"WHAT HAPPENED?" Chris asked Mandy as she entered the kitchen. He was leaning against the counter, holding his coffee mug. He pointed to her hand.

"I…uh, I broke the mirror last night."

"On purpose?" he asked. "Or were you sleepwalking again?"

"I'm not sure," she lied. "I might've been."

He shook his head. "I worry you're gonna hurt yourself. I think you should talk to someone about it."

Mandy sat at the dining room table. "Yeah, maybe. Ethan heard it —he came in and fixed me up."

Chris raised an eyebrow. "Ethan? *Our* Ethan?"

"I know." She smiled. "And he did a good job too. You would've been proud of him."

He nodded, sipping his coffee.

"I missed you last night," Mandy said.

"Yeah, me too."

There was a break in the conversation. Mandy told herself it was time. It was her moment. Her chance to tell Chris what she'd learned. What she'd done.

But the words still didn't come.

Chris cleared his throat. 'I'm gonna wrap up a few things today and take the kids back to the hotel for the night. I already booked us a room. I didn't wanna leave any projects half-finished, not if I could help it. Not much I can do about the electricity right now. You'll have to figure that one out on your own, I guess."

"Does it have to be this way?"

He looked at her. "Are you gonna sell the house, Mandy?"

"No. But, I called Harlan. And I told him to back off."

"Ooh…well, great. That just fixes everything." Chris laughed, shaking his head.

"I think he'll listen now."

He sighed. "We're so far apart on this we're not even having the same conversation anymore. I'm not gonna keep the kids here if there's even a remote possibility it's dangerous. But love…I hope you change your mind. I hope you come with us. I really do."

———

Grace hated the idea of going back to the hotel, and the thought of leaving her mother behind was worse.

As she wandered along the creek, breathing in the grove—the sweetness of the wildflowers, the musk of damp bark, the earthiness of the moss that lined the water, and the crisp, almost metallic scent of the water itself—she fought against a sadness, a heaviness that was new to her.

She didn't want this part of their story to be over. It didn't feel over.

Her father had told them to be ready to leave in an hour. Ethan had said he'd come to the trees with her, but he'd gotten distracted charging his electronics, so, she'd come alone. Now, after crossing the old bridge over the creek, Grace wandered through the woods.

Their woods.

Her woods, or so she'd hoped.

Perhaps they'd never been hers, not even for a moment.

Perhaps they held too much sadness for others to be happy. Too much darkness to make room for anyone else's light.

But she'd been up for the challenge.

Lost in thought, Grace didn't realize she'd wandered into the clearing. As she looked up at the headstones, her breath caught.

She froze.

Standing behind the graves were five figures, silent and still, one behind each headstone.

Two of them were similar-looking men, almost the same age, a bit older than her father was now. Another was a much older woman, her hair gray, her face gaunt and tired.

The two others she recognized immediately.

One was the old man with the scraggly gray beard who'd scared her and Ethan away from the creek that afternoon with his shotgun.

The other was the little blonde girl, sad and small and so full of pain.

She stared at them. And they stared back.

Their eyes were dark and blank, as if they were looking right through her. Something about them felt so familiar to Grace that it made her heart ache. She didn't understand it, but she was beginning to have her suspicions.

"They're not really here," she whispered to herself. "They're not gonna hurt you."

She wished she hadn't come alone.

The figures remained unmoving, locked in an eerie silence.

Grace began to back away, keeping them in her sight, taking slow, measured steps in the direction she'd come. The sound of dry leaves crunching under her sneakers was amplified in the unnatural silence of the clearing.

Step by step, she backed away—until she ran into something behind her. Something warm. Flexible. Something *human*.

Startled, she yelped and stumbled back, almost losing her footing. Spinning around, she realized that she recognized the person. It was the boy who'd made her so uneasy that day by the bus. Ethan had said his name was Hunter.

He stood, looking at her, hands at his side, a smirk on his face. "Well, lookie here. *Told ya* I'd be seein' ya again."

Her stomach lurched.

She glanced back at the graves, suddenly *wishing* the figures were still by the headstones. Their presence, however unsettling, had been better than this. Seeing them would've made her feel like she wasn't alone, like she wasn't so vulnerable.

But the clearing was empty now.

Hunter took a step toward her, his smirk widening. "Reckon it's a good time to get to know each other, now that your brother ain't around."

Grace stepped back, moving into the clearing, her pulse quickening. She didn't want him near her. But with every step she took back, he countered with one forward.

"I gotta get back home," Grace said. "I'm already late. My daddy'll come lookin' for me."

Hunter nodded like he understood, but his eyes were still studying her. "That's okay. We can wait for him together. I'd love to say hi." He shifted, stepping in front of her, blocking the path.

She moved away from him again, toward the graves.

Hunter's smile deepened. "Ya sure are a pretty one, ain't ya?"

Grace forced a nervous laugh. "I'm just a kid."

"We grow up fast 'round here," he replied with a shrug. He reached into his back pocket and pulled out a pack of cigarettes, tapping it against his hand. Fishing one from the pack, he stuck it between his lips. Then swapped the pack for a lighter. He wrapped a hand around the cigarette, shielding it from the breeze, until it was lit.

After taking a drag, he blew out a cloud of smoke. He took the cigarette from his mouth and offered it to Grace.

She shook her head. "I…don't *smoke*. I'm only a kid."

"So am I," he shrugged again, taking another drag before stepping closer again. "You don't wanna try? Gotta start sometime. Why not here? With me. I can show you how."

Grace stepped back again. The edge of one of the gravestones pressed against her lower back and legs, the coldness of it seeping through her clothes.

A shudder ran through her.

There was nowhere else for her to go. The only other option was to run, and she was sure he would be faster.

Though her skin was cold, her palms and forehead were slick with sweat. Her heart was thudding in her chest.

She kept her eyes fixed on the boy's face. He was too close to her now. So close she could feel the heat from his skin. She could smell him—a stale, acrid mix of smoke, sweat, and…something *sour*.

"I don't wanna smoke," Grace said, her voice firmer this time. She set her jaw, attempting to hide her fear behind a mask of boldness.

Hunter cocked his head, his smile fading now. "Girls need to be submissive to men. Don't ya know that? *Have a quiet spirit.*" His voice was slow, patronizing, as if he were teaching her something she should've already known. He was mere inches away from her now. "Aint' you ever read your Bible?"

Grace shook her head, her brow furrowing as a wave of loathing rose up within her.

"See, that's the problem these days," he said, speaking to her as if she might not be smart enough to understand. "Girls don't know how to be girls. That's what my old man says." He reached out, the cigarette smoldering in his hand, and let his fingers graze her cheek. His touch made her skin crawl and she flinched. "Y'all should be soft," he continued, "learn your role."

Grace curled her hands into fists. Hunter was much bigger than she was, but she didn't care. She didn't like him touching her. And she wouldn't let him do it again. If he tried, she would hit him. And she would run.

"Don't touch me," she whispered, her teeth clenched, her voice quivering. She stared into his eyes, her lips tight, her breathing fast and anxious. There was heat in her cheeks. And her pulse throbbed behind her ear.

Hunter scoffed—the sound wet and grotesque—and blew his foul breath through his nostrils. His eyes narrowed, his lip curling as his curved smile returned, revealing crooked teeth.

He reached for her again.

Grace observed his hand moving toward her in slow motion. The moment seemed to stretch out endlessly. And her mind was filled with a chaotic flurry of thoughts.

Should I? Could I? Would it be worse if I did? Or if I didn't? Will I get in trouble? Will he hit me back?

The questions came fast, crashing into one another, but as his fingers got closer to her face, they all coalesced into one, crystal-clear idea, burning within her: *I am not yours to touch.*

Her fist shot out, small but fierce. She watched it fly as if it weren't her own. As if it weren't connected to her body, controlled by her, fueled by her anger. Her knuckles slammed into his chest—right below his sternum, and above his stomach. A flash of pain shot through her hand, but she ignored it.

Hunter's eyes bulged. His air escaped in a guttural "Ooooof" as he doubled over, wilting, his knees buckling.

RUN!

The word was loud in her mind.

Grace didn't hesitate. She shoved off from the gravestone and bolted. Hunter swiped out at her as she passed him, his fingers grazing her jeans, but she tore free and kept moving.

She realized her punch had been lucky. She'd taken him by surprise —that was all. It had slowed him down, but it wouldn't stop him.

She glanced back over her shoulder.

The boy was already on his feet, anger in his eyes. He started to follow.

Then Grace collided with something. Solid. Jarring. She stumbled back. Something? No—*someone!* Her heart sank. *One of his friends*, she thought. *Two against one.*

Hands gripped her shoulders. Grace shoved them away, raising her fists again as she looked up.

Ethan.

Grace had never seen him like this before—so still, so focused. His jaw was clenched, his nostrils flaring, his eyes dark and steely.

Relief washed over her, mingled with a creeping fear.

"*Go*," Ethan whispered. He nodded toward the house.

She hesitated, but did as she was told, moving around him and sprinting out of the clearing. When she was far enough, she stopped behind a tree. She turned and crouched down, watching, trying to catch her breath.

Hunter had been ready to pursue her, but he'd stopped short when he'd seen Ethan. Now, the two boys stood facing each other. Ethan's body was rigid, his feet planted and his hands clenched into fists at his sides.

"We was just horsin' 'round," Hunter said.

"Not what it looked like to me," Ethan replied, his voice steady. He called to Grace. "Were you two *horsing around*, Grace?"

"No," she answered.

"See?" Ethan said, firm but quiet. "Can't have a game if both people don't want to play."

Hunter laughed. "Pussy-ass California bitch. Ya think you're a tough guy now?"

Ethan tilted his head, as if considering the question. "Nope. Not a tough guy. But you can't mess with my sister. That ain't okay."

"Or what?" Hunter smirked and took a step closer.

"Or…" Ethan shrugged. "I'll make sure you hurt."

Hunter laughed again, his movements exaggerated, taunting. "*You* really think you're gonna beat me in a fight?"

Ethan paused. When he spoke again, his voice was calm and even: "That's not what I said."

This answer gave Hunter pause. Grace could see his confusion, the slight shift in his stance.

The two boys stood still, studying one another.

Ethan was so still it was almost unnerving.

"Stay off our property," Ethan said finally. "This is *our* home now. I don't want to see you anymore."

"Or?" Hunter repeated. But this time, Grace didn't think he sounded as confident.

Ethan let the question hang.

Then, without another word, he turned and walked toward the tree where Grace was hiding.

Grace continued to watch, her heart in her throat, scared that Hunter might attack her brother from behind. But he stayed where he was.

By the time Ethan reached the tree, his expression had changed, softened. He nodded toward the house. "Come on."

She moved to walk beside him, her legs trembling as they went. She kept glancing over her shoulder, watching Hunter, until she was positive he wasn't going to follow.

"Thank you," she whispered, her voice still quavering.

"Naw," Ethan said. "You had it under control, you little badass."

Grace chuckled.

"But I'll always be there to help you."

She gave him a small nod but said nothing. She grabbed his hand, and they walked the rest of the way back to the house in silence, her mind still racing.

———

"You guys almost ready to go?" Chris asked, slinging a backpack over his shoulder and picking up a box of supplies from the dining room table. "Just make sure you have what you need for the night. We can pick up more stuff tomorrow."

Grace stood next to Mandy in the living room, holding her hand.

Mandy tried not to show any emotion as they prepared to leave, but her composure was faltering. She'd always been the stoic one in the family, but since breaking the mirror, something had splintered inside of her too. She felt raw. On the verge of tears. And fragile—as if one wrong word, one misplaced gesture, might break her.

"Are you okay with the tents still up?" Chris asked, motioning to them. "I wanted to pull them down, but I ran out of time. I can do it tomorrow."

"It's fine," Mandy said.

Chris smiled but it didn't match the sadness in his eyes. He mouthed the words, *Love you.*

Mandy mouthed back, *Love you too.*

"Ethan, buddy, will you grab that bag and help me load the car?" Chris asked.

Without responding, Ethan picked up the bag by the front door and headed outside, holding the front screen door open for his father to follow.

"Mom, I don't wanna go," Grace said, looking up at Mandy with doleful eyes. "I wanna be with you."

Mandy bent down so that they were face to face. "Me too, honey. I hope it won't be long." She tried to force a smile, to appear optimistic, but it didn't work. "I'm gonna miss you tonight."

"Me too," Grace whispered, wrapping her arms around Mandy's neck.

Mandy held her tight, fighting the tears that were once again threatening to come. When the hug ended, Grace lingered, looking as if she wanted to say something else.

"You okay?" Mandy asked. "What is it, Gracie?"

"I don't want to worry you…but I saw the little girl again."

Mandy blinked. "Where?"

"Down by the tombstones."

Mandy tried not to let Grace glimpse her concern. "When?"

Grace nodded. "This morning. A little while ago. She was with all the people who are buried down there."

Mandy's blood froze. "What—what do you mean by that?"

"I saw them, Mom. All of them. The ones buried there," Grace said, as if the words weren't fantastical, as if it were an ordinary thing to say.

Mandy shook her head. "I don't think so, honey. How would you know who's buried there?"

"I know," Grace insisted. "And I *did* see them. All *five* of them."

"I don't know what you saw, sweetie," Mandy said, "but only four people are buried down there."

Grace looked Mandy in the eyes. She seemed thoughtful, almost patient, as if she were waiting for Mandy to catch up. She shook her head. *No.*

Mandy's skin crawled. She opened her mouth to speak but no words came.

"I can show you," Grace said.

"What are you gonna…*show me?*"

Grace moved across the room to the credenza. Mandy followed. Her stomach twisted as Grace began rearranging the family photos, moving several to the front. One by one, Grace picked up the frames, blew the dust off, and wiped the glass clean with the hem of her shirt, before setting them back down on the credenza.

She gestured to the first photo—a faded color picture of Mandy's uncles, Harlan and Malcolm, just home from hunting, holding ducks. Grace pointed at Malcolm. "Him."

She moved to the next—a photo of Mandy's parents together, taken right before Mandy left Rosebury. Grace pointed at her father. "Him. But he was older, and his beard was wild. He's the one that scared Ethan and me by the creek the other day."

Mandy's breath slowed.

Then, Grace turned to a black and white photo of the Caulder family, posed together on the back porch of the house. "Her," Grace said, pointing at Mandy's grandmother.

"That's my Mamaw," Mandy whispered, her voice breaking. "She was always kind to me."

"And him," Grace said, pointing at Mandy's grandfather.

"No," Mandy said, shaking her head. "That's not… No, he went missing, honey. He was never buried in the yard. There's only a headstone."

Grace's expression didn't waver. "No, he is," she insisted. "He's there. I *saw* him."

Mandy's mind reeled. She felt dizzy.

It didn't make any sense, but nothing had in recent days.

Grace's finger slid down the photograph, landing on another figure. "There she is," she said. "*The little girl.*"

Mandy made a noise—not quite a gasp, not quite a cry. It was raw and primal. She tried to catch it, to hold the sound back, to stop it from emerging, but it clawed its way out of her.

Her knees were weak. Her heart was pounding.

How had she not seen it before? How had she not recognized her sooner?

There, in the family photo, standing next to her grandparents and her uncles as young boys, was the little girl.

Blonde hair. And sad eyes.

The phantom Mandy had seen her entire life.

Her mother.

Chapter 30

Locked Away

Mandy watched as Chris's truck backed down the driveway. Grace's face was pressed against the back passenger window. Mandy waved at them, her cheeks straining to hold her big, optimistic smile, trying her best to maintain the façade, to keep her heartbreak from slipping through.

Ya know why you're gonna be here forever, don't ya?

"Not now," she whispered between clenched teeth.

Ethan waved from the passenger seat, concern in his eyes.

'Cause ya want to be. 'Cause, deep down, ya reckon it's what ya deserve. And where ya belong.

"Shut. Up."

It's the truth, Amanda Jean. Otherwise, you'd argue. Otherwise, you'd do somethin' to change it. But ya don't. And ya won't.

"Enough!"

It wasn't until the truck was halfway down the block that Mandy allowed her faux smile to wane.

This place is a part of ya. Forever.

Mandy was tired of the voice. It was wearing her down.

She took a deep breath and went inside. It was only her and the house now. But it felt more crowded than it had since she'd arrived.

Every inch of it was occupied by phantoms of her past. She couldn't move without colliding with a memory. All alone, and yet the claustrophobia made her want to scream.

The day hadn't been hot, but the humidity had been high. Her skin was itchy with perspiration, and her clothes were saturated.

She made her way down the hallway. She didn't turn to look into the bathroom or her childhood bedroom. She kept her eyes focused dead ahead, for fear of what might be lurking. Waiting for her. Wanting to show her things.

But she didn't need to see any more.

Didn't want to. Not now.

She was too tired for that.

Mandy went into the primary bathroom and turned on the shower, letting the water run to warm up. Then she went to the bedroom and stripped off her clothes.

She unwrapped the bandage from her hand. Though Ethan had done a good job, the dressing was near saturated with blood. Looking at the wound for the first time since she'd cut herself, she winced at how deep it was. She probably should've gone for stitches. As it was, the wound would likely result in a scar, but at least the bleeding had stopped.

What's one more scar?

She stepped into the shower, keeping her hand out of the direct stream. The water was hot. She wanted it that way. She wanted it hot enough to melt her skin away. She scrubbed at her body with an unusual ferocity. If only she could scrub her brain in the same way.

Mandy ignored the shadow wavering right outside the frosted glass of the shower door—another apparition, no doubt, waiting to show her something. Another important something. Another *revelatory* something.

If she just ignored it, perhaps it wasn't ever there at all.

When she was done showering, Mandy wrapped a towel around her body and reapplied the bandages to her hand. She should've asked Ethan for help before they left. He would've done a better job using two hands than she was using only her left.

Once she deemed the dressing acceptable, she went back to the bedroom, lay down on the bed in her towel, and stared at the ceiling. She stared straight ahead and paid no mind to the figures that lingered at the sides of the room. The ones that crept right outside the door. And when they began to demand her attention, she closed her eyes.

Mandy didn't mean to fall asleep, but she did.

———

WHEN SHE WOKE, the light through the bedroom window had taken on the ruddy hue of late afternoon. Her head was throbbing. In fact, she felt hungover. Her body was shaky and her mouth was dry. She needed food.

She got up and began to get herself dressed. She grabbed a pair of jeans off the floor, turning them right-side out. As she did, something small slipped from the pocket and landed on the carpet.

It took her a moment to realize what it was—where it had come from.

It was the key she'd found in her mother's medicine cabinet. She'd shoved it into the pocket of her jeans and forgotten all about it.

Then it struck her.

A hidden key. A locked metal box. Could the two things go together? Could it be that easy? Why hadn't she made the connection before?

Mandy went to the nightstand, opened the top drawer, and retrieved the lockbox from inside. She sat on the bed and placed the box next to her.

With a jittery hand, she inserted the key into the lock.

When it turned and clicked, she gasped.

She opened the lid of the lock box and peered inside.

On top was a folded newspaper clipping. It was yellowed and frail from age. Mandy was careful as she unfolded it. The article had been clipped from the *Knox County News*. Though it wasn't a front-page story, the clipping included a date: June 25, 1969. The head-line of the article read: LOCAL VETERAN REPORTED MISSING.

Mandy read the story:

ROSEBURY, TN — Authorities are searching for J.T. Caulder, a well-known resident of Rosebury and a respected World War II veteran, last seen on the evening of June 21.

Caulder, 48, was last spotted at Buck's Bar, a popular local establishment. Friends and family members have expressed concern, noting that, while Caulder is known to take day trips for fishing or hunting, it is unusual for him to be gone more than a day without notifying someone. His car remains parked at his home, deepening concerns about his disappearance.

Sheriff Orville Greer told the Knox County News that the case is being treated as a missing person investigation. Sheriff Greer indicated that, while no evidence of foul play has been uncovered, the nature of the case remains troubling. Deputies, assisted by local volunteers, have conducted searches of the Caulder property and surrounding wooded areas, but no significant developments have been reported. His wife and the couple's three teenage children are reported to be cooperating with the investigation.

Though some have suggested illness or an accident as possible explanations, authorities have found no supporting evidence. Sheriff Greer has urged the public to remain patient and avoid undue speculation. He encouraged anyone with information to contact the Rosebury Sheriff's Department.

Further updates will be provided as information develops.

Mandy folded the paper back, just as it had been, and laid it on the bed.

Looking back into the box, she saw a photograph. It was a polaroid picture, yellowed and faded but still clear enough to show her uncle Harlan. He was young in the picture, in his late teens. He was standing next to his father in front of a bar counter, drinks in hand. Behind the bar were shelves of various beer and liquor bottles, and a neon sign that read BUCK'S.

At the bottom of the photo in the white caption area, hand scrawled in blue ballpoint pen, was the date: JUNE 21, 1969.

She'd have to compare them to be sure, but the handwriting appeared similar to the one in the diary—her mother's.

Mandy squinted at the picture. She only knew her grandfather from photos. And now, from the descriptions of his brutality in her mother's diary. She examined his face, the long lines and wrinkles, a smile that disguised a scowl.

If the date was right, this was the last night anyone had ever seen the man—and Harlan was standing right beside him.

Mandy placed the photo on the bed next to the newspaper article and exhaled. She was aware that she shouldn't jump to any conclusions, but this box had been buried for a reason, and the contents had been carefully chosen.

She picked up another folded sheet of paper from the box, raggedy on one edge from being pulled from a spiral notebook. And, as she did, she gasped at what was hidden underneath. A pocketknife, blade still extended and speckled with dark red stains.

As she stared at it, she almost forgot to breathe.

The notebook paper shook in her hands.

She hadn't expected to find anything like this. Not something real. Not a knife.

But there it was.

Caked in dried blood.

She blew her air out slowly. And, with still trembling hands, she unfolded the paper.

In large scrawl, it read:

HARLAN CAULDER KILLED OUR DADDY ON THE NIGHT OF JUNE 21ST. THIS IS THE KNIFE HE USED. IF ANYTHING HAPPENS TO ME, THIS IS MY TESTIMONY.

It was signed:

DEBORAH CAULDER, JUNE 23rd, 1969

Mandy dropped the letter. Her eyes darted back to the knife.

She couldn't process it. Her fingertips were tingling. Numb. She tried to swallow but couldn't. She needed a moment.

Could this be real? Had her mother written this note in fear? In anger? Or in desperation?

But there was a picture. *The knife.*

She began to think about events since she'd arrived in town. Harlan's eagerness to buy the property. Travis talking about their mother rambling with dementia, saying *"Somethin' 'bout Harlan bein' scared of gettin' caught."* And then she thought of her phone call to Harlan early that morning, and the words she'd said: *"I know what you did now. Do you understand? I know everything."*

Panic flooded through her. *What had she done?*

She stood, a sudden urge to flee rising within her. She paced back and forth in front of the bed, frantic—unsure of what to do next.

She glanced at the lockbox. And at the knife.

Is this really a murder weapon? The thought was too much to comprehend.

Mandy shoved the papers back into the box and slammed the lid closed, then pushed the box back into the nightstand. She raced through the house, checking doors. Checking windows. Making sure everything was locked.

As she passed her childhood bedroom, she recalled the headlights on the window again. The way she'd crawled from her room, racing to keep her uncle from getting in the house.

She felt as small and afraid of him now as she had then.

Mandy picked up her phone, found a number in her sent call log, and dialed it again.

———

"No, I don't think you're bein' silly," Bo said. "I'm glad you called me."

He sat in her kitchen, across from her at the dining table. In front of him were the newspaper article and the polaroid with the handwritten date, sitting next to a can of Coke. Behind him, through the back door window, Mandy could see the darkness beginning to intrude. The day had disappeared.

"Have you ever heard anything about this before? About Harlan being involved in the disappearance of my granddad?" Mandy asked.

Bo hesitated, pursing his lips. "Amanda, this has been… Well, hell, they talked about this…even when we were *kids*. Folks have always talked about it being a possibility. But folks *talk*. You had to have heard about it too."

Had she?

Mandy shook her head, uncertain.

She'd heard so many rumors about her and her family growing up that they'd turned into white noise. Perhaps people *had* spoken to her about Harlan and her grandfather, about something scandalous like this, but she couldn't remember.

"What about the original police investigation back in the sixties?"

Bo shrugged. "Nothin'. If they *did* have evidence pointin' to your uncle, it wasn't enough to charge him. And it's long gone now. We're talkin' 'bout a *very* cold case here." He pulled the polaroid closer to him and tapped on it. "And this…this doesn't really count as anything. The date is the only thing that puts Harlan with your granddaddy on the night he went missin', but anyone could've written that on there."

Mandy had also told Bo about the diary entries detailing her grandfather's abuse, but she hadn't shown him the diary.

Nor had she shown him her mother's handwritten note accusing Harlan.

Or the bloody knife.

She didn't know how far she should go. She'd put herself in the middle of this, simply by virtue of investigating her parents' deaths. If she introduced *actual* evidence of a murder, there was no going back. And if she did and nothing came of it, her uncle would be free to torment her for the rest of his life. Or *worse.*

"Hypothetically, if Harlan *was* involved in his father's *murder,*" Mandy said, "wouldn't it be *possible* that he could've killed my parents too? To protect himself? To keep his secret? He has a lot to lose now. And Travis told me Mama started sayin' weird things toward the end, 'cause of the dementia. Things that got Daddy upset. What if—"

"Amanda." Bo cut her off. "You're gonna drive yourself crazy with this stuff. What good is gonna come of it? What's the best possible scenario? An old man goes to jail?"

Mandy thought about it. "At least I'd know the truth. At least I'd be free of him."

Bo nodded. He appeared understanding, but unswayed. "Tell me more about these threats you say Harlan made."

Mandy sighed. "He didn't make any *specific* threats, just…*hints* at threats. He told Chris he'd make life hard for us. And he's already told contractors and local businesses not to work with us."

"Well…maybe that's all he meant by it." Bo shrugged.

"Ain't that enough?" Mandy asked. "We're underwater here."

"Maybe let it be for a spell. See if it don't resolve itself."

Mandy rubbed her hands together. "There's somethin' else. I… called him. This morning. Told him to stay away from us. And I told him… I said I knew *everything,* but I didn't mean *this.*" She motioned to the polaroid. "Now I'm worried. I don't know if I'm safe here. I think I really screwed up."

"What *did* you mean?" Bo asked.

She hadn't anticipated that question. "Uh, it was…uh, another matter. Family stuff. It was personal."

"I ain't meanin' to stick my nose where it don't belong," he said, looking around the empty house, his eyes darting back and forth. He took a sip from his soda can. "I'm only tryin' to *make sense* of things here. So, forgive me if it ain't my place, but…*where* has your family gone?"

"Chris…" Mandy stopped. She realized she was about to frame Chris as the bad guy, and that wasn't right or fair. She started over. "I told Chris I wouldn't sell the house to Harlan. He doesn't understand why I won't. It's been a sore subject between us, and it sorta came to a head. Because of the…*threats*, he didn't think it was safe for the kids to stay here, so he took them to a hotel."

Bo nodded, his lips thin and tight. "I gotta be honest, Amanda. I don't reckon I'd understand either. Seems like it'd solve everything."

"No, not everything," Mandy said. "And sure as hell not if he killed my folks."

"I understand. But I don't know what else I can do here. I don't doubt your intuition on this, and I ain't dismissin' your concerns. I'd be right upset too if I was in your shoes. But there's no evidence of any wrongdoing."

"Yeah." Mandy thought of the knife. She should tell him. Show him everything. But then she thought of Harlan and swallowed hard. "I get it."

"That bein' said, I'd hate to think this has hurt your relationship." He reached across the table and placed his hand on top of hers. "He is…lucky to have you. I hope you know that."

She glanced up at him and saw the same kind, caring eyes she'd fallen in love with as a girl. He looked at her now like he had then.

The events of the last week had brought up so many emotions for her. They were swirling inside of her, muddled and confused. And he seemed just as he always had for her: a safe place. Shelter in the middle of a storm. Calm amongst chaos.

"I never stopped thinkin' 'bout ya, ya know," he said. "Always wonderin' where you'd gone. Never had the guts to ask—'fraid I might hear somethin' I didn't wanna hear. Always hopin' you…might come home again."

Mandy placed her hand on top of his. "We were only *kids*."

"Don't do that," he said. "Please."

"You…" She trailed off. "I don't think you realize how important you were to me back then. You were the *only* one who made me feel seen. Who made me feel *special*. Loved."

"But then you just…cut things off between us. And never even explained why."

Mandy looked down at their hands together, hers on top of his. The effects of time were evident on both—lines and scars and marks from the sun. Lives lived.

"I didn't want you to see any more of me," she confessed. "I didn't want you to learn who I was—what my life was like. It was like you and I were in this…perfect little *bubble*. And I wanted it to stay that way. I didn't want that feeling to end. And I was terrified that if I told you the truth, it would. That you'd reject me."

Bo opened his mouth as if he was going to say something, but he just slumped, and let out a weary, wavery breath.

Mandy looked at him, tears threatening to escape. "Ever since I got back to Rosebury, I've been so confused. This stuff with Harlan. My folks. I keep rememberin' things I've tried so hard to forget. Things I *had* forgotten. It makes me question everything—my life, who I am. Since I've been back, I even started to question my sanity. And as jumbled up as I am, it would be *real* easy to…*find comfort* in what's safe and familiar. But it ain't what I want no more." She patted the back of his hand, a gentle touch, and then she withdrew. "Chris is… well, he's everything to me that you might've been, if I'd let you. And I love him very much."

Bo nodded. "I don't want you to think I came here to—"

"I don't. We both feel the same way."

Bo sighed and wiped his eyes, clearing his throat. "I'm glad you finally found what you deserve, Amanda. Someone you're comfortable enough with to let in completely. To share yourself with. Who knows what your life was like back then. Someone you know won't leave you when you tell them the truth 'bout things."

It was as though Bo's words had knocked the wind from her.

A wave of nausea and shame washed over her.

For seventeen years, Chris had been right by her side. For seventeen years, he'd been all-in. And the whole time, she'd kept him at arm's length. She'd obfuscated. And denied. And hidden. But still, he had stayed.

"Do you think you'll be safe here tonight?"

"I don't know," she said. "I'll be okay."

"I'll wait in my car outside for a spell, and I'll drive by from time to time to check on you."

"Thank you, Bo. That means a lot. You're *exactly* who I remember."

———

"ARE YOU OKAY?" Chris said as he answered the phone.

"Yeah, why?" Mandy replied.

"I'm not used to you using the phone as, you know, a phone." He chuckled.

"I wanted to say goodnight to the kids," she said. "And you."

Chris put Grace on first, and they chatted for a few moments. "I wish you were here," Grace said.

"Me too, honey."

Ethan was next. Their conversation was shorter. Mandy realized she didn't know how to talk to him, but she wanted to do better.

"How is your hand?" he asked.

"I had a good nurse," Mandy replied. "Thank you, honey."

When Ethan handed the phone back to Chris, Mandy wanted to ask if she could join them at the hotel. She was certain he would welcome that. Instead, she said, "Look, I…still haven't changed my mind 'bout selling the house." She hesitated. "But maybe…" Her heart was pounding, her palms were covered in sweat. She forced the words out. "Maybe…you'll let me try…to explain why."

There was a moment of silence. Long enough that the fear began to creep in.

Then Chris spoke. "I'd like that. Very much."

Hearing him say it nearly brought her to tears again. "I love you."

"I love you too," he said. "I miss you bein' here with me."

Chapter 31
Buried

Guns had been a part of her life growing up, but Mandy had never been comfortable with them. She'd been around them. She'd even been taught how to use them. But she'd never liked them.

Despite all that, fear had driven her into the closet, searching for the pistol she'd hidden away. She could almost reach the top shelf, but not quite. She retrieved a chair from the kitchen to stand on.

When she found it, she placed the gun on the nightstand next to her bed. She realized having it around might be more dangerous than not, but it still made her feel better. She wasn't sure if it was loaded. It had been so long she didn't remember how to check safely. If confronted, she would use it as a prop. If threatened, she would pull the trigger, and they would both find out if it was loaded.

Mandy lay in bed, tense, aware of every sound. She couldn't quiet her thoughts. She tossed and turned for several hours—haunted by memories, replaying events, thinking of words spoken—before finally falling asleep around midnight.

Then—

BANG! BANG! BANG! BANG!

A pounding at the front door.

She shot up out of bed, startled, her heart racing.

Who was it? Who was at her door? Her Uncle Harlan? Chris? The police? Was something wrong? Were the kids okay? Was someone there to hurt her?

She flashed back to the night she and her brothers were alone in the house. Headlights on the window. The truck horn blaring. Her uncles pounding on the front door, eager to get inside.

Mandy reached for the nightstand, clamoring for the gun, but it wasn't where she'd left it. Without turning on the lamp, she fumbled for it in the dark, using both hands, panic building inside of her.

BANG! BANG! BANG! BANG!

She dropped to her knees on the carpet, searching the ground. Under the bed. But it wasn't there.

BANG! BANG! BANG! BANG!

Mandy stood again, crouching low.

She'd creep out to the kitchen. She'd find a knife.

As she turned to the doorway, she came face to face with the little girl.

Her nose was an inch away from Mandy's. Her skin was gaunt, her blue eyes open in terror. She was so close that Mandy could feel her icy breath.

The little girl began to scream.

Mandy screamed too.

And then her eyes snapped open.

The little girl was gone.

But her relief lasted only a moment. She was on her back, staring into the tops of the oak trees as they loomed above her. Beyond them, the sky was dark, speckled with stars.

She was outside, lying on the ground. In the back yard. Near the creek.

Still dreaming, she thought.

But her heart was still racing, the taste of adrenaline in her mouth.

Mandy stood and brushed herself off.

In the distance, she heard digging.

CHUNK! A shovel bit into the earth. It was followed by the fluttering cascade of rocks and soil falling to the ground.

CHUNK!

The sounds repeated.

She followed the sound, and realized she was approaching the clearing where the gravestones lay. Her footsteps made no sound at all. It was as if she were gliding through the woods, floating toward the clearing.

Once there, she saw a man, lit only by the moon. He was busy. Digging a hole in the ground, right in front of the headstone that read: JAMES THOMAS "J.T." CAULDER

Mandy watched him.

As he finished digging—the figure of his body dark against the night, haloed in blue light—he pulled himself from the hole and moved nearby, crouching in front of a large object draped in a plastic sheet. He grabbed the edge of it and began to drag, letting the entire object slide into the hole. It fell with a thud.

The man dropped back down into the hole and began to adjust the package.

Mandy peered through the darkness, trying to catch a glimpse of his face. But she already *knew* who this was. His thin—almost bony— frame was unmistakable. On his head was the baseball cap he nearly always wore. It hid his hair, except for what hung long in the back, untidy.

"Harlan," she whispered to herself.

He stopped, as if he'd heard her.

His head whipped around, and he stared right at her, his eyes illuminated in the darkness. *Glowing.*

Mandy gasped and backed away,

He slithered out of the grave, coming after her. His movements were quick, jerky. Unnatural. Like a wolf learning to walk on two legs. As he came toward her, he hissed between crooked teeth, "Youuu… caaaan't… juuuust… LEEEEEAVE!"

Mandy moved as fast as she could, but she tripped and stumbled, falling, twisting, landing on her back. The impact shook her. Knocked the air from her lungs. Her eyes closed, but she forced them open again.

She jolted upright, gasping for breath, body tensed, ready to run.

But Harlan wasn't there anymore.

She was still in the clearing, but it wasn't as dark now. The sun was threatening to rise, lightening the sky, though still unseen. The grave was filled in. It hadn't been fresh in many years.

Mandy blinked.

Was she awake? *Really* awake? She thought that she might be this time. But the line between dreams and reality had blurred too far for her to be certain.

She stood.

She was dressed as she had been when she went to bed: a white t-shirt and thin, brown sweatpants, no shoes.

Her back ached from the hard ground. Her bare feet were dirty. Leaves were tangled in her hair. The air was crisp, fragrant from an early morning dew.

This was real, she decided. She was out in the yard, and it was real.

Sleepwalking, she thought. *Again.*

But when had she come here? How long had she been lying on the ground?

The sound of birds beginning their day began to fill the grove.

Mandy stretched, her neck and spine cracking.

Then she started to walk back toward the house, negotiating the grove shoeless—as she had so many times when she was a girl.

———

MANDY NEARED THE HOUSE, the dream replaying on a loop in her mind. The little girl screaming. The unceremonious burial. Harlan's voice, echoing the words that had been haunting her since her return.

As the back porch came into view, she saw that she'd left the back door standing open. Though hesitant—worried that *someone* might've gotten in while she was away—she proceeded inside, closed and locked the door, and listened.

The house was still.

She glanced inside the tents, then went down the hall and checked her childhood bedroom. She went into Travis's old room, peeking into the closet. And then into the primary bedroom.

The gun was still on the nightstand, right where she'd left it. A part of her was concerned she might've done something with it during her sleepwalk.

She checked in the primary closet and bathroom.

As Mandy left the bedroom, she glanced over at the closed door to Shane's old room, the room that had first been hers, once upon a time. She experienced the same pang of panic just looking at it, a visceral reaction every single time.

But she was tired of feeling this way. Ruled by fear, by the whims of others, the lingering pull of the past.

She was tired of running.

Almost violently, she threw open the door.

She lingered on the threshold, inhaling the musty air. It was a room, like any other. And it had terrified her for her entire life.

Only a room, she told herself.

Mandy stepped inside and stood there a moment. She took a quick peek in the closet. Empty. She wanted to bolt out, as she always had, spending no more time inside than necessary, but she fought the urge and stayed a moment longer, defiant in her own way.

Doing it on her own. Not because she was trapped there by Harlan. Against her will.

It gave her strength, being here, facing it.

Then she found herself doing something she hadn't planned and hadn't anticipated. She left Shane's old room and walked down the hall toward the kitchen, taking determined steps toward the basement.

She stepped around the tent and opened the door.

She flipped on the lights and stood at the top step, looking down at the rickety stairs.

The scent of the basement hit her. And she gagged. For a moment she thought she might throw up. It was different than it had been, in a way—layers of odors, built up over years of neglect—but at its core, the scent was the same.

Her mind began to revisit the events of that night. But she resisted. She didn't want that. This wasn't about that. This was about *her*. About her facing the past for what it was—a collection of memories, both good and foul—and not for what she'd allowed it to become, a monster pursuing her through life.

She stepped down one step.

The stair creaked under her foot, a raw and chilling sound that elicited more feelings. More images of that night. Of seeing him come down the steps toward her.

"These are my stairs," she said, her voice soft.

She took another step down. "I own them."

With each step, she reassured herself. "They belong to me."

When she reached the bottom, she stopped in front of the washer and dryer. She stood still a long moment, looking around the room. At the boxes and the clutter, as chaotic and disorganized as it ever was. In many ways, just the same.

Mandy placed her hand on the washer.

Another memory flashed: the droning hum of a wash cycle. The scent of detergent returned to her.

She steeled herself against it.

"This is my washer," she whispered, and took another deep, cleansing breath.

She glanced at the spot on the wall near the washer, the one shaped a bit like a fish. And another memory began to intrude.

"That is my wall," she said, pushing the memory away.

Not *down*, but *back*. She wouldn't allow it to be buried anymore. She'd seen it. She'd acknowledged it. But she wouldn't let it bully her either.

Not anymore.

It was a thing that happened, she told herself. *It is a part of me, a part of the very fabric of me. But it is in the past, and I will not let it control me.*

More memories came at her, clawing for space in her mind. But one by one, she stepped past them. Pushed them back. Pushed them aside.

She closed her eyes and allowed herself to be quiet, to exist in the space where it had happened.

"This is my house," she whispered.

After a moment, she opened her eyes and turned, starting up the stairs. But before she could reach the top, her eyes opened again. She was back in front of the washing machine.

"This is *my* house!" she said it louder this time.

She turned and started up the stairs again. But once more—right before reaching the top—her eyes flew open, and she was back in front of the washing machine.

In her mind came the whisper of words. The ones that had gripped her and held her, kept her from moving forward.

Harlan's words.

You can't just leave.

Mandy closed her eyes again. She gritted her teeth. She tilted her head back and screamed at the roof. "THE. FUCK. I. CAN'T!" She shouted the words as loud as her voice would allow, louder than she knew she could.

And then she screamed some more.

Until her throat burned, raw from the force of it. Until her chest ached.

The scream rose from the very depths of her.

It carried weight. Torment. Anger. *Loss.*

When she finished, Mandy became dizzy. She held onto the washing machine to steady herself, so that she wouldn't collapse. There were no tears. Only energy, unfiltered and palpable.

And it was hers.

Mandy glanced around the basement again. She addressed it as if it were a living creature. Maintaining a quiet, respectful tone, yet showing no deference, she repeated herself, "This is *my* house. *Mine.* And I will leave here whenever I want."

Then she turned and walked back up the stairs. She took one last look at the room from the landing. At the top, she switched off the light and shut the door.

———

MANDY DIDN'T KNOW if she was slowly unraveling, or if she had never been clearer. But she was about to do something that would've seemed insane and unimaginable to her only months before.

Even a week ago, for that matter.

The shovel and spade rested on her shoulder as she walked through the yard, heading back toward the clearing again.

She waited for her inner voice to say something—to tell her she was batshit for even *thinking* about doing this, or that Chris was gonna put her in a home for the mentally ill—but it said nothing.

It wasn't there.

In fact, Mandy felt like she was the least crazy, the least chaotic she'd been in as long as she could recall. As if she were thinking with a clear head for the first time since hearing the news of her parents' deaths.

When she reached the clearing, she stopped in front of the grave marker for JAMES THOMAS "J.T." CAULDER, a stranger who was her grandfather, a man who'd gone missing, a wife beater, a child abuser.

She wasn't doing this for that brute of a man. She wasn't even doing it for her parents. Nor was she doing it to spite her Uncle Harlan, another wretch of a human being. No. If she found what she thought she might, it was for her. For her own sanity. For her peace of mind. And for the truth.

Mandy began to dig.

She only used the shovel. Unlike digging near the tree, there were few roots and rocks here. That made sense if her dream had been accurate. This ground would have been dug up once already.

After an hour or so, she stopped and stretched her fingers, wiping her hands on her jeans. She mopped at the sweat on her forehead with her shirt sleeve. She should've brought water. It wasn't as cool digging here in the clearing as it had been in the shaded grove.

It seemed like so much had happened since she'd woken up here this morning. It was hard for her to believe it wasn't even noon yet.

After taking no more than a minute to catch her breath, she gripped the shovel tight and began to dig again. This time, it didn't take long for the shovel to hit something—something that wasn't dirt or root. Nor was it the clink of stone.

It was the soft, unsettling tear of *plastic*.

Holy shit.

Mandy's pulse raced.

A mix of excitement and terror surged through her as she hurried to clear the dirt away, her hands shaking but precise. Bit by bit, the outline of the package emerged.

The milky-white plastic, brittle from more than fifty years underground, disintegrated like old paper under her touch. Silver tape clung to the mess, a tangle of decomposing material: the torn white strips, shreds of fabric that used to be clothes, and—beneath it all—bones.

Mandy didn't know what to do next. She wouldn't be able to lift it out without it falling apart. Perhaps it would be best to let professionals handle it from here.

She leaned in and examined the fabric. Her heart skipped. She recognized the pattern of the flannel, having seen it only *yesterday*.

It was the same shirt J.T. Caulder was wearing in the polaroid picture.

"Got you, fucker," Mandy whispered. She pulled the phone from her back pocket and snapped several pictures, making sure to get a close up of the fabric.

She left the tools behind and hurried back. When she got to the house, she gathered up the diary and the lockbox. She took them with her to her car and placed them on the front passenger seat. Once inside, she hit REDIAL on her phone.

Bo answered.

Mandy didn't take any time for pleasantries. "I'm sending you some pictures from my phone. Can you look at them right now. It's *important*."

"Of course."

Mandy started the car.

After a prolonged silence, Bo whispered, "Oh my god."

"Yeah. It's exactly what you think it is. And there's more. I'm on my way to the police station right now." She pulled the car away from the curb.

"Alright. I'll meet you there."

Harlan pulled his truck across from 33 Stillwater Lane and put it in park. He sat a minute, letting the vehicle idle, taking it in. Amanda's car was usually parked on the street in front of the house, but it was gone. And her husband's truck wasn't in the driveway.

He wiped a hand over his mouth. He tapped his fingers on the steering wheel. He didn't like getting his hands dirty if he didn't have to, but it didn't appear he had much choice anymore.

After a quiet moment in thought, Harlan threw the truck in reverse and eased it down the block, rounding the corner before parking it just out of sight.

He switched off the engine and opened the glove compartment. He pulled a pistol from within, checked the chamber, and tucked it into the back of his jeans. As he climbed out of the truck, he patted his right front pocket to make sure his knife was there. And then his left front pocket to make sure he had his kit as well.

Harlan strolled down the block toward the house, whistling "You Are My Sunshine." Just a man enjoying the day. He did nothing to raise any suspicions or draw attention to himself. He strode up the lawn with the ease of a man returning home.

And why shouldn't he? It was his family's home once, after all. And it would be his again soon.

As he stood on the porch in front of the door, he glanced around to see if anyone was watching. He pulled the kit from his pocket, and rapped on the front door—not too hard, but enough to make sure that no one was home. Then he opened the kit and found the right pick.

The lock was new, tighter, harder. A minor delay, but not enough to stop him. Once he had it open, he slipped inside, closing and locking the door behind him.

———

Grace stood on the hotel balcony, restless.

Her father and brother were watching something uninteresting on the hotel television. She decided she'd rather be alone with her melancholy. She leaned against the railing, the warm summer air on her face, and listened to a train pass in the distance.

Then the train horn blew.

It started small. And then it surged—rising, swelling, until it swallowed everything else. Until it was all she could hear. It pierced through her, sharp and bright, like a dentist's drill.

Grace clamped her hands over her ears, but it was useless. The sound was *inside* of her, under her skin, ripping through her skull. She clenched her teeth, and a soft groan escaped her lips.

Then—from somewhere deep within the noise—her mother called out.

Grace's breathing quickened. She felt woozy. She winced at the relentless sound, squeezing her eyes shut tight.

Focus. Find her. See her through the noise. She's buried in the noise.

After a long moment, the sound vanished, leaving her body aching, her mind tired.

Grace took a deep breath.

She knew what needed to be done.

She raced back into the hotel room, where her father and Ethan were sitting on separate beds, watching a sports show and chatting. She stood in front of the television, blocking their view. "Daddy, I need you to listen to me," she demanded. "It's important."

Her father stopped talking and muted the TV. He looked at her and nodded. "Okay, I'm listening. What is it, honey?"

"Mom is in trouble. And we need to go and help her…*right now.*"

Grace was worried that he would require a lot of convincing. She studied his face, bracing herself for a fight.

But he got up from the bed. "Okay."

"Right now," she repeated.

"*Alright,*" her father said. "I'll go. You guys stay here."

"We *all* have to go," Grace said. "Together."

"No way. If there's danger, I have to go alone. I'll go and—"

"We *all* have to go," she stressed. She looked over at her brother on the bed. "Ethan too."

Ethan sat up straight.

"And we need to go now," Grace said. "*Before it's too late.*"

CHAPTER 32

SHADOW MAN

CHRIS PULLED INTO THE DRIVEWAY, BUT MANDY'S CAR WASN'T there.

"Mom's not even here, honey," he said to Grace, who was riding shotgun. Ethan had taken the back seat, and hadn't said a word since they'd left the hotel.

"She will be," Grace said, her gaze fixed on the house.

Chris dialed Mandy's number again. For the sixth time, it went to voicemail. He switched off the truck and ran a hand across his chin, considering the situation. "I'm gonna go inside," he said, "and make sure everything's alright."

Grace broke off her stare to look over at him. "We *all* have to go," she insisted.

Chris shook his head. "I know. I heard you. And we're all here, like you wanted. But you two need to stay in the car while I go inside and take a peek." The thought seemed to distress Grace. She opened her mouth, but Chris cut her off before she said anything. "No arguing. I mean it. If you are certain there's danger, I'm going in first."

He got out of the truck and leaned against it, hesitating. He looked at the house and then back to his daughter's face—earnest and concerned. He smoothed his shirt and straightened his spine. "It's silly, but you have me all creeped out now."

"Me too," Ethan said from the back seat, his voice small.

Chris opened the back door, reached under the seat near Ethan's feet, and pulled out a heavy-duty Maglite flashlight. He slapped it hard against his hand to feel its weight. "Okay," he said. He was trying to appear calm, assured, but he was unable to hide his nervousness.

Before he shut the doors to the truck, he said, "I'm leaving the key so you can run the air. But keep the windows up and the doors locked."

He walked around the truck bed and up toward the porch. As he reached the front door, he jiggled the handle. It was locked, just as he hoped it would be.

He pulled the key from his pocket and slid it into the lock, but it seemed to have trouble going in. The lock felt rough and there was a catch as he turned the key. Had it always been this way? Was he over-analyzing because he was on edge?

After stepping inside and closing the door, he began to move through the house, gripping the flashlight like a club.

First, he looked around the living room and the kitchen, peeking inside the tents, checking the back door. He went to the kitchen pantry. He didn't know if someone would be able to fit inside, but he choked up on the flashlight and yanked the door open. No one. Not even enough room.

His muscles were tight.

This is ridiculous…isn't it?

He started down the hall but remembered the basement and turned back. If he was going to search the house, he might as well be thorough. He opened the basement door, switched on the lights, and started down the stairs. With every creaky step, he winced. There was no sneaking up on anybody down here.

When he reached the bottom step, he glanced around the room, at the shelves and random, scattered junk. Plenty of places down here where someone might hide.

What the hell am I doing?

Was he being irresponsible by participating in Grace's fantasies? Or did he actually believe her? He thought of his conversation with her at breakfast—*I see things sometimes,* she'd said, so matter-of-factly. In his gut, he knew she was being truthful. And though he didn't understand her, on some deeper level, he believed.

He switched on the flashlight and swept the beam across the basement. But more than helping, it only cast long, disorienting shadows, creepy overlapping silhouettes thrown from decades of accumulated rubbish.

With slow, deliberate movements, he searched between the stacks and shelves, scanning every shadow until he was confident he was alone. Then he walked back up the squeaky stairs, turned off the light, and closed the door.

He continued down the hall, first pushing the door to the bathroom open. It was a small room, with no shower curtain in place. Nowhere to hide.

He crossed the hall to Mandy's childhood bedroom and pushed that door open as well. The mirror was shattered, but there was no glass on the carpet. When Mandy had said she'd broken a mirror, this wasn't what he'd pictured. No wonder she'd cut herself.

This room had several places that someone might hide.

Chris leaned down and peeked under the bed. He checked behind the mirror and inside the open closet.

Next was Travis's old room. It still retained the musk of weed and Axe Body Spray.

The closet door was shut.

Chris crouched and checked under the bed, then moved to the closet, trying not to make too much noise. Again, he held the flashlight up, ready to strike, if necessary. He placed his hand on the knob and pulled. Nothing inside but old clothes and other miscellaneous items.

He exhaled, shaking off the tension in his neck and shoulders.

Oh, your nine-year-old daughter had a vision? Well, of course, go into red alert mode!

The last stop before the primary bedroom was Shane's old room, where Chris had slept the night before. Again, not that many places to hide in here. Another glance under the bed, and then he moved to the closed closet door. It occurred to him that some of his shirts were still hanging inside. He'd have to remember to take them when he left.

He pulled the closet door open.

Harlan sprung out toward him, growling, knocking Chris back.

Chris stumbled, his shoulder slamming into the bed frame before he fell backward onto the mattress.

Harlan was on top of him in a flash, knocking the flashlight from his hand. It tumbled to the floor out of reach.

Harlan straddled him, pinning him down. And began throwing punches, hitting Chris in the face and neck again and again. His wiry frame was tense, solid as a rock. His arms tore through the air, moving with a ruthless intensity. His eyes were wide and unblinking, as if possessed. His yellow teeth were clamped together in an almost inhuman snarl.

Chris thrashed, wrestling with Harlan, trying to block his fists. But they came down on him like a jackhammer—relentless. *Ruthless.*

Harlan was nearly *seventy. How* was he moving so fast? *How* was he so strong?

One of Harlan's furious blows connected with Chris's cheek. Everything went blurry and dipped to black, but only for a moment. Chris put his hands up to cover his face. He shook his head and blinked, trying to clear his vision. Harlan's weight shifted. His hand disappeared behind him, and then—a glint of metal.

He had a pistol.

Chris panicked. This was as bad as it could get. No way out. No way to fight back. It might be the end. He thought of his children, waiting for him in the car, vulnerable. He thought of Mandy returning home, unaware. The thought of being unable to protect them was almost unbearable.

He began to shout. He leaned his head back as far as possible, aiming his voice toward the window, hoping the kids might hear him. "Go! Get out of here! Run! Call the police!"

Harlan sneered. He gripped the pistol on its side and raised it up, before swinging it down *hard*, smashing it against Chris's face.

An explosion of pain.

And everything went black.

ETHAN DIDN'T LIKE THIS. Not one bit. He didn't like Grace's quiet. Her deliberate seriousness. Her worry. It was unlike her, and it made him anxious. He'd come to understand, even appreciate, her ability to sense things. To *know* things.

But she'd sensed *their mother* in danger, and he couldn't shake that thought.

His hands were trembling.

Grace hadn't said a word since their father had gone inside. She'd only stared at the house, her eyes fixed. Ethan thought about trying to make conversation, lightening the mood. Maybe asking her if she wanted to listen to the radio.

Out of nowhere, Grace said, "Dad's yelling."

Huh? Ethan strained to listen, but there was nothing.

He rolled down his window a few inches and listened again.

Nothing at all.

"We've got to go help him," Grace said.

She was out the door before Ethan could say anything, running toward the front porch.

Ethan grabbed the door handle. Should he follow? Or run to the neighbors and call for help?

Grace disappeared into the house.

Crap.

He opened the door, his breathing heavy. He swallowed hard, before following her in.

As he entered the house, he spotted Grace at the end of the hallway, standing at the threshold of the third bedroom, motionless. Something was definitely wrong.

Ethan ran toward her.

And as he came up behind her, he saw what she was staring at.

The old man in the baseball cap had a gun in his hand, and he was hovering over their unmoving father, whose face was covered in blood.

Dad's dead. No. No, he's—this man killed our father!

Ethan started to spiral, but then another thought forced its way to the front of his mind. *Take Grace! Now! Take her and run!*

He put his hand on her shoulder, but as he did, the old man turned to them and chuckled.

"Well, lookit here…if it ain't my kin come callin'," the man said, his voice low. "I'm your great uncle, Harlan. I didn't think your folks were ever gonna let us meet."

Ethan pulled at Grace, whispering, "C'mon," but she didn't move. She stared ahead at the old man.

"He was hiding," she said quietly, as the man stood up from the bed.

"What?" Ethan whispered.

"He was hiding," she repeated as Harlan stepped toward them. Her voice was so soft it was almost a whisper. "In the closet. In the dark."

———

As Mandy left the police station and climbed into her car, she realized that she had six missed calls from Chris. She'd been so caught up in what she was doing that she hadn't been paying attention to her phone.

Chris wasn't the type to panic and call multiple times in a row. The fact that he'd done so concerned Mandy in and of itself. She tried to dial him back right away, but the call went to voicemail. As she drove back, she kept hitting redial, but the call went to voicemail every time.

At first, she was relieved to find his truck in the driveway of the house. But that quickly gave way to dread. What had been so urgent that it had prompted him to call her so many times? And what had brought him back to the house? And why wasn't he answering her now?

Mandy pulled up to the curb, climbed out of the car, and listened. Nothing seemed unusual. Only the normal sounds of late summer in Tennessee.

Pulling her keys from her pocket, she walked across the lawn and up the front steps. As she reached the front door and attempted to insert her key, the door swung open.

Mandy's pulse quickened.

She pushed through the doorway and stood in the living room, listening.

"Chris?" she called.

No response.

"Chris?" she called again, her voice shaking. "Where are you?"

Silence.

Then she heard Ethan. He was calling from the direction of the basement, his voice almost too muffled to decipher. The words sounded like: *"Mom! Run!"*

Her son was in trouble. And he was warning her to go.

But it only served to turn her fear into anger.

This was her house. And that was her child. She wasn't going *anywhere.*

Mandy pulled the phone from her pocket, scrolled to the outgoing calls, and dialed Bo again. After putting the phone back in her pocket and letting it ring, she opened the basement door and made her way down the stairs.

She was so focused on Ethan that she didn't notice the creaking of the steps.

As she turned the corner at the landing, she saw Harlan.

He had Ethan. No, not only Ethan. *Both* of her children.

They were standing in front of the washer and dryer, with Harlan looming behind them, a gun in his hand.

The sight of him near them—threatening her *babies*—was almost too much.

Mandy was enraged. She wanted to attack. To bite and claw and tear and rend, until nothing of him remained.

But she didn't. She told herself to remain calm.

Behind Harlan, in the dark of the basement, something moved. Big. Hazy. Long teeth and empty sockets. Horns curling. The thing hid within the shadows, hovering just beyond the light. Right behind her children. *Waiting.*

Mandy inhaled, holding her breath for a long moment before exhaling.

"You're an idiot," she said, staring Harlan in the eye. "And you've *always* been an idiot."

Harlan sniggered but stayed silent. His eyes were fixed on her, his mouth twitching. After a long moment, he said, "This is what they call check mate, Amanda Jean. This is what happens when ya got more stubborn in ya than sense."

"My name is Mandy," she said.

She looked at Ethan and Grace, trying not to let the fear in their eyes unravel her. "Are you guys okay?"

They both nodded.

"Where's your dad? Is he okay too?"

Harlan answered for them. "Your fella's still breathin'. Least for now. But I don't see how else this is gonna end. You just had to go stickin' your nose where it didn't fuckin' belong, didn't ya? And ya didn't think I'd learn about ya pokin' around? Askin' questions?"

"You're not gonna slither out of this one, Harlan," she said, her tone calm and measured. "Not this time."

Harlan chuckled again. "Oh, I think I'll be just fine."

"Yeah, I don't know 'bout that. You probably should've made Mama show you where the *evidence* was…'fore you killed her."

He didn't laugh at this. His smile disappeared.

"I figure you must've known she had somethin', right? At first, I assumed all the damage to the house was from Travis, but a lot of it was you, wasn't it? Trying to find what she had. Where she'd hidden it."

His mouth straightened into a thin line. "The hell you talkin' 'bout?"

"Knowin' she had somethin' kept you at bay a little, didn't it? An understandin' of sorts. But then her dementia got too bad. And you couldn't control her anymore, could ya? Couldn't control what she was gonna say. Not when she couldn't control it herself. But I found it. *I got it.*"

For the first time since she'd gotten there, anger crept over Harlan's face. He stepped toward her, his body coming in line with the children. "You think that's gonna help ya, ya dumb cunt?" As he spat the invective, his nostrils flared, and the whites of his eyes shone in the dim light.

The massive thing shifted behind him in the dark, leaning in.

There was a moment of stillness.

And then—Ethan moved.

With all his might, he elbowed Harlan in the groin. Harlan doubled over, grabbing his crotch, and the gun fell. Ethan grabbed Grace's hand and ran toward Mandy.

Mandy moved aside, ushering them up the stairs. "Go!" she shouted.

Before Harlan could react, Mandy kicked the gun. It spun across the concrete floor and slid under the dryer.

It all happened in seconds.

Then Harlan was up and moving again, going after the children. Mandy stepped in front of him at the base of the stairs, flinging her arms out, obstructing his path.

His eyes flared.

He grunted, clenched his teeth, and swung, the back of his hand cracking across Mandy's face. The blow sent her flying back. As she landed hard on the concrete, Harlan started up the stairs.

Mandy blinked, her vision blurring.

The thing was still there, lingering in the dark. Watching.

———

As they reached the top of the stairs, Ethan faced a moment of decision. Go left—out the front door to the street, the obvious path. Or go right—out the back door, where they might lose Harlan altogether. He went right, pulling Grace along behind him. He unlocked the back door, and they went out as fast as possible. He made sure to close it behind them.

At the bottom of the porch steps, Ethan turned to Grace and said, "You need to hide under the porch. Let him follow me. When it's safe, run to the grove and hide in the old bus, alright?"

Grace nodded and hurried under the porch.

The back door slammed open with a crash.

Ethan didn't wait—he darted right, toward the side yard. He ran. Fast. And he didn't look back to see if Harlan was following.

Damn. He'd wanted more time.

———

MANDY PUSHED herself off the floor, grimacing. Her head pounded. Her ears rang. Her jaw throbbed.

Using the stair rail to steady herself, she started up the steps. She realized it was dangerous to climb them in her condition, but she could think of nothing but her children. And Harlan running them down.

She pulled herself up, step by step, blinking her eyes, trying to clear her vision.

As she reached the door, she lurched through it into the kitchen, stumbling and falling forward, landing on her knees, catching herself before her face hit the ground.

Dizzy and dazed, she glanced around the room.

She didn't know which way they'd gone.

What would she do? Where would she go? How would she find them?

But it wasn't a decision she would get to make.

Harlan burst through the back door, flinging it open with force. He came to stand before her.

"Figures your goddamn kids would be as aggravatin' as you and your mama," he growled. "Now get the hell up and help me find 'em."

Mandy glanced up at him and started to laugh.

"What's so goddamn funny?" he snapped.

"Oh, nothin'," she said, struggling to her feet. "Picturin' you behind bars."

"Ain't *nobody* puttin' me nowhere."

Her vision was sharpening. Mandy swiveled her head back and forth, closing her eyes against the pain. She didn't want him to know how much she was hurting. She didn't want him to have the satisfaction.

"I couldn't figure out why you wanted this place so bad," she said. "I knew it wasn't legacy. You never gave a *shit* about that. Money, yeah. But not family. *Now* it makes sense. It was *self-preservation*."

"You're babblin', girl," he said, reaching for her shoulder.

Mandy pushed his hand away and stood tall in front of him. "No!

You don't get to touch me anymore, you old fuck." She clenched her jaw. She was quivering, but she stood firm and stared him in the face.

"*You knew* she had evidence here that could prove your guilt," Mandy said. "So, you figured…why not just buy the place? And tear it to the ground."

He huffed. "You sound batshit crazy," he said. "Like yer mama."

Mandy laughed in his face. "That ain't gonna work no more, Harlan. I ain't crazy. And neither was she. I *remember* what you did to me. And I know you did the same thing to her. I also know you killed your daddy. Did you kill my folks too? To keep them quiet?"

Harlan put his hands on his hips and cleared his throat. "Load of horseshit."

"Are you really this dumb? *I found the evidence!* You're *done*, you piece of shit!"

———

ETHAN HID under the abandoned truck on the side yard for a few minutes, waiting until he was certain the old man hadn't followed him. Then he backtracked. He thought of running to the neighbors. Checking his father's truck for some sort of weapon. But no. Not enough time.

As he passed the back porch, he spotted the man through the window and crouched down. He hoped that the door to the primary bathroom was open. But he realized it wasn't likely—they'd done such a good job keeping everything locked up. He stepped up to the door and turned the knob, but it didn't budge.

He noticed that the window on the primary bedroom was open, only slightly. Maybe it wasn't open wide enough, but he had to try.

He ducked down and tried to wedge his head through the opening. It was tight enough that it hurt, but he thought he might be able to fit if he was persistent and calm. He pushed through the discomfort, and then—*yes!* His head was inside. Next were his arms and his torso, much easier. He'd never been so thankful he was slim.

Ethan braced himself against the edge of the window frame and hoisted one leg up.

He was terrified he might break the glass, or come crashing down on the other side, but he kept going. Once he had one leg over and was straddling the sill, it was easy enough to lower himself down to the carpet.

He didn't really have a plan. He'd try to wake his father. His father could help. He'd know what to do. *If he was still alive.*

But then he saw it. A gun. On his mother's nightstand.

———

MANDY THOUGHT she sensed the doubt in Harlan.

"Ya ain't found nothin'," he said.

"Where do you think I was just now, ya dumb ass? The police have *everything*, and they're on their way here *right now* to *finish* diggin' up yer daddy. Oh, you musta thought you were so clever buryin' him out there."

Now, Mandy was sure she could see it. The concern in his eyes.

She hoped it was true that the police were coming. They *were* coming. She just didn't know when. She hoped that Bo had heard enough of her phone call. And, if not, perhaps the threat of them coming would be enough to convince Harlan to go.

Either way, good or bad, this was going to end soon.

Mandy stepped toward Harlan, lifting her chin to face him. "You best get runnin'."

Harlan scoffed, but uncertainty had crept into his face. He studied her, but she did her best to keep her expression neutral, her eyes unreadable.

He sighed. "Ya always were a nosy little bitch, Amanda Jean."

"*My name*—is Mandy."

Harlan smiled. He reached into his front pocket and withdrew his pocketknife. "Mandy it is," he said, unfolding the blade. "I'll let 'em know, for your eulogy."

He reached for her again, his face twisting into a feral rage.

Mandy staggered back, still dizzy. She kept her eyes on the knife, trying to avoid its edge. She couldn't help but think of the time that

Harlan had driven a similar knife—the very *same* knife?—into her father's gut.

Then the house rumbled. The sound was deep and rolling, like a beast stirring in its slumber.

Harlan shoved her and Mandy fell, landing on her back. He was on top of her immediately. She gripped the wrist that was holding the knife with both hands. Even as an old man, lean and bony, Harlan still possessed unusual strength.

His other hand wrapped around her throat.

The house rumbled again, stronger this time. And the windows began to rattle. Glass broke somewhere in the house. But Mandy focused on Harlan.

Don't let him kill you. Gotta get outta here alive.

Mandy choked as Harlan's hand tightened on her windpipe. And from the sides of her vision, the darkness began to creep in.

One by one, the kitchen cabinets began to fly open, and what few dishes they'd managed to unpack began to fall, crashing to the floor around them.

"What the goddamn—?" The glass breaking was enough to distract Harlan, and his grip loosened for a moment.

It was enough. Mandy gasped. And as the air filled her lungs, her vision expanded again.

From another room, something heavy fell.

And—with a loud crack—the roof of the kitchen split open down the middle.

Harlan looked up, startled. Confused.

For a moment, Mandy thought he might flee. But he refocused, narrowing his eyes, and began to squeeze Mandy's throat again.

She fought hard against it, but she started to lose consciousness.

"Let her go!"

It was Ethan.

He was standing in front of the basement door, aiming Travis's pistol at Harlan.

Harlan looked over at the boy. And, after a long moment of indecision, he released his grip on Mandy's neck.

She gasped and scurried out from under his body, crawling back through the broken glass.

Harlan stood.

Mandy scrambled toward Ethan.

And the house continued to rumble around them.

"Ya know how to use that thing?" Harlan called to Ethan over the noise.

Ethan shook his head. "I think I just pull this trigger?" Harlan stepped toward Ethan, but the boy didn't move. "Want me to try it?" he asked.

Harlan scowled, grumbling.

"Are you okay?" Ethan asked Mandy, his eyes still locked on Harlan.

"Ye…yeah," she said, coughing up the word through a bruised windpipe. She was bleeding. She had new cuts on her hands, but nothing that was too deep.

"Dad's in the third bedroom," Ethan said.

"Will you be okay?" she asked.

Ethan nodded.

Mandy stood and started down the shaking hallway. The house was moving so much now, she couldn't walk in a straight line. She found Chris unconscious on Shane's old bed, his face covered in blood. Her heart sank. She rushed to his side, crouching as she pressed her fingers to his throat.

A pulse!

She sighed, relieved.

It took her a few seconds to roust him. He opened his eyes to chaos—things breaking, walls cracking—as the house continued to shudder. Mandy helped him up. Supporting him, they shuffled back toward the kitchen.

Something made Mandy turn and look back down the hall. There, the little girl—her mother—was sitting on the floor, her stuffed animal in her lap. Behind her was the dark thing with the curled horns. As it stood over her, its darkness surrounded her. Still. Watching. Waiting. Even as the house broke around them.

Slowly, the little girl stood and took the thing by the hand.

A beam split in the roof of the hallway and dust poured in around them like smoke. When it settled, they were gone.

Mandy swallowed and nodded, tears in her eyes.

As she and Chris reached the end of the hall, Ethan spotted them. He began to back toward them, toward the front door, keeping his focus on Harlan. He didn't lower the gun until they were all safely outside.

Even from the lawn, the noise of the house shaking was pervasive, the sound of things breaking inside. As they hurried to Mandy's Corolla, a car with temporary police lights on top pulled to a stop at an angle in the driveway, its siren wailing.

Bo emerged, sidearm drawn.

"He's inside," Mandy shouted.

Bo hurried to the front porch. He hesitated a moment before going inside.

Chris was groggy. Still bleeding. Ethan helped Mandy put him in the passenger seat.

"Where's Grace?" Mandy asked.

"I told her to hide in the old school bus until I came to find her," Ethan said.

"School bus? You mean *Mama's bus?*"

Two marked police cars arrived.

Mandy gave Ethan a hug, squeezing him tight. She told him to stay with the sheriffs, and to find Grace only when they said it was safe.

As she pulled away down the street, she glanced back at the house in her rearview mirror. Harlan was being dragged into the yard in handcuffs.

She exhaled.

It was over.

MANDY STOOD at the door to Chris's hospital room.

The doctor told her he had two broken ribs, a fractured cheek bone, a broken nose, and a severe concussion. It was bad enough for them to keep him, at least overnight.

Chris had large bandages wrapped around his chest, more around his head, and another across his swollen face. When he spotted her, he lifted his hand an inch or so off the hospital bed. A small, tired wave.

"I didn't want to wake you, if you were sleeping," Mandy said.

"I wanted to see you," he replied.

She crossed the room and stood next to his bed, placing her hand on top of his.

"Well, aren't you…*pretty*," she said.

"Don't make me laugh. It's painful."

She smiled and nodded. "Okay. I promise."

"Are the kids…?"

She nodded again. "You would've been so proud of them. Ethan's just like you."

Chris started to smile. But coughed and winced at the pain from the movement.

"Babe…do you want me to let you rest?"

"I want you to stay," he said. He held her fingers.

She was happy to hear those words.

Mandy took a deep breath. "I have a lot to tell you. Whenever it's a good time," she said. "About my life. My past."

Chris nodded, his fingers tightening around hers, his lips curling into a small smile. "I've got time."

EPILOGUE

Dear Shane,

I heard the news of Travis's passing and wanted to reach out. I tried calling, but you didn't answer. Perhaps a letter is best. This way, I can say just what I want to say.

You know how I felt about Travis, and I can't pretend otherwise now. Death makes saints of the least of us, but Travis died as he lived—selfishly. He was a stranger to me even when we lived ten feet apart.

Now that he's gone, it's just you and me. The last of the Holloways. I suppose that doesn't mean too much, really. You left home as soon as you could, and we were never a close family to begin with. Still, I think it's important that we stay in touch.

I wanted to tell you it was a kind thing you did putting Travis in the sober living home. He told me it was you footing the bill. I hope you don't have any guilt about him overdosing. We can hand people the tools they need to better themselves, but we can't swing the hammer for them. He was on this path since he was a boy. You generously offered a lifeline. It's regrettable he didn't use it. But not a surprise.

I saw that Harlan was denied bail again. The prosecutor said we might have to appear at the trial. I told her we will if needed, but I hope it doesn't come to that. Harlan will fight until his last breath. And Lord, I hope that breath comes soon.

I still haven't heard if they're going to pursue charges in regard to the deaths of our folks. I sure hope they do. Maybe it doesn't matter to anyone, but it would be nice to have the truth on record. Maybe there isn't enough evidence. Travis was their best witness. And now he's gone. Hopefully, Harlan's at least found guilty of his father's death. That should be enough to put him away.

As for us, it's been a few months since we returned to California. With the Stillwater house falling apart, we didn't get near as much from the sale of the property as we'd hoped. The reason for its collapse remains unconfirmed. It felt like an earthquake, but none were detected. The insurance company attributes the damage to natural age (of course they do).

Still, the money was enough to move us back and help us start a proper handyman business. Chris will handle the physical stuff, while I take care of operations, marketing, and sales. It's a very different thing for me, but I'm enjoying the challenge so far. (We'll see how Chris and I fare working together. Haha.)

The kids are doing well since we got home. They're happy to be back in familiar, sunny CA, but I think Grace misses the woods. She's been writing stories about them. Ethan has shown interest in shadowing his father in the business, which makes me happy. Our relationships have never been stronger. I wish you'd gotten to meet them while we were nearby. Maybe if we return for the trial, or for a visit, as Grace has asked us to do. They're better people than they have any right to be, considering who their mother is.

While I am kidding (somewhat), I find it ironic that it took returning home for me to realize I wasn't who I wanted to be. Wasn't present for them like I needed to be. Maybe it was all the memories of our parents and our childhood. I always knew I didn't want the same for my kids. So, I guess I'd kept them at arm's length. I was afraid I'd be a negative influence, but keeping my distance meant I wasn't a positive one either. I don't want that. I love them too much. I'm not Mama. I know that now. I will do better.

Hope your foot's feeling okay. Give my best to Sharon and the kids.

Your sis,
Lil Bit

Afterword

I've loved the Southern Gothic tradition since I was a young reader. I always hoped I'd find the right story to try my hand at it. I finally did.

The individual pieces of this novel have existed in my mind for years. They circled each other—flirting, finding their way to one another, forming bonds. They are inexorably linked now, inseparable in my mind, as if they've always belonged together, as if they've always fit.

This novel is about a haunting. At least that's how it started.

The idea that I can dictate the direction or tone of a story is a lie I tell myself repeatedly. What entered the chrysalis as a straightforward haunted house tale emerged quieter. Sadder. Something more meditative than I anticipated. At some point in the telling, the characters take over and decide their own path.

Maybe it's not about ghosts at all anymore, except for the ones from our past that cling to us and won't let go. It's just a story now— *Mandy's story*—existing on its own, exactly as it decided to be.

You Can't Just Leave is my first published novel in over a decade— though not the only one I've written in that time.

Writing is a habit, and I didn't keep it.

Between loss, grief, existential spirals, and political chaos, it was easy for me let writing slip down the list. It became easy to ignore. Even to forget.

It felt selfish, almost. Frivolous. *Unimportant.*

But that's a lie. Art matters.

I'm reminding myself that it's one of the things that makes life bearable. Worth enduring. Worth fighting for.

I'm glad to be here with you again, shaking off the rust and getting back to work. I grew through the process of telling this story. I hope, in some small way, you find something in it too.

As always, the journey matters,

John Mulhall,
    May, 2025

Acknowledgments

I'd like to thank the following people. This book wouldn't have been the same without them.

Naz Keynejad and Linda Larson, for assisting with developmental editing. Both of you are not only treasured friends, but valued collaborators, and I am always indebted to you for your feedback and the support you provide.

Dayna Bennett, for the copy editing, the collaboration, the impromptu therapy, and for the years of friendship. You're the best!

All the focus group readers, for being the first audience to take the book for a spin, and for providing your thoughts and feelings. In alphabetical order: Sonia Agredano, Kerri "Simba" Bacon, Amanda Bennett, Christopher DePalma, Melinda Girard, Melanie Groover, Deborah McQuerrey Gow, Chris Hamel, Jamie James, Dana Johnson, Jeannine Marquie, Erin Moody, Tammy Porter, LaVaughn Powers, Jessica Rickards, Veronica Rush, Teresa Stone, and Holly Winsor.

Cheryl Armstrong for the use of your eagle eyes. Thank you for proofreading!

Cheri Fox, for the cover art.

Rick Simonton, for helping me with the title treatment.

Victor Curtis, for taking my author photo. I respect and appreciate your talents, my friend. Thank you!

Maria Marquis, for providing her voice and acting talent to the audiobook version. Fantastic job!

Jolene and Harley Heft, for sharing your experiences as paranormal investigators with me, and for inspiring the title of the book. (One of the perils of hanging out with a writer is that we're always listening!)

Wendy Stephens, for being my consultant about all things Tennessee. Thank you for your love and support. Your contributions to this book cannot be understated.

You, dear reader, for picking it up and giving it a chance.

About the Author

John Mulhall writes about the monsters we fight—those in the world, and those within ourselves. He is the author of *Geddy's Moon*, a supernatural thriller that became a #1 Amazon horror bestseller; *Dark and Broken Things*, a haunting psychological tale currently in development as a film; and *You Can't Just Leave*, a modern Southern Gothic ghost story. He's also released two collections of poetry and several short stories. He lives in Southern California, where he spends his time cooking, arguing with his cat, watching movies, and lying to himself that the next book will be easier.

www.ingramcontent.com/pod-product-compliance
Lightning Source LLC
Chambersburg PA
CBHW031242310726
48971CB00004B/1134